GANGSTERLAND

GANGSTERLAND

A NOVEL

TOD GOLDBERG

COUNTERPOINT | BERKELEY, CALIFORNIA

Goldberg

Library of Congress Cataloging-in-Publication Data

Goldberg, Tod.
Gangsterland : a novel / Tod Goldberg.
ISBN 978-1-61902-344-4 (hardback)
1. Mafia—Fiction. 2. Criminals—Fiction. 3. Mystery fiction. I. Title.
PS3557.O35836G36 2014
813'.54—dc23
2014014920

Cover design by Michael Fusco
Interior Design by Neuwirth & Associates

COUNTERPOINT
2560 Ninth Street, Suite 318
Berkeley, CA 94710
www.counterpointpress.com

Printed in the United States of America
Distributed by Publishers Group West

10 9 8 7 6 5 4 3 2 1

For Wendy, my North, my South, my East and West.

The foolish man knows not an insult, neither does a dead man feel the cutting of a knife.

—THE TALMUD

GANGSTERLAND

April 1998

When Sal Cupertine was going to kill a guy, he'd walk right up and shoot him in the back of the head. Shoot someone in the face, there's a good chance they'll survive. Sal never messed around with a gut shot or trying to get someone in the heart. It was stupid and made a mess. You get told to kill a guy, you killed a guy. You didn't leave it up to variations in the wind and barometric pressure and all that Green Beret shit he saw on TV. No, Sal knew, you just went up and did it. Be professional about it and no one suffers.

Still, he'd begun to appreciate that sometimes a little distance wasn't a bad thing, particularly since he'd been picking pieces of those Donnie Brasco motherfuckers off himself for the last three hours. One of the guys had a mustache, and Sal was certain that the hair he'd finally been able to dig from beneath his thumbnail was from him, since it was coarse and light brown and didn't have any blood on it, which meant it probably got jammed in there when he was choking him out. A mistake all around, that's what that was. But what could he do now? Three hours sitting in the backseat of a Toyota Corolla aside Fat Monte, who wasn't even fat anymore since he'd done six months and got hooked up with some steroids and had apparently hit the weights pretty hard, and all Sal had come to conclude was that he was probably only a few hours, at most, from his own death.

Not that Sal was actually afraid, at least not yet. Fat Monte hadn't taken his cell phone from him, which was a good sign; but it kept vibrating in his pocket, which to Sal meant his wife, Jennifer, was wondering where he was. She knew he wasn't exactly a nine-to-five guy, knew that when he was off doing Family business that he could be gone until the next day, or might need to jet down to Florida or over to Detroit, but even in those cases he was pretty good about giving her a heads-up that he wouldn't be back for dinner. The bosses understood that he couldn't just disappear for weeks on end without a word, now that he had a kid. Because once the wives got talking, it was everybody's problem. And on this day, of all days, he told Jennifer he'd pick up a prescription for her over at the twenty-four-hour Walgreens. His son, William, was in preschool over at Mt. Carmel Academy and brought home a dozen infectious diseases a week, or at least that's what it felt like, all three of them constantly battling some kind of respiratory shit that winter. The codeine cough medicine was helping, and Sal promised to pick up a refill on his way home, and that all would have happened if he hadn't lost it on those Donnie Brascos. And now here he was, maybe two hundred miles outside of Chicago in the middle of the night, nothing but black farmland on either side of the highway, Fat Monte breathing through his mouth next to him, two young guys up front—a half-Latino kid called Chema riding shotgun and Fat Monte's cousin Neal driving, though he spent more time looking in the rearview mirror than at the road, which wasn't helping Sal's sense of dread.

He wasn't afraid to die, but he was afraid of how it would feel to leave Jennifer and William behind. It wasn't something he'd thought about before, but today had been full of revelations. Dying was fine. He could handle that. He was only thirty-five, but he'd had enough close calls in the past that he wasn't mystical about the process. He knew there'd come a time when he was on the other end of a gun and that would be that. But he didn't want Jennifer and William to suffer for his stupidity. This whole deal was different. Preventable. That's what kept niggling at him: Somehow all this was going to roll back on them.

He fished his buzzing phone out of his pocket. If he was going to die tonight, at least he'd see his wife's name one last time.

"The fuck you doing?" Fat Monte said, though he didn't snatch the phone from Sal's hand. Interesting.

"It's been going off all night," Sal said. He didn't answer to Fat Monte, and he wasn't about to start, so he kept himself calm, went the honest route. "My wife's sick."

"Man, cops can triangulate that shit. You gotta lose that thing."

"You think they're looking for me?"

"Oh, you think your fingerprints aren't on record? Your first mistake, and it was a doozy. A little restraint, Sal, and you'd be home right now."

"Yeah," Sal said. "Well, things got clumsy. I admit that."

"You don't have to admit shit," Fat Monte said. "Everyone already knows it's true."

Everyone. Sal hated to think about what that meant. Monte still hadn't asked for the phone, so Sal just turned it off and stuffed it back into his pocket.

One thing for certain, if it were Monte who'd fucked up, Sal would have already killed him. That much he knew. And he wouldn't have bothered with any witnesses, either, especially not the half-Latino kid, whose neck Sal could see was covered in sweat; the bosses were all about diversifying lately, not keeping to the strict Italian edict, particularly not with so many good soldiers doing time. Supply and demand and a lack of good staff turned everything upside down.

That's what got him in trouble in the first place.

Three new guys started hanging around the fringes of the Family, trying to get inside any way they could, coming up with stashes of top-of-the-line televisions, heroin, even a truck full of leather office furniture, to the point that the bosses couldn't ignore them. The TVs and office furniture were one thing, but when they produced bags and bags of the highest-grade heroin—Sal was no good on heroin, it made him twitchy and overly aggressive, but he'd been convinced to give it a taste and had something like a religious sexual experience that night—the bosses began to wonder where they were connecting from, since the Family had controlled the heroin in Chicago for the better part of a century. So they told Sal to dig around, learn what he could, and report back when he knew anything definitive.

This truth-digging expedition was a significant growth in his duties. He was good at the whole stalk-and-kill process, that was simple work, but now the Family wanted him to be the point man on the business side, too. Not just lurking in the shadows. Out in the daylight and everything. He hadn't ever shown his face to a stranger in the game. At least not a stranger who wasn't about to become a corpse. But this was a chance to become a legit player, no more midnight murders, more time with his wife and kid. Whatever. It was a chance for something better than the business of killing. He even hazarded to tell Jennifer that big things were coming for them, that if everything went right, in the next year maybe they'd be able to take a vacation or see about moving somewhere warmer, both of them sick of freezing every winter in Chicago. Jennifer was taking art classes at City College—she enrolled at Olive-Harvey all the way down on the South Side so no one would recognize her, which Sal thought was stupid since no other wives were going to go anywhere near a community college—and every other week or so she'd bring in a painting of the ocean or a drawing of palm trees swaying in the wind. Though she wasn't really much of an artist, Sal liked the idea of her one day sitting on a beach chair all day and drawing.

Plus, the downtime between jobs could be maddening for Sal, to the point that he started doing outside work just to make ends meet around the holidays and such—it was nothing to drive down to East Saint Louis to take out some Crip for a shop owner, or even over to Springfield to put one in the head of a cheating spouse—but that was also dangerous. The bosses allowed a little freelance work, but not to the level Sal had entered into recently. But when the kid is sick every other week and you don't have health insurance, man, you do what you have to do.

■

Sal was pretty sure they had been driving aimlessly for hours. Chema, the mixed kid, consulted his map every now and then and told Neal to take exits, and then Neal would drive around for a bit before getting back onto the highway in a different direction, not saying a word the whole time. Even Sal could sort of appreciate the irony of the situation: He'd been killing people for the Family for over fifteen years, and now he was on a night ride into the fields for shooting three of those Donnie Brasco rejects in the face that afternoon and choking out the fourth. It was amateur hour on his part, really. Just one simple mistake.

He'd gone to a fancy hotel just off Michigan Avenue—the Parker House—to meet the Donnie Brascos and their Mexican connect on heroin. The meeting had gone well enough; the Mexican guy let him get a taste of some shit called Dark Chocolate Tar that immediately turned Sal's brain into a fuzzy, calm place.

Just a dab of Dark Chocolate Tar on his tongue gave him a serene feeling of total clarity. He left the hotel room feeling . . . good. The world was softer. He'd had a nice meeting with some enterprising businessmen, that's all, and they seemed like perfectly decent people, relatively speaking. He wouldn't have to kill them. They'd die in their own time—probably sooner than later because they were criminals—but he wouldn't be the instrument of their death.

He was already out on the street and thinking about maybe getting some goulash over at the Russian tearoom when a random thought struck. *Who was actually staying at the hotel?* Which was followed by: *Why were they even meeting at a hotel?* They could have done this whole deal in the parking lot of a Krispy Kreme. He stopped on the sidewalk and tried to remember the exact layout of the room he'd just been in no more than ten minutes earlier: a king-size bed; bags of heroin spread out on the desk next to the bed, buffet-style; and four guys in tracksuits standing around smiling. He'd gone into the bathroom to take a piss before leaving because when he was high he actually loved the way taking a piss felt, just one of those weird things, and he was impressed by how nice the bathroom was, how everything gold-plated shined.

But why wasn't there a tube of toothpaste on the counter? Why wasn't there any luggage in the room? Sal closed his eyes, right there in the middle of the sidewalk, and focused on every last detail he could remember, because if there was one thing he was known for, it was his memory. He hated it because guys called him Rain Man, but facts were facts: He saw something once, he saw it forever.

Sal turned around and walked back to the Parker House. By the time he was inside the lobby, the soft fuzz from the tiny bit of heroin he'd tasted had turned jagged, and all the mirrored surfaces inside the hotel were making him angry. The hotel was done up like it was 1935, pictures of Al Capone on the wall and Tiffany-style lamps everywhere, their light magnified a thousand times over by the ornate floor-to-ceiling-mirrors and shined marble floors. Every step Sal took toward the registration counter was met with another glint, another flash, until Sal swore people were snapping his photo.

Oh, he thought, *this will not do.*

He approached a young woman at the front desk.

"Can I help you?" she asked.

"I need to check out," Sal said, and he gave the woman the room number. The woman stared at her computer screen for a few seconds, tapped at her keyboard a few times, and then sighed. "There a problem?" Sal asked.

"Oh, no," the woman said, "I'm sorry. It's just that it looks like this is going through corporate. Did you make the reservation yourself?"

"No," Sal said, thinking now, realizing where this was all going, "my office made it."

"Ah, okay," the woman said. "Well, it looks like you've got a government purchase order, so we can just go ahead and charge your incidentals to a card, or you can pay cash."

"Cash," Sal said. "And could I get a copy of the bill?"

"Of course," she said. She made a few more taps on her keyboard, and within a few seconds Sal was looking at a bill for just over five hundred dollars in room service charges. He looked at the name on the bill—one Jeff Hopper with an address on Roosevelt Road in Chicago, the motherfucker not even bothering to hide the fact that he worked at the FBI. What an insult.

Sal patted his back pocket. "Oh, darn it," he said, "I think I left my wallet in the room. Could I get a key and then I'll come right back down and finish checking out?"

"Sure," the woman said, because who wouldn't trust an FBI agent named Jeff Hopper with a government purchase order and five hundred dollars in room service charges?

General etiquette suggested that killing an FBI agent, let alone three, maybe four, presuming the Mexican was one of theirs, too, was not good business. You could kill a cop if he was crooked, or you could put a bullet into a city councilman if it looked like he was going to go running to the law to get out of his debts. But you just didn't go around lighting up FBI agents. For the better part of the last decade, at least, the Family had a quiet détente with the authorities since although they moved a huge sum of heroin in and around Chicago and even up into Canada, they didn't go around killing innocent children or housewives, and no one ever died in cross fire at the mall, not like the fucking kiddie gangsters in the baseball caps and baggy pants and lowered Pontiacs. They were running a professional business, and as long as the Family didn't act too egregiously, the feds didn't get involved. But in the last year, with the economy all moving to the Internet, the world got so much smaller, which meant you didn't need to know someone locally to get your drugs or to get you a clean piece, and thus things had heated up between the Chicago Family and their rivals down south in Memphis for a smaller marketplace. And then there was online gambling—two months ago Sal was sent to Jamaica to kill a guy and ended up taking down five others just to make a point—all of which had caused the Family to retrench and consider different revenue streams. Killing everyone who took an interest in the business would be a twenty-four-hour-a-day proposition and would include half of Hollywood, too. But killing feds, specifically, was like asking for a RICO hailstorm.

Sal knew and understood all that. But what became crystal clear to him on the walk from the registration counter to the elevator was that if anyone was going down, it was going to be him alone. They'd yank his ass into the FBI field office and start showing him pictures of his family, start talking to him about how his son was going to be a foster kid raised in some butthole town or maybe even moved out to Indiana for "his own safety." And then they'd show him some video of Jennifer getting boiled, showing her pictures of every person he'd ever killed, and then, what could she do? She'd have to roll on him. She sure as shit wasn't going to do time, right?

Sal did some quick math. How many people had seen his face? The three Donnie Brascos. The Mexican. The girl at the counter. There was surely a camera over the registration desk, which meant some rent-a-cop in the bowels of the hotel had probably put an eyeball on him.

Six people. He could kill six people. Hell yeah. He'd done that plenty of times.

But if he killed the girl and the rent-a-cop, he'd need to kill another dozen people just to get out of the hotel alive, and, frankly, he didn't have enough bullets for that, nor any real desire for it. That wasn't something he could return from.

Shit.

He'd control what he could control on his own, let the Family figure out how to take care of the girl, get any videotapes. They were good at that sort of thing, particularly at a union hotel like the Parker. But the feds, those guys needed to go.

An old hotel like the Parker was actually a good place to kill a person: Thick walls and dense carpeting absorbed sound well, and, unlike some fucking Marriott, these old hotels didn't lump rooms together as densely. Plus, they didn't have huge banks of supermodern elevators shuttling hundreds at a time, opting instead for the charm of flying into the air in just a few ornate oak coffins. What really made the old elevators nice was that they still had stop buttons you could yank out to freeze the elevator in place, which Sal did when he got to the eleventh floor. In the amount of time Sal would take to do his job, if he did it right, no one would think twice about the elevator wait time.

In retrospect, Sal should have found out if the Mexican was on the take, not that it mattered, really, since he was the first one Sal shot when he opened the hotel room door. In that case, it wasn't personal; it was just about getting shit taken care of as quickly as possible. The first two Donnie Brascos went next, no problem, but the third guy decided he wanted to O.K. Corral the place; Sal eventually wrestled him to the ground and broke his windpipe. It was all done in maybe two minutes. Three at the most. And then Sal calmly walked down the hall to the service elevator and left.

At first, he was going to pick up Jennifer and William and make a run for it, but he knew that would end poorly for everyone. So he did the only thing that made sense to him: He called his cousin Ronnie Cupertine, his only direct relative still in the Family, but who now split time between Chicago and

Detroit, since he had used-car dealerships in both cities. Ronnie was one of those guys people on the street assumed was connected, mostly because he looked like such a cliché with his affinity for pinkie rings and pin-striped suits. He ran ads in the *Tribune* where he'd make used-car buyers "offers they couldn't refuse" and comical spots on TV where he dressed in a zoot suit and carried a tommy gun, called the other dealerships "dirty rats," and promised that the credit agencies would be taking "dirt naps" when he was done with them. The joke, of course, was that he was a real fucking gangster, and most of the cars he came upon and was thus able to sell at such a cheap rate were chops from Canada, bought in bulk.

"I fucked up," Sal told Ronnie. In the background, Sal could hear a cartoon playing on the television. Ronnie had four kids, all under thirteen, all in private school. A real bastion of society.

"What happened?"

"I took out some company guys," Sal said. It was probably the wrong thing to say. Sal was using a cell that he ripped new SIM cards from about twice a week, but Ronnie always thought he was being bugged, even though he routinely went around his house with a metal detector and the Family always kept a couple guys in the phone company. The whole world was changing, and no one in the Family knew dick about computers or technology. They knew only enough to be paranoid.

"Where are you?"

"Driving around," Sal said, but in truth he was parked across the street from Ronnie's Gold Coast manor. Built in the 1950s, the house was three stories high with a basement that Ronnie had turned into a fully operational sportsbook, though he'd become so rich that he used it now only to host parties and Vegas Night fund-raisers for the Boys & Girls Club. Used to be in the late '80s and early '90s, Ronnie would run a full casino out of the place, but the Jamaicans with their online books and the Indians with their casinos had made all that sort of high-roller action obsolete. Why bother getting in with a bunch of gangsters when you could do it legally?

The house was surrounded by a six-foot wrought iron gate and towering old-growth hackberry and bur oak trees, which gave the place the appearance of a fortress, even if there was now a hopscotch course chalked on the sidewalk out front. If someone wanted to roll up on the place, they'd need a team of well-armed arborists with them.

"Get off the fucking road," Ronnie said. "They got cameras everywhere."

"Where should I go, your place?" Sal teasing him now, letting him know that he could bring Ronnie down with him if he wanted. Sal didn't want to do that, not yet, but he wanted to make sure Ronnie knew the stakes.

"No," Ronnie said, "are you crazy? My kids are here."

"So I can't see my cousins anymore, Ronnie? That's how it is?"

"Sal," Ronnie said, "let's not get melodramatic here."

"Then where, Ronnie? You tell me where to go."

"I can't have you here if it gets hot," he said. "You have to understand how that would look."

"Maybe you should try to understand how I look," Sal said. "I'm picking brains out of my hair, okay?"

Ronnie didn't say anything for a minute, which Sal didn't like. Ronnie was one of those people who thought he always knew what was what, which struck Sal as funny since Ronnie hadn't even graduated high school. Now he was a self-made millionaire, or that's what people thought, when in truth he was just another link on the same crooked chain.

"Fifteen minutes," Ronnie said eventually, "that place where we played kickball."

Ronnie was fifteen years older than Sal, but all the kids in the family—the actual family—had lived around the block from the Winston Academy and used to use their big grassy field up over on the other side of North Seminary to knock the ball around. It was a pretty good neighborhood to grow up in, but now the boutiques and espresso joints were creeping in, replacing everything. It had been years since Sal had been over there during the daytime, not since he'd gone into the school to break the principal's arm. Gave the guy a compound fracture on orders from way up the line. Guy didn't even owe anything, which made Sal think there was something larger at work, but he never bothered to ask. Asking wasn't his job.

"Okay," Sal said.

"Monte will be there. You go with him while I sort this shit out."

"You need to get Jennifer and William to a stash house," Sal said.

"We'll do that," Ronnie said. "One thing at a time."

"I'm sorry I fucked up," Sal said, because he was.

"I know you are," Ronnie said.

"I just, you know, lost it. I saw that they were feds, and, you know, I just saw all the dominos at once. It seemed like the only thing to do."

"Are you high?"

"No," Sal said. "A little."

"You should have walked away," Ronnie said.

"I don't walk away," Sal said.

"See," Ronnie said, "that's the problem."

Ronnie cleared his throat, then didn't say anything. For a few seconds, Sal listened to the sounds of his little cousins screaming in the background. This was not good.

"Jennifer's sick," Sal said.

"Yeah, okay," Ronnie said.

"The kid, too," Sal said.

"Sal," Ronnie said, "I can see you on my security cameras."

"I'm just saying that she needs to be taken care of, that's all."

"Just meet up with Monte. We'll get this shit done with. Sunday, you'll come over and we'll watch the Bears."

"Yeah," Sal said, "we'll do that." He hung up without saying good-bye because it was April and no one was going to be playing football for another six months.

■

And now here he was, bumping down a pockmarked road off the highway, Neal hitting every possible divot, no one in the Corolla saying shit, everyone just acting like they always drove out to a farm in the middle of the night. Where were they? Missouri, maybe. No, they hadn't been gone that long. Indiana? Wisconsin? Sal was disoriented from the darkness and nauseous from the smell of Fat Monte's sweat.

"Where the fuck are we?" Sal finally asked.

"Ronnie said to bring you out here," Fat Monte said.

"Where is here?"

Fat Monte shrugged. "I didn't ask."

Great. Sal ditched his nine in a gutter after the Parker and now had only his five-shot .38. He was pretty sure he could take out Fat Monte without a problem, but trying to get at

Neal and Chema would pose some problems. They were dumb kids, but you didn't need to be smart to shoot a gun, plus they both surely had automatics.

"What about you, brown boy? You know where the fuck we are?"

Chema turned in his seat and glared at Sal. Fat Monte then said, "We're almost there."

"I thought you said you didn't know where we were going," Sal said.

"I don't," Fat Monte said, "which is why Chema has the map. Tell him we're almost there, Chema."

"We're almost there," Chema said, no emotion in his voice at all.

A few minutes later, Fat Monte's cell phone rang. He looked at it and then handed it to Sal. "It's Ronnie."

"You okay?" Ronnie asked when Sal picked up.

"Yeah," Sal said. "Should I be worried?"

"You caught three feds, so yeah," Ronnie said.

"What about the Mexican?"

"Not sure yet, no real chatter on him," Ronnie said. "Probably a legit guy working both sides. Channel 7 didn't mention him. Channel 2 called him an informant, so who the fuck knows."

"They say my name?"

"You don't kill three fucking FBI agents and not get on the news."

"They put my face up?"

"Yeah," Ronnie said. "Cops are at your house right now. It's not a good situation."

Shit. That meant the last phone call he received from Jennifer was likely not really from her. "You didn't get my family out?"

"Maybe you're not understanding the magnitude of this situation."

"Jennifer," Sal said, "is solid, Ronnie. You know that."

"Everyone breaks sometime."

"She won't," Sal said, but he really didn't know. She knew what he was, or at least she knew the version he gave her, and that was basically the truth: He did bad things to bad people. And she knew that other people considered him one of the bad people, too, had no notions that he was somehow a superhero or vigilante. They'd talked over the years about what to do in the event the police came looking for him, so she knew to keep her mouth shut, knew that she couldn't be made to testify against him, knew that if the police were looking for him, he was likely already gone.

She also knew that *gone* could mean a lot of things.

"We'll see," Ronnie said. "Meantime, we got you a bus out of town."

"Listen to me," Sal said, he turned away from Fat Monte and tried to lower his voice, but it's tough to be discreet in the backseat of subcompact. "If it comes down to it, I'm not going to be all polite and shit. Just be aware of that. This isn't some movie. I'll take a couple with me."

"We're aware of that," Ronnie said, and he hung up.

We. All this *we* shit. Ronnie's way of telling him that he'd pissed so far up the rope that it wasn't just Ronnie deciding his fate. Sal clicked off the phone and handed it back to Fat Monte, who then opened the back of it, took out the SIM, and crushed it under his shoe before tossing it out the window. "You wanna give me your phone?" he asked Sal.

If he did, Jennifer would have no way of reaching him. Maybe ever.

"Not just yet," Sal said, and Fat Monte just shrugged again. It wasn't as if he was going to call 911. And it wasn't as if he could call his wife. Nevertheless, he liked the idea that he still had one small connection to the outside world. As long as that lasted, he was still alive.

The Corolla veered right, and suddenly the rough patch of road turned smooth—or smoother, anyway—and Sal could make out the farm with a bit more clarity. There was a main house, what looked like a several warehouse-size barns just adjacent to the house, and half a dozen grain silos. The headlights passed over the glint of thousands of eyes out in the pasture. Cows. As the Corolla got closer, Sal could also make out a big rig and two smaller trucks as well. There were figures milling about—maybe ten men moving back and forth between the barns and the trucks, each with a dolly stacked high with boxes.

Sal rolled down his window and was immediately assailed with the stench that can come only from a slaughterhouse: a mixture of piss, shit, the iodine stench of raw meat, and the earthy smell of grain. It reminded Sal of road trips when he was a kid—his father always stopping at big corporate farms that had diners or restaurants attached to them, convinced that they had the best food on earth because they had everything fresh. His father dead now, what, twenty-five years? Thrown off a fucking building.

The Corolla pulled to a stop next to the big rig, but Neal didn't bother to kill the engine. "This is the spot?" Neal asked.

"Yeah," Fat Monte said. He got out of the car and walked toward the sprawling barn, none of the guys with their dollies giving him even a second glance. With the Corolla's headlights illuminating the landscape, Sal could see that the men all wore matching uniforms—navy-blue Dickies, gray button-down work shirts with a logo over one pocket, blue baseball caps, and gloves, though it was a pleasant evening, all things considering—and that the trucks all had the same logo, too, on their sides: Kochel Farm Fresh Meats. Condensation flowed out of the back of the refrigerated trucks, which explained the gloves.

Sal reached down and touched his .38. He'd put one in Chema, one in Neal, and then he'd make a break for the darkness. With all these civilians as witnesses, Sal had to hope Fat Monte wouldn't open up on him, though who knew what people were capable of anymore. He didn't want to kill Neal. Didn't even want to kill Chema, but Sal recognized he was about five or ten minutes from being ground into a patty and loaded into a refrigeration unit bound for a supermarket somewhere between here and California.

He looked out his window one last time to make sure he knew where he was running to, and when he did, he saw something that made him sit upright: Fat Monte was standing maybe twenty feet away, talking to a bald guy holding a couple of blankets, a toddler by his side. Three, maybe four years old. Hard to tell in the dark. What the fuck was a little kid doing there?

"Chema," Sal said, "I want to apologize." The Latino kid nodded his head but didn't turn around. So tough, he couldn't even take an apology like a man. "And I want you to thank me, too." This got him to turn around.

"Yeah, why's that?"

"Because I was about to shoot you in the back of the head, and I decided against it." Chema swallowed once, but stayed silent. "Way I figure it, you owe me a pretty big favor."

"What about Neal, were you gonna shoot him, too?"

"Probably," Sal said, "but Neal and I got some history. I used to watch you when you were a baby, whenever your mom had to run an errand or had one too many White Russians. Maybe you don't remember that."

Neal looked at Sal in the rearview mirror and said, "I thought that was just a joke."

"Nope," Sal said, "true story."

Outside, Sal saw the bald man hand the toddler one of the blankets, and the kid ran it over to the big rig. Fat Monte and the bald man shook hands, and Fat Monte started to make his way back to the Corolla. The two smaller trucks pulled away then, too, leaving just the big rig.

"So what is it you want me to do?" Chema asked.

Sal pulled out his wallet and handed it to Chema, who immediately pocketed it. "Couple weeks from now, mail this to my wife. Same address as on my license."

"That's it?"

"That's it," Sal said. "There's maybe two grand in there. Make sure there's two grand in there when my wife gets it, too."

Chema bit at his bottom lip but didn't say anything for a second. "Your wife," he said finally, "she like Mexican food?"

"Not really," Sal said.

"My girl makes these Mexican wedding cookies, maybe something like that?"

"Sure," Sal said. "If not, my son would eat them."

Chema bit at his lip again, and Sal couldn't help but wonder what was going through his head.

Fat Monte opened the car door before Chema could respond.

"Neal, Chema," Fat Monte said, "give your coats and shirts to Sal." Neal and Chema looked at each other once in mild surprise but did what they were told. At the same time, Fat Monte took off his jacket and handed it to Sal, too. "Put all this shit on over your clothes."

"Where am I going?" Sal asked. He was out of the car now, layering shirts and jackets on top of his own suit jacket and button-down, the way he always dressed for a business meeting.

"I don't know," Fat Monte said. "But my guess is you're gonna be in the fridge until you're at least a couple states away. The truck is only gonna be at forty-five degrees, so it'll be like springtime in Chicago."

Forty-five degrees. Sal could live with that.

Fat Monte walked Sal over to the big rig, and the two of them stood for a moment at the bottom of the loading ramp. They watched one of the uniformed guys inside the truck clear a spot. There were maybe ten blankets, a pillow, a flashlight, a couple of bottles of water, a box of Ritz Crackers, a walkie-talkie, even a chair. All the comforts of home, surrounded by boxes of ground beef. When the worker saw the two of them, he said, "This gonna work, boss?"

"That'll be fine," Sal said.

"You start having a problem, just get on the walkie-talkie and the driver will pull over," the worker said.

They had all the angles worked out, which made Sal think maybe this wasn't the first time the Family had smuggled a man out of town this way, which gave him an odd bit of relief.

"This is where we part ways," Fat Monte said.

"How long we know each other?" Sal asked.

"Couple concurrent sentences," Fat Monte said, being funny now, which gave Sal pause. Fat Monte wasn't exactly known for his quick wit.

"Ten years for robbery," Sal said. "Another fifteen for assault."

"That's about right," Fat Monte said. "Listen, I need your phone and your piece."

It was polite enough, not an order, which made Sal willing to hand them over. Fat Monte threw the phone onto the ground and then crushed it under his shoe, but didn't bother to pocket the .38.

"You ever come back to Chicago," Fat Monte said, "I'll have to kill you and your entire family, and I don't want to do that." Fat Monte clapped Sal once on the shoulder and then walked back toward the Corolla.

It wasn't five minutes later, after he had found a reasonably comfortable way to sit wedged up against a wall of meat, that Sal heard the two quick gunshots.

CHAPTER ONE

David Cohen. Sal Cupertine rolled that name around in his mouth. *David Cohen.* When he was a kid, he hated his own name, probably because every kid on the block had an uncle named Sal. But as he got older, he started to like it, started to see how it conveyed a sense of power and menace, two things he liked, at least in the abstract.

David was biblical, which had its own worth. Sal wasn't a religious man, never had been, and he certainly couldn't be if he killed people for a living. Residual guilt and remorse he could deal with, but trying to reason with an entire *other* life, one that started after death? Sal couldn't be bothered with that shit.

Cohen. Well. That was something else all together. Sal had known a fair amount of Jews in his life, and the Family always got along with the Kosher Nostra that moved ecstasy and counterfeit paper around the college campuses; those guys were mostly Israeli and Russian Jews, the days of Bugsy Siegel and Meyer Lansky pretty much a thing of the past once they figured they could get rich by owning Hollywood and the banks. The Israelis and Russians in Chicago were young and respectful since they viewed the Family like something mystical they'd seen only on television and in the movies.

All those guys were named Yaakov or Boris or Vitaly or Zvika, and they had thick accents and wore vests and big watches and drove Range Rovers, so everyone knew they weren't your local Rosenblatts and Levys. With real business, though, they were ruthless. They'd send a message by killing a guy's dog and girlfriend; fuck him up emotionally for the rest of his life without ever actually putting hands on him. Someone owes you money, you break their spirit and they will pay you forever, they said, and though he hated to admit it, Sal saw the wisdom in it. The problem was that the only way the Family had stayed in business for so long was that they didn't hurt innocent civilians or pets. You kill a guy's kids or dog, that's the sort of shit that ends up in the newspaper and actually gets investigated. Kill some shitbag, it's just a dead shitbag. Kill four federal agents, and your entire world could change.

But *David Cohen*? That wasn't a tough guy. That was a guy who fixed your glasses. That was your lawyer.

"David Cohen," Sal said, but it didn't sound quite right and probably wouldn't for another two weeks, or at least until he got his jaw unwired.

Six months he'd been gone, and during that time no one had addressed him directly or looked him in the eye. Seven days he'd spent in and out of refrigerated meat trucks while they figured out what to do with him before they finally dumped him in Las Vegas.

Or at least he was pretty sure it was Las Vegas.

The local newspaper, the *Review-Journal*, had a columnist named Harvey B. Curran who spent half his time writing gossip about all the "wiseguys" in town and the other half writing gossip about the people who were taking bribes from the "wiseguys" in order to further whatever their aims. And there was the fact that Oscar Goodman was probably going to run for mayor, every night on the local news another feature about how he'd revitalize the city and bring back that Rat Pack vibe, no one even giving a shit that he was the mouthpiece for fucking Mount Olympus—Lansky, Leonetti, the whole Scarfo family.

Everything was all out in the open. Except, of course, for Sal. Six months he'd been in the same house, not allowed to walk out the front door, only out back, only at night. Not that he'd been up for any travel, not with the litany of surgeries he'd gone through: a new nose and chin, a bunch of teeth ripped out and replaced with permanent implants. They'd lasered off his tattoos, shaved his head, got him to start wearing glasses. And the last thing, he hoped, was this new jaw. Even the surgeries had been done in secret—driven in the back of a windowless van in the middle of the night and hustled into a doctor's office, Sal shot up full of anesthesia and then waking up back in the house. It was at the point now where he didn't even bother taking the pain medication. Every part of his body hurt, and all the Percocets in the world weren't going to make it any better, not while he was being held captive in an elegant two-story house with a saltwater pool, indoor hot tub and sauna, full gym, and a good five hundred cable channels pumped into every room in the joint.

And now this: David Cohen.

Sal was doing curls in the gym when Slim Joe, the kid who lived with him, came in and handed over a stuffed manila envelope.

"What's this?" Sal asked.

"Bennie told me to give it to you," Slim Joe said. "I didn't ask any fucking questions." Slim Joe didn't ask about shit. Which was probably good. But Sal could set the house on fire and Slim Joe wouldn't bother to ask why, he'd just sit there and watch it burn, particularly if Sal told him that it was being done on Bennie's order. Bennie was Bennie Savone, a name which didn't mean much to Sal when he was living in Chicago but which apparently carried weight in Las Vegas . . . enough so that he showed up in Curran's gossip column fairly regularly. He ran a strip club in town called the Wild Horse, but what the column always alluded to was his marriage into a religious Jewish family, the Kales, who weren't involved in any wiseguy business. Unless you counted Bennie's father-in-law, since he was the rabbi at Temple Beth Israel.

Not that Bennie had mentioned any of this to Sal. In fact, Sal still wasn't entirely sure how he'd ended up hiding out with the Savone family, since the Family in Chicago wasn't in business with them prior. It wasn't his place to know or to ask, but the way Bennie treated him—respectful, but also clearly as a subordinate—indicated to Sal that whatever deal had been made was not a short-term arrangement. That, and all the surgeries to change his face.

Sal took the envelope into his bedroom and emptied its contents out onto his bed. There was a birth certificate, a social security card, college transcripts from Hebrew Union College in Cincinnati, even old utility bills, all in the name of David Cohen. And affixed to a copy of a rental agreement for the very house he was already staying in—an agreement that was drafted that very same day between himself and the temple—was a Post-it note written in Bennie's careful cursive: *This is you. Commit it to memory, Rain Man. All of it.*

Rain Man. He hadn't heard that name since Chicago.

There was more: a family tree that showed David Cohen's genetic history, all the way back to Poland in the 1800s; a weathered gold-leafed copy of the Talmud; a yarmulke.

"David Cohen," he said again.

Sal Cupertine got up from his bed and walked into his bathroom. It was the nicest bathroom he'd ever had: travertine floors, a sunken Jacuzzi tub, two sinks, a stand-up shower with a rainfall shower head and built-in seating area. At first, Sal couldn't figure out a pressing need for the seating area, unless you took a lot of showers with other people, which then made him miss his wife, Jennifer, so acutely he felt sick. He covered the seating area with shampoo bottles and soaps and towels, whatever he could find, really, so that it was now just a shelf. At the far end of the bathroom was a walk-in closet roughly the size of the bedroom he and Jennifer shared in their house in Chicago. It was so big, in fact, that it had a closet of its own: a cedar-lined coat closet that was kept cooler than the rest of the house by a separate air-conditioning unit. The closet was filled with designer clothes: a dozen suits, dress shirts, slacks, sweaters, shoes . . . all still with the price tags on them. One pair of shoes was marked down from seven hundred dollars to five hundred, or about what Sal would reasonably expect to spend on shoes for an entire year.

The whole house, really, was beyond what Sal could ever have afforded, though it was certainly within the grasp of someone like his cousin Ronnie.

Or maybe someone like Rabbi David Cohen.

The truth was, for the last six months Sal had been trying to figure out a way to escape. He didn't know where he planned to escape to, exactly, since he knew that going back to Chicago would be murder—either at the hands of the cops or at the hands of the Family. Fat Monte made that clear enough. No one had said anything to him about what went down in Chicago with the Donnie Brascos, but Sal knew for certain that if the Family let him live, they had a higher purpose for him or, more likely, managed to get something in exchange for him from the Savones, since killing the feds had to have caused a big problem, the kind of problem that would ripple through all the families, would cause innocent (or relatively innocent) men to get strung up on other charges, just so the *Tribune* and *Sun-Times* would have something positive to report.

Besides, if he showed back up in Chicago, he'd have, at most, only an hour to get in and out before someone caught wind of his presence. Between the snitches, the cops (even the crooked cops would turn his ass in—that went without saying), and the feds, never mind average Joe Q. Publics out there looking to pick up a reward, the odds of him getting dimed were high. Still, he entertained ideas of snatching Jennifer and William in the middle of the night and riding off for Canada . . . but then he was always struck with a question he simply did not have an answer for: *And then what?*

It was a question that paralyzed him with its simplicity. Ronnie had promised to get his family out in due time, a promise Sal realized was empty almost as soon as the meat truck took off that night, but he still woke up each morning and searched the bed for Jennifer. Sal had managed to survive fifteen years in the game by keeping strict habits. Even the smallest ones were not easily broken.

Sal leaned down and turned on the Jacuzzi and watched for a few moments while the tub filled with water, the jets sputtering to life. *A year*, he thought. A year of being Rabbi David Cohen, and he'd have some money, some connections, a way to get out of this mess. He'd already done six months, after all. What was another year? Maybe he could get Jennifer and William to Las Vegas, though he knew the feds would be watching them for a good long time, just in case he tried to make contact. So maybe two years. Yes. Two years. Two years and he'd make his move.

So the Rabbi David Cohen went back into the bedroom, picked up all the paperwork he'd been given, and set it all on a chair next to the Jacuzzi. He then stripped out of his clothes and got into the tub, let the jets pound away at his back and neck until he began to understand that Sal Cupertine—all the things he'd done, all the people he'd loved—was, for the foreseeable future, dead.

And then he began reading.

◾

It took three more weeks, but by the time David Cohen was due to have his jaw unwired, Bennie deemed it safe for him to go out the front door of his own house. It was two weeks before Thanksgiving, and David had spent the previous weeks reading and reading and reading, every day some new rabbinical text dropped off at the house with specific instructions of what should be read. David appreciated the attention to detail that was going into his cover, but he couldn't help but think it was all a bit overboard. Was anyone going to walk up to him in the grocery store and demand to know his opinions on different parts of the Midrash? Or when he was putting some guy out, was he supposed to stop and educate the fucker on what it meant to be a veteran of history and the whole idea of noblesse oblige? It seemed excessive. The readings all came with corresponding quizzes—ten or fifteen questions written in florid cursive that David was to complete and return. He didn't bother to cheat. He just answered the questions and hoped whoever was grading him took into consideration that he'd only barely passed high school, though that had more to do with falling for Jennifer in senior year than anything else.

The weird thing—one of the weird things, anyway—was that since David received his new identity, Bennie hadn't bothered to show his face at the house. He usually showed up for the midnight doctor's appointments to check on the progress of David's various operations, firing questions about healing time and when it might be appropriate for David to increase his physical activity, ironic since Bennie was a good one hundred pounds overweight. So David knew his concern wasn't entirely altruistic. David didn't mind his visits. It was better than trying to make conversation with Slim Joe.

On this day, however, Bennie pulled up in front of the house and then called Slim Joe, who then handed the phone to David. "You ready to get that shit out of your mouth?" Bennie asked.

"Since the day it happened," David said.

"Then let's go," he said. "I'm out front."

"Really?" David said.

"It's a blessed day, Rabbi," Bennie said, and then he hung up.

David walked out the front door, and he felt mostly normal, except for the fact that he didn't have a gun on him. He hadn't had one all this time, of course, but now here he was out in public, or as public as a house behind a private gate can be, and he realized that it was the first time in twenty years that he didn't have a weapon of some kind on his person.

"You look good," Bennie said when David slid into the passenger seat.

"I'm down thirty pounds," David said. He hadn't been able to open his mouth for almost six weeks. He'd gone to sleep in some doctor's office one night after midnight and woke up the next morning with incisions on either side of his head, back behind his ears, that felt like someone had hit him with a hammer, which, in fact, they had. They'd broken his jaw with a hammer and chisel, moved it down, smoothed out all the rough edges, and then locked him up. Talking was hard enough; having Slim Joe make him protein shakes nearly induced suicide. "Maybe I should get my jaw wired," Bennie said. "My wife's dream."

Bennie drove down the long driveway and waited for the gate to open. It was at least twelve feet high, David saw, and there were cameras mounted on each corner, though David had never seen a closed-circuit TV in the house. He'd remember to ask about that. Bennie turned right, and David realized for the first time that he was in a neighborhood of homes just as sprawling as the one he'd been living in. Just as sprawling and, he noted, just the same. No character, David thought as they drove, just a bunch of houses painted somewhere between brown and mauve, each with a fountain with spitting cherubs out front. Where were the walkups and Craftsman homes? Weirder still were the street names: Anasazi, Hualapai, Turquoise Valley.

As they drove, David also noticed full neighborhoods on one side of the street and then nothing but empty lots on the other with elaborate signs promoting the next new community, always with names like The Lakes at Town Center Commons, and always with a smiling white family rendered in a drawing. Not even a pretense of being politically correct or multicultural. His own housing development was called The Lakes at Summerlin Greens, not that he'd seen a lake or any greens. Though judging from the land movers he saw out in the empty fields, both were coming at some point.

"Where the fuck are we?" David finally asked.

"Summerlin," Bennie said.

Summerlin. David had read about this place in the newspaper. A master-planned community built by Howard Hughes. "Why does everything look the same?"

"Welcome to Las Vegas," Bennie said.

They drove in silence for a few minutes, David soaking in the world. They kept going around traffic circles, made all the more absurd by the lack of other people on them. "Where are the casinos?" David asked.

"The Strip," Bennie said. He pointed to the south. "And then there's a bunch of little shit holes around town. Places to play cards. Get a drink. See Eddie Money play. That sort of thing."

"The casinos," David said, "that part of what you do?" He'd avoided asking any questions about the operations of the Savone family, but now that it was clear he was going to be spending some time around these parts, it felt prudent.

"Nah," Bennie said. "Not on the front side. We got influence in restaurant and hotel unions, we got a few cement and steel contracts, we run a couple construction outfits, we get some influence on the books, but you can't just buy a casino anymore. It's not like it used to be. Place like the Bellagio? You're talking ten thousand employees. And anyway, it's an open city. Half these other families aren't smart enough to figure how to avoid prison time just by signing the wrong box, so I just let them, and if they come to me for advice, I'll give it to them. We're all better off if we can work together out here, but if you don't know how to form an LLC, that's not my problem. I'm happy to let some other family try their luck on the low-hanging fruit, find out how rotten it is these days, you know?"

David didn't, not really. He was straight muscle in Chicago, paid primarily not to know, and that had been fine, at least until recently. He understood that the Family in Chicago made a lot of their money on heroin and cocaine, but the real money came from garbage and landfill, mostly. City contracts, he understood, brought in the real cash. And that was another reason why the feds typically kept their distance: No one wants to have garbage piled up on the streets. But the nuts and bolts of the economy were left to people further up the line, like his cousin Ronnie.

"This Jew stuff," David said, but then he stopped himself. He'd forgotten about Bennie's wife and kids. "No disrespect intended," he continued, "but I don't understand it."

Bennie scratched at something on his neck. He turned onto the Summerlin Parkway and then onto I-95 heading south and all the while staying quiet. Which was fine with David. He was content not to say another word for the rest of his life.

"Let me ask you a question," Bennie said finally. There was an edge to his voice. Annoyance, maybe. Maybe he was going to pull over and shoot David in the face. There was no telling, but David was pretty sure that Bennie wasn't the kind of guy who'd want to fuck up his upholstery, never mind his suit, a perfectly tailored Armani number that must have been expensive. "You go to college?"

"No," David said, though it felt like all the reading he was doing now was making up for that.

"You ever been overseas?"

"Canada a couple of times," David said. He didn't mention an overnight business trip to Jamaica, figuring there was no good reason to let Bennie know about that. Three hours there trying to decide how best to dispose of five dead Jamaicans.

Bennie scratched that spot again on his neck, and David noticed that he had a bunch of little red bumps running from his Adam's apple all the way to his chin. Razor burn; but the spot Bennie was scratching was actually a fine raised line that was a deeper shade of red. He'd noticed it before, not thinking anything of it, but now that he was up close he could see that it was a surgical scar. That or someone tried to slit his throat.

"Why not?" Bennie asked.

"Why not what?"

"Why haven't you left the country?"

"My wife," David said, "is always getting on me about wanting to go to the Bahamas. Once we had a kid, though, you know how that shit goes."

"You don't have a wife," Bennie said. Annoyed again. Or just being nasty. The prick.

"No," David said, "I guess I don't."

"What about college?"

"I was already in the business full on by the time I was nineteen," David said.

"You ever hear of a place called Harvard?" Bennie asked.

"Yeah," David said.

"You ever hear of a place called Europe?"

David thought he knew where this was headed. "Yeah, I've heard of both of those places."

"You think there's a bunch of guys like you and me running around Harvard and Europe? You think if you walked into Harvard just to ask where the toilet was that they'd tell you?"

"Me or the new me?"

"The guy-who-shoots-people-in-the-back-of-the-head you."

"I don't know," David said.

"Sure you do," Bennie said. "Some gangster walks into Harvard and asks where the toilet is, they're gonna take him down the service elevator and show him where the janitors piss. Same thing in Europe. Say you walk into, I don't know, The Hague. Do you know what The Hague is?" David told him he didn't. "It's where they have trials for war crimes. The courtroom of the world, basically. It's in the Netherlands. You know what happens if you and me walk in there right now? They throw us against the wall and frisk us, ask us if we're fucking Cosa Nostra, like either of us even speaks Italian, throw us in a cell with a bunch of guys with towels on their heads."

"What are we doing in the Netherlands?" David asked.

"Forget the Netherlands. The point is this: You ever see any Jews getting shown to the service elevator or on trial for war crimes? You ever see anyone named David Cohen getting jacked up on RICO charges?"

"The difference is," David said, "they got half the world trying to kill them all the time."

"Exactly," Bennie said. "You mess with one Jew, you're messing with all of them."

David thought about this, thought about how he was seriously concerned about his own cousin pulling his card over the shooting . . . which was a valid concern, considering he was pretty sure Fat Monte had killed *his* cousin Neal that same night, just to close the circle of information. Even the Kosher Nostra were all about family, literal family and cultural family. David couldn't think of a single instance of one of those guys getting lit up.

"So," David said, "you want me to be your guy on the inside with the Jews?"

Bennie started to smile, but then stopped himself, rubbed at that spot on his neck. He was a strange cat. There was something cunning about him, about the way he never came at you directly with information, instead let you come up with questions. "You really able to remember shit like they say?" Bennie asked.

"I guess so," David said. Up ahead, David could see the looming casinos of the Strip, including one that looked like a giant syringe.

Bennie got off the freeway on Rancho and turned left, wound around a few streets, and then pulled into a parking lot beside a sprawling park. There was an RV in front with two black guys sitting on plastic chaise lounges on the blacktop, smoking cigarettes and roasting hot dogs over a tiny barbecue. The RV had a painting of the sun setting over a mountain lake across its entire back end. It had a personalized Arizona license plate that said RAMBLER, and the license plate frame said RALPH & LINDA'S WAGON.

"These guys, they're gonna get that shit out of your mouth."

"They doctors?" David asked.

"The guy who did your surgery had an accident," Bennie said.

"I'll wait for him to heal," David said.

"It wasn't that kind of accident," Bennie said, and he pointed at one of the black guys—he was maybe fifty-five, had a thick gray beard, and wore frameless glasses—"He used to be a doctor. He knows what he's doing."

"When was he a doctor? Vietnam?"

"He's someone we go to when we can't use our Blue Cross," Bennie said. "All he needs to do is snip a couple tension wires."

"That are in my mouth," David said.

"Your choice, Rabbi. Either he does it or maybe we go back to your place and have Slim Joe do it. He has pretty steady hands when he's not on the meth."

David didn't think Slim Joe was on meth. The kid was too lazy to cook. But he got the point, so he stepped out of the Mercedes.

"Which one of you is the doctor?" David asked. He wanted to make sure at least Bennie knew who was who.

"That would be me," Gray Beard said. He didn't bother to look up or even to stop turning his dog over the open flame.

"This is the guy I was telling you about," Bennie said. He reached into his pocket and pulled out his wallet—took five bills out and handed them to Gray Beard, who then handed the money to the other man, who counted the money, nodded twice, and slipped it into his sock. "How long is this gonna take?"

Gray Beard stood up and walked over to David. "Smile big," he said, and David did. Gray Beard peered into his mouth and shook his head once, almost imperceptibly. "Who did this work?"

"Dr. Crane," Bennie said.

Gray Beard took a hold of David's chin and moved it from side to side. "That hurt?"

"Yeah," David said.

"Less or more than it did a month ago?"

"Less," David said.

"That's good, at least," he said. David didn't like that *at least* part. "You get titanium rods in there?"

David had no idea, so he just shrugged, but Bennie said, "Yeah, for the elongation."

"I'm going to stick my finger in your mouth," Gray Beard said to David, not asking, just letting him know it was about to happen. The finger smelled like a combination of cigarette smoke and deli mustard, tasted like that, too, and for a moment David thought he might vomit, which would be a particularly difficult proposition in his current position. "Just breathe through your nose," Gray Beard said quietly. He began to poke around toward the back of David's mouth, pressing alternately on the gums on the top and bottom of his mouth. "That hurt? You just nod your head."

David nodded his head.

"Dr. Crane, he tied the wires too high up around the bicuspids and molars so that your gums would grow over the wires," Gray Beard said. "He was old-school that way. He wanted people to really hate their doctors." Gray Beard took his fingers out of David's mouth and then disappeared into the RV for a moment, returning with a small compact mirror, which he handed to David. "Take a look at your gums," he said. "You're about eighty percent infected."

His gums were dark red and, he could see, had grown around the wires holding his jaw together. He'd noticed this before but figured that's just how it was done. Bennie came over and looked, too.

"So, what are you saying?" Bennie asked.

"This is going to be bloody," Gray Beard said. "Another hundred, I'll shoot your friend up with enough Novocain that he won't feel a thing. Two hundred, I'll put him under."

"Just get this shit out of my mouth," David said.

"You don't want to be numb?" Gray Beard said.

"I just want this shit out of my mouth," David said.

"We're talking two hours of me cutting and pulling wires out of your soft tissue," Gray Beard said. "He even wired up your wisdom teeth. That's going to be a real bitch. I'm being real candid with you."

"Just get this shit out of my mouth," David said.

Gray Beard looked at Bennie, presumably for approval, and Bennie threw his hands up. "Whatever he wants," Bennie said.

"Give me and my assistant here a couple minutes to get everything sterilized," Gray Beard said.

Gray Beard and his assistant went inside the RV then, leaving Bennie and David alone. David thinking that if they brought out their needles and shit to be sterilized on the barbecue that he'd just pull the wires out himself, infection be damned.

"I would have paid another hundred," Bennie said.

"I appreciate that," David said, and he did. "But I'm not letting that motherfucker shoot me up with anything."

"I think his assistant does that," Bennie said.

"Even worse," David said.

Bennie smiled then. An actual, genuine smile. "I'm going to make this worth it for you," Bennie said. "Five, ten years from now? When you and me are running this city? We're gonna sit somewhere and laugh about this."

Ten years from now, David thought, *I'll be on a beach somewhere with my wife and kid. And you'll probably be dead, and I'll probably have killed you.* It was a good thought. A thought that made David smile, though with his jaw wired shut, he was pretty sure no one could really tell what emotion he was trying to convey. And that was good, too.

CHAPTER TWO

When Jeff Hopper was still studying for his MA in criminology at the University of Illinois, he'd occasionally stuff his books and lunch into his backpack and jog the one mile to the FBI field office on Roosevelt to study between classes. It was a silly thing, really, since he wasn't allowed inside. This was the late 1980s, and Jeff was already in his early thirties but still somehow felt like everything was possible, including working as a special agent for the FBI. He knew it wasn't a glamorous job, not like how the recruiters who came to campus said it was; that it, in all likelihood, was just as mundane on a day-to-day basis as any job. But at least there was some grander purpose to it, which appealed to Jeff.

He'd been a cop in Walla Walla, Washington, for a decade prior, and while the work was steady and not terribly dangerous—he unholstered his gun once the whole time, to break up a fight between two drunk migrant farm workers—it also wasn't the kind of heroic thing Jeff had imagined for himself while growing up in Seattle. He certainly never saw himself living in a city like Walla Walla, with its charming downtown and flowing wheat fields and . . . that was about it. He'd made a life there, even bought a house over by the country club, had managed to find a little romance with the occasional visiting professor at Whitman College (Jeff liked knowing these affairs were on a clock, since no one visiting Walla Walla dared to stay in town very long). But when the city announced it had to cut its police force in half during a particularly ugly budget crisis, Jeff readily stepped forward to take the parachute the city offered. He had a bit of money saved, the result of being single and well paid in a shitty place, and he started looking at graduate schools.

He knew he couldn't get into the CIA since he wasn't ex-military and his undergrad degree from the University of Washington probably tabbed him as a tad too liberal for those guys. Age was likely a factor, too. The FBI, on the other hand, liked guys who were a bit older, more mature, happy to do investigative work from a desk if need be, and so that became Jeff's goal. Not the desk, exactly, though Jeff figured that was where he might start out. And if the FBI didn't pan out? Maybe the NSA. And if NSA didn't work? Jeff had a full list of options written out on a yellow legal pad, and he even conceded that a job doing special investigative work for the IRS would be cool, maybe catching mob guys in tax evasion schemes or something. What Jeff Hopper wanted most of all was to wear a suit, a really nice suit that concealed a gun, and he wanted to stop bad guys and save America.

More than a decade later, though, standing in his office and staring out the window at that berm he used to sit on (even during clear days in the winter), Jeff wondered just what the hell he thought he was trying to prove. Did he think the ghost of J. Edgar Hoover would walk across the street and offer him a job? Did he think he'd assimilate some divine intelligence simply by breathing the same air as the agents he saw walking in and out every day? How did he not know that it would take him so long just to get into that building, that he'd bounce from Quantico to Kansas City to Cleveland to Rochester and then, finally, to Chicago, at which point his romantic vision of being in the FBI would be trumped by the hard understanding that he hated the feel of a tie around his neck? Had he even *learned* anything while sitting out there, what with all the exhaust from passing cars and trucks? It didn't seem possible.

Few things seemed possible to Special Agent Jeff Hopper anymore. For the last six months, he'd spent more time in his therapist's office than his own. He knew intuitively that he wasn't responsible for the death of his three colleagues and their CI, that he hadn't pulled the trigger on them, that legendary hit man Sal Cupertine had done it. If he knew anything about Sal Cupertine, it was this: If he wanted you dead, you were dead. And he understood that those men—Cal Hodel, Keith Baldwin, and Derek Lewis, he reminded himself that they were *people* and not just *men*—knew that working undercover came with its own unique set of dangers, including death. All that was clear to him. You deal with wild animals, you can't be surprised when they act like wild animals, his therapist told him, and he agreed.

That didn't change the fact that Jeff had lacked specific attention to detail—the billing information on the hotel bill, of all things—and that the result had been fatal. Four times fatal. And though his therapist told him not to blame himself, not to doubt his own abilities, the FBI had already made a few decisions for him: They'd knocked him down a grade, from senior special agent to special agent, and though they allowed

him to stay on the task force looking into the workings of the
Chicago crime families, he'd been completely shunned by the
other agents. Not that Jeff blamed them. It had been his idea to
get Cal, Keith, and Derek into the Family, and for the previous
year that's all he'd done, little by little, getting those three estab-
lished locally.

Used to be the best way to get information was to hope for a
snitch; the problem these days was that the Family was simply
too good. They hadn't made an arrest that stuck for almost
a decade—at least not of anyone significant, just soldiers, the
kinds of guys whose level of information was so limited they
couldn't snitch. So the only way in was to go that whole Donnie
Brasco route. But Cal, Keith, and Derek were serious men. Jeff
liked that. Liked that they wanted to get bad people off the
streets. Liked that they didn't think the FBI's policy of staying
away from the Chicago families since they were better than the
Crips and Bloods and Mexican gangs was worth shit. A criminal enterprise was a criminal enterprise, and Jeff was proud
that those three men agreed with him.

It had been Jeff's idea to let them meet up with Sal Cupertine without a strike force in the next room. Jeff knew that Sal
was a careful and considerate killer—if such a thing existed—
that he wouldn't shoot up a public place. It wasn't his style,
which is why on that day six months earlier, he was still a
free man. Plus, if what everyone said was true and Sal had
the memory of an elephant, it wasn't safe to have a bunch of
other guys waiting around in case something happened. If by
chance Sal saw one of them and then saw him again on some
later date . . . well, it would be trouble. Besides, it was just an
exploratory meeting. The guys went for it, and why not? There
were three of them, after all, plus their CI, and all three were

top-notch FBI agents. Sal Cupertine, at the end of the day, was just a man with a gun.

"Excuse me, Agent Hopper?" Jeff turned from the window and saw a young man in his doorway with a cart stacked high with boxes. Jeff didn't recognize him, which probably meant he was one of the clerks who'd been hired in the last few months. Maybe even a criminology student like he'd been. "Where would you like these?"

"Just leave them in the corner," Jeff said. He watched the clerk unstack the boxes, each one marked s. cupertine in black marker with a date starting from 1983, and wondered how it was that a guy who'd been killing people for the mob for over fifteen years had never spent even a night in jail, but had ten boxes of intelligence in an FBI office just down the street from his house. The last box the kid unpacked was the one Jeff was most interested in—marked 1998, it contained the report on what was purported to be Cupertine's body. There were no dental records or fingerprint records to be found, because there were no teeth left in the head when it was located, nor even a jaw, and no hands or feet, either.

In fact, all the cadaver dogs turned up (conveniently in a garbage dump owned by the Family) was half of a head, charred to the skeleton, with a hole from a .38 in the back, attached to just the trunk of a body, also burned to the bone. Helpfully, Sal Cupertine's wallet was also found nearby. His driver's license, which Cupertine inexplicably kept current, contained the only verified description of the man in the last decade: six foot, 215 pounds, brown hair, hazel eyes. He had an olive complexion, which made him look a bit more exotic than he was, since both of his parents, and their parents, too, were born and raised in

Chicago. His file said he had a tattoo on his arm of an eight ball, which would have been a good identifying mark if the corpse happened to have had an arm.

It was all too convenient, though not without precedent, that the Family would kill one of their own and make his body so easy to discover. The Family hadn't done business in Chicago for the better part of a century without knowing how to make amends, even to the authorities. How many dead crooked cops had turned up over the years? Twenty-five? Fifty? Enough to be both a shame to the city as well as a tidy solution. Yes, there were bad cops . . . and this is what happened to them. So here was the body of Sal Cupertine, offered up as a peace offering to the FBI. The FBI hadn't bothered to investigate much further to see if it really was Cupertine—Jeff knew it wasn't, it just wasn't possible—because the point was clear enough: *We've given one back to you.*

"Can I get you anything else?" the clerk asked.

Jeff looked up from the paperwork and saw that the clerk had arranged all the information into a kind of order—boxes containing information on Cupertine's presumed victims were put into a nice pyramid, boxes about his close family members in another, boxes of general information in another—which Jeff rather appreciated. "What's your name?" Jeff asked.

"Matthew Drew."

"You a student?"

"I graduated UIC last December," he said. "Quantico sent me back here to see if maybe it would be a good fit. So I'm just waiting to see where I'm assigned."

"So you're an agent?"

"Yeah," he said. "I guess I am."

"What's your specialty?"

"If it were up to me, I'd be on Hostage Rescue," he said. "I qualified for an assault team."

"Why are you running boxes for me?"

Matthew shrugged. He was young—maybe twenty-five, Jeff guessed—but big through the shoulders, maybe played small college football. "I guess I'm the guy who runs your boxes until I'm otherwise directed."

"This case," Jeff said, "what do you know about it?"

"Just what I saw on the news."

"C'mon," Jeff said. "You spend the whole morning hauling up boxes on big, bad Sal Cupertine, and you don't stop to read one or two files?"

This got the kid to smile. "I might have looked over some stuff," he said.

"What do you think? You think that body was Cupertine's?" Jeff handed the file he was reading to Matthew, but he didn't open it right away, which told Jeff he'd probably spent some time with it already.

"You want my opinion or an educated guess?" Matthew asked.

"Both," Jeff said.

Matthew opened the file and started thumbing through the documents. "Body was found three days after the killing, but with garbage that had been picked up five days earlier," he said. "So he was stashed, I'd say, not put in a garbage can somewhere. They actually carried him and pushed him under a bunch of trash. No teeth. No hands. No feet. I mean, no nothing, really. It's a pretty brutal way to kill a guy who'd done a lot of good work for you, isn't it?"

"You tell me," Jeff said.

"Seems excessive. I mean, he was their top muscle. So he messes up and kills a couple good guys . . . bad news, right? But not as bad as if he was skimming or planning a coup. If they killed him for messing up, my guess is that they'd do him decently. The wallet? That's too sloppy for them. No way they'd let his wallet get into the mix."

"So?"

"So that's not him."

"Why fake his death? Why kill *another* guy?"

Matthew closed his eyes for a moment. "Maybe his cousin Ronnie's influence. Maybe as an appreciation for his services. Maybe they were scared to go after him. Maybe all that. It doesn't make a lot of sense. I think that's the problem. Easier to just make it him and get on with things. Easier for the families of those guys and for us, too."

Matthew was right about that, but the thing that niggled at Jeff had nothing to do with the four men Sal Cupertine had killed at all. Certainly their deaths *mattered*. Certainly. What got to Jeff was that he knew Sal Cupertine believed the agent named Jeff Hopper was dead. That he saw Jeff's name on the bill and decided he'd go upstairs and take Jeff Hopper out, put a bullet in his face, or choke him to death like he did Cal, and how, in his mind, that was an okay thing. How wherever he was now—and Jeff was certain he was out there somewhere— he thought he'd killed Jeff Hopper.

And maybe he had killed Jeff Hopper for a while. Six months, give or take. Now Jeff Hopper wanted Sal Cupertine to know: He was alive, and he was coming for him.

"You have a sport coat or something in your cubicle?" Jeff asked.

"No," Matthew said. He had on a pair of tan slacks—probably Dockers—and a nicely pressed white polo shirt that now was dotted with smudges of dirt and dust from unloading the boxes.

Jeff checked his watch. It was a little past two o'clock. "You live nearby?"

"Yeah," he said, "just down by the college."

"You got a suit there?"

"Yeah," he said.

"Okay," Jeff said. "Go change your clothes and come back. We're going into the field."

"Sounds good," Matthew said calmly, though Jeff could tell he was excited. He apparently didn't know yet that Jeff Hopper was a pariah. "Where are we headed?"

"Sal's house," Jeff said.

■

Jeff Hopper was always surprised by the houses bad people lived in, since they tended to look just like the houses good people lived in. In the case of Sal Cupertine's house in Lincolnwood, there was even a white picket fence out front, which went along nicely with the brick driveway shaded by a towering blue ash. The blue ash even had a tire swing, something Jeff had always imagined he'd have one day, too, if he ever managed to have children, though at this point in his life that likely meant stepchildren. Turning forty-five without a wife, and with no clear prospects in sight, had confirmed that.

Hopper had Matthew make another drive around the block so they could rendezvous with the surveillance car at the end of the street, which was a peculiar place to watchdog a house, since they had to spend their whole day looking through their rear and side mirrors. Jeff couldn't help but wonder how long that detail would last. Maybe another month? Two months? The house was likely bugged, and Jennifer Cupertine's car had a tracker on it, so there was no real cause for concern that she'd skip out of town to find or meet up with her husband without the FBI being aware, though there was still the small chance that Jennifer and her son were in danger from the Family, an idea Jeff found unlikely. That was some Russian mob shit that even the Italians looked down on.

Matthew pulled up next to a black Chrysler, and Jeff rolled down his window so he could talk to the agents inside. There were two of them, both about Matthew's age and build, which meant they were probably spending their free time cursing the recruiter who'd told them they'd be on the front line in the war on crime.

"Anything we should know?" Jeff asked. He didn't recognize either man, which meant they probably didn't recognize him, either. Better all around.

"Been pretty quiet," the one in the driver's seat said.

"How long?"

He looked at his watch. "I don't know, maybe ninety days. Coop, that sound right?"

Coop, the agent in the passenger seat, had a row of playing cards spread out on the dashboard and was too busy playing solitaire to even look at Jeff. "Yeah," he said. "Give or take a month." He flopped down a nine of hearts but didn't seem to know where to put it.

"Okay," Jeff said. "When was the last time anyone from the Family stopped by?"

"Never," the driver said. "It's all wives and girlfriends. Ronnie Cupertine's wife came by with two little ones about a week ago. Stayed about ten minutes and left in tears. That was a fun day."

"Yeah?" Jeff said.

"Yeah," the driver said. "The next hour, Jennifer stood out on the front lawn with a hammer and beat the shit out of that big tree next to the driveway. When she got tired of that, she came out into the street with a picnic basket filled with food and spent the next, I dunno, twenty minutes throwing fruits and vegetables at us."

"She has a pretty good arm," Coop said.

That explained why they were parked so far down the street.

"Okay," Jeff said. "We've got some questions for her, so if Al Capone shows up, call me on my cell."

Jeff handed the driver his card, and when the agent looked at the name, it was clear he recognized it. "Yeah," the driver said, "I'll do that," and then he crumpled the card up and dropped it onto the pavement between the two cars.

Matthew didn't give Jeff an opportunity to say anything, hitting the gas fast enough to make it clear he was polite enough not to say a word. He drove their same black Chrysler down the block and then pulled onto the Cupertine's driveway, just as the manual suggests. Let the suspect know that you're comfortable enough to park on their property . . . while also, obviously, blocking their ability to drive away. Matthew took off his seat belt, but Jeff put a hand on his chest. "Hold up," he said to him.

"What are we doing?" Matthew asked.

"Waiting for Mrs. Cupertine to come outside," Jeff said.

"What if she never comes?"

"She'll come," Jeff said. "And when she does, feel free to ask questions."

"I don't feel comfortable doing that," Matthew said. "I'm not familiar with all the particulars of the case."

"You know that this lady's husband killed three agents and a CI," Jeff said. "Isn't that enough?"

"I guess so," he said. "Should I turn off the engine?"

"No, let it run," Jeff said.

Matthew sat there quietly for ten minutes, didn't even turn on the radio, didn't roll down the window. Jeff was impressed. It wasn't like an FBI agent, even a new one, to sit quietly by. But the kid did fidget in his seat a few times. Then he cracked his knuckles.

"You play a sport? In college?"

"Lacrosse," Matthew said.

"Some place with a bunch of ivy around it?"

"Tufts," Matthew said.

"That a good school?" Jeff messing with him now.

"Better than some," Matthew said. "More expensive than most." He cocked his head and then did roll down his window. "I think the venetian blinds are moving."

"Yeah," Jeff said, "Mrs. Cupertine has taken a couple looks."

"You know," Matthew said, "it's not like she killed the agents."

"I know that," Jeff said.

"Then why are we sweating her to come out? Why not just go to the door?"

"I want her to get a good look at us," Jeff said. "That way she won't be scared to come outside and talk. We go knock on the door and badge her, maybe her kid gets all flustered and starts screaming and crying and throwing a tantrum. Then the dog starts barking and it's all gone to shit. I don't want that. When she's ready, she'll come outside and ask us questions."

"That standard procedure?"

"No," Jeff said. "Standard procedure would be that we just go about our business and pretend that body in the dump was Sal Cupertine."

"Those guys back there," Matthew said. "Did that bother you?"

"A little bit," Jeff said.

"Here's what I don't get," Matthew said. "And I mean no offense in this. But how do you still have a job?"

"Because I haven't quit," Jeff said.

Matthew rapped his fingers on the steering wheel. Jeff liked that the kid wasn't scared to ask a question. Didn't seem worried that he might say the wrong thing, or if he was, had determined that Jeff wasn't the kind of guy to pull rank on him. Truth was, six months ago, he *was* that guy. He was that guy going all the way back to Walla Walla. Maybe all the way back to his crib in Seattle. Raised like that by his father, a man he despised until he died. Then just as soon as his dad was six feet deep, their relationship improved markedly.

"Here we go," Matthew said. The front door opened, and a young boy ran out, followed in short order by his mother. William was just a small child, Jeff could see, no more than four or five. He had Jennifer's blonde hair but his father's olive complexion and deep-set eyes. If William was lucky, Jeff thought, his mother would get rid of all remnants of his father and let him start fresh. Move to Nebraska or something and live his entire life thinking his father had never been a part of his life. Could you do that to a four-year-old? Probably. At three, for sure. But by five, they'd retain too much. The kid still had a chance not to be infected by the Family.

Jennifer stood on the front porch and watched her boy. He ran around the side of the house and came back riding a Big Wheel. He pedaled past the car and out into the street and then turned back around and cut up the passenger side and down the long driveway, before banking left and disappearing. A few moments later, he came shooting back around the house. Jennifer stepped off the porch then, sidestepped what looked to be several dinosaurs engaged in battle with each other on the front lawn, and came over to the Chrysler. She was tall—maybe five feet nine—and her long blonde hair spilled into the car. She had green eyes, though they were mostly red on this day, and the deep, dark circles around them weren't doing her any favors, either.

"Please get off my property," Jennifer said. Polite. Nice. Like it was just another inconvenience in her life, like having Jehovah's Witnesses showing up when you're watching television.

"I just have some questions for you," Jeff said.

"Who are you? FBI or cops? Not the press, that's clear enough by your nice ties."

"FBI," Jeff said. Jennifer gnawed at the skin surrounding her right pinkie nail. It looked raw, and Jeff wanted to reach across Matthew and pull it from her mouth, as if she were a child. Jeff couldn't remember everything they had on her in their files, but what he did recall indicated to him that she wasn't the average Family wife: the former Jennifer Frangello was in art classes at Olive-Harvey, getting good grades, parents were both dead—cancer and heart disease—and neither were related to any known crime families. She was just a person who happened to fall in love with a sociopath. Happens every day, and if he could figure out why, well, he'd retire and get his own afternoon talk show. "If this is a bad time for you, we can come back."

"This is a good time," she said. "Most of my neighbors are still at work, so they won't come outside to watch the freak show." She stopped to examine her finger. It had begun to bleed, so she gathered up the hem of her T-shirt and squeezed it around her hand. "I'm sorry about whatever you think my husband did," she said. "I mean, I'm sorry about your friends. Were they your friends?"

"They were," Jeff said.

"No one deserves to go out like that," she said.

"That's where we agree," Jeff said.

"My husband," Jennifer said, "he's a good person. I know you don't believe that. He loves his son. He's a caring person. A very caring person."

For some reason, Jeff didn't doubt that. He'd listened to all the wiretaps they had on him from his meetings with the boys—even the last one—and what Jeff took away was that he seemed . . . professional. Had an okay sense of humor. They'd even caught him briefly, and unexpectedly, on a wire a few months earlier, when they were working on the Russians, and he'd spent a good fifteen minutes standing outside a Subway near the college talking on his cell phone about cough medicine. Called his wife "baby." Told her that he loved her before he hung up. Went inside and ordered a tuna fish sandwich. Just like a normal person.

"Your husband," Jeff said, "is a hit man for the Family."

"He's never been arrested, do you know that?"

"Of course," Jeff said.

"You know these people you call the 'Family' threw his father off of a building? So why would he work for people who did that to him?" Jennifer began to tear up, and Jeff wondered how hard it would be to live her life for one day. He didn't try to empathize with the people he investigated, generally speaking, but then Jennifer wasn't someone he was investigating.

"I'm not here to harass you," Jeff said.

"The cops keep showing up whenever I go out. They don't come here, because they probably know you guys are listening to everything, but they'll roll up behind me when I'm out getting groceries. William, he loves it. But you know Chicago cops. They aren't investigating anymore. The ones that stop me now, they think Sal is off somewhere going state's evidence, so they're here making sure I'm doing okay, asking me if I need anything, offering me money or whatever. Last guy? He came up to me at Tino's pizza down the street, asked me what I needed, so I told him the best thing he could do would be to pay my electric bill. I was just joking, though I wonder if he did it, you know? Maybe next time I'll ask him to get my cleaning."

"Is that what you think?" Jeff asked. "That he turned state's?"

"I think if I sit out here and talk to you, Ronnie will send his wife over to talk to me again."

"Would that be why you didn't hold a funeral?" Matthew asked.

Jennifer cocked her head and regarded Matthew with a look that Jeff thought was a mix between amusement and utter sadness. "Look at you," she said. "Have you ever wanted for anything in your life?"

"Everyone wants something," Matthew said, the young agent composed, cool, maybe a touch condescending, which was okay; he was FBI, after all. Then Jeff saw for the first time that Matthew had a wedding ring on his finger, and it all made some sense. He might have been a young agent, but he still had a life, still had more shit going on than Jeff, really. "It boils down to how they go about getting what they want, doesn't it? For me, anyway."

"Aren't you smart, with your Brooks Brothers suit and your class ring. You think that gives you the right to talk to me like that? You're not even old enough to valet my car."

"Let's take it easy," Jeff said.

"No, to answer your question," she said. "I didn't have a funeral because I don't want to believe he's dead. Don't want his son to believe he's dead, either. Maybe he did turn state's and he's living out in Springfield or something, eating steak every night and telling you everything he knows about his cousin Ronnie's used-car business."

"Is that what you want?" Jeff asked.

"It's what I hope," she said. "It's the best-case scenario. Otherwise I have to believe the shoe box of ashes in my hall closet is my husband, and I can't handle that." William came around the front of the house again on his Big Wheel, his legs pumping away on the pedals. Jennifer stood upright and watched as he spun around the car again before heading toward the backyard. "William, be careful," she said, though it wasn't loud enough for him to hear. It seemed almost reflexive.

"Your son has a lot of energy," Matthew said. "My son is about his age. Never gets tired. My wife, Nina, is always looking for new ways to wear him out."

"Get him a puppy," Jennifer said absently. "Or a brother."

"He's adorable," Matthew said.

"Right now he is," Jennifer said. She shook her head just slightly, and then her pinkie went back into her mouth. She was only thirty-five, still a young woman, but Jeff wondered how much pressure she could take. Jeff took off his seat belt and got out of the car then, not bothering to put on his suit coat. He didn't imagine she had a lot of allies in this world. He wanted to put an arm around her, let her know it was going to be okay, though of course he knew it never would be. So, instead, he handed her his business card. She looked at it briefly and then stuck it in her back pocket.

"Your husband," Jeff said, "is not in state custody, and that body? That's not him, either."

"You have his DNA or something?"

"No," he said. "But I don't need it. I know the truth."

"What's that?" Jennifer said.

"We'll get a court order and DNA your son at some point, compare it to the samples we have, and then it will be a big deal in the newspapers and such. It wouldn't be good PR to do it now. Might not even be good PR for another year."

"I don't know where he is," Jennifer said. "I don't care if you believe me."

"I believe you," Jeff said.

"You do?"

"You've got no reason to lie," he said, though of course she did. Everyone Jeff had ever known had a good reason to lie; it's just that those reasons rarely panned out in the long run.

Jennifer Cupertine nodded twice and then took a deep breath through her nose and let it back out slowly through her mouth, then did it again. It occurred to Jeff Hopper that he shouldn't have come here. Not because he didn't appreciate the small amount of information he'd received, but because he was sure that this was another bad day Jennifer Cupertine would remember for the rest of her life. Another in a series of shitty days, this one featuring Special Agent Jeff Hopper and Kid Agent Matthew Drew, the lacrosse superstar who was now in the middle of his own career suicide, or would be once he got back to the office and was quizzed by the senior agents about what the fuck he was doing out at Sal Cupertine's house when he was supposed to be running boxes.

"Why are you here?" Jennifer asked.

"I wanted you to know your husband was alive," Jeff said. "And to tell you to keep away from Ronnie Cupertine and his people. They don't have your son's best interests, Mrs. Cupertine. This is a chance for you, for him. Make a different life. Get out of Chicago. This is your opportunity to get away from this gangster bullshit, Mrs. Cupertine."

"No," she said. "This house is paid for, and I'm going to stay in it until Sal comes back."

"Sal comes back, he's going to prison," Jeff said. "If he's lucky."

"That's fine," she said, "but he'll come here first, and I will be here, no matter when that is."

"Fair enough," Jeff said. He extended his hand toward Jennifer, and, surprisingly, she took it. "You hear from your husband, call me. I can help him."

This made Jennifer laugh. "Okay," she said, "I'll be sure to do that."

Jeff watched as Jennifer Cupertine gathered up the stray dinosaurs on her front lawn and then called for her son to put his Big Wheel away and come back inside. A simple domestic scene. And maybe what Jennifer Cupertine said was true—maybe Sal Cupertine was the most loving man on earth. It didn't change the fact that he was also a murderer.

Something else Jennifer Cupertine said started to bother Jeff, so before she went inside, he said, "Mrs. Cupertine, just one more question."

"What's that, Agent Hopper?"

"How did you pay off your house?"

Jennifer Cupertine smiled. "Don't you know?"

"If I did, I wouldn't be asking."

"Cousin Ronnie paid it off," she said. "An early birthday present for William."

CHAPTER THREE

For the first week, Rabbi David Cohen still couldn't open his mouth more than half an inch, just enough room to shove in a fork and do some good chewing. Soft foods mostly. Potato salad, pasta. On the Monday before Thanksgiving, as he brushed his teeth with the fancy electric toothbrush he'd picked up after Gray Beard had finished his wire excavation, David realized his mouth had regained nearly full mobility.

His jaw still hurt at the joints, which made long conversations somewhat painful, not that he and Slim Joe were having long and involved chats. David had learned that Slim Joe's main job was working the door at the Wild Horse, a job he'd gone back to after David was allowed out the front door, and that he was nominally in charge of shaking down the pimps who brought their girls in to work the club. It was a small percentage of the two hundred or so girls who worked on a weekend night, enough to keep him in Nike tracksuits and gold chains. His other job, David had gleaned, was to provide a bit of de facto security for David. The closed-circuit TVs were in

Slim Joe's closet, along with an armory to put up a good long siege if that came to pass.

David had also learned that Slim Joe had two big ambitions: He wanted to open up a cart on the Strip serving all kinds of different hot dogs, as well as slices of homemade pies that he envisioned his mother would be in charge of fixing. It would be open from midnight to 5 a.m. when all the drunks and tweaks were fiending and when the dancers got off shift. "I'd do it real classy," Slim Joe told him. "None of that taco truck shit where you don't know what kind of cheese you're getting. I'd be cutting fresh cheeses, too, deli-style. It'll be off the hook."

"You need a permit for that," David said. "You really want the state looking into you?"

"On the real?"

"What's your other idea?"

"Bennie had me take some classes over at CCSN," Slim Joe said. "Computers and shit. I had this idea of making a website where people would just, like, put up their thoughts every day. Like two sentences about what was on their mind. Call it Expressions, but with a *z*."

"Why don't you just call it Snitches?"

"Don't be a bitch," Slim Joe said, like they were friends.

David told Slim Joe that if he ever called him a bitch again, he and his mother would be selling hot dogs and pies in the middle of the desert from the trunk of a burnt-out Cadillac. It was the first time he'd threatened Slim Joe, the first time in six months he'd threatened anyone, and it made him feel great.

Like he was back in the game.

But all the books he'd been reading were having some kind

of residual effect on David, because his elation was short-circuited by the honest look of hurt on Slim Joe's face. And then he thought about something he read in the Talmud: *Hold no man responsible for what he says in his grief.* Because the truth was, he didn't give a shit if Slim Joe called him a bitch or anything else. Those were just words, and it's not as if Slim Joe even knew what he was saying; the kid was practically illiterate. David was just mad about . . . everything. The whole nut of his life had been cracked open.

"Look," David told him, "there's nothing more boring than hearing someone else's dreams, right? But these are good ideas. You should save some money and do it."

"Really?" Slim Joe perked right back up, like a dog that's chased a ball into the street, only to get hit, but still wants to get that fucking ball. "I ain't told no one about this shit because I don't want no one biting my game. So you think, on the real, that it could work?"

"On the real," David said, and then he went back upstairs for the rest of the night. He just couldn't listen to anything more about anything.

David spit out his toothpaste, wiped off his face, and went into his closet to pick out a suit. He was supposed to meet Bennie in thirty minutes at something called the Bagel Café. "Bring all of your fancy Jew books with you," Bennie told him. "You're gonna meet someone important."

David had no idea who that might be, though the idea of bringing all his books with him set up a bit of a practical dilemma. The nice thing about Christians is that they had just one book, the Bible, and inside of it were all the secrets of life. The Jews, however, had the Bible, and the Torah, which was really just the five books of Moses from the Bible, and the Talmud, which ran six thousand pages, or what David thought of as his sleeping pill.

And then there was the Midrash, which was like someone went through the Bible, Torah, and Talmud and filled in the empty parts, or explained what everything meant, or what they thought everything meant, since some of it was pretty clear to David and, yet, there was an explanation that was completely contrary to his understanding. Finally, there were the stacks and stacks of books on "Jewish thought" that had been dumped off at the house over the weeks, which were like reading a combination of someone's diary filled with their thoughts on all of the other books combined.

All this for a fucking cover? David thought it would have been a lot easier to say he was a butcher.

David picked out a gray Hugo Boss suit and put it on with a white shirt and a blue tie and those five-hundred-dollar black Cole Haan dress shoes, found a handkerchief and put it in his breast pocket, and then called downstairs to Slim Joe to help him with his books.

"You look like a pimp, dog," Slim Joe said when he saw David, and then, quickly, he added, "that's a good thing, yo. Just on the real."

All this time, Slim Joe had treated him like nothing. Didn't fear him. Didn't respect him. Didn't *dis*respect him, either, but generally regarded him as nothing but a warm body he was tasked to bring food to and help change bandages for early on in the process. But since David threatened him twelve hours earlier, the kid was now acting deferential, maybe even a bit scared, which struck David as funny since he looked less menacing than he ever had. His words, though, still carried weight. He liked that.

"You think so?" David said. "I don't look like a pussy?"

"Never, dog," he said. He examined all the books stacked up on David's dresser. "You need to take all these?"

"That's what Bennie said."

"Sometimes, I think he just says things to say things, you feel me?"

"He's the boss," David said.

"Is he your boss?"

Slim Joe had never asked him a single organizational question; it was as if he'd been strictly informed to steer clear of any such talk, which seemed like a reasonable possibility, which made his sudden boldness questionable.

"Just put the books in the car," David said.

                ■

Back home, David drove a 1993 Lincoln Town Car his cousin Ronnie got for him. When he had to do a job for the Family, someone would show up with a car for him to use, something that could be torched or cleaned and resold. When he had a freelance job, he'd take the bus over to O'Hare or Midway and steal a car from long-term parking. Weird thing was that he always had his license with him, even on the jobs he did freelance, on the odd chance he was pulled over for speeding or running a stop sign—not that he'd gotten a ticket since he was a teenager. Having a valid identification was a good way to avoid ancillary problems.

He had a temporary Nevada license in his wallet—Bennie brought it by over the weekend, along with another test, this time about what happens to Jews after they're resurrected, which was some of the most absurd shit Dave had ever read, as it involved Jews rolling from their graves all the way to Israel, which made no sense whatsoever—and had been told over and over again that his paperwork was legit and not to worry, which was easy enough for Bennie to say. He wasn't the guy driving around in a gold Range Rover with tinted windows, which made David feel as inconspicuous as the Sears Tower and just as big. So David drove from his house in Summerlin to the Bagel Café, located five miles away on the busy intersection of Westcliff and Buffalo, at about ten miles below the speed limit, which brought him to the restaurant fifteen minutes late.

When David walked in, he noticed first all the old people. There was a bakery section at the front of the house, and the seniors were lined up five deep by the pastry windows, the din of their hearing-aid-loud conversation bouncing off the walls of the place, the cacophony reminding David of a bingo parlor the Family ran back in the day on the South Side. On the other side of the bakery was the seating area—a U of booths around the perimeter, which looked out to the street and the parking lot, and then a dozen or so tables in the middle. David had always been freaked out by old people, never able to imagine himself living past fifty or so, not even after Jennifer had William and his life began to feel . . . different. More valuable. It just didn't seem feasible. His father was dead by forty. Never knew his grandparents. His mother remarried and moved to Arizona as soon as he graduated high school, and he'd lost complete contact with her, though he guessed she was probably still alive. His dream of retiring to California as a top dog was just a dream, something to put in the back of his head when he was doing contract killing in Champaign. As it turned out, Sal Cupertine *was* dead. David thought he might start keeping a list of all life's cruel ironies, just to be sure he wasn't imagining half of the shit that was happening.

He spotted Bennie sitting alone in a booth at the near corner of the restaurant, a bunch of papers spread out in front of him, three waters on the table. He had a pair of reading glasses in one hand, something David had never seen before.

"You're late," Bennie said when David slid in across from him.

"It took Slim Joe a while to get all the books downstairs," David said.

"How's that working out?"

"He's fine," David said, though the truth was he really wanted him out of the house, David not having any time to himself since the day of the shooting.

"He's an idiot," Bennie said.

"He's all right," David said, not really sure why he was defending Slim Joe.

Bennie put on his glasses and examined David's face. "Any pain?"

"Nothing I can't manage."

"Swelling?"

"Around my chin some," David said. "Probably couldn't take an upper cut, if that's what you're asking."

"Jaw looks good," Bennie said. "The beard is coming in nicely."

"I don't recognize myself when I look in the mirror."

"That was the point," Bennie said. He gathered up some of the paper in front of him—they looked to David like blueprints and spreadsheets, actual business work—and slid them into a manila envelope. "Anyway," he said. "You ready to start earning?"

"Yeah," David said, not sure what he was agreeing to. Anything was better than sitting around reading and watching the local news. Maybe Bennie would send him out to hit the weatherman on Channel 3 who needed a dog to sit next to him every day while he told Las Vegas it would be eighty-eight degrees for the fiftieth straight day, as if the stress of blue skies, dry air, and a city full of strippers was too much to handle by himself. "I need to get out of the house."

A waitress walked up to the table then and smiled warmly at Bennie. "Hi, Mr. Savone," she said. She was maybe eighteen, no more than twenty, tall, brown hair, had a hole in her nostril where David presumed she usually kept a ring, a little butterfly tattoo on her ankle just above her no-show socks and white Keds. The servers—male or female—all wore the same outfit: tan shorts, red polo shirt, white shoes. It looked to David that this waitress had hemmed her shorts a little higher than most of the other ladies. Not that he had a problem with that.

"How are you, Tricia?"

"Super," she said. "How's your wife? I haven't seen her at temple in forever."

"She's been sick lately," Bennie said.

"I hope it's nothing serious."

"Lady problems," Bennie said. David marveled at how Bennie showed absolutely no embarrassment at all. "What's it called? Endometriosis? When it gets bad, she just can hardly get up. But what can you do, right?"

"Oh, no," Tricia said. "Well, when she's feeling better, if you guys need someone to watch the kids for a date night or whatever, I'm happy to come over to help anytime."

"I appreciate that," Bennie said, and it sounded to David like the truth.

"Are you waiting on Rabbi Kales?"

"He just went to the restroom, so maybe just get him his usual," Bennie said. "And I'll have bacon and eggs, scrambled wet. Bring me a plate of sausage, too."

"And what about for you?" Tricia gave David that same warm smile, which immediately made him feel uncomfortable. When was the last time he'd even *seen* a woman, much less spoken to one?

"Rabbi," Bennie said, "you want some bacon and eggs, too?" Bennie not just fucking with him now, but also letting him know that he needed to act like a Rabbi in this place.

"I guess I'll have an onion bagel and coffee," David said. A plate of fucking sausage would work, too, the mere thought of it making his mouth turn on for the first time in months. No, no, not sausage. A plank of honey ham and a couple eggs fried in the ham fat and some corned beef hash. Glass of buttermilk to wash it down. Why were they meeting at a deli when Bennie knew Rabbi David Cohen couldn't eat anything he might want?

Tricia took down his order but didn't scurry on, which David really wanted her to do. The combination of his ham fantasy and her legs, which had to be ten feet long, was distracting. "So, I have to ask," Tricia said, "are you going to be the new youth rabbi we've been hearing about?"

"He is," Bennie said before David could answer. "He'll be taking over in a couple of weeks."

David couldn't help but think of something he'd read a few mornings ago about the nature of good and evil, which basically said that no man was born entirely one or the other, that the moral freedom to be a complete asshole is inherent in all men. If you were largely a decent human, that was called *yetzer tov*. If you were not, that was called *yetzer hara*. Bennie Savone, the fat fuck, with his order of sausage and bacon, with his complete inability to inform David of things like the fact that he was about to become some kind of youth rabbi, clearly had made his choice. This was a personal choice to surprise him, put him off-center, show him that he had no control over anything. The Jews, they were always going on about personal liberty and truth—what did they call truth? *The seal of God*, not that David believed in God, but the sentiment was concise enough.

"That is so cool," Tricia said. "We all totally miss Rabbi Gottlieb."

"I've heard only good things about him," David said, thinking, *I can't just sit here like an idiot and let Bennie push me into corners*, though, at the same time he realized he had no choice, his own response a calculated answer to make this pretty young girl appeased. What was happening to him?

"He was so young, so it's totally sad," she said, and David realized Rabbi Gottlieb hadn't just moved to Reno. "The way he spoke Torah . . ." She couldn't continue, as the power of whatever she was talking about was just too palpable.

Bennie patted Tricia lightly on the small of her back. "A tragedy," he said. "And Tricia, be a doll, and make sure my bacon is soft. I can't eat that crispy stuff." Bennie watched her walk off before he said, "Her father used to own half of North Las Vegas. Jordan Rosen. You'll meet him at temple."

Great. "What happened?"

"He started coming down to the Wild Horse," Bennie said. "Fell in love with a girl we used to have. Said she was Iranian when shit was bad with the Iranians, said she was Iraqi when shit was bad with them, but truth was she was just brown. Real name was Karen but on stage she went by Sholeh, which she said meant 'flame' or 'fire' or 'hot pussy.' She had the game she played. You get these idiots in from Kansas who want to get some towel head to push her tits in their face while they say trash to her, that's a good time. Tricia's dad, he just wanted some strange, you know? He couldn't stand having these tourists abusing her, so he'd buy her all night long, drop five, ten thousand a night on her. That adds up." Bennie paused and took a sip of his coffee, put his glasses back on. "The pictures we sent him did the rest."

"You had to do that?" David said, testing him now, still thinking about what he'd read, pondering exactly how he was going to address this whole situation, seeing if Bennie ever made the right choice.

"He started putting dances on his credit card, and he kept getting declined," Bennie said. "First time, whatever, we let it slide. He's a good customer, so I tell the manager to pay the girl for her time and that we'll double up next time. Next time comes, same shit, so now I'm out twenty K. I gave him a few days to make good, you know, gentleman to gentleman, and he didn't come up, says not to worry, he's good, owns half the city, just having some liquidity issues, and so I'm reasonable, right? You'd say I'm reasonable?"

"Yeah," David said, thinking: *Reasonably mad.*

"Two months he pulled this shit," Bennie said. "He lives three houses from me, his wife and kids practically cousins to my wife and kids, so what can I do?" Before David could answer—and his answer would have been *Beat it out of the fucker, because a debt is a debt and somehow, if you owe, you gotta pay*—Bennie pointed at a tall, well-dressed older gentleman walking through the restaurant. "That's Rabbi Kales," he said. Rabbi Kales stopped and had a few words with the people at almost every table, his hand always on someone's shoulder. "Watch how he works the room. That's your lesson for the day."

Rabbi Kales didn't really look like a rabbi, at least not what David thought a rabbi looked like, which is to say he thought he was going to be wearing that black getup, have the long beard, the hat, all that Hasidic garb. Instead, Rabbi Kales looked like a bank president—blue suit, not too flashy, but clearly expensive, nice shoes, though not as nice as the ones David had on, tie with a big Windsor knot, and what looked to David like a pretty decent watch. (David had a Rolex once, though he hadn't earned it. He just took it off of a body. It eventually started to creep him out, so he traded it to a Russian for a nice GSh-18 self-loading pistol when the Family had him proctor an arms deal a few years back.) Rabbi Kales wasn't even wearing a yarmulke, which came as a great relief to David, since he realized he'd be able to do likewise.

When Rabbi Kales finally finished his tour of the restaurant, he sat down beside his son-in-law in the booth and gave him a handful of checks. "Take these to the bank for me, Benjamin," he said.

Benjamin? For some reason, David had never thought of Bennie as having any other name. The mere thought of this gave David his first reason to smile in a very long time.

Bennie went through the checks, one by one, nodding each time. "Not a bad pull," he said. "Maybe we should come back at dinner."

Rabbi Kales didn't reply. He was too busy eyeballing David, that jovial table-to-table demeanor David witnessed now long gone. "So," Rabbi Kales said finally, "you're him."

"I guess so," David said.

"Did you bring your books?"

"They're in the car," David said. "You want I should get them?"

Rabbi Kales gave a short laugh, not much more than a snort. "In your entire life," he said, "have you ever heard anyone, other than the people you worked with previously, use a phrase like *You want I should get them?*"

David felt his face getting very hot. "I don't—" he began, but Rabbi Kales cut him off with a wave of his hand.

"You're smart," Rabbi Kales said. "Speak like it."

David didn't know if he was smart. He liked to think he wasn't dumb, even sort of liked learning new things, provided it didn't come at the expense of doing something he really wanted to do. He didn't believe in street smarts, since that meant you were a failure in some other part of your life but somehow were cagey enough to make shit work out among the uneducated trolls who lived under the bridge. But David was aware that he didn't *sound* smart. "I only know how to talk one way," David said.

"We'll fix that," he said. Not rude. Not condescending. Just factual. David admired that. It was a different kind of toughness. "Rabbi Gottlieb, you should know, was a very popular man. You have your work ahead of you."

"Where did he go?" David asked.

"Right off the side of a boat," Bennie said.

"He was a fine boy," Rabbi Kales said quietly. "And an excellent rabbi. He didn't deserve his fate."

"Yeah, well, who does?" Bennie said.

"He was a religious man, Benjamin," Rabbi Kales said.

"Then he should be happy," Bennie said. "He's in a better place."

"You know nothing of our religion," Rabbi Kales said. He spit the words out with such venom that David actually backed away from the table and banged his knee on the underside of it with a force that knocked water out of the glasses, all of which seemed to get Rabbi Kales to settle down a bit. "For my grand-daughters, at least," he continued, "you might want to know what happens to them when they die. It's the sort of question children tend to ask."

Yeah, David thought, *yetzer hara for sure.*

Thankfully, Tricia reappeared then with everyone's orders: plates of pork and eggs for Bennie, lox and onions for Rabbi Kales, David's lone bagel. David had never been happier to see a waitress in his life. Everything he'd witnessed thus far had him completely confused: There was, apparently, some belief by Bennie and his father-in-law, Rabbi Kales, that he'd be *working* as a rabbi. Not pretending to be a rabbi as a cover story while he chilled out for a few months, years, whatever.

There was no good reason either Bennie or Rabbi Kales should think he was qualified for any kind of work with kids, or any kind of work that didn't involve killing people. It was his unique, cultivated skill set.

What David really couldn't figure out was Rabbi Kales. What could Bennie possibly have on him? Bennie was married to his daughter, they had kids, and apparently Bennie was somehow involved enough in the day-to-day operations of the temple that Rabbi Kales wasn't in the least bit worried about being seen giving him money in the middle of a restaurant.

"Listen," David said. He leaned across the table and spoke as quietly as he could while still being heard. "I've been a good soldier here. You guys wanted to change my face? Fine. Change my face. You want me to read five hundred books on Judaism? Fine, I'll read the books. You want me to take tests? Write essays? No problem. Give me a number 2 pencil. You want to coop me up in solitary confinement in that house with that half-wit Slim Joe for six months, I grin and make it through. Now, either someone tells me what the plan is, or I bounce. And when I bounce, people get hurt. That's all I'm saying."

No one said anything for a moment, so David sat back, took a bite of his bagel, and chewed it angrily, or what he presumed Rabbi Kales and Bennie would see as anger, though really he chewed it with relief for finally speaking his mind (plus he could finally *chew* with actual purpose, which was a nice surprise). Whether or not he'd made the wrong play was a slight concern.

Both Bennie and Rabbi Kales seemed surprised, neither of them used to getting told what was what, but if there was one thing he'd learned in his life, it was that as soon as you let someone else dictate the terms of your survival, you are a dead man. That's why even though he'd been part of the Family all these years, he still worked freelance and didn't concern himself with whether or not someone got pissed about not getting a pinch of his take. If they wanted a bite, they could try to come and take it.

"Tell me something, David," Rabbi Kales said, his voice perfectly calm, his whole demeanor at ease. "Do you understand what you've read, or do you just memorize?"

"I get what I get," David said. "Some things, they just seem like weird stories that someone came up with after a meth run."

Rabbi Kales took a bite of his breakfast—lox and onions, neither of which appealed to David, at least not in their raw form, seemed to be popular in the place, David noticing half the octogenarians had big slabs of the pink fish on their plates—and chewed for a few moments, his eyes still on David, everything about him placid. "Give me an example," Rabbi Kales said.

This was all getting too strange. David had essentially threatened to kill both of the men sitting across from him, but neither seemed to take any offense. Back home, someone would already be dead. Nothing was the same in Las Vegas, not even the deli they were sitting in, which was like someone had cut and pasted a Chicago deli into the middle of the desert. Even David: sitting in a booth in a thousand-dollar suit making threats he didn't even know how to make good on anymore. And now he was getting quizzed on sacred religious texts, as if he were a normal person, not someone who'd put, what, fifty people into the ground? Maybe more like seventy-five. Shit, maybe one hundred. He'd never kept count, had never tried, really, but he could see each of them. Remember all the details. Because that's what he did. He kept that on file in his head, ready to be accessed at any time. It was his risk-management plan, knowing that the softest part of the windpipe is actually down by the clavicle, and that if you want to be humane, you press on the carotid artery for about thirty seconds and the guy will pass out first, and then you can break his windpipe without much struggle. But what was he gonna do now? Reach across the table and stab a rabbi in the throat with a butter knife? Suffocate him with his bagel and schmeer? And then kill a couple dozen senior citizens on his way out the door?

"Well," David said after some more thought, "that Ezekiel is a piece of work. The Orthodox drop his vision of the Valley of Dry Bones into half their writings. I mean, that guy was a complete whack job of the first order, and yet every other book I've got in the car talks about him like he's this creature of the divine. My opinion? He's got dementia or schizophrenia. Not a level guy in the least."

Rabbi Kales tried to stifle a smile, but it didn't work. "Well," he said, "you're lucky that Temple Beth Israel is Reform. You won't have to deal with much of that sort of thing." He took another bite of his lox and onions, took a sip of tea, wiped the corners of his mouth with his napkin, which somehow made him look elegant, and then sighed. "You see these people in here, David?"

"Yeah, I see them," David said.

"Do you know why they are all here?"

"I don't know," David said. "The bagels aren't bad."

"They're here because it's their community," he said. "This is not the best food in the city. It's not even the best bagel, you should know. But this deli stands for who they are, their traditions. This food I'm eating? It's a connection to my father. In 1919, as a little boy, he was smuggled out of Russia, Ukraine, to be accurate, across the Black Sea to Romania inside a bag of potatoes, with his own baby brother in the bag beside him, dying. Can you imagine what that must have been like?"

"I've got some idea," David said.

"You have no idea," Rabbi Kales said, "because you've never been pursued for being born, for what exists *spiritually* and *metaphorically* in you. But all of these people here? They have the same ancestral stories, or, many of them have worse stories. The books you have? They have the same books. The food you're eating? They have the same food. Ezekiel may seem to you to be insane, and maybe he was. But for everyone here, whether they know it or not, he is a witness to both the beginning and the end, and that is at least worthy of some respect. Sitting here, just to have a simple meal, is a connection to a collective history, much of it born out of misery that had nothing to do with any of them directly. You, you've had to accept the consequences of your horrible choices."

"If you'll pardon me," David said, though he made sure he kept his voice down, "what about your horrible choices, Rabbi?" David knew enough about Jewish history through his reading to know that what Rabbi Kales said was absolutely true, but that didn't mean he wanted the lecture, nor the sanctimony. "You're sitting here, too, and you're sitting with me and with Bennie, not your, uh, what is that word? *Mish* something or other."

"*Mishpocha*," Bennie said. "That's the word you're looking for."

"Right," David said . . . and he suddenly felt undercut by Bennie, who, as it turned out, actually was Rabbi Kales's *mishpocha*, at least through marriage. "That."

"*Your people shall be my people*," Rabbi Kales said. "I'm sure you're familiar with that?"

Truth was, Jennifer had a framed print of that passage from Ruth in their bedroom, right under a photo of them on their wedding day, May 5, 1988. The memory of this suddenly paralyzed David, the realization—one he'd had several times—being that he was beginning to forget details of her face already. Not how she looked, but specific lines and moles and dashes of pigment, and how they both looked in that picture. He couldn't conjure his own face anymore, either. And then a new level of sadness ran through him: He'd missed their ten-year anniversary. Rabbi Kales was right, that was the problem: This was all a consequence of his own profound mistake.

"You feeling okay?" Bennie said.

"I, uh," David began, but he couldn't say anything. All the tables surrounding them were filled not just with old people . . . not just old Jews . . . but old men and women, together. Staring at each other across their meals, kibitzing about their lives, their pasts, just the minutia of everyday existence. Couples. Old married people.

David needed to get out of this deli.

"My jaw," David said. He kept his eyes focused on his lap, didn't dare look up at Bennie, since he was pretty sure he had tears in his eyes. Christ. Had it come to this so quickly? Six months and a few weeks and a couple thousand pages of Judaica, and he was suddenly a big fucking puss. The Jews, the thing was, they didn't get down with this woe-is-me shit. They took vengeance, you fucked with the wrong person, you woke up with Mossad standing over your bed. "It's, uh, I need a Percocet. It's tightening up. Shooting pain into my eyes."

"Fine," Bennie said, all business. "Why don't you take Rabbi Kales back with you to get your baby aspirin, and then we can meet back at the temple in, say, thirty? Give you both some more time to argue about what the food means."

Rabbi Kales hadn't taken his eyes off David the whole time, or at least that's what David felt. Rabbi Kales exuded a sort of kindness that David had never experienced. The man was a hard motherfucker, that was clear enough; weird thing was that he also seemed like he had a real vested interest in other people's wellness, something David was not particularly familiar with.

"That would be fine," Rabbi Kales said. When David finally got his shit together enough to look up, he saw that Rabbi Kales was still staring directly at him. He looked profoundly sad.

CHAPTER FOUR

"**Y**ou ask good questions," Rabbi Kales said. They were weaving through the streets of Summerlin, David still keeping his speed low, though with Rabbi Kales periodically waving at people in the cars beside them, David didn't know why he even bothered. "Inconspicuous" was apparently not a word in Rabbki Kales's vocabulary. He had a volume of the Talmud on his lap and was flipping through it, not reading, just looking at the pages and at the notes David had left in the margins. He closed the book, but kept his hand on it, his thumb running back and forth over the gold-leafed pages.

"When you know a test is coming," David said, "it's easier to figure out what you don't understand."

"Is that your philosophy?"

"No," David said, though, now that he thought about it, it was probably better than "everybody dies," which had managed to get him through the previous thirty-five years. "Just something I've noticed."

"Yes, well," Rabbi Kales said, "it is the basis of much of what you've been reading. Trying to figure out the unknowable. Place order onto chaos. All anyone wants to know is how they'll find happiness, what it will feel like to die, and what happens next."

"And do you know that?"

"Of course not," Rabbi Kales said. "Nobody does. Not definitively."

"I thought all the Jews rolled to Israel," David said. "And the Mount of Olives opens up. Isn't that what Ezekiel said?"

"That's when the Moshiach returns," Rabbi Kales said. "It's one of the thirteen principles of our faith. But no one knows. How can they? Even the prophets, they just speak prophecy." Rabbi Kales made a tsking sound. "Everyone so concerned about what's next. No one cares what they're doing now. There's no present anymore."

"So it's a racket," David said. You want to run a racket, you've gotta give people the hope that there is a tangible result in the end—money, sex, a free futon, TV, trip to Tahoe, whatever. God, it seemed, was the biggest racket of all. You sell people the afterlife, you sell them resurrection from the pine boxes they're buried in down in Palm Springs, you're not gonna be around when they find out if you were right or not. In David's books, the Orthodox Jews were always talking about how everyday items could be cloaked in radiance, how a wet towel in the bathroom suddenly bore messages.

"Yes," Rabbi Kales said, "I suppose you could look at it that way." David stole a look in his direction, saw that the Rabbi was staring out the window, but still with his hand on the Talmud, his thumb moving over the edges of the pages.

"Tell me something," David said. "What does Bennie have on you?"

"He loves my daughter," Rabbi Kales said.

"Bullshit," David said.

"I believe that's honestly true," Rabbi Kales said.

"No," David said, "I meant bullshit on that being all he has on you. Guy like you doesn't just fall into a racket. Don't try to play me like that. At least show me that respect."

Rabbi Kales tapped on his window. "You see all this land out here? All these houses? When I was your age, this was actual desert. Just thirty, thirty-five years ago. No buildings. No people, maybe a few living off the grid, as they say now, but then, just living. I could come out here and walk and think and imagine what my life might be like without worrying about getting run over by someone driving the equivalent of an aircraft carrier. Coyotes, rabbits, desert squirrels, field mice, all of them gone now. For what? Who is going to live in all of these houses? Has anyone given any thought to this?" Rabbi Kales paused, then tapped his window again. "You see those mountains?"

"The Red Rocks?" David said.

"Yes," Rabbi Kales said. "When I first arrived from New York—this was 1965—you could actually see their real color. What you see now, that's a product of the air quality we now have, all that carbon monoxide, because all of these houses and buildings and casinos have changed the way the shadows fall, changed the way light works. Just in the last ten years, it's all changed. Everything has become diffuse right before my eyes."

"Could just be your eyes," David said, finding that parlance again, the way he used to talk to the old-timers in the Family, give them a little hell as a backward way of showing respect. David was learning that dealing with retired Family members and religious figures wasn't all that different: They both wanted you to solve your own problems and be a man and listen to the stories of how things used to be, the past always a pristine vision of a golden age, the present always a bag of shit, the future a vast, unknowable wasteland. Sometimes being a man meant showing that you were bold enough to tease a little, confident that your intention was clear—that you were a person who knew the score, whatever that score might be.

"Could be that, I suppose," Rabbi Kales said. He pondered that for a minute, though the thing of it was, David already had similar thoughts about the mountains, too. Here, everything was the color of old, rusted blood; the mountains jagged and ripped, at night they sat against the sky like pieces of broken glass. "My son-in-law," Rabbi Kales continued, "offered me an opportunity to fill that desert with my faith, to see my dream come true, to provide education and culture to my people. He offered me an opportunity to create a place of understanding and faith. With opportunity comes sacrifice." He shrugged, like this was nothing, starting up a temple funded, apparently, by the Mafia. "We have big plans for Temple Beth Israel."

"Bullshit," David said again.

"I have made mistakes in my life," Rabbi Kales said. It came out with such finality that David didn't feel he could question what those mistakes were, though he sensed that if Bennie were his chief benefactor, it must have been bad. "My son-in-law offered me a chance to start with a fresh ledger. So maybe we aren't that different."

"You don't know what I've left behind," David said, "so don't try to tell me we're the same."

"Why don't you tell me something," the Rabbi said. "Who are you?"

David hesitated. He wasn't supposed to speak that name. His own name. "I can't say," he said.

"I'm your rabbi," Rabbi Kales said. "We have the privilege of confidentiality. Nothing you tell me can be repeated, legally."

"Really? Even if we're not in the temple?"

"Where I am is the temple," Rabbi Kales said. "That's the law." And there it was, again, that sense of radiance. Bennie, man, that guy was onto something. If Rabbi Kales was a rabbi, and if David Cohen was a rabbi, there was an awful lot of wiggle room in that. Here was a hustle that David was finally beginning to see. "So why don't you at least tell me what you've done to end up here?"

"Killed some people," he said, nonchalant, like back at home, talking to the boys.

"Some?"

"That's my job. I kill people. And then I killed the wrong people, and here I am."

"What made them wrong?"

"They were feds."

"Oh, yes," Rabbi Kale said. "I read about this. In Chicago?"

"You read about this?"

"Harvey B. Curran wrote about it in the *R-J*," Rabbi Kales said. "I think he said you were found dead. Dismembered and burnt, as I recall."

That sounded about right. Poor Chema or that retard Neal, maybe both of them, dead just for knowing his name, knowing where he was last seen. Jennifer, she'd know it wasn't true. Maybe Ronnie would give her some kind of hint, nothing concrete, because nothing was ever concrete anymore; everything was about conditions and consensus, everything done to protect the brand, the Family now like a McDonald's franchise. "What else did that cocksucker have to say?"

This brought a smile to Rabbi Kales. He was an odd man. Holy, sure, but whatever he was mixed up in with Bennie was another side of his game that didn't add up yet; no matter what his "mistakes" were, whatever skin they were cutting, he had to have some take in it beyond the spectral. "Only that it was the sort of screw-up that would have all the families watching their backs for the next decade or so."

"I made a mistake," David said. "I snapped."

"How does a professional killer snap?" Rabbi Kales asked. Again with the calmness. The man was like a glass of warm milk.

It was a good question, David had to admit. "It's like anything else," David said. "Bad day, I guess." Though, of course, it was much more than that, but he needed to get Jennifer out of his head. He needed to get William out of his head. He'd been so sharp on this for the last several months, and then he meets this rabbi and all he can think about is what's been left behind. "Fact is, Rabbi, one day, something bad was going to happen one way or the other. This mess probably saved my life. Too high profile to actually kill me for it, you know?"

Rabbi Kales processed this information for a few moments and then said, "You cost Benjamin quite a bit."

"What does that mean?"

"It means what I said," Rabbi Kales said. "He paid a great deal of money for you."

"He bought me?"

"There was some understanding that you had special skills," the rabbi said. "The amount of reading you've done, the amount you recall, is astonishing. Do you know that?"

"I have a lot of free time," David said.

"You're smart," Rabbi Kales said again. "If you actually believed anything you were reading, I have every faith you could be an excellent rabbi."

"Why don't you think I believe?"

"If you did," he said, "you wouldn't have threatened to kill me in the Bagel Café."

David turned left from Alta onto Palmer Lane and came through the ornate front entrance to his neighborhood, the Lakes at Summerlin Greens. Normally—or at least for the last week, since he'd been given freedom to drive himself—David went back and forth through the rear gate, since there was never anyone there, no gardeners, no kids on their bikes, no old ladies in terry cloth walking their golden retrievers, still feeling like he needed to keep a low profile. Now, David decided to bring Rabbi Kales in through the front door, show him how he was living, suddenly feeling like he needed to let the rabbi know he wasn't some kind of beast who went around threatening to kill people over breakfast. Not every day, anyway.

The front entrance had a blooming fountain surrounded by five-foot-tall white rose bushes in the middle of a half circle paved with replica Spanish brick, which was like driving over a dry creek bed. Ingenious. It was the one thing David and Slim Joe really agreed on: that if given the chance, they'd find the guy who designed the entrance and drag him over the bricks a few times, let him know that what looked nice wasn't user-friendly.

He turned right on Trevino Way, then left on Nicklaus Street, then turned onto his own street, Snead Place.

David pulled through his own front gate and up his driveway. "I'm just going to run in, take my pill, and then I'll be right out," David said after he'd parked, not that he needed a pill for the pain, though he now thought about finding one of the Xanax he'd been given a few months ago. "Unless you want to come in."

"No," Rabbi Kales said. "It's bad enough seeing you in Rabbi Gottlieb's car. I step foot in his house, and I'm morally complicit in his death."

"This is his house?"

"It was, yes," Rabbi Kales said.

"I'm sleeping in his bed? Using his bathroom?"

"And living with the man who killed him," Rabbi Kales said. "I don't suppose Benjamin mentioned these details to you?"

"No, he skipped all that," David said. Slim Joe didn't seem like the killing type. Plus, Bennie said Rabbi Gottlieb had gone into Lake Mead. Guess he was pushed. "Truth is, I don't need a pill. I just had to get out of that deli. That place was making me nuts. But now I come to find out I'm sleeping in a dead man's bed. Next thing you're gonna tell me I'm wearing his clothes."

"He wasn't quite as flashy as you. He dressed for the people, not himself. You'll do the same."

David didn't know about that. What he did know was that he wasn't going to spend another night in Rabbi Gottlieb's bed. You sleep in a murdered man's bed, that's inviting doom. David didn't believe in much, even Rabbi Kales could tell that, though what he did believe in was that you didn't go around courting cosmic reparations. David didn't even bother turning the car around—he just backed up all the way down the driveway.

"Tell me how to get to the temple," David said.

■

Temple Beth Israel was only a few miles away, just on the other side of the Summerlin Parkway, on a mostly barren stretch of Hillpointe Road . . . which meant it was a few blocks away from hundreds of houses and gated colonies that looked suspiciously like the very one David lived in. For a people that spent forty years lost in a desert, David found it more than a little dubious that they'd parked themselves in a place where it could happen just as easily, the replication of precisely manicured lawns, pastel and cream homes, and gold Lexuses a desert in itself.

The temple took up an entire square block and was abutted on either side by expanses of open field that, at that very moment, were being graded and watered. On one side was a sign that read FUTURE HOME OF THE NEW BARER ACADEMY: NOW ENROLLING K-12! and on the other was a sign that proclaimed it the FUTURE HOME OF THE TEMPLE BETH ISRAEL COMMUNITY PARK & LEARNING CENTER. Across the street was the Temple Beth Israel Cemetery and the Kales Mortuary & Home of Peace, which gave David his first bit of understanding regarding where the good Rabbi's shake was coming from.

David pulled into the temple's parking lot and saw that Bennie was already there, pacing back and forth in front of a playground filled with young children—they couldn't have been more than five years old—while he talked on his cell phone. Though David could tell that the temple was fairly expansive just from its width on the street, he wasn't expecting to see that the place was more like a campus of buildings in the back. There was a sign pointing to the DOROTHY COPELAND CHILDREN'S CENTER, which was a one-story building just adjacent to the playground, and another sign pointing toward the TIKVAH PRESCHOOL. Both were modern glass-and-steel buildings that looked to David more like the FBI office in Chicago than any place he ever went to school. The playground itself was like something from the model-home signs he saw all over Summerlin: a jungle gym that resembled a Navy SEAL training regiment, complete with rope jumps, tunnels, pools of percolating water, monkey bars over a padded blacktop, and a pegboard for climbing.

"All this," David said to Rabbi Kales as they walked across the lot toward Bennie, "and you couldn't afford a sandbox?"

"If you're paying a thousand dollars per week for preschool," Rabbi Kales said, "I'm afraid a sandbox isn't sufficient."

"A thousand dollars per week? For how many weeks?"

"It depends," Rabbi Kales said. "Most do it for at least six months. Many do it for nine months, like a traditional school year. You can do the math."

There must have been sixty kids on the playground. A couple million. And no blood.

"How many years?"

"Usually two," Rabbi Kales said.

"Jesus fucking Christ," David said.

"When the private school opens next fall," Rabbi Kales said, "it will be more."

"How much more?"

"The high school students will cost thirty-five thousand dollars per year, maybe more. The younger children will be less than that, but not by much."

"And people will pay that?"

"People will line up to pay that," Rabbi Kales said. "And those that can't afford it will be offered loans."

"And what happens if they can't pay back the loans?"

"We'll put a lien on their property, that sort of thing," he said. "But I suspect that won't be a problem."

"Everybody defaults," David said. "Trust me on this."

"Well, then it will be your problem to solve," Rabbi Kales said.

Bennie then waved them over, though he was still on his phone. In the time David had been in Las Vegas, he'd gotten the sense that Bennie was a pretty busy guy. He had the Wild Horse, which he went to most nights, and then he had his other business interests, which David didn't know too much about. David knew what Bennie had told him about his involvement in the construction game—he'd put good money on those land graders belonging to Savone Construction—and the union shit, which probably took a lot of time and energy; he just didn't have a sense of how the Savone family soldiers went about making their nut or how Bennie collected. Slim Joe shook down pimps, which didn't sound like a great way to make a long-term nut if he was already thinking about getting into the hot-dog-and-pie game.

Back home, even though he was just a gun and therefore not expected to be pulling jobs, he knew, for instance, that Fat Monte's main job was the low-grade heroin distribution, the shit they gave to college kids and Canadians. So he had his whole operation, and he kept his take and kicked the rest upstairs. Or a fool they called Lemonhead, because he was always sucking on Lemonheads, he was in the offtrack betting they ran out of a couple of different restaurants. Perfectly legal, except that Lemonhead ran the side game, running the crazy bets and parlays, along with a little bit of girl business, too.

In Las Vegas, though, with so much stuff actually legal, David couldn't see Bennie collecting much on that. When you can jack someone for their toddler's tuition, maybe it didn't matter.

"That was your daughter," Bennie said to Rabbi Kales. "She wants to know what you want for Thanksgiving and whether or not we should invite over the new rabbi, since apparently it took Tricia Rosen all of five minutes to let her parents know they met."

"Perfect," Rabbi Kales said.

"Perfect?" David said.

"It's important that you don't just show up one day," Rabbi Kales said. "But if you're here for a few weeks, showing up periodically, people will get used to you. Won't be a big deal when you start doing actual work."

"You think Curran saw us?" Bennie said.

"He was sitting at his usual table," Rabbi Kales said.

"Good," Bennie said.

"Wait a minute," David said. "The columnist was in the restaurant?"

"Every Monday," Bennie said.

"Then why do you go there?" David asked. None of this lined up, David thinking that whatever amount of money Bennie paid to get him to Las Vegas would have been better spent on decent legal counsel.

"So that he sees us sitting there," Bennie said. "I thought they said you were smart."

"It's not how we did shit in Chicago, is all I'm saying," David said.

"And yet here you are," Bennie said.

David needed to stop looking for evidence that anything in Las Vegas was like it was in Chicago. He didn't want to be like one of those guys from New York who could see things only as a compare-contrast with New York.

"I just," David said quietly, "I don't want to wake up and find a bunch of U.S. Marshals on my front lawn because you want to keep up appearances."

"The only way for you to avoid the marshals will be to keep up appearances," Rabbi Kales said. "No one is looking for you here, David. That's what you need to understand."

Bennie pointed at his watch. "I've got an hour," he said, and started walking toward the main temple. "Either keep up and learn something, or fly back to Chicago where everything is candy canes and pillow fights."

■

Religious places freaked Rabbi David Cohen out. He knew intellectually that a church or a synagogue was just a place, just dirt and wood and cement and glass. He knew that the priests or rabbis or whatever were just men (and, occasionally, women) that had once been kids, had once watched Daffy Duck cartoons and *The Brady Bunch* and saw Spot, Dick, and Jane run and then, at some later point, decided they wanted to devote themselves to a book. Still, there was something about religious places that made David aware of how different his own life was, how if any of the people in the building (save, in this case, for Bennie and Rabbi Kales) knew what he was, they'd throw holy water on him and try to cast his demons out. He was a bad guy, he knew that. Was he evil? No, David didn't believe he was. Fucked up? For sure. He watched enough of those shows on the Discovery Channel to understand that maybe his brain didn't work like other people's brains, though David also had to consider that people who celebrated the purported holy day of Easter by eating marshmallow baby birds were just as twisted.

So as he followed Bennie and Rabbi Kales through the temple and they told him bits of information that was probably very important, he had to do his very best to concentrate, what with all the stained-glass windows, Hebrew letters on walls, memorial candles for dead Jews, notices about Shabbat and daily services and holiday services and the upcoming Hanukkah celebration. Weird thing was, it was the first time in his life that he'd been in a place like this and actually knew what everything *meant.* Not that he could read Hebrew, though he had a sinking feeling that soon that would not be the case. Some things had become so familiar to him from his reading that he kept getting a strange sense of déjà vu.

"There are one hundred thousand Jews in Las Vegas," Rabbi Kales said as they turned down a long hallway toward the temple's administrative offices. "And six hundred Jews move here each month, which, as you can imagine, has created a need for more and better facilities. We built the cemetery and mortuary here in 1990, and we'll have the Barer Academy built by next fall, ready for all grades. The Learning Center should open at the same time. The next phase will be the Performing Arts Annex, though that may be a few years down the line, depending upon funding."

"How many of them die every year?" David asked. The preschool kids grossed the joint a cool two million dollars, though someone probably had to teach them something, and feed them, and that preschool looked like it cost more than a few bucks, too. But funerals? That was another kind of beast. When Carlo Lupino died a few years back—and granted he was old-school Chicago Family, so there was a whole production—David remembered hearing it ran over seventy-five thousand dollars once you factored in food, flowers, embalming, the casket, the service, all that. Even a simple service was going to run ten, fifteen, maybe twenty-five Gs. There was cash in the body business, David knew that firsthand; burying them, however, that's where the real money was.

"What did you say?" Bennie rubbed that spot on his neck again, that spot that looked like someone had garroted him. Rabbi Kales looked pale.

"He asked how many," Rabbi Kales said. He actually sounded rattled for the first time.

"Yeah," David said, "that's what I asked."

"Depends," Bennie said. *He* wasn't rattled in the least. He seemed fairly giddy. "Good year? Usually between 750 and 900. Of course, we don't bury all of them. Some get shipped back to Boca Raton or Seattle or Palm Springs. Some get buried across town at the old Jewish cemetery, though I don't see that happening much in the future. Anyway, we've had a lot more lately."

"Lately?" David said.

"Next year is already looking good," Bennie said.

Rabbi Kales pushed on past Bennie and made a show of fumbling in his pockets for something. David took this to mean he didn't want to hear whatever was coming next.

"How is this week looking?" David asked.

Bennie shrugged. "Who is to say?"

"It's okay," David said, getting it now, or thinking, maybe, getting part of it. "I'm a rabbi. We have the privilege of confidentiality."

"Thanksgiving is usually a slow week," Bennie said. "But the first of the month tends to be a busy time."

"Here?"

"Everywhere," Bennie said. "We've got a few wealthy clients who've found that they prefer our cemetery services to those in their own hometowns."

"These clients," David said. "They live in Chicago?"

"Some of them. Some of them live in New York. Some of them live in Los Angeles. We've got some new clients in Cleveland. Detroit just opened up a few opportunities."

"And they're all . . . Jews?"

"They are when they get in the ground," Bennie said.

"Who presides over these funerals?"

"Why you do, Rabbi Cohen."

The Jews, they were pretty specific about their funerals. No embalming. No open caskets. No waiting around, either. The Jews wanted you in the ground within twenty-four hours, bad to wait more than three days. They also advocated simple pine boxes; they were big on their people returning to the earth and doing so as quickly as possible.

Bennie Savone. The guy was a genius. What better place to bury war dead than a cemetery? Feds would need an act of God to get a court to agree to start disinterring bodies in a Jewish cemetery. Even if they did, what would they find and how would they find it? They could pile a couple bodies into one coffin, and who would ever know?

"Who knows this?" David asked.

"It's a small circle," Bennie said. "The three of us. My guy Ruben, who you'll meet, who works on the bodies across the street."

"Slim Joe?"

"He knows you," Bennie said. "But not for much longer. I didn't like that shit he said today."

"You got my place bugged?"

"Number one, it's not your place," Bennie said. "Number two, I did it for your own safety. You want that dumb fuck turning state's on you?"

It made sense. All of it. Why Bennie was willing to buy him from the Family. His new face. The reading . . . all the reading . . . and now this more direct revelation.

"What's my take?" David asked.

"You'll be provided for," Bennie said.

"What's my take?" David said again.

"Depending upon how effective you are," Bennie said, "twenty, twenty-five percent."

"Of what?"

"Of a lot," Bennie said. "Plus, I see you doing some additional work around town, starting with your friend Slim Joe. You comfortable doing that?"

"Who gets the other seventy-five?" David said, not bothering to answer Bennie's question.

"This place look cheap to you?"

How much would it take for him to get back to Chicago? How much would it take for David to get back to Jennifer and William? To buy the kind of freedom he wanted, he'd need more than just a few hundred thousand dollars. How much would he need to get Sal Cupertine back? He'd need millions. "I want an accounting," David said.

"Now you're a businessman?" Bennie said.

"I guess I am," David said.

"Fine," Bennie said. He looked at his watch. "Any more demands? I've gotta pick up my wife and take her to the doctor."

"No," David said, and then he added, "not at this time."

"Great," Bennie said. He took an exaggerated look over both of his shoulders and then reached into his sport coat and pulled out a nine and handed it to David. "Don't make a mess unless you want to clean it up."

"When do you want it done?"

"Yesterday," Bennie said, "but give the kid his Thanksgiving. Give his mother her last good memory, then we'll maybe do her, too. Last thing I need is for her to start yapping."

"Root pulls aren't my thing," David said.

"She's my cousin," Bennie said. "So don't think it hurts you more than it hurts me, okay? Anyway, if you're lucky, she'll be back on a plane by Sunday and you won't need to deal with it. You make the call. You think she knows about you, we'll make it look like an accident. You any good with poisons?"

"No," David said. The idea of killing Slim Joe's mother didn't appeal to him in the least, but he understood the message that was being relayed: No one was off-limits when it came to this proposition.

"I'll figure something out," Bennie said.

Rabbi Kales found what he was looking for then—his key chain—and unlocked a wooden door just a few feet from the main office entrance, which was glass embossed with a huge Star of David. David could see a middle-aged woman sitting behind a reception desk. She had a phone to her ear and was absently flipping the pages of a magazine. She looked up when Rabbi Kales opened the office door wide and sunlight flooded into the hallway, along with a plume of dust. She gave David a vague half smile, which made sense when Rabbi Kales said, "This was Rabbi Gottlieb's office. It will be your office now. You'll bring your books in here." He stood in the doorway while he said this, only the side of his face visible to David. "We'll meet each morning at seven for your lessons. I can't have you working with the children until you are up to speed, you understand." He turned then and regarded David. "You do understand, don't you?"

"Yes," David said. For the first time in seven months, he understood everything.

CHAPTER FIVE

Paid administrative leave. Special Agent Jeff Hopper thought about those three words as he walked across the parking lot outside of the Chicago field office. Taken separate from each other, they didn't mean much. Put them together, at least in FBI parlance, and they meant that you'd flamed out in spectacular fashion, not worthy of actual firing, as the FBI didn't like to fire full agents unless they did something that might get them arrested. It was easier to put them on paid administrative leave and reassign them into oblivion—the Anchorage, Alaska, field office, or, worse, San Juan, Puerto Rico—after two or three years' worth of investigation into their actions (or, occasionally, inactions). The idea was that the time on paid administrative leave and the weight of the investigation would cause the agent to quit and find other work. The FBI even offered kind letters of recommendation when agents on paid administrative leave were interviewing for private sector jobs. Hopper knew this all too well: As senior special agent, he'd once been the guy writing the letters.

He wasn't surprised by the timing—the day after Thanksgiving—since that's when he liked to discipline agents, too. Do it before Thanksgiving, you're asking for the agent to do something crazy. Do it too close to Christmas, same deal. But the day after Thanksgiving is a dead period, everyone so stuffed with cholesterol and saturated fat and tryptophan that it's impossible to get too worked up about anything. What surprised Special Agent Jeff Hopper—now on paid administrative leave—was how quickly the FBI had acted. It usually took a good three or four weeks for agents to go over wiretaps on low-impact surveillance subjects, like Jennifer Cupertine, though Jeff realized now that they had probably hot-buttoned any mention of Sal Cupertine.

Jeff thought Senior Special Agent Biglione, a man he'd known for the better part of five years, a man he'd gone fishing with the previous winter, a man who once confided in Jeff that what he really wanted to do with his life was become a pastry chef, took far too much joy playing the tape of Hopper telling Jennifer Cupertine that her husband was alive. "Is that your voice?" Biglione asked him when the tape concluded.

"You know it is," Jeff said.

"This is unacceptable behavior," Biglione said. "You're aware of that, I would imagine?"

"Just give me the form," Jeff said.

It took less than fifteen minutes, including the time it took the woman from Human Resources to give her speech about how he'd retain his full benefits but that he'd need to surrender his gun, his company laptop, his company cell phone, and his keys.

Jeff got into his Ford Explorer and tried to stifle a laugh. He was certain that someone, somewhere, was watching him (particularly since the parking lot was circled with cameras), and it just wouldn't look right for him to be caught on film giggling after being put on paid administrative leave. All things being equal, this was the best possible turn of events for Jeff—he'd spent most of Thanksgiving copying the rest of the relevant materials from the files—and he could now look for Sal Cupertine without the burden of being an FBI agent. He'd find Sal Cupertine—and then what?

He didn't even want revenge. He had no intention of killing Cupertine if he found him, though he had the sense that Cupertine wasn't the kind of guy who would throw up his hands and say, "You got me!" if and when the time came. He simply wanted justice and to clear his name, not that he thought he could clear his name with the FBI—that ship had sailed, hit an iceberg, and sunk to the bottom of the ocean—but with Cupertine himself. The idea that Cupertine thought Jeff was a fool, was so stupid as to leave his own name on the bill, and that he surely thought he'd killed Jeff—either by shooting him in the face or choking the life out of him, face-to-face, Cupertine's own saliva on the man's forehead—enraged Jeff, kept him awake for three months, and wasn't letting him rest even now.

Not that the FBI gave a shit. They had their body. They had their continuing investigation into the Family. No one other than Jeff was losing sleep.

Jeff pulled out onto Roosevelt and glanced over to the berm where he used to spend his lunches. There was so much to do, so many things to get started on, but the first thing was that he needed to get home and sweep out all the bugs. Probably sweep the car, too. Might as well yank the phone from the wall and do everything on the cell . . . though, he'd need to get one of those, too. He had a gun, that wasn't a problem. He had some money saved up, about twenty grand.

It wasn't until Jeff Hopper turned down Morgan Street and saw the university dusted in the first significant snow of the season, saw the few students who were walking into the library on a holiday weekend, that he realized Matthew Drew had probably been fired.

■

Matthew Drew lived on the seventh floor of an apartment building in the Medical District, just a few miles from the FBI offices and down the street from the university, but it took Jeff an hour to figure that out. The FBI was good about hiding the addresses of their agents, so Jeff had to go about things the old-fashioned way: He had to try to remember the name of Matthew's wife. He thought it was . . . Sarah? Gina? Something like that. He spent thirty minutes outside on a campus pay phone, freezing his ass off, calling 411 and asking for different women's names with the last name Drew. He'd then ask for the addresses, hoping to find one that was within a few miles of the offices, since he recalled that Matthew was able to get back and forth to the office within thirty minutes. He had two good leads—Trina Drew, that sounded right, and Nancy Drew, which couldn't be possible, but the operator said someone with that name did in fact live in greater Chicago, and as an FBI agent he almost *had* to check that one out—before he decided to ask for information on Nina Drew and came up with an address just blocks away. That had to be it, he decided, and sure enough when he got to the apartment building and scrolled through the names on the security keypad he found it to be the home of both Matthew and Nina Drew.

He tapped in 713 and waited beside the intercom. There was a camera pointed directly at the door, which probably meant all the tenants had closed-circuit access. It was amazing to Jeff that things that were spy technology ten or fifteen years earlier were now regular amenities at middle-class apartment complexes. It also meant Matthew could decide whether or not he wanted to answer the door.

"Yes?" It was a young woman's voice on the intercom. Nina, presumably.

"Yes, uh," Jeff said, "this is Special Agent Hopper. I'm here to see, um, Agent Drew?"

"You should have been here yesterday then," she said. That answered that. "Come on up," she said, and then front door buzzed open.

Jeff spent the elevator ride trying to think of what he'd say to Matthew's wife, and yet, when he knocked on their door and a young woman opened it, he found he had absolutely nothing to say. Part of this was because he still hadn't settled on the exact words of his apology, and part of this owed to the fact that the young woman who opened the door looked very young. Eighteen, no older. Even though it was freezing outside, she had on only a white V-neck T-shirt and pink shorts, no socks or shoes. "Are you Nina?" Jeff said.

"Yeah," she said, "come on in. Matt is in the shower."

Jeff stepped into the apartment and looked around. There was a leather sofa pushed against one wall, a coffee table in front of it stacked with textbooks—*Introduction to Western Civilizations*, *The Norton Anthology of Contemporary Fiction*, a thesaurus—and two dirty plates. On the other side of the room was a papasan chair covered in magazines, a treadmill with dry cleaning, still in the bag, hanging from the hand bars, and a muted television, which sat on the floor. There was a VCR perched precariously atop the television and a Nintendo system on the floor beside it, along with a stack of games. On the TV was an old Harrison Ford movie, though Jeff couldn't tell which one. He was either chasing someone or being chased, but with the sound off, it was impossible to tell.

There was a small galley kitchen and then two bedrooms separated by what Jeff presumed was the bathroom. He could hear a shower coming from the general vicinity. There was no evidence of any children.

"So," Jeff said, "you're Matthew's . . . wife?"

"Yuck, no," Nina said. She plopped herself down on the leather sofa and picked up the Western Civilizations book. "I'm his sister."

"Right," Jeff said. "Where do you go to school?"

"UIC," she said. "I just started, and it's kicking my ass."

"It gets easier," Jeff said.

"You went there?"

"Graduate school," Jeff said.

"Yeah, it's totally different undergrad," she said. "Everyone says the first two years are cake, that it's just basic retard stuff— history, math, comp—and that when you get into your major, that's when people jump out of buildings from the pressure and all that. So. Yeah. Not looking forward to that if I'm already underwater."

A small bookshelf by the sofa was filled with books on criminology, forensic investigation, and counterinsurgency methods, and it also held framed photos of Matthew and Nina with their parents from a cruise, everyone posed in front of the ship's bow. There were also photos of both kids playing lacrosse.

"So, you guys share this place?"

"Yeah, it's cheaper that way," she said. "Or, I guess it was. I don't know what we're going to do now. I don't think Matt has anything saved up. His loans are insane."

Shit.

"Yeah, well, I've got some news for Matthew that will help alleviate that," Jeff said, not even knowing what the hell he meant as he said the words.

"Cool," Nina said. She got up off the couch then, like she'd forgotten something, and headed into the tiny kitchen. "I'm being totally rude. Do you want some turkey or string bean casserole or something? Our mother sent us this huge care package, and we've been gorging on it since last night. We've got, like, three different pies, too."

Before Jeff could answer—he would have liked some string bean casserole—Matthew came out of the bathroom wearing a pair of sweatpants and no shirt, a damp towel in his right hand. No wedding ring on his left.

"What are you doing here?" he asked. He didn't seem all that surprised, just mildly annoyed.

"I wanted to talk to you," Jeff said.

"I got fired, did you know that?"

"I had some idea, yeah," Jeff said.

"You knew ahead of time?"

"No," Jeff said, "they put me on leave today, so I figured that you got the axe. It's how I would have done it." Matthew rubbed at his head with the towel and let out a grunt of exasperation. "Look, I want to apologize. I dragged you into something stupid."

"You know they didn't even give me a severance?" Matthew said. "Two weeks short. Can you believe that? Apparently the twenty weeks I spent at Quantico didn't count."

"I know," Jeff said. He'd fired plenty of people like Matthew during his time in the FBI, their positions were at will during their probationary period, and though he always felt bad about it in the abstract, his feeling was that the best severance for these people was that they could put FBI on their resume and land a nice corporate security job. "Look, I have a proposition for you. Something temporary so at least you can pay your bills." He pointed to the ceiling and then to his ear, let him know people were probably listening, though he doubted the bureau bothered to bug Matthew's place, since he wasn't even really an agent yet. Still, it gave the proceedings a bit more weight. "Let me buy you a cup of coffee somewhere we can talk about it."

Nina came out then holding two plates full of food and handed one of them to Jeff. "Hey," she said to her brother, and then she went and sat back down on the sofa. "He thought I was your wife."

Matthew didn't say anything for a moment, so Jeff took his plate and sat down beside Nina on the sofa and got to work on some casserole. "Give me a couple minutes to get dressed," Matthew said.

"Take your time," Jeff said. He was suddenly starving.

■

The White Palace Grill was one of those places Jeff used to go to all the time when he didn't have any money. They'd let you sit in a booth all night long for the price of a cup of coffee, particularly if you came in with textbooks, and they'd keep refilling your mug without ever getting snooty about it. It was up on Canal Street, so it had a crowd that was equally mixed with college students, hookers, cops, and the occasional wiseguy.

It had been almost a decade since Jeff had stopped inside, and yet, as he sat across the booth from Matthew, he recognized everyone in the joint. The waitress with the tattoos on her neck; the two detectives sitting by the door, a mountain of paperwork spread between them; the hipsters wearing their sunglasses inside; the young woman in horn-rim glasses sitting at the counter next to another young woman, also in horn-rim glasses, though it didn't look like they were there together. And then the solitary old folks eating chicken salad and drinking tea. He wondered if they recognized him, too, curious about where he'd been all these years.

The waitress with the tattoos on her neck came by and dropped off their food and drinks—Matthew had ordered a strawberry shake and french fries, figuring, he said, that he didn't need to worry too much about staying in shape now, which sounded like fairly wise, if shortsighted, counsel, so Jeff ordered chili-cheese fries and a chocolate malt.

Jeff had spent the better part of the previous twenty minutes explaining to Matthew his plan . . . a plan he'd developed mostly on the fly, as he spoke, but the nut was simple: He was going to find Sal Cupertine. Wherever he was, he was going to track him down. And if Matthew wanted in, he was willing to pay him for his services.

"So, you're gonna pick up my whole salary?" Matthew asked after the waitress left.

"No," Jeff said. He wasn't sure how much GS-10s made these days, but whatever it was, Jeff couldn't afford it.

"So, I'm hourly?"

"I haven't really worked it all out yet," Jeff said. "But don't you worry, if your wife and kid need a place to stay, I've got a guest room at my place."

"That's funny," Matthew said.

"Not as funny as you telling me you had a wife and kid," Jeff said.

"I never told you that," he said. "I told Jennifer Cupertine. You just assumed I was telling the truth."

"The ring was pretty convincing."

Matthew leaned forward. "All my life, I worked toward getting a job at the FBI. When I got there, I didn't want a bunch of guys like you calling me *kid-this* and *kid-that*, asking me if I was too pussy to go out drinking with them after work. So I bought myself a simple gold band, and all of a sudden, I'm a guy with a bit more going on than just the job. And you know something? Maybe it worked too well, since now I'm sitting here with you and you're not trying to provide me with teachable moments."

"I said I was sorry," Jeff said.

"No you didn't," Matthew said. "You said, 'I want to apologize.' That's not actually saying you're sorry. Let's just agree that you went out there and did exactly what you wanted to do with Mrs. Cupertine and didn't take into consideration that maybe I'd lose my fucking job because I was I dumb enough to go with you."

"Fine," Jeff said. "We're in agreement."

"Great," Matthew said, and then he sat back in the booth and spread his arms across the top of the banquette and seemed to notice the restaurant for the first time. "How did you find this place?"

"I used to come here," Jeff said.

"A mile from my apartment and I've never even noticed it," he said.

"Hiding in plain sight," Jeff said.

"That a metaphor?"

"Unintentional," Jeff said, "but probably true." Jeff had spent the last several days going over everything he could find on Sal Cupertine, all the transcripts, all the witness information, even put a feeler out to an old Family CI named Paul Bruno, who was now living in Milwaukee and selling real estate but who'd grown up with the Family and who probably still had a couple skeletons, actual skeletons, in his closet. He was going to drive out to see him on Saturday, see what he could glean about Cupertine's habits, see if Bruno had heard any gossip. What Jeff had already gleaned on his own, however, and what he told Matthew, was that he couldn't imagine Cupertine being holed up in some safe house somewhere, at least not forever. If the Family felt it was important enough to keep him alive, then there had to be a tangible purpose for his continued existence. If Sal Cupertine was alive, and Jeff was sure he was, he was working.

And it wasn't just because that made the most organizational sense. The FBI profile developed on Sal Cupertine was extensive: He was a professional, a workaholic even, who had a sociopathic view of violence, but only as it related to his business, which suggested he wasn't a true sociopath, though his freelance work suggested his morality had a price. The death of his father, who was murdered in a coup within the Family, and which Sal Cupertine supposedly witnessed, likely had a disassociating effect on him from a young age . . . but, really, who knew? He might have just liked killing people, though Jeff didn't believe that was true. It was his job, and almost everyone hates their job.

Thing was, no one had ever even been able to question Sal Cupertine. He'd never been arrested. The only time he'd ever left prints at one of his killings was at the Parker House.

Everything the FBI had used to develop Cupertine's profile was based on supposition and secondary evidence, which was usually enough to catch a serial killer, since serial killers were often insane, which made it easier to catch them since their insanity usually fell along predictable medical lines. A sane person was much more difficult to figure out.

"You don't actually think he's in Chicago, do you?" Matthew asked after Jeff shared his thoughts.

"No," Jeff said. "I doubt he's even in Illinois."

"Canada?"

"Maybe," Jeff said, "but I can't see Sal Cupertine fitting in with the syndicate in Windsor. They're all white-collar fraud these days. Tech stuff. Mortgages. Not a lot of violence, just a lot of money. They don't have a good reason to harbor an international fugitive. It would bring too much heat on them. Even if he went to Toronto or BC, it's a different kind of Mafia. For one thing, they speak Italian."

"Cupertine doesn't?"

"No," Jeff said. "And I don't see him picking up French, either."

"But he's smart, right? Isn't that what the files said?"

"Yes," Jeff said. "Or at least he has a good memory. They called him Rain Man."

"Nice to know even the Mafia goes to the movies," Matthew said. "So maybe he just moves to Canada and lives a nice humble life."

"He doesn't have any skills," Jeff said. That was the problem with all the mob guys Jeff had ever managed to get into witness protection. They never knew how to do anything but rip people off. He heard Sammy the Bull was already back into the game in Arizona. Just asking to get killed.

"Mrs. Cupertine, she was believable to me," Matthew said. "Perhaps that makes me naïve. But I feel if Sal Cupertine is within a couple hundred miles of her, there's no way he's not already back in town." He pulled the straw out of his milk shake and gulped down half of the glass and then wiped his mouth with the back of his hand. *He is a kid,* Jeff thought, there wasn't any way of disputing that. That wasn't a bad thing; perhaps he could look at things with a fresh perspective. "What about Vegas?"

"Too hard to keep him hidden," Jeff said. "There's a mob gossip columnist in town. He covers the comings and goings of the families like they're members of a boy band."

"Don't you think Ronnie Cupertine knows where he is?" Matthew said.

"I'm going to guess he'd say he's in the landfill, right where we found him."

"That's bullshit," Matthew said. "Why doesn't someone grab him, put him in a dark room, and spray him with a fire hose until he gives up the information?"

"Because we're not the CIA," Jeff said. "Or the KGB."

"I bought my car from him," Matthew said.

"You and half of Chicago," Jeff said. "That's part of the problem." Ronnie Cupertine wasn't just connected in the mob sense, he was part of the very fabric of Chicago—benefit lunches with the mayor, golf with Gold Coast politicos on both sides of the aisle, luxury suite to see the Bulls, black-tie events at the Field Museum, the entire city driving his chop shop cars. Word was he had a deal with an Albanian syndicate in Canada for the high-end rides, but there was never anything solid on that.

That Sal Cupertine was still alive was all thanks to Ronnie Cupertine; Jeff was sure of that. A savvy businessman, he'd figure out a way to get the most out of his cousin Sal. Jeff really wanted to sit across from Ronnie Cupertine and have a conversation, but that wasn't going to happen. At least not yet. Ronnie Cupertine was the kind of guy who knew his rights, the kind of guy who kept lawyers on his speed dial, the kind of guy who wasn't going to get suckered into admitting the sky was blue.

"I'm going to need at least two thousand dollars a month," Matthew said then, "plus expenses."

"What expenses?"

"How should I know?" Matthew said. "I've never been a private detective before. Between that and unemployment, I'll be fine for a few months. Keep my sister off the streets."

"I don't think it will take a few months," Jeff said. "I feel like we'll be able to track him down before Christmas."

"What gives you this confidence?" Matthew asked.

Jeff had no idea why he thought this. With no leads—the FBI having announced he was dead didn't exactly cause the tip lines to light up—and not even a solid clue as to where Sal Cupertine might be, Jeff would be starting from below ground. But Matthew was right: Someone knew where Sal Cupertine was, and if one person knew, two people knew. And if two people knew, there was a pretty good chance four people knew. A criminal organization requires a hierarchy—there was no way Ronnie Cupertine was going to have blood on his hands, literally or figuratively—and that meant there were probably several moving parts between Sal Cupertine killing four men at the Parker House and the charred body found in the dump.

Jeff thought about his savings—the twenty grand he'd stashed away. If he caught Sal Cupertine, Jeff Hopper could write his own ticket, even if that meant he just went back to eastern Washington and sat around in his underwear all day.

"Look," Jeff said, "give me three months, that's all I'm asking. If after three months we aren't any closer, you go your way, I'll go mine, and I'll pay you another two months' salary as severance."

Matthew picked up a french fry and blew the salt off of it before putting it in his mouth. "What if we catch him?"

"Same deal," Jeff said.

"So you're going to give me ten thousand dollars whether or not we catch Sal Cupertine?"

"I need your help," Jeff said. There was no way he could take this on by himself. And in a more tangible sense, he needed Matthew physically—if it came down to a fight, Jeff Hopper felt like he could do what needed to be done, could still handle himself with a gun, but there was no denying that having someone qualified for assault team duty as his backup wasn't a bad thing.

Matthew ate another fry and finished off his shake. "This is insane," he said.

Jeff agreed.

"We do this, we get him," Matthew said, "do you think I have any chance of getting picked back up?"

"No," Jeff said. "Not by the bureau. Maybe NSA will like the self-determination angle, but who knows. I've got some contacts in private security, guys doing paramilitary and intelligence jobs on contract, things like that. That's where the real money is."

"It wasn't about the money for me," Matthew said.

"I wanted to be a superhero, too," Jeff said, "and here we are."

Matthew shook his head. Jeff couldn't tell if it was in disgust or resignation or just simple frustration. Maybe it was something else all together. Either way, he followed it up with a brusque laugh and said, "What time do we leave for Milwaukee?"

■

The first time Jeff Hopper met Paul Bruno was in late 1995. Bruno had just been released from county—in fine Chicago form, he'd done two months after getting picked up for assault after trying to collect on a gambling debt, and then pled down to a minor racketeering charge, a term that didn't even exist until 1927, when the Employers' Association of Greater Chicago coined it in response to the constant shakedowns from organized crime figures in the Teamsters—and came sniffing around the bureau for opportunities to snitch once he realized a jail cell was not a place he ever wanted to visit again.

He wasn't a made guy in the classic sense—as in, he'd never been made part of the Family—but he had a foot in their business interests in that he was good with numbers. He helped run a couple of books by setting spreads and the like, and since he worked with his father, Dennis, at the family butcher business—Bruno's Fine Meats—he knew his way around dead bodies.

Paul Bruno had two problems, however: The first was that he was a closeted homosexual, which wasn't exactly a great secret to have while trying to be a tough guy. Not that he wasn't tough, but it opened him to blackmail by other syndicates or anyone else who might want to hurt him or his business interests, which was primarily with the Family. Paul was smart enough to realize this himself, which is why he kept himself outside the lines as much as possible. Sure, he'd aid and abet, provide a few key services, even; he just wouldn't saddle up all the way. That made him even more valuable, since he'd been

GANGSTERLAND

able to befriend guys up and down the chain of command. It helped that he'd grown up with them.

The second problem was far less pronounced, or at least was until Bruno landed in a jail cell: He had claustrophobia, which led to anxiety, which led to panic attacks, which led to crying, which led, every time, to vomiting. Jeff knew of Bruno's first problem long before Bruno landed in county and revealed his second issue, though that revelation was the impetus for putting a CI into the cell with him for the last few weeks of his sentence to put some ideas into his head.

For the next year, in exchange for getting his record expunged and for financial help with tuition toward his real estate license, Paul Bruno provided information to the FBI, though because his operational knowledge was slight—he'd helped teach some Family members the art of cutting up bodies and knew the Family had cut up some bodies but didn't know who those bodies actually were—what he knew about the books was practically common knowledge, so that was largely worthless. So Jeff tended to use Bruno for insight on the men themselves, find out their peccadilloes, their habits, interesting things about who they were outside the crimes they'd perpetrated. Bruno became a good CI because he was so secretive and low-key in his normal life that becoming a snitch was easy work for him.

Now, as Jeff and Matthew pulled up to a new model home tract located just outside of Milwaukee in the lake country town of Oconomowoc, it was impossible not to notice how things had changed. First, there was the series of billboards featuring Bruno and his "gold pro team" of real estate agents that lined Silver Lake, the long street that wound through Oconomowoc toward a subdivision called Pleasant Farms Lakes, that pronounced Bruno the "king of lake country home deals!" Then there was the yellow Hummer Jeff saw in front of a half-built two-story house at the entrance of the tract. It had a picture of Bruno and his "Gold Pro Team" emblazoned over the whole driver's side of the vehicle.

"I thought you said he was a quiet guy," Matthew said.

"He was," Jeff said. When they spoke on the phone, Bruno suggested they meet at the development since it was a good place to do business—good guys wouldn't bug a house that's being built, and bad guys wouldn't be smart enough to do it in the first place—which made Jeff think Bruno was still doing a bit of crooked work on the side. Which was fine. As long as he wasn't piling up bodies, Jeff didn't really care anymore about a little white-collar stupidity—in the larger scheme of things, everyone was at some point getting robbed.

Jeff parked down the street at the sales office—which was actually the garage of the Saddle Rock model home, a modification that would be changed once the development was built out—and waited outside, near a blue minivan and a ten-foot-wide map of the proposed community. Pleasant Farms Lakes boasted that space had been carved out for over two hundred homes; a multihole putting green; a dog park; a day care center; three man-made lakes, each one stocked with different kinds of fish; and, the map noted, "several lots scaled for Devotional Worship development."

"Nice place," Matthew said.

"It has the same basic layout of a federal prison," Jeff said. "Minus the dog park."

"I could see myself living in a place like this one day," Matthew said. "Once I'd lost all hope." He pointed three fingers at the map. "I'm trying to figure out the wisdom behind man-made lakes in lake country."

"Easier to dump pesticides into a lake you own," Jeff said.

Bruno's yellow Hummer came down the street then and stopped a few feet from Jeff. The doors opened, and a family of four came tumbling out, followed by Bruno himself. The family looked happy, or at least normal: The father was maybe thirty-five, dressed head to toe in L.L.Bean, while the mother looked like she'd robbed J.Crew, as did their two small children, both girls. Bruno, however, looked completely different from how Jeff remembered him. He was the kind of guy who had a sweat suit for every occasion, but now he was in tan chinos, a black cashmere sweater over a white collared shirt. He had a Movado on his wrist, leather band, black face, classy. He'd grown a beard recently—or at least since the photos that appeared everywhere had been taken—and had a suntan, which meant he was spending his free time in a tanning bed, since it was already in the low forties and thirties in town and the skies had been gray for a good two months.

The father thanked Bruno for showing them around, and then the entire family systematically climbed into the blue minivan and drove off. Bruno waved at them as they meandered down the road, his face all smiles, his eyes wide and bright and filled with the kind of bottomless optimism all real estate agents seem to have when they stare at you from the calendars left on your doorstep. Jeff couldn't help but wonder about the intersection in Bruno's mind between cutting up bodies for the mob and showing nuclear American families real estate they probably couldn't afford.

When the van finally turned the corner, Jeff got his answer.

"Fucking maggots," Bruno said. He pulled his cashmere sweater off, balled it up, and tossed it into the Hummer, then walked inside the sales office and came back out with a bottle of Windex and some paper towels. He opened the back passenger door and started scrubbing at the seats. Jeff walked over and peered in. Brown leather, built-in TV monitors. State of the art. Matthew stayed a few feet back, probably trying to figure out what the hell was going on.

"Fucking kids spilled a full Coke on my backseat," Bruno said, not that Jeff had asked. "Splashed it up on the back of my fucking sweater, too. Two-hundred-dollar sweater and now it's sticky as shit. They don't make sippy cups anymore? You gotta give your kids a full can of soda?" He stopped his rant for a moment, appeared to notice Jeff and Matthew for the first time, and said, "I thought you were coming alone."

"Good to see you, too, Bruno," Jeff said.

He regarded Jeff with a look of exasperation, like they'd been together on some kind of horrific experience, then he just got back to scrubbing. "Two hours I spend with that family. And what do they tell me? They're just looking. You know, look on your own time."

"This is Matthew," Jeff said. "He's working with me."

"And one more thing," Bruno said, "if you got a problem with two-story houses, then move to the Saharan desert and get a tent, okay? What is wrong with people these days? A two-story house *is* America. It's the dream. Am I right?"

"I live in an apartment," Jeff said.

"You don't count. You work for the government." Bruno finally paused and gave Matthew the once-over. "What about you, Encyclopedia Brown? You want a two-story house? Basement, wet room, big yard. You want that, right?"

"I'd just be happy not to have any more student loans," Matthew said.

"When I was a kid, you know what I wanted?" Bruno said.

"To be an adult?" Jeff said.

"That's right, that's right," Bruno said. "I just wanted to be bigger. You know? These kids, they kept telling their parents what they needed in a house, like they were gonna bust their asses on the mortgage. The gumption. That's what gets to me."

"This doesn't sound like the sort of talk that made you the King of Lake Country Home Deals," Jeff said. "Hardly what one would expect from a person who has his own Gold Pro Team."

"You wanna know the truth?" Bruno said.

"I don't know," Jeff said. "Do I?"

This got Paul Bruno to laugh. "There is no Gold Pro Team. I'm it. These other people? I just found them in some clip art book. They don't exist."

"I believe they call that a racket," Jeff said.

"Just false advertising," Bruno said. "Anyway, I've sold more houses in this shit hole than anyone. This is my baby out here. You know more people move to Wisconsin than any other state in America?"

"That can't be true," Jeff said.

"It isn't," Bruno said. "So I always say it like that. Make it a question. People, they'll hear what they want to hear, right?" He looked at his watch. "I got another client in an hour. Come on, get in the Hummer. I'll drive you down to this development I'm buying into. We can talk in the car."

Jeff slid in the front seat, left the sticky backseat for Matthew, who didn't seem to mind. Bruno got behind the wheel and fired up the engine. It sounded like a bomb going off. Jeff couldn't figure out one good reason for anyone to own a Hummer unless they had designs on attacking Baghdad. He knew several agents who drove them, but they were always ex-military types who wanted you to know just how comfortable they'd been riding in armored vehicles, so much so that they bought them to drive around the South Loop, too.

Bruno drove them through Pleasant Farms Lakes, pointed out where all the amenities were going to be, all of which were just mounds of dirt, and then pulled out of the development and headed down a road that had only recently been paved. Up ahead was a gate and a sign that proclaimed the development, called Legacy at the Lake Country, was Oconomowoc's first "over 55 luxury retirement destination." Jeff saw only dirt and gravel behind the gate. Bruno hit a button on a remote control, and the gate opened, and the Hummer pulled through and then came to a stop a hundred yards in, near a construction trailer. In the distance Jeff could make out two land graders moving back and forth near a low outcropping of tamarack and shagbark.

"This place," Bruno said, "is my secret nest egg."

"How secret is it if you're showing it to us?" Jeff said.

Bruno considered this. "You got the can, right? For the Cupertine shit?"

"Paid leave," Jeff said.

"Same shit. What about you, Encyclopedia Brown?"

"Fired," Matthew said. "Just for knowing Agent Hopper."

"So neither of you is officially FBI right now, right?"

"Correct," Jeff said, though officially he was.

Bruno turned in his seat to face Jeff and Matthew. "So I tell you the plan, you tell me what kind of legal trouble I'm looking at, okay?"

"Fine," Jeff said. He'd had conversations with Bruno like this before. He always had a scheme of some kind.

"So the builders? They're friends of mine, plus, you know, I've got cash in the deal. Whatever. It's a good deal, right? So they're gonna put in these windows and sliders with locks. Everyone afraid of the world, they all want locks. Every single house is going to be Fort Knox, because these old mother-fuckers will be moving in here with all their worldly goods, waiting for the Rapture and all that. Thing is, I'm going to have a master set of duplicates to every house. I fall on hard times, need a quick score to get me out of the city, on a boat to Hawaii, or I just want some extra cash to buy my groceries, whatever, I got my own mall right here. All I can steal. What do you think of that?"

"That's a sound plan," Jeff said. "I'd say ten years, maybe fifteen. Could probably plead down and get five."

"Nah," Matthew said. "I bet he'd only get two years. Non-violent crime? They'd process him out in a year."

"Maybe so," Jeff said. "Maybe plea insanity, Bruno, hope the people you're ripping off get Alzheimer's before they need to testify."

"These old motherfuckers," Bruno said, "they won't know if a ring or two is missing. It's not like I'm going to be housing the whole joint. Just diamonds, Baccarat crystal, easy stuff to move. Just little things, here and there. Maybe a car if I need one. Free and clear, I think."

"It would be hard to get caught," Matthew said. "Having a key makes it easier to be discreet. Having a car key makes it even easier in the event you decide to move into full GTA mode."

"That's what I'm saying," Bruno said. "See, Agent Hopper, Encyclopedia Brown here knows a good score."

"Of course," Matthew said, "you might break into the wrong house and there's some old man who did a couple tours in Korea waiting for you with a shotgun. Or maybe someone's grandson with a nine and good aim. Things could take a turn."

"Risk of doing business," Bruno said. "What do you think, Agent Hopper? My feeling, if it works, I do this all over the country."

"I wouldn't bank on it," Jeff said, though of all Bruno's scams, it did have the highest degree of possible success, "but if you feel like in the future you're going to need extra money, who am I to tell you who not to rob? But why not just make it simple and have the builders put in a false wall for you, something on the side of the house, near the garage, something you can just pop in and out and have it open into the back of a closet or something."

Bruno pondered this. "Tongue and groove it, essentially?"

"Sure," Jeff said.

"Maybe make sure there's a shrub in front of it, make sure it's a guest room closet or some shit, right?"

"Right," Jeff said. He'd spent his entire life trying to stay one step ahead of crooks, and this had been the one idea he'd really appreciated stumbling on. A small arms dealer operating out of Rochester had a similar setup in his home as an escape route.

"That's a pretty good idea," Bruno said. "Why the fuck did you tell me that?"

"I need you alive," Jeff said. "This seems like a better way to keep you above ground."

"The FBI really dump your ass?"

"Really," Jeff said.

"Just for Cupertine killing your boys?"

"No," Jeff said. "I might have harassed Cupertine's wife, telling her I thought her husband was still alive and it was being covered up by the FBI."

Bruno snickered. "How's Jennifer doing?"

"Tough," Jeff said.

"Nice girl, that one," Bruno said. "Her dad and my dad used to bowl together."

"Yeah?" Jeff said.

"Yeah, the Frangellos were good people. Jennifer, she fell for Sal hard. Her dad, you know, he hated that she was married to a gangster. He was no idiot. I mean, everyone knew that Sal Cupertine was a killer, right? But I guess he told old man Frangello that he'd never bring that shit home, that they'd live a normal life, and I guess maybe they did. They had that little house in Lincolnwood, right?"

"White picket fence and everything," Jeff said.

Bruno laughed at something.

"What's funny?" Matthew said.

"I was just thinking," Bruno said, but then he paused for a second. "Did I know any of your boys who got killed?"

"Not as FBI agents," Jeff said. "You ever do any business with a guy calling himself Gino Ruggio?"

"Furniture guy? Always with the nice leather shit?"

"Yes," Jeff said. "He was one of ours."

"Huh. Good guy."

"Two kids," Jeff said.

Bruno laughed again. "I'm not laughing at your friend getting it," he said quickly. "I'm just thinking how here I am, ninety minutes away, showing real estate to people, living a pretty good life, right? And all that same shit is still going on. End of the day, I'm forty now, I just want a comfortable place to sit, maybe someone to sit and talk to, periodically go see a flick, whatever. All that shit they're still doing in Chicago doesn't make sense to me anymore."

"Money," Jeff said. "But not what Cupertine did."

"Don't kid yourself, it's always about money," Bruno said. "No call to kill a fed. But if you don't think there was some kind of financial reason behind it, you deserve to be on leave, Agent."

"Three *people*," Matthew said. "Three people got killed."

"I said I was sorry to hear that," Bruno said, a little edge to his voice now.

"And a confidential informant," Matthew said. "Bullet right between the eyes. Brain matter all over the Parker." Matthew toying with Bruno now, reminding him that he knew what, exactly, Bruno was. Jeff respected that, even if it was a bit misguided.

Jeff watched Bruno, to see if what Matthew told him made him pause to rethink his current status in life. If the Family was now in the business of killing federal agents and snitches, well, Bruno could have a short life expectancy.

"Did you tell Encyclopedia Brown how you saved me from my life of crime?" Bruno asked Jeff.

"I gave him the basics," Jeff said.

"He tell you I like men?" Bruno asked Matthew.

"He did," Matthew said.

"How you feel about that?" Bruno was testing now. Each of them trying to find their margin, Jeff just happy to sit back and watch.

"I don't care," Matthew said.

"See," Bruno said, "that's how all the kids are now days." He shook his head. "I bet if I were coming up now, my life would be easier. Probably be a capo by now." He paused for a moment and looked back out the front window of the Hummer. "You hear my dad died?" he asked Jeff.

"No," Jeff said.

"Yeah, he got Lou Gehrig's. All his life, you know, he was about being as precise as he could be cutting up steaks and shit. One day, he comes to work, can't cut straight. Hand's all shaky. I hear this from my mother, because my dad wouldn't have shit to do with me. Anyway, you know what that fucker did? He swallowed a bunch of my mother's Valium, put a bag over his head, and, just like that, good night, world. You believe that?"

"That's how I'd do it," Matthew said.

"Really?" Bruno said.

"Absolutely," Matthew said. "Less pain for everyone."

Bruno sniffed once, rubbed his face, and then didn't say anything for a few seconds. "Reason I tell you that, man, you just never know how people are going to go, right? Gotta always be getting right with the people you care about. Him dying, that had an effect on me. I've been thinking about that a lot since you called me, Agent Hopper, asking about Sal and about that body in the dump."

Normally when Bruno came in to give information, it was quick. This long conversation had Jeff off-center. He'd never known Paul Bruno to be an overly emotional guy, at least not one prone to introspection. There was something more here.

"What do you know about Sal?" Jeff said.

"Good guy," he said. "Smart as fuck."

"If he's so smart," Matthew asked, "why did he kill those men?" *Good*, Jeff thought. *Just like that.*

"I've been trying to wrap my head around that," Bruno said. "There had to be money involved, like I said, one way or the other. The Family don't send out Sal Cupertine just to hang out, you know? I mean, you ever get his prints, anywhere?"

"Never," Jeff said.

"I knew the guy his entire life," Bruno said, "and from the time he started doing hits until today? I never once saw him in the daylight. I mean, the man was a shadow, but that was his shit, too, you know? He wasn't dumb. Made him sound like the boogeyman."

"He took out my guys in broad daylight," Jeff said. "His DNA was everywhere."

"Then there's no way it was a hit," Bruno said. "No way."

"No," Jeff said, and then he told Bruno about how Sal Cupertine had figured out he was dealing with agents, how he got Jeff's name, how he'd gone back upstairs and killed the whole room.

"That's why you're here?" Bruno said. "You're taking a personal affront to this?"

"I am," Jeff said.

"Dumb," Bruno said. "Sal Cupertine will kill you and not even miss a meal afterward. Personal vendettas are stupid, and this is coming from a person who has a lot of personal vendettas."

"It's about justice," Jeff said.

"You keep telling yourself that," Bruno said. "Anyway, my thinking? Sal must have snapped. Just exploded."

"Do you recall him ever doing that before?" Matthew asked. It was a phrase hammered into young agents: *If possible, find a pattern.*

"When we were kids, yeah, sure," Bruno said. "After his dad got thrown off that building, he had some anger problems. But last ten, fifteen years? Nothing. I mean, I never got why he went into the killing business, except that he was good at it. And Ronnie was his only family. Sal didn't have shit. Murdered father, mother was a nut job. For a time, rumor was she was fucking the principal at Winston so Sal could get free lunches. I mean, crazy shit like that. That was his life. That's what he dealt with before he fell in with Ronnie. So I don't begrudge him a few problems, you know?"

"So why now?" Matthew asked. "He's methodical. He's smart. He's got this nice family now. Living the perfect gangster life. Why just lose it?"

"There any drugs involved?"

"Heroin," Jeff said. "The initial report was that he sampled a bit of everything."

"He was a mean fucker on heroin," Bruno said. "Once he had a kid, he stopped doing any kind of junk. But you know, if some good shit came through, he'd have a taste. Last guy you wanted paranoid at a party was Sal Cupertine."

"Then you go home, get your family, and run away," Matthew said. "You don't murder four people."

"Normal person, maybe," Bruno said. "This isn't a normal person. Killing is what he does, that's his nature. You put him in a situation where he might kill someone, he's gonna do that. So, probably realized he was caught. Realized everything he'd been doing for fifteen years was gonna get undone, and he did what he could to get out. Frankly, I'm surprised he didn't kill everyone in the whole Family for putting him in that position."

"He didn't have the time," Jeff said.

"Still," Bruno said. "Ronnie Cupertine shows up somewhere missing his head, don't act surprised. Only reason Ronnie would send Sal out in the day would be to get caught. Ronnie, he's the one with problems. On TV playing a gangster. The perfect cover. A fucking embarrassment, you ask me. Sal was just doing what he was told and if he blew, it was because someone put him in a position where that was the only choice."

That was the problem. Sal Cupertine was consistent. By acting inconsistent, by being reckless, he'd thrown everything off. Jeff couldn't figure out what his next move might have been, couldn't even figure out where he was. Once they got the records, the FBI had pinged his cell phone off towers close to Ronnie Cupertine's and then, hours later, it looked like he was driving in circles around southern Illinois. And then . . . nothing. He surely ditched his phone, but that there was no chatter at all about him, that the Family all spoke of him in the past tense, and that Jennifer Cupertine was alone and not exactly prospering made it all clear enough.

"What about the body in the dump?" Jeff asked.

"Not him," Bruno said. "My opinion? That body was a kid called Chema, real name Jose Espinoza. Half Mexican on his dad's side. Couldn't have been more than twenty-two, twenty-three."

Jeff hadn't heard of any half-Mexican members of the Family, though he supposed it wasn't beyond possible. The Gangster 2-6 street gang ran a lot of the cocaine and heroin in the city for the Family, so it reasoned that they might occasionally find an able body there. Still, that Bruno had a specific idea on who had been murdered and then dumped was curious. "How do you know him?" Jeff said.

"He used to come up to Milwaukee to hit the rainbow clubs," Bruno said. "So I recognized him. His brother Neto used to courier H for the Family before he got sent up to Stateville. I'd check and see if he's dead, too. My guess is he is. Family is good about that sort of thing. If Neto is dead, then for sure that's Chema they dumped."

Bruno fell silent for a moment, and Jeff realized he needed to ask a question he really didn't want to ask, had to ask the question he was hoping Bruno would explain on his own. "So," Jeff said, "you two were a couple?"

"Not in the traditional sense," Bruno said. "You know, we had fun, but he was a dumb, confused kid. Had a girlfriend, was Catholic, also, which fucked him up. Plus, he thought he was going to rise up in the Family, even though he saw what happened to Neto."

"You know who he was working for?" Jeff asked.

"He just got on Fat Monte's crew," Bruno said. "Day your boys got hit, he called me to say he couldn't drive up to see me. He had an errand to do for Monte. I never heard from him again."

"That doesn't mean he's the body," Matthew said. "Maybe he just didn't want to see you anymore. Maybe he decided to make it work with his girl. Could be a hundred different things."

"Could be, could be," Bruno said. "What's it been now? Seven months? How many people stay on Fat Monte's crew for seven months and don't end up getting pinched for some stupid gangster shit?"

Bruno let his last statement hang there.

"If Neto is dead," Jeff said, "then I'd advise you to get a new address. Maybe a new name. You still have chits in the bureau."

"Fat Monte don't scare me," he said.

"You're not a gangster, Paul," Jeff said. He used his first name on purpose, to remind him that he was a guy named Paul, not Bruno the Butcher, the name people on the street knew him by. Maybe he'd been a tough guy at one point, but he wasn't on the level of a Fat Monte. Not now, anyway. "You don't need this shit."

"I see that motherfucker," Bruno said, "I'll roll over his ass with my Hummer, drag him out here, and have my guys put him in the foundation of a nice three-bedroom. Give him a view of the pool and everything." Paul Bruno turned away from Jeff and Matthew then and started shaking his head. "I told myself I wasn't going to do this," he said quietly, and then he abruptly jumped out of the Hummer.

"What was that?" Matthew said.

"I think he's finally realizing his boyfriend is dead," Jeff said.

Jeff Hopper recognized two essential truths, as well, as he watched Paul Bruno walking off into the distance, his hands clutching at his scalp, his gait slow and deliberate: The first was that there was only one way for Paul Bruno to die, and it wasn't from breaking into some old lady's house to steal her furs and diamonds. Eventually, just as he'd told Jeff all this information, someone, somewhere, would give information to Ronnie Cupertine about Paul Bruno's activities in Milwaukee, how he had this nice new legit business going and didn't Ronnie think Paul owed him something for all their years of friendship? And did you know he was a queer? And then one day, Paul Bruno would wake up and find Fat Monte, or someone a lot like him, holding a gun on him. Diming out Fat Monte wasn't something he had to do. It was something he wanted to do.

The second truth was that Paul Bruno had been in love.

"Wait here," Jeff said to Matthew, and then he got out of the Hummer, too. It was cold outside, and Jeff immediately wondered just where Bruno hoped to find the seniors who would want to move here to live out their golden years.

Bruno walked over to the construction trailer and sat down on the second of three stairs that led to the door. There were no lights on inside, so Jeff made his way over, too, and sat down beside him, and the two of them waited there for a few minutes without speaking, the only sound Bruno's periodic sniffling and the chirping of birds.

"I'm sorry," Bruno said eventually. "I think I'm going through menopause or some shit."

"It's all right," Jeff said.

"He was just a dumb kid," Bruno said. "We never even did it. He was working out his shit and trying to figure out where it all went, and that was cool. I mean, who was I to pressure anyone? But to be done ugly like that?"

"Look," Jeff said, "I need your help on Cupertine. I find him, I can put a lid on this whole Family. Get all of them what they deserve."

That got Bruno to laugh. "You even hear yourself? This shit will just keep going on. You might find Cupertine, but don't think it's gonna change shit. You think Eliot Ness thought he'd solved it all? Poor motherfucker didn't even make sixty, you know that? Dead at fifty-four. True story. And he didn't stop shit. You find Sal Cupertine, just be content with that."

"You got any ideas?" Jeff said.

"Where was the last place you spotted him?"

"His cell phone had him in south Illinois, near the border to Missouri," Jeff said. "Last solid hit was outside Divernon."

"Nothing but farmland out there," Bruno said. "Slaughter-houses, too. Could be we're both wrong and you ate Sal Cupertine last time you had a Big Mac."

That thought had occurred to Jeff, too, when he'd seen the map. "You think of any safe houses the Family has outside of Chicago? Any other families they're close enough with to have them harbor Cupertine?"

"No one is gonna take that weight without a return," Bruno said. "You wanna look for a syndicate that can use him for something, someone who'd *buy* him from Ronnie, not the other way around."

It was an idea so simple, so reasonable, and so fundamentally in line with Ronnie Cupertine's way of doing business—selling people the things he didn't want to hold on to for more than a month at a time was the very basis of his used-car business; the reason the feds had so much trouble making any case against him on his cars was that they were out the door before they could even be tracked—that it made Jeff feel foolish. It was also something Jeff had never heard of—the trading of assets between crime families. "That happens?" Jeff asked.

"I worked for a lot of people," Bruno said. "They all seemed to know how to find me. I assume they paid Ronnie for that information."

What Jeff couldn't understand was what another syndicate would want with Sal Cupertine. Yeah, he was an efficient killer, but there were plenty of efficient killers working in all the families. "Who middled for Ronnie?" Jeff asked.

"Might be a nice thing to ask Fat Monte the next time you see him," Bruno said. His cell phone rang then. He pulled it from the clip on his belt and examined the number. "Oh, fuck me," he said, and then he answered it after the second ring. "Paul Bruno," he said, his voice an entirely different tenor. Mellifluous, even. "Uh-huh. Uh-huh. Yes, well, I'm happy to hear that. Yes, of course, it would be my pleasure. I do think a two-story is something to really consider. Those girls of yours will be making a racket in a few years, and you'll want the refuge! Yes, yes, of course. Okay, we'll do that then. And thank you for calling, Mr. Stubbs. Thank you again." Paul Bruno clicked his phone off and slipped it back into his belt clip.

"They want to buy a house after all?" Jeff said.

"Looks like it," Bruno said. He stood up then and stuffed his hands into his pockets. Jeff stood, too, and for a moment they both looked at the view. It was a bit desolate, though Jeff could see the potential. The air was crisp and clean. The trees tall and stately in the distance. A little imagination? A few man-made lakes? Maybe it would be paradise. Stranger things had sprung from the dirt.

"You get this place built," Jeff said, "maybe in fifteen years I'll come back and buy a condo."

"I shouldn't have said all that about Fat Monte," Bruno said.

"No," Jeff said, "you probably shouldn't have."

Bruno sniffled one last time. "Fuck it," he said. "I trust you won't mention my name to anyone?"

"Of course."

Bruno pointed at the Hummer, where Matthew was still sitting. "What's his skin in this?"

"I feel a debt to him," Jeff said. "I cost him his job. He's a good agent, or will be."

"He doesn't like me," Bruno said.

"No," Jeff said, "he doesn't. Probably better for both of us, really."

Bruno spit through his teeth then, a nasty habit of his Jeff had forgotten. "I never understood you, Agent Hopper," he said after a while.

CHAPTER SIX

David had his own preferred method for handling the guns he used for killing, and it involved buying them himself and making sure they were used only once and then immediately melted.

Not sold.

Not thrown in a river or a lake or buried or hidden under the dog house.

Not even destroyed. *Melted.*

It was a time-consuming process. In Chicago, he rented out a spot in a converted warehouse on West Fulton, near the old Kinzie Industrial Corridor, that had been turned into an artists' space complete with a metal lathe, foundry, press, and furnace. He'd go straight there after a job to dispose of all his evidence, even the clothes he was wearing. If there was reason to be concerned that evidence had somehow ended up in the stolen car he was driving, he'd disassemble and melt the car doors, or trunk linings, or, one time, the whole front console of a Gran Torino. You don't spend fifteen years killing people without learning how not to get caught.

David killed young men, middle-aged men, even old men. His first sanctioned hit was that German fucker, Rolf Huber, who'd been running girls in the suburbs since the 1950s and, at eighty, after the Family decided to colonize Batavia, started to talk about writing his memoirs for the feds. That was a gimme. Got him as he was walking out of his bar, the Lamplighter, on Christmas Eve. One shot, side of the head.

Not how he'd do it now; the side of the head sometimes didn't work, too many variables. But that was before he knew exactly what he was doing. He was only nineteen, and everything he knew about killing he'd picked up watching Cousin Ronnie. Ronnie was more of a bludgeoner, didn't feel like he'd done a job until he was covered in someone else's blood. No one knew shit about forensics and DNA back then.

Now, parked a few doors down from Ibiza Tan, the salon Slim Joe visited every other day in order to keep his nice orange hue, David couldn't believe how lucky he'd been. Killing disposable people helped. No one was sad to see another gangster dead. Besides, in those days, all the Chicago cops were on the take, and the FBI's attention was focused on New York, everyone working John Gotti.

Back before he was the Rain Man, back before he had any reputation to uphold, he was out hitting street dealers Ronnie said were skimming. Didn't matter if the kid was seventeen. David would stalk the kid for a week, two weeks, however long it took to figure out how to take him out with no collateral damage, follow the kid on the train out to Aurora, watch him shoplift from Lord & Taylor in the Fox Valley Mall, the next day show up outside his high school, see if there was any recognition on the kid's part, show up a few days later on his block, walk right by the kid, see if the kid started to mad-dog him, act tough, flash the gun in his waistband, whatever.

Nothing.

No one ever recognized him. His simple secret to killing was that he was always behind the guy about to die, days, weeks, sometimes months before it actually happened. It was the part of his legend he happily cultivated over the years. He was like an embolism: Just because you couldn't see him didn't he mean he wasn't there, waiting.

The only thing that bothered him now was that he knew he'd been trained, that the dealers he killed probably had done nothing in the least to deserve their fate, that it was all Ronnie manipulating him into a perfect killing machine. Ronnie building a legend on the streets to control his bigger business, so that when he had to hit actual hard targets, it was just a job.

David checked his watch. He had a lot of shit on his agenda, and Slim Joe was taking forever. He'd spent the last several days trying to figure out how he'd kill Slim Joe. David didn't want to do it in the house, not with his own genetic material all over the joint, and he certainly wasn't going to kill Slim Joe and then clean up afterward. Not after the last job he'd done in Chicago, a few months before the Donnie Brasco fuckup.

That was Frank Picone, the Windsor Syndicate's guy in Chicago. Ronnie told David at first that he wanted only intel on the guy, find out what the Mounties were doing in town, but not to kill him. It was no use killing a guy if it meant it would open up a job for some other, more capable asshole.

In Canada, the Windsor Syndicate was into the computer and mortgage shit Ronnie and the rest of the Family had no interest in. Ronnie didn't seem to mind when he found out that they'd moved down into Detroit, and then Chicago, running cons at nursing homes, stealing the identities of the patients, taking their whole portfolios out from under them, selling stocks, moving the cash back into Canada. It was irrelevant and frankly too risky for Ronnie. "That's civilian business," he told David. "Civilians have relatives. Relatives call the cops."

But when Picone started freelancing, flipped his cash into oxycodone, began dealing on AOL message boards, created a network of faceless buyers that handled their business with dead drops like they were the CIA, flooded the streets with an opiate cheaper and easier to handle than heroin? That was some shit Ronnie would not abide. The opiate business in Chicago belonged to the Family. And this asshole had just walked right around the Family, and in the process had taken intimidation and fear completely out of the game. That was a hanging offense.

Not that David cared about any of that. The only thing that concerned him was that Picone was indiscriminate, that he was able to get the thread of his actions by following him for under a week, was able to break into his house twice without incident, even sat behind Picone and his wife at a Chili's on a Tuesday night, the two of them talking about their business like they were discussing an episode of *Law & Order*.

Picone and his wife rented a redbrick house all the way out in Evanston. It was the kind of neighborhood where everyone drove an Audi or BMW, and the only American car on the block belonged to the nanny, so David had to keep stealing nicer rides than he preferred, just so he wouldn't be made. Picone spent his days either sitting around the house in his underwear, working on a laptop, or making drops at the Field Museum, or the sprawling Hilton on Michigan Avenue, Gene's & Jude's in River Grove, Buckingham Fountain, out in front of Wrigley

Field, wherever there were a lot of people. His big spy move was to have his buyer tape an envelope stuffed with cash on the underside of a bus stop bench. If everything was in order, Picone would leave a duffel bag of pills in a bush or garbage can. If the envelope wasn't there, or the money was short, he'd just keep moving, no deal, no problem, no one sticking guns in anyone's face, and he could go see a dinosaur or get a red hot and be on his way. He didn't even carry a gun.

Still, David couldn't very well shoot Picone in front of Wrigley Field. He also couldn't walk into Picone's house and put one in his head while he slept—he *could*, it just wasn't prudent. A murdered Canadian citizen in a solid upper-middle-class suburb was the kind of thing that ended up on the news. That wasn't going to work. Plus, he wasn't real keen on killing Picone's wife.

He needed a work-around. So, he did the only thing that seemed sensible. He called the cops.

On Saturdays, Picone did a big drop on Navy Pier, usually in front of the Children's Museum. He'd park blocks away and drag a suitcase behind him, pretend to take photos, talk on his cell phone, look frustrated, sometimes stop and ask directions. It was a whole bit. If he hadn't been so predictable, it would have been a decent cover. When David picked him from the crowd, he was walking along the promenade wearing a Hawaiian shirt, jeans, big sunglasses, a baseball cap. The only thing that stood out were the two Latin Kings with the neck tattoos waiting over by the bike racks. Seemed Frank Picone had at least one other tail.

A few yards behind Picone, an old man pushed himself along in a walker.

Perfect.

David called 911. "There's a guy in a walker out front of the Children's Museum flashing his dick at the kids," he said, then he hung up, ditched the phone in a planter, and stepped behind Picone, kept pace with him for a few minutes, until the Navy Pier security and cops started to stream out of every corner. Picone tensed up, and David put a hand on his back, pulled him close.

"You've been made," David whispered. "Walk back to your car." Picone nodded once, kept moving toward the museum for a few more seconds—there was a science fair going on, kids and parents and cotton candy and clowns and a bunch of rent-a-cops simultaneously putting walkie-talkies to their ears—then turned heel, David now a step back.

"Who the fuck are you?" Picone asked, trying to sound hard, not that it was working. They'd made it to Gateway Park, Picone still dragging his suitcase full of oxy.

"Ronnie Cupertine would like to have a conversation," David said.

"I don't know anyone named Ronnie Cupertine," Picone said.

"He's interested in doing business with you," David said.

"I'm not a decision maker."

"You are now," David said.

Picone brightened, hazarded a glance toward David. "He thinks so?"

"Yeah," David said, "you're the guy he's looking for."

When they got to Picone's car—a black 5 Series BMW with tinted windows and Ontario plates—David directed him to drive to his warehouse. He'd never actually killed anyone in his warehouse space—he killed a local gangster, he just shot them in the street; if he was doing some contract shit, it was easier to just make it look like a robbery gone wrong and do it at a victim's house or job, preferably the job, since no one brought their kids or pets to work—but this called for special circumstances. When they walked inside, before Picone could say a word about the foundry or the metal press, David put one in the back of his head.

Then he got to work.

He called Air Canada using Picone's cell phone and, using Picone's Visa, booked Picone a ticket to Windsor, one-way, leaving that night out of Midway. He called Kirkpatrick's Florist in Evanston, ordered two dozen red roses, and had them sent to Picone's wife, along with a note that said he'd been called out of town. His wife was smart. She'd know that if he hadn't called and just sent flowers, maybe he had a job to do and wouldn't ask questions. Two dozen roses would make anyone happy for a few days. Maybe a week. Eventually she'd get antsy, but then she'd see the Visa bill, and that would keep her another week. Still, she wasn't going to file a missing person's report. Gone meant gone in this business. She'd know that. Besides, the guy's name probably wasn't even really Frank Picone.

Ronnie didn't want any evidence of the guy's existence, which meant no body, so David first cut him up, then used the metal press, then used the furnace, then used the foundry, but it was a terrible mess. The metal press had been an inspired idea, but it took him hours to clean, so long that he had to drive Picone's car to a long-term parking lot, leave it, catch a bus, and come back to scrub even more. He was the fucking Rain Man. He didn't do floors. It ended up taking him three full days with industrial cleaners, some selective melting, and then a meticulous black light check to even feel confident about it.

He didn't have a secret place like that in Las Vegas, wasn't even sure how to go about looking for one. There was nothing old in this town. Once something wasn't useful anymore, they'd just implode it and start again, or do it like Fremont Street and throw a million lights on it and call it an "Experience" and give everyone a souvenir football filled with beer. Besides, he was a respected member of the community now, or would be beginning on Monday; he even had a set of keys to the temple, and that meant he needed to conduct himself a bit differently. He couldn't exactly rent a murder shop.

That meant trusting Bennie.

Slim Joe finally walked out of Ibiza Tan five minutes later—he'd gone in for a full thirty-minute bake—his cell phone already up on his ear, like the idiot didn't have enough radiation coursing through his veins. It was only ten in the morning, and David couldn't imagine anyone Slim Joe knew was actually awake yet. No one would miss Slim Joe for at least another ten, fifteen hours, and even then, no one who might miss him would be in the business of contacting the police. His own mother had just seen him, so even she wouldn't notice his absence for a few days. And maybe by then she'd be dead, too, though David was hoping to avoid that.

David watched Slim Joe get into his car—a black Mustang with a rear spoiler you could land a plane on—and tried to figure out how Bennie came to associate himself with such an obvious liability, cousin or not, particularly since the first thing Joe did when he got in his car was roll down the windows and begin bumping rap music. That he was still pretending to talk on his cell phone at the same time filled David with such an uncommon disdain that he nearly shot him right then.

Instead, he got out of the piece of shit Buick Bennie had secured for him, double-checked to make sure there weren't any cops lingering around—not that David believed the Summerhill

Plaza was a hotbed of criminal activity, though there was a Gold's Gym in the corner of the center that was filled with guys who must have thought they looked pretty tough hanging out in front of the elliptical machines—and headed over to the Mustang and got in. Slim Joe recoiled immediately and practically jumped out the window. David thought he even heard Joe scream a little, but he couldn't be sure with the bass creating sonic booms every other second. David tried to turn the volume down, but Slim Joe's stereo had more lights and buttons on it than a fucking spaceship, so David just reached over and yanked the keys from the Mustang's ignition.

"That's better," David said.

"Fucking Christ," Slim Joe said. "You scared the shit out of me, dog."

"What's that smell?" David said.

"What?"

"There's a smell in here," David said. "Like fruit mixed with grass and piss."

"That's my bronzer," Slim Joe said.

"What's that?"

"Makes my tan stick," he said. "Dog, you scared the shit out of me. I could've put a cap in you."

Slim Joe was wearing his usual outfit—a wifebeater, Nike sweatpants, white Pumas, a watch the size of a hubcap. Not much room to keep a gun, not that there was any need to bring a gun with you to a tanning salon. Bullets and intense heat don't usually have a good, safe relationship. Not even Slim Joe was that dumb. Maybe he kept a gun in the glove box.

"This bronzer, what does it run you?"

"I dunno, fifteen bucks. Whatever, man. No disrespect, but what the fuck are you doing here?"

No disrespect. Two words David had grown to hate. Someone said *no disrespect*, it immediately meant they were about to disrespect you. The Jews, they had it right: They basically told the Palestinians they could either have a piece of crap land or they could fuck off. Being polite got you exterminated. They killed first now.

"Maybe I've been thinking about getting a tan," David said. "It's the one thing I haven't really addressed since I got into town. You think I need a tan?"

"Naw, dog, you look good." Slim Joe gazed up into the rearview mirror and then turned around to look at the parking lot. "You drive here? I don't see your ride."

David could see that Slim Joe was agitated, which was good. He wanted him agitated. When you're off-balance, you're not as prone to seeing the obvious things. Better to keep someone engaged.

David put Joe's keys back into the ignition but didn't turn the car on. "We need to have a conversation. You willing to have a conversation with me?"

"You know I'm down for whatever."

"Then let's go for a ride," David said.

"We can't do this at the crib?"

"House is bugged," David said. "What I want to talk about wouldn't include Bennie. Just be something you and I get some skin on."

"Oh, shit," Slim Joe said, though it wasn't clear to David if he was happy or frightened by this prospect. "How long?"

"How long have I been there?"

"Oh, shit," Slim Joe said again. "All the rooms?"

"That's my guess," David said.

"You think Bennie listens to everything?"

"He's your cousin," David said. "I barely know the man."

"Oh, shit," Slim Joe repeated.

"You get it now?"

Slim Joe didn't say another word. He pulled out of the shopping center, and David told him to head toward the temple. Slim Joe kept stealing glances at his cell phone while he drove.

David picked up the phone and examined it. As expected, Slim Joe hadn't made or received a call since the previous night. David wasn't sure when it became cool to appear to be talking to someone. He'd read something the night before that stuck with him: *Reason is a small word, but a most perfect thing.* Some old Greek Jew said it when he was talking about being grateful for the natural powers men possess—life, death, soul, imagination, all that. None of these Jews ever talked about trying to be cool, or trying to impress anyone. They never got down and demanded respect, or complained about being disrespected. It was always about being aware that your deeds were your legacy and how you were viewed wasn't based on something as illusory as respect. Content was the thing.

It was a point that didn't exactly sit well with David. Not that he didn't believe it, only that he hoped it wasn't true for everyone. Because if so, he was fucked.

As it related to someone like Slim Joe, however, it seemed apt: What the fuck was he grateful for, really? All he wanted was for people to stare at him, maybe fear him. Normally, David tried not to think about the people he was about to kill. Once they became people, you could sort of imagine them being someone's husband, someone's brother, someone's son, and then you started to imagine them as babies, and his job became harder. Usually, David tried to depersonalize the experience as much as possible. The world was usually a better place for his work.

Even when he did contract work, he tended to kill bad guys as much as possible, not just cheating spouses, though he'd done that on occasion, too, like when Jennifer was pregnant and they didn't know how they'd afford all the prenatal care.

David opened up the Mustang's glove box, and, sure enough, there was a TEC-9. Of all the guns to keep in your car, the TEC-9 was among the worst, since they tended to jam more often than shoot. TEC-9s looked cool, though, which David assumed was enough for Slim Joe to choose it over the arsenal of practical assault weapons inside the house. David pulled out the gun and put it on his lap, then tossed Slim Joe's phone into the glove box and closed it.

"Why'd you do that?" Slim Joe finally asked.

"You expecting a call?"

"Nah, man, I'm just freaked out," he said. "You just roll up on me in a parking lot and tell me to drive, man, I'm a little on edge about that shit, you feel me? Now you got my TEC on your lap."

"I feel you," David said, the words sounding absurd coming out of his mouth, and David made a note to himself never to put those three words together again.

"Are you here to kill me?" Slim Joe said. Maybe he wasn't so fucking stupid.

"Suppose I am," David said. "There something you'd want to admit to, so maybe I don't have to torture you first?"

"I'd want you to know," Slim Joe said, "whatever beef I got with Bennie, that's got nothing to do with you. That's family shit, you feel me? Me and you, I feel like, you know, we bonded and shit while you were getting your face put back together."

"Sure," David said. He turned the TEC-9 over in his lap, inspected the clip. It had a full thirty-two rounds. That solved a problem. The gun was fairly light—two, maybe three pounds—which meant you really had to use some force if you wanted to beat someone with it, but it could be done. Metal versus flesh tended to have predictable results.

"So we're straight, right?"

"Right," David said.

"That's a relief, dog," he said.

"You tell anyone about me?"

Slim Joe swallowed. It looked like he was having some difficulty with general body functions, particularly now that David could see bulbs of sweat dotting his forehead. "Nah," he said. "Bennie said keep your name out my mouth, so that's what I've done."

"So, your friends ask you where you've been living these last few months, what do you say?"

"Just that Bennie got me up in a big-ass crib for doing him a favor," Slim Joe said.

"Rabbi Gottlieb?"

"Yeah," he said, excited now, as if David wasn't sitting there playing with his TEC-9. "You heard about that? Cuz Bennie said I couldn't say shit about that."

"It's all right," David said, the dumb motherfucker practically jumping out of his seat to tell the story. "How'd that go down?"

"Basically? I tied him up and forced about twenty shots of Jack down his throat, right? Make it look like he was drunk if they ever find his body, cuz Bennie, he was like, don't beat him or nothing, but then the rabbi, he got mouthy on me so I ended up breaking some of his fingers and toes. I thought that shit was gonna come back on me, but then the boat motor pretty much ate him up, so it worked out fine."

"Where was this?"

"The crib," he said. "In the weight room. I put him right up against the mirror so he could see. I thought that was pretty hardcore, some *Reservoir Dogs* shit." Slim Joe was giddy now.

David had always treated killing people as something you did with as little fanfare as possible. He'd done some torturing when he was younger, even broke the kneecap of a guy once. Frank Moti, an alderman in the First Ward, who Ronnie said had screwed him out of money on a zoning deal. You smack someone in the kneecap a few times with a ball-peen hammer, they throw up from the pain, there's a mess everywhere, they can't speak, they can't walk, and then you try to send them to the bank to get your money and they crumble on the street, or someone sees them with their bones sticking out of their pants and they call the cops. Moti didn't do that, instead he had a stroke right there in Ronnie's basement, so Fat Monte ended up dumping him a block from a hospital. Guy ended up serving another dozen years at city hall with a limp and a frozen eye. Moti never said a word, and Ronnie still didn't get his money. What was the use?

If the Family sent him out to kill someone, it was usually to make sure a secret remained a secret. Or maybe it was to keep some larger peace, or, and this wasn't as frequent as it used to be, to exact revenge. That was street-gang shit, and it only led to bigger problems. That David himself was still alive, and not killed to keep a larger peace, in this case with the feds, weighed on him somewhat. He knew it meant either Chema or Fat Monte's cousin Neal or, more likely, both, were dead because of it.

Though, it occurred to David that just having this conversation with Slim Joe was a kind of torture, prolonging the inevitable and all, but in this case David needed to know certain things.

"So you killed him in the house?"

"Naw, I just beat him there," Slim Joe said. "Drowned him in Lake Mead and then dumped him, let the boat roll up on him." David could hear the excitement in his voice, the memory of killing Rabbi Gottlieb firing him up. "So many bodies in there, it's amazing anyone found him. That's like our fucking cornfields, on the real."

"Why'd they have you do him?"

"Bennie didn't tell me that," Slim Joe said.

"You didn't beat it out of him?"

Slim Joe smiled. "I might have tried some words on him."

"And what did he say?"

"He mostly just cried," Slim Joe said. "Then he said he wouldn't tell no one about Bennie. I guess he heard about some job Bennie was planning."

David was both confused and surprised. Confused that they'd even attempt to run the body business under the nose of a real rabbi since it seemed far too risky a proposition, and surprised it had taken so long for Bennie to act on what would be a readily apparent situation. If Bennie had something on Rabbi Gottlieb, like he did on Rabbi Kales, it was more likely that Rabbi Gottlieb would have run to the police, so David assumed that whatever Rabbi Gottlieb learned was not because Bennie or Rabbi Kales tried to get him into the business. The poor fucker probably found out about it by being a good and diligent human being. The wrong kind of guy to kill, in David's opinion.

"Personally?" Slim Joe said. "I think it had more to do with him touching the kids. That's what I heard."

"He was molesting the kids?"

"Allegedly," Slim Joe said. "Bennie told me he had to go."

David doubted that. If it had been true, Bennie would have done the ugly himself. One of his kids was in that school, after all. Sounded more like a way to get Slim Joe interested in doing the job. A little motivation beyond the chance to just kill someone. He remembered needing that starting out. "That your first job?" David asked.

"Yeah," Slim Joe said. "It was fucked-up at first, but now I feel like I got a taste for it. Hoping you'll show me some moves down the line. Heard you were the fucking Grim Reaper in Chicago."

"Where'd you hear that?"

"You know," Slim Joe said, "I got the Internet."

"So you know my name?"

Slim Joe licked his lips, reached over and flipped on the AC, even though it was only about fifty degrees outside, and then didn't say anything. His silence was answer enough.

"You tell anyone else my name?"

"Nah. I keep the omertà like it's my job, homie."

Clearly, David thought. "You didn't mention me to your mother?"

"Naw," he said. "I mean, I told her I met someone who was down with our idea, like, who had some real faith on it, because she knows Bennie thinks it's bullshit, but she's been knowing him for all her life and knows he's all about big-dollar gigs, not this small-business shit."

"So," David said, "at no point did you say my name to your mother."

"That's what I said." Slim Joe was getting angry now, which meant he was probably lying. He'd have to tell Bennie that. "On her grave, I swear it."

"You don't swear on someone's grave before they're dead," David said. "That's like asking for them to be killed."

"Really?" Slim Joe seemed baffled by this.

"That's what the Torah says," David said, not that he thought that was true, but sometimes, like right before you're about to kill someone, it's just easier to lie.

■

Ten minutes later, they were pulling down Hillpointe, the temple coming up on the right, the cemetery and funeral home on the left, signs everywhere for the schools, Stars of David poking out around every corner. It was Sunday, so there was no construction going on, but there were a few cars parked in the temple's lot. Across the street, however, the cemetery was empty, and though there were lights on at the funeral home, there weren't any cars in the front lot, which was good. This was going to work out fine. David instructed Slim Joe to pull through the service entrance to the funeral home and then back behind the main building, where there was an alley between the home and the actual morgue where the bodies were unloaded. The entire lot was surrounded by a seven-foot brick fence and then rows of full-grown weeping willows, which must have cost a fortune to have planted, though David again had to admire Bennie's forethought. It looked pretty, sure. More importantly, between the brick wall and the trees, all views were completely obstructed. Sound was duly muted, too.

"Park here," David said, "and keep it running." Slim Joe did as he was told, because that's what he'd been trained to do, though David could see he found this whole proposition dubious.

"So, what's this job?" Slim Joe said. "We gonna rob some graves?"

"You don't know about this place?" David asked.

Slim Joe looked around. "Well yeah," he said. "Isn't this Bennie's big deal?"

"Is it?"

"Yeah, I mean," he said, "it's why I had to off the rabbi and it's why you're here, right? Run this game? You thinking we cut out Bennie and go it together? Bonnie and Clyde style?"

"No disrespect?" David said, and Slim Joe just stared at him, not getting it. Whatever. David had learned enough. Slim Joe knew too much and probably told at least his mother about David, maybe even his real name. He reached over and turned on the stereo until the car filled with the sound of nothing but bass. There were some lyrics in there somewhere, David was sure, but he couldn't make them out over the dusty-sounding *boom-de-boom-de-boom-boom* of the bass and the *boo-ya* of the shotgun fire the song employed as, David assumed, menacing authenticity. Like anyone still used shotguns.

Slim Joe opened his mouth to say something, and David shoved the TEC-9 in, felt Slim Joe's front teeth crack and give way, and squeezed the trigger once, putting a bullet right through Slim Joe's medulla oblongata, David's preferred sweet spot, and into the headrest. The human skull was the best silencer in the world, and the nice, new ergonomic safety design of modern headrests provided plenty of sound cushion, too. The rap music, however, really did the trick.

He set the gun back on his lap, took out a small packet of wet-naps from his pocket, and carefully wiped the gun down and then put it in Slim Joe's hand, made sure his prints were all over it, and then dropped it on the floor. He then took a few moments to wipe down all the surfaces he'd touched, pulled out Slim Joe's phone and wiped that down, too. It was more than he needed to do, more careful than he needed to be by a mile, since no one would ever find Slim Joe's body or this car, but still: You were either a professional or you weren't. No need to be sloppy just because you feel like you're in control.

David checked himself in the rearview mirror, made sure there wasn't any spatter on him—last thing he wanted was to be walking around with bits of Slim Joe stuck to his face—then killed the Mustang's ignition, took one last look around the car to make sure he hadn't left anything important sitting about, and then stepped out into the late morning.

It was brisk outside with a nice breeze, not like the gales that came off the lake back home, and Rabbi David Cohen caught the whiff of cooking meat coming from somewhere in the neighborhood. It was about ten thirty, pretty early for someone to be having a barbecue, though not outside the realm of possibility in a twenty-four-hour town like Las Vegas. Steak and eggs, that's probably what it was. Yeah, that would work, the idea of red meat finally starting to sound palatable. Hit the whole plate with a little Tabasco, maybe get some breakfast potatoes, maybe a nice cigar, call it brunch.

David walked across the street to the temple, where his Range Rover was parked, let himself in the back door with his keys, avoided the actual synagogue, where he heard some laughing and talking, like maybe there were a couple of people having a normal conversation, unaware that there was a dead gangster about one hundred yards away, and then entered his office. It was still dusty and dark with all the books stacked up on the shelves and the floor, plus all of Rabbi Gottlieb's non-personal effects—stacks of probably unread issues of *The New Yorker*, articles clipped out of the *Review-Journal*, a corkboard filled with coupons for free car washes. He'd clean the place himself, let a little light in, see what he could get rid of. This was his place of business now, so he didn't want to get too cozy, because cozy was soon lazy, and he wasn't ever going to be that.

He fished a scrap of paper from his pocket, then dialed out on the office phone.

"You done?" Bennie asked. Not even a hello.

"Yeah," David said. "He's back behind the mortuary, just like you said."

"Anyone see you there?"

"Only Slim Joe," David said.

"Okay," Bennie said.

"Listen," David said. "His mother, she probably knows my name."

There was silence for a moment, followed by a long sigh. "Shit," Bennie said. "He could've been running the Wild Horse in a couple years, you know? Dumb fuck." He paused for what seemed like a long time. "Well, she would have begun to wonder why he wasn't calling anyway. All right. I'll send someone out to Palm Springs in the morning, get it taken care of. You good? You need anything?"

"Steak and eggs," David said.

"What's that?"

"I want some steak and eggs," David said. He thought for a moment, then added, "and buttermilk pancakes."

"Go get yourself some steak and eggs and buttermilk pancakes then," Bennie said.

"You want your new rabbi out eating a nonkosher meal?"

"Jesus," Bennie said. "You think you're on a cruise ship? Anything else?"

"Couple cigars," David said. "And some breakfast potatoes, with the skin on. Maybe some of that blueberry shit. Compote."

"Jesus," Bennie said. "You should've told me this before you did your job, I would have had Joe get this shit together." David heard Bennie cover the phone and then shout for his wife, Rachel. David couldn't make out what Bennie said after that, but when he came back on the line, he said, "How you want your steak, Rabbi?"

CHAPTER SEVEN

For the first two weeks of December, Rabbi David Cohen woke up each morning at 5 a.m. and ran a few miles on the treadmill while listening to a series of Hebrew language tapes. Rabbi Kales gave him the tapes the day after David took out Slim Joe. David had gone into the office that Monday morning, as he was ordered to do, and Rabbi Kales began saying things to him in Hebrew, and when David didn't respond, he stopped and examined David's books, which David still hadn't completely unpacked, and pulled out a slim workbook titled *Modern Hebrew for Children*.

"You didn't read this?" Rabbi Kales asked.

"I tried," David said.

"What do you mean you tried? You've read a hundred books; you've read most of the Midrash! And you only tried to read this?"

David didn't think he could learn another language. He'd read the first ten or fifteen pages, about the alphabet and phraseology so that kids could figure out how to say prayers and maybe prime them for their bar mitzvahs, and it just wouldn't stick. He'd never had any facility with Italian, either, though he thought that had more to do with his mother. After his dad was thrown off the building, she didn't let anyone speak Italian in the house, said it was the sound of his father's stupidity and malice, the sound that had left her a widow, the sound that left her to raise a son alone.

"I'm not good with other languages," David said. "You're in America, speak English, that's my opinion. Otherwise, get the fuck out."

"Your xenophobia is lovely," Rabbi Kales said, and when David didn't respond, he added, "Only Jews speak Hebrew, and even then, in America, not a great many. But a rabbi who doesn't know passable Hebrew is like a fish that cannot swim."

Rabbi Kales gave him a series of cassettes, narrated by what sounded like an entire city of thousand-year-old Jews; he told David it was important for him not just to learn the *words*, but also to get familiar with the *voices*.

At first, David couldn't find the thread of the talks—the accents were too pronounced—and sometimes he couldn't tell if the person speaking was a man or a woman, their voices so thick with age all he could hear was syllables. It wasn't until he realized that whenever they spoke he started to run faster, began to sprint, that it all made sense: He couldn't understand them because he didn't want to hear what they were saying.

Knowing that Rabbi Gottlieb had been tortured just a few feet away from where he was attempting to learn Hebrew began to bug him, which is what got David to start jogging outside.

Out in nature—in the re-created nature of his gated community—with hills and curves and stones in the road and 7 Series BMWs blocking part of the communal sidewalk, which David was sure was against the HOA rules, he found himself forced to concentrate more on his own footfalls than what was coming into his ears, and the result was that he began to hear the stories, began to understand the old voices, began not to be creeped out by them.

It was beneficial, the tapes and jogging out in public, Rabbi Kales telling him how he needed to get integrated into society, to not fear his congregants, to start acting like a rabbi, particularly with the holidays coming up, where he'd be asked to take on a more *interactive* role. Since killing Slim Joe, he'd spent most of his time getting schooled by Rabbi Kales at the temple, meeting a few people here and there, learning functional Hebrew directly from Rabbi Kales and the tapes. It was hard, particularly since Rabbi Kales had him learning two new languages: Hebrew and what the rabbi called "dignified language," which basically meant he wasn't allowed to swear anymore. At least not out loud.

While he jogged, he'd talk back to the tapes, which meant he did little more at first than nod at the other joggers he encountered, or the people rolling into their homes after the conclusion of their 9 p.m.–5 a.m. shifts at the hotel (or casino or strip club or wedding chapel or wherever else all these people seemed to flow in from), the neighborhood as busy at 5 a.m. as it was at 5 p.m. The town kept meth hours, which was unnerving. David had spent so much time over the last fifteen years doing work in the dark that he'd become comfortable alone in the shadows. Here, everyone moved under the cover of darkness. It made David feel unbalanced. Or more unbalanced, anyway.

So he shouldn't have been surprised when at five thirty in the morning on the first day of Hanukkah, he came around the corner of Pebble Beach Way, heading toward Sawgrass Street, and found a man in a suit standing there. He was about David's size—a little over six foot, fit, but not overly so—but looked to be a decade up on David in age. The first thing David thought was that he was a fed. He reminded himself he wasn't supposed to be paranoid, that no one in Las Vegas was looking for him, and that he didn't look like Sal anymore, a fact that surprised David every time he looked in the mirror, particularly now that he had a full beard speckled with bits of gray.

Still, his first inclination was to snap the guy's neck and keep moving. There was something wrong with this idea, David now understood, even if it seemed simpler than whatever was going to come next.

The man approached him without any trepidation, already talking, though David couldn't hear him over the cassette he was listening to. The man didn't appear to have a gun, or handcuffs, or any kind of walkie-talkie or a cell phone, and was standing next to an idling Mercedes. Not even the best fed got to roll in a Mercedes, so David removed his headphones and tried to look surprised and not murderous while still maintaining enough distance that, if need be, he could act on whatever volition he had. Not paranoid. But not a fucking pussy, either.

"Sorry, sorry," the man said. "I didn't see you had phones on." He extended his hand, and David shook it. "Jerry Ford. Like the president, except I've got all my hair, at least for now."

David didn't respond. He was trying to figure out why this man had been lying in wait for him. He looked vaguely familiar in the same way people in dreams look vaguely familiar.

"I live right here," Jerry said, when the pause became awkward, "and have been meaning to come out and chat with you. Seen you every morning and just didn't make the connection before. Sort of expected the whole *mishegas* with the crap hanging off of your clothes and whatnot."

The butter-yellow house was three blocks from David's, and the Mercedes—a butter-yellow convertible—registered, too.

"Not *crap*," Jerry kept on, "never *crap*, God, but, what do you call that stuff that the Hasids wear around their waist?"

"*Tzitzit,*" David said. Rabbi Kales had warned him that once people knew he was a rabbi, they'd have all kinds of questions, the pressure of which made David stay up every night and, even before the jogging, wake up early every morning. It was the same schedule he kept back home, anyway, just with more reading.

Jerry snapped his fingers. "That's it, that's it," he said. "I don't know why I was expecting the full black getup with the . . . how do you pronounce that again?"

"*Sit-sis,*" David said.

"Oh, like you're telling your sister to take a seat, right?"

"Right." David wasn't positive this was correct. He was positive, however, that he had the authority to be wrong and not be challenged, which he rather liked.

"I don't know why I thought that," Jerry said. "Rabbi Gottlieb, Rabbi Kales, they're both like you, right?"

"I never knew him," David said. "Rabbi Gottlieb."

"Helluva nice guy," Jerry said, in a way that made David doubt the sentiment. "Never took him for a drunk. Never took him to be much of a boater, either, but then who knows, right? Private lives of rabbis must be a thing of great mystery."

"I'm sorry," David said. That was something Rabbi Kales had imparted to him lately: Start conversations by saying *I'm sorry*, and people will assume you're apologizing for being very busy, even when you're just trying to get away from them. Then just say *but*, and if you're lucky, the person on the other end of the conversation will get to their point or leave you be.

"No, no, I'm sorry, you're a busy man, I'm sure," Jerry said. "And I just ambushed you on your run like some kind of criminal. I keep odd hours, like you, and thought this might be the one chance I had to chat with you for a minute, finish a business conversation I never got to finish with Rabbi Gottlieb." Jerry fished a business card out of his suit jacket pocket and handed it to David. "I own my own biomedical business, and I've been trying to get into a conversation with the funeral home at the temple, where, it should be noted, I am a member in excellent standing."

David stared at the card trying to make sense of what was happening. He couldn't. "I'm sorry," David said again, and, tried to hand Jerry his card back.

"No, no, hold on to it," Jerry said. "I'm not trying to sell you anything. Rabbi Gottlieb and I talked about this at some length before his accident, and then Rabbi Kales wouldn't take any of my calls. I tried to go through the rabbi's son-in-law, and he gave me the runaround, said he was just a fund-raiser, which I totally get. Need to keep business and family separate, right?"

"I haven't gotten to know Mr. Savone very well," David said, "but the Talmud tells us that business is a test of our ethics. And I know Mr. Savone is an ethical man."

"No argument," Jerry said. "My business is in tissue, and tissue doesn't discriminate. We do a lot of work with the dental school at UNLV and the med school out in Reno, plus private medical interests around Nevada, little bit in Oregon, trying to move out into Utah, but the Mormons are a *golem*, am I right?"

Jerry stared at David like he was looking for some kind of approval. It was one of the weird things David had noticed about the Jews. They wouldn't always come right out and tell you they were Jews once they found out you were a rabbi, or even just with strangers they thought were also Jews; instead they'd drop these code words into the conversation, these bits of Yiddish, just to let you know on the sly that they were in the tribe. It was like how the wannabe gangsters used to talk, every other word was *whacked* or *respect* or some shit they picked up watching *The Godfather*, like everyone was running around talking about going to the mattresses.

"You shall inquire and make search and ask diligently," David said. He'd read that in the Talmud, and it sounded like something Rabbi Kales might roll out without explanation, so he gave it a spin.

"I get that, I get that," Jerry said. "Thing is, I'm trying to develop a partnership with a funeral home or two locally for those people who want to donate their tissue, and, quite honestly, we have some of the cleanest bodies around. Even the old ones live pretty clean, right?"

"I'm sorry, but," David said.

"No, no, I understand. It's not pleasant conversation. But, *for our people*, you understand, this is a great opportunity to give back to the local community. And, of course, there are rules about this stuff. The temple would be compensated. That was the thing Rabbi Gottlieb and I were talking about, and he just couldn't wrap his mind around Rabbi Kales ever getting into it. But I'm seeing you out here running every day, and I'm seeing a sophisticated young man, who, I understand, has the rabbi's ear now. And I'm thinking, you know, maybe there's a better chance for a symbiotic relationship to develop here." Jerry paused, as if trying to find that final bit of noninformation that might interest David, not knowing he'd already stumbled through it when he mentioned some form of compensation. "It would be a *mitzvah*, is what I'm saying. Good for the Jews."

"How much?" David said.

"A big one," Jerry said. "A very significant *mitzvah*."

"No," David said. "How much would the temple be compensated?"

"Oh," Jerry said. He seemed honestly surprised. "It depends on your service."

"So we wouldn't be getting paid for getting you the . . . what did you call it? The tissue? Just for our actual removal of things. Am I understanding you?"

"Right, right," Jerry said. "That's the law."

"How much do you get?"

"I do all right," he said. "I'd like to do better, which is why we're having this conversation."

"If I'm to explain this to Rabbi Kales," David said, "I need to explain to him how this might return to the temple in some positive light, you understand."

"I see," Jerry said. "You're talking about getting press for this?"

"No," David said. "No press. Never."

"Right," Jerry said. "Say we're talking about some corneas. We have an excess of good corneas here in the United States, but I can sell them to companies in China, India, places like that, really help people all over the world. I don't know if that's what you're talking about."

It wasn't. But it was interesting. "How much do you make on a deal like that?" David asked.

"I get maybe fifteen or twenty thousand for them," he said. "Not all pure profit, of course."

"Of course," David said, thinking: *Yeah, maybe only 99 percent profit.* "And this is legal?"

"You think I'm going to present an illegal idea to you, Rabbi?"

That Jerry didn't come talk to David at the temple, instead waited out on the street like he was selling watches out of his briefcase, raised David's bullshit detector, but he liked this guy's gumption. Las Vegas was the only place he'd ever been where everyone was squeezing you. There was a tip jar at the cleaners he used down on Rainbow, like you should give an extra buck because they got the starch right; a tip jar at the automated car wash, presumably so the robots would feel appreciated; and at the Borders on Decatur, where he'd sometimes go to hide out during the day, he'd see people hand the girl with the pierced nose at the info counter a few bucks for showing them where to find the self-help books.

But he could actually appreciate a business like Jerry's—it was called LifeCore—which aimed to help others. Thing was, the more Jerry talked, the less David believed him to be all about the altruism. Like how he hadn't answered his yes-or-no question with a yes or a no.

And if he was on the take? So what. The whole town was on the take, even people like Rabbi Kales, all done under the cover of escapism of some kind.

One day the *Review-Journal* would run a big piece on how a mob museum would be a great way to lure nongambling families and history buffs to the Strip, better than *Star Trek: The Experience* at the Hilton or the septic water park next to the Sahara, and then the next day Harvey B. Curran would have a blind hit piece about how he heard New York families were muscling into the monorail project and if it were thirty years ago, there would be blood on the streets and the streets would be better for it. A week later, there'd be a splashy feature on how Steve Wynn was saving the arts by bringing rare Cézannes, Monets, and van Goghs to the Bellagio for the world to see, people seeming to forget every piece was bought on the backs of a generation of assholes losing on rigged games of chance.

Never mind the locals he saw every day at Smith's, buying their groceries with an attitude, dressed in sweat suits, gold chains, those hard stares, like they were going to intimidate a box of Cheerios into giving up the money it owed. And the tourists. Somewhere along Interstate 15 they stopped being accountants and file clerks and started being tough guys in shiny shirts. David wouldn't be surprised if in fifteen or twenty years, after he was long gone, the city built a roller coaster on top of the temple's cemetery and renamed it Gangsterland.

Maybe Jerry Ford was trying to play David for a rube.

Maybe he didn't think someone like Rabbi David Cohen would want to find a way in, rather just see the good of it. Which made David think he should probably at least act slightly concerned about how all this was going down. Last thing he wanted was for this shyster to think he was a shyster, too. But that's what made this all interesting to David: Something about David's mere appearance made Jerry think he could approach him about this business deal. And maybe it was just a business deal. Maybe David was reading it all wrong, but he didn't think so. Jerry Ford had probably been marking him for a week or two, just waiting to pounce with this little shell game. Maybe even saw him with Slim Joe once or twice in the neighborhood, probably wondering why the new rabbi was consorting with a thug.

"Why aren't you standing outside a hospital right now?" David asked.

"You know how many people die in Las Vegas every day?" Jerry asked. "Hospitals don't have the time for these tissue donations. Lungs, hearts, kidneys, they do the big jobs, and even still, they subcontract that work out most of the time to organ banks. So say Mrs. Rosenthal passes on, she's a tissue donor, we come get her, bring her to your shop, if you pardon the term, and your guy handles the process. I assume you've got a guy who's qualified for that?"

David had no idea. Bennie had yet to introduce him to the funeral home staff, figuring it was better to keep him away until the last possible moment, make sure he was, as Bennie said, as "Jew'd up as possible" before he started interacting with the staff.

"Yes," David said.

"Might be good for business overall, steering more funerals up here to Summerlin," Jerry said. "Not that what you do is a business of course."

"Of course," David said.

The sun was starting to come up, David's favorite time of the day in Las Vegas. It was the only time when the place looked clean. He needed to get back to his house, shower, and then get over to the temple. Today was going to be a busy day with the Hanukkah celebration, and, according to Bennie, he was going to officiate his first funeral, maybe two. The whole week was a mess of meetings, and services, and God knows what. Then, after Hanukkah, Bennie told him there might be an influx of body work, that some shit was going down in Reno that could end up lucrative for them. But Jerry had opened up some ideas for David, maybe a way to keep something on the side, even, work his way back to Chicago a little faster. He'd need time to ponder that.

"I'm sorry," David said to interrupt Jerry's monologue. Jerry was talking about how hip bones were the new wave, what with all the hip replacements being performed now that people were living longer. "My point here was that I think Rabbi Kales would be interested in knowing what you intended to donate back to the temple." David couldn't quite understand how he'd managed to put those words together in that way, how he was actually starting to talk like a straight guy. Small steps for mankind and all that.

"Oh. I guess I didn't understand . . ." Jerry stammered for a moment, tried to take in what David was telling him. "What would a good percentage be?"

"Ten percent," David said. "Fifteen. Maybe even twenty." This kind of talk felt normal. Shaking people down was second nature to David. He knew if he talked to Jerry in his own voice, he could get fifty out of him. Maybe sixty. Hell, he could probably get seventy.

"Fifteen percent," Jerry said. "Like a tip, basically?"

"People tip twenty percent now," David said.

"*Machers* tip twenty percent," Jerry said.

"And you're a *macher*, aren't you?" David slipped Jerry's card into the pocket of his sweatpants, where he thought he might start keeping a switchblade, just in case. "I'll talk to Rabbi Kales," he said.

"All I can ask, Rabbi Cohen," Jerry said. They shook hands again, and David was surprised to feel sweat on Jerry's palm.

"Tell me something," David said, not yet letting go, his smile wide and friendly, or at least trying to be, his jaw still not quite right in his opinion. "How did you know my name?"

"Oh, right." Jerry tried to pull his hand away, so David covered up their grasp with his other hand. He'd seen Rabbi Kales do a similar move when he wanted to keep someone from ending a conversation before Rabbi Kales was ready. "It was in the HOA newsletter. It's a big deal when a rabbi moves in. Good for home values."

■

It was just after noon, and Temple Beth Israel was filled with kids, all of them screaming or crying or running, or all those things at once, the temple's Children's Hanukkah Party in full swing. The entire playground had been turned into a carnival area, with face-painting stations, booths filled with cooking food—latkes, hot dogs, burgers and fries, funnel cakes, because it was David's understanding that you couldn't have a carnival without funnel cakes—a guy making balloon art, a ten-foot-tall inflatable dreidel that the kids could get inside of and make spin, and, surrounding the perimeter of the playground, the parents, including Bennie and his wife, Rachel, sipping coffee and ignoring their children entirely, letting the teenagers who'd volunteered to take the brunt of the abuse.

David stood on a small stage in the middle of it all, trying not to feel sick while Rabbi Kales made a speech welcoming everyone to the annual party. David had lived his entire life lurking in the background, a shadow, the person in the room no one wanted to speak to, and now here he was front and center, minutes away from being formally introduced by Rabbi Kales.

After, David feared the adults would want to talk, make polite conversation, something David had never done in his entire life. What if he got something wrong? What if he said something that was completely contradictory to the Jewish faith? Rabbi Kales had told him not to worry, that if anyone questioned anything he ever said, all he needed to do was tell them that it was from the Talmud and he'd be covered, because no mere quasi-practicing Jew (which is what the temple was mainly comprised of, what Rabbi Kales called "pork-eating Jews") ever cracked open the Talmud. Besides, Rabbi Kales told him, it was all about interpretation. He could have an interpretation that was different than any other rabbi in the world. That was the nice thing about being a Reform rabbi, Rabbi Kales said, they were open to the idea that maybe another rabbi had a different slant to the same set of beliefs.

He had a pretty good feeling that was going to be true.

"Some of you may have noticed a new face here at Temple Beth Israel," Rabbi Kales said. David searched the playground for a soft landing place and instead found Bennie Savone, who at some point had moved directly in front of the stage, along with his wife. She was smiling at him with genuine warmth, and it occurred to David that she thought he was an actual rabbi, like her father was an actual rabbi. They'd met in passing only twice—she'd come to the temple to pick up her daughter while he and Rabbi Kales were in conversation, so she just stuck her head into his office and said hello, told him if he needed anything not to be afraid to call, that sort of thing, which struck David as extremely polite for a woman married to such a fucking prick—and somehow his mere countenance had been enough for her to believe.

David thought maybe that was the thing. People wanted to believe that you were who you said you were.

Rachel had an expensive haircut, nice makeup, white angora sweater, simple gold jewelry, a significant diamond on her wedding ring—maybe two, two and half carats—but it was nicely inset, not like his cousin Ronnie's wife, who had a diamond so big it could send SOS signals on sunny days. Rachel didn't wear gaudy hoop earrings or huge clusters of ice on every appendage. The Orthodox, they were big on the idea of *tzniut*, keeping modest in dress, particularly the women, which meant they all dressed as though they'd just escaped from Russia with the Cossacks hot on their tail. Rachel wasn't that modest, comparatively, though up against the other women he saw in Las Vegas, particularly the ones he could see staring at him now from behind their Starbucks cups and huge bug-eye black sunglasses, she looked like a nun.

David focused on Rachel, tried to imagine that she was rooting for him, thought about how disappointed she'd be if he started vomiting, and that seemed to soothe him a bit, until the sound of Rabbi Kales voice once again pierced through the roaring of blood rushing to his ears. He was talking about how the Maccabean warriors took it upon themselves to live or die nobly, some fairy tale about, when you got right down to it, how noble it was to be a killer, provided you happened to be killing people for your freedom to believe in something. It was the same bullshit the Family tried to press on the new meat. Problem was, as time wore on, you started to realize you were just part of the same bureaucracy found in any business. The only thing noble about it, as it related to the Family, was at least you knew your friends were more likely to stab you in the chest than in the back.

Rabbi Kales paused in the middle of his speech and turned to look at David. David smiled, still feeling like if he moved too quickly or even opened his mouth more than a crack he might hurl. The rabbi looked pained for a brief moment, just a flash, really, probably not long enough for anyone to notice, and then he cleared his throat and started in again.

"No one can replace Rabbi Gottlieb," Rabbi Kales said, "not in our hearts, nor in mere presence, and we all wear the tragedy of his passing each day here at Temple Beth Israel, particularly today, on the first holy night of Hanukkah, when we celebrate the onset of a true miracle. I think you will come to find Rabbi Cohen to be a kind and faithful servant of the Torah." David saw the adults in the audience nod, almost imperceptibly, and David understood that the rabbi was proving David's very point: He was telling them what to believe, and because they believed *in* Rabbi Kales, they believed what he said. "Like all of us, Rabbi Cohen is still learning that life looks somewhat different here in Las Vegas." The audience laughed, since no one was actually from Las Vegas, at least not according to the statistics David read in the paper. Even Bennie chuckled, though probably for entirely different reasons. "So please do keep in mind that Rabbi Cohen is still in training, both as a rabbi and as a Las Vegan, which means I don't want to hear of anyone inviting him to any poker games for at least another six months, and he is never allowed anywhere near the Strip when the rodeo comes to town, and that's an order!" More laughing, the rabbi putting on a nice little nightclub patter now, full of inside jokes, bringing the room back up. It was a holiday, after all. "Especially not in the company of my son-in-law." And the house came down, as much as a house can come down when it's also filled with a bunch of sticky six-year-olds, wealthy Jews, and a Mafia boss who happened to own the Wild Horse strip club and was inexplicably married to the rabbi's daughter.

Rabbi Kales stepped away from the podium and motioned for David to take his place. They'd practiced this moment earlier in the morning; Rabbi Kales told him to simply thank everyone, tell them how happy he was to be in Las Vegas and how he hoped to be of service to the temple, and then get the hell off the stage.

It sounded simple enough, yet when he stepped behind the podium and looked out at the playground filled with Jewish children, smelled the cooking food, heard the polite applause from the adults, and saw Bennie Savone with his arm around his wife, his wife whose father was the rabbi, his wife whose father the rabbi had done something depraved enough that he was now in bed with a gangster who was going to build an empire on corpses, in a way no other Mafia boss ever had, and had selected David to be his guy, had seen enough in him that he was going to let him be responsible for the growth and the prosperity of not just his criminal plan but, it seemed, also his noncriminal plans to grow a temple Las Vegas . . . well, he felt a huge surge of pride.

All this time waiting for something big to happen. All the years he told Jennifer that they were going west to get beyond that Chicago shit. All the ways he'd wondered if he'd ever see fifty, or if he'd be thrown off a building. All the nights he'd driven back across the Illinois state line in a stolen car, ten grand in his pocket from a freelance job so they could get the transmission fixed, get a stove that didn't leak, help Jennifer's dad pay his medical bills after he got his hip replaced, or just to get them through the slow time during the coldest, frozen months of winter.

All that . . . and here he was, he'd done it, he'd made it. Now all he had to do was bide his time, do what Bennie asked, listen to Rabbi Kales, make all the right moves. And when the time was right, he'd be done with all this *tsoris*, he'd have money in the bank, and then, then, he'd go get Jennifer and William. Maybe it wouldn't be only a year or two. Maybe it would be more like five or seven. And that would be fine. The Jews had wandered the desert for forty years. He could do five standing on his head.

David opened his mouth slightly at first, to make sure he wouldn't wretch, found Rachel in the audience, realized what he was looking for wasn't even her, wasn't any friendly face in particular, more like the idea of a friendly face, because he knew at some point in his life he was going to disappoint Rachel, would probably leave her a widow, because that's how the game always ended for people like Bennie, and then he leaned into the microphone and said, "Shalom."

CHAPTER EIGHT

That afternoon, after David helped the teenagers wrangle the last of the sugar-addled kids off the playground and break down the tents and deflate the dreidel, he walked across the street to the funeral home, where he found Bennie pacing out front.

"You have a good time today, Rabbi?" Bennie asked. He was still on the phone, so he covered the receiver with his hand.

"It was fine."

"Looked like you were going to puke for a minute there."

"I don't like public speaking," David said.

"You want me to get you some Valium? Maybe another steak?"

"I'll make it work."

Bennie put a hand up to indicate he was back on the phone. "Here's the deal," Bennie said, "you tell Danny to get out of town, I don't care where he goes. Let this shit blow over, and then we'll deal with it after the holidays. Last thing I want is to get subpoenaed on Christmas Eve, because that's how they'd do it, right? Okay." Bennie closed his phone and slipped it into his pocket, then gave a snort. "You know what's unsatisfying? You can't hang up on anyone anymore. You can't slam the phone down. I just get to flip it closed. Used to be you could get some aggression out on a phone, not anymore. Now I just get to stand here and be pissed off."

"You got a problem?"

Bennie eyed David curiously. "You want to know?"

"Doesn't matter one way or another," David said.

"So you're my consigliere now?"

"That's a bullshit word," David said.

"Yeah," Bennie said, "I always thought so, too. I blame Coppola for that stupidity." He rubbed that spot on his neck absently. "I'd kill someone for a cigarette right now."

"Easier just to have a cigarette and leave the killing to someone else."

"Can't," Bennie said. He pointed to his scar. "See that? Thyroid cancer. Seven years clean of the bug. Not gonna start inhaling cancer just to feel better about myself. Nearly died from that shit. Probably will die from it at some point. Cancer's the one thing more efficient than you ever were." He rubbed the scar again. "Some shit went down last night at the club. Guy gets his hands all over one of the girls on the floor, so the bouncers tell him to knock it off or go to the VIP room. The guy tells one of our bouncers to go fuck himself, and so they dragged him out back and stomped the shit out of him."

"That who I'm burying?" David asked.

"No," Bennie said. "He's over at Sunrise Hospital. Paralyzed from the neck down, apparently bit off his own tongue, lost an eye. They tossed him in a Dumpster when they were done with him, didn't realize he still had some buddies inside."

"That's stupid," David said.

"No, what's stupid is that it's all on camera," Bennie said. "Pawn shop next door records everything. Only legit pawn shop in the fucking world and it's next to my club."

"The bouncers are your guys?"

"Yeah."

"Were you there?"

"Yes and no," Bennie said. "If my wife asks, yes. If someone else asks, no."

"Were you doing something illegal?"

"No," Bennie said. "This new dancer, Sierra, she wanted to suck my dick, I wasn't gonna deny her." He actually looked remorseful for a moment. "Rachel's been sick for almost a year."

"You trust this Sierra?"

"I don't even know her real name," Bennie said.

"You should give them up," David said.

Bennie considered this. "Gang enhancement, they could get twenty on this," he said.

"They get twenty, you might get life if they decide to really probe; which sounds better to you?" David said. "Unless they're the type who'd flip, get them a decent lawyer, maybe he gets a plea and they get five years, out in three on good behavior."

"These aren't good-behavior guys," Bennie said. David could see the wheels turning in Bennie's head, however, the idea taking root. "That how you do it in Chicago?"

"We don't get caught in Chicago."

"I wouldn't be so sure of that." He checked his watch. "Jesus, I gotta get to the mall before sundown to pick up presents for the girls. This eight nights of presents thing is a real slog. I've been trying to convince Rachel we should just light the candles and sing the Neil Diamond songs for eight days and give out presents on Christmas. She's not hearing it. We've got a tree.

That's her one concession. When I was a kid, my dad used to climb up on the roof on Christmas Eve and would leave a bunch of reindeer prints in the snow, throw some glitter down the chimney." He paused, lost in the memory. "What about you?"

"My dad was dead by the time I was ten," David said. "I don't really remember much before that."

"How did he go?"

"Straight off the IBM Building."

"The IBM Building? Like off the top?"

"It was still being built," David said. "They tossed him out a window on the thirty-second floor."

"Chicago does its business, I'll say that," Bennie said. A minivan pulled down the street, and Bennie waved at the driver, motioned for him to pull over, which he did, directly in front of the funeral home. The doors slid open, and six old men stepped slowly out onto the sidewalk. Two of them had walkers, the rest of them should have; David thought that if they were under eighty years old, he'd eat his shoe. Bennie shook each man's hand warmly, others he also hugged, one he actually kissed on the cheek. A bunch of old thugs, David realized, their gangster suits and tommy guns traded in for Sansabelt pants and oxygen tanks.

Bennie handed the driver a roll of bills. "Give them a hundred each," he told him. "Walk them over, then go pick up some pasta over at the Venetian and bring it back in, say, ninety minutes. Keep whatever's left."

"What was that?" David asked when the driver walked away after the meandering men.

"Those are your mourners," Bennie said. "Bring them in from Sun City."

"You're not worried about that?"

"You know what it would take to get a warrant for a wire on a funeral home? A cemetery? Much less a temple? Besides, I have no business interest in this place. I'm just a concerned member of the temple, happy to lend my checkbook to worthy causes."

The front door of the funeral home opened, and a Mexican guy in a dark gray suit stepped out. David had seen him on a few occasions in the last couple weeks, usually walking back and forth to the temple with paperwork for the business office. Whenever they made eye contact, the Mexican would drop his eyes, like he was afraid he'd catch on fire just from looking at him. "Mr. Savone," he said, "everything's ready if Rabbi Cohen would like to begin." He handed Bennie two manila folders.

"Thanks, Ruben," Bennie said. "Give us five minutes."

"Of course," he said, and he disappeared back inside.

"That's Ruben," Bennie said. "You haven't met?"

"No," David said.

"Good," Bennie said. "He was my first project. Plucked him out of the pound and sent him out to Arizona to get a degree in mortuary science. He's been here for five years."

"What does he know?" David asked.

"Just enough," Bennie said. "He's solid. He does his job, gives everybody that comes through the respect and dignity they deserve, unless otherwise directed."

"What's his take?"

"Salary and benefits," Bennie said. "And as far as he knows, you are what you are, and Rabbi Kales is what he is, so don't start thinking about how he's just another person you'll eventually have to kill."

It didn't matter to David what Ruben was paid. He just wanted to know how Bennie was keeping him quiet and what

David would need to do if he wanted to keep him quiet, too, if this shit with the body tissue came to fruition. Though, the more he thought about it, the more it seemed prudent to clue Bennie in, give him a cut of the action versus being forced to cut him in at some later date.

Bennie gave David the folders. "This is who you're burying today," he said.

David opened the first folder and read for a moment. It said that the person was named Lionel Berkowitz, that he was sixty and that the family requested a private service and simple headstone noting his life and death. A simple recitation of the Kaddish and a few remarks would be sufficient. A full sermon was typed out for him to recite, the Hebrew prayers rendered phonetically, just in case. "Why even bother with this?" David asked.

"That's what the family wanted," Bennie said. "We do what the families tell us."

It was a curious thing to say, more mysterious than Bennie was prone to be, so David opened the second file and saw that it was for a woman named Rhoda Kochman, age seventy-three, born Rhoda Heaton in Saint Louis to Lonnie and Edith Heaton, preceded in death by her beloved husband Raymond Kochman, a founding member of Temple Beth Israel, survived by . . .

"What is this?" David said.

"Your four o'clock," Bennie said.

"Someone hit a seventy-three-year-old lady?"

"I don't know how she died," Bennie said. "Rachel probably does. They were on a bunch of planning committees for the book drive. Lady was at my house more than I was."

It dawned on David then that he wouldn't just be presiding over the funerals of the war dead, that he might not know one body to the next who was a natural death versus a murder. Probably better all the way around, David realized, and certainly a smart decision by Bennie. But it got him wondering about something. "Rabbi Gottlieb," David said, "he do both?"

"A few times. But it wouldn't be prudent to speak poorly of the dead," Bennie said. "Rabbi Kales wouldn't approve." Bennie checked his watch again. "I need to get moving, and you need to get to throwing dirt."

"If someone comes from Chicago," David said, "I want to see them first."

"Closed casket," Bennie said. "No can do."

"I wasn't asking permission," David said.

Bennie stared at David without speaking for ten, fifteen, thirty seconds. "Fine," he said, eventually. He paused again. Another fifteen unblinking seconds. "But that means you see every body that comes through. You prepared to do that?"

"Nothing I haven't seen before."

"You see a dead kid before? You ever see that? Like a toddler? A newborn? You ever see a *stillborn*?"

"Know that the reward unto the righteous is not of this world," David said.

Bennie took a deep breath, then another. "You better go tell Ruben you want to see the bodies. Tell him you want to do some sort of religious shit to them. He won't know any better."

Bennie started to walk away, then turned around. He already had his phone out. "You really think I should give them up?"

"They know anything important?" David asked.

"They're just muscle," Bennie said.

"This guy they paralyzed, he a local?"

"A dentist from Omaha," Bennie said. "In for some implant convention at the MGM. Wife, couple kids."

"Give them up," David said.

"My insurance is going to go through the roof. Would have been easier if they'd killed him." Bennie looked out toward the Strip. You couldn't see any of the casinos from this vantage point, couldn't see anything other than houses and palm trees and blue sky. "You know what Bugsy Siegel said about this place? It turns women into men, and men into idiots. If he saw this place today? He'd think he walked into an insane asylum."

"Maybe give that newspaper guy a call," David said.

"Curran?"

"Beat him to the punch," David said. "Give him a quote. Tell him you're ashamed of what happened and that you're going to see that this guy gets the best treatment available. All that."

"And then, what? Go in and smother him?"

"Maybe do the right thing," David said, "and pay his bills."

Bennie pinched his mouth, contemplated for a few seconds. "Happy Hanukkah, Rabbi," he said.

"You, too," David said.

■

Dead bodies didn't bother Rabbi David Cohen. He'd seen plenty of them over the years. That's what David believed to be true, anyway, as he followed Ruben into the mortuary to look at the bodies of Lionel Berkowitz and Rhoda Kochman.

David and Ruben walked through the funeral home—the portion that actually looked like a home, in this case someone's grandmother's house, replete with couches covered in velvet, thick curtains, ornate coffee tables, pastoral art, and, inexplicably, plates of butter cookies everywhere, which is maybe why it was called Kales Mortuary & Home of Peace, since it was hard to imagine feeling anything but drowsy and restful in that joint. And then they were outside, back where David killed Slim Joe, the mortuary only a few feet away and closing fast.

"You ever see a dead body before?" Ruben asked.

"Yes, of course," David said.

"Someone who's been in an accident?"

"Yes."

"Not like a drowning or an OD," Ruben said. They were at the door now, which had a sign that said AUTHORIZED PERSONNEL ONLY, and Ruben was visibly nervous.

"I get it," David said.

"Because, as you know, we don't do much restorative work unless the family asks for it," Ruben said, "and in this case, uh, Mr. Berkowitz's family was very specific that he be left alone."

"Ruben," David said, "do you mind if I call you Ruben?"

"Of course not, Rabbi Cohen."

"Ruben, do you know what happens to the Jews when the End of Days comes?"

"No disrespect," Ruben said, and David had to stop himself from grabbing Ruben by the throat and choking him to death, "but I'm not really up on a lot of the more religious aspects of Judaism. I appreciate everything you do and Rabbi Kales, too, but I'm just not a believer in that way."

"That's fine," David said. "What happens is that the dead are flushed with the Dew of Resurrection, and we return as our most vibrant selves, and then we roll through a series of underground tunnels to the Mount of Olives in Israel."

David hoped Ruben wouldn't question him on that, since it was one of the strangest things he'd learned in all the eschatology he'd read. "The point, Ruben, is that even the most horribly disfigured Jews will eventually be whole again," David said. He paused for a moment, trying to think of something else he could add to convince Ruben that whatever he was about to see was not going to make him pass out. "It is one of the thirteen principles of our faith, Ruben, and when the time comes, it will make sense. That is what we believe."

"Okay then," he said. Ruben opened the door, and David followed him past a reception desk, where a young woman sat reading *People* magazine, and down a narrow hallway, which led to the morgue. Ruben stepped through a set of double safety doors, and the first thing David saw was the body of a naked man, belly up on the embalming table.

There was another young Mexican kid, this one in medical scrubs, cleaning the body. The room smelled like a mixture of disinfectant and body odor, though David didn't know if that was coming from the dead guy or the one cleaning him, along with a pungent smell that reminded David of rotting lamb (and which, he realized, would forever preclude him from eating lamb). There was a refrigeration unit against one wall and then three other tables, which David was pleased to see were empty, and the room was lit with bright halogens that gave the space a white glow. He didn't know the guy on the table; all he knew was that he didn't have a funeral the next day, so it must have been one Rabbi Kales was doing, or someone working freelance was coming in.

"Miguel," Ruben said to the kid working on the naked dead guy, "this is Rabbi Cohen. He's taking over for Rabbi Gottlieb."

"Pleased," Miguel said, and he gave David a shy smile. He was just another person doing a dirty job, David thought, which made David examine Ruben more closely. He was wearing a conservative suit, but it was cut precisely, and he had a thick gold watch on his wrist, an absurd topaz pinkie ring, perfectly shined black shoes on his feet. In fact, the more David examined the suit, the more familiar it looked, since he had a matching one in his own closet. *Salary, benefits, and probably whatever they could pinch off the dead or get on the cheap from Bennie's contacts*, David thought.

David followed Ruben through another set of double doors and into a well-lit waiting room that housed two coffins—both simple pine boxes—on wheeled platforms, two chairs, and another velvet sofa. A door led out of the room and onto the service road that wound through the cemetery. David saw through the one window in the room that there was already a hearse parked outside, the driver standing next to it, sipping coffee from a Styrofoam cup.

"From now on," Ruben said, and David realized he didn't know if Ruben had been talking the entire time, he'd been so focused on keeping everything as normal and blasé as possible, "maybe it would be easier if you just came down in the morning before a service, so that we don't need to reopen the coffins, since I know that's against Jewish law."

"Yes," David said. He didn't know if that was strictly true, though he figured if Ruben knew that fact, it probably had some truth in it.

Ruben went around and unlatched the top of both coffins, but didn't open them. "Should I step out?" he asked. Polite guy. Probably was a real comfort to the actual grieving families. His manner even made David feel at ease.

"Yes," David said, "because of the Jewish law."

"I'll be outside," he said. "Just let me know when you're ready, and then we can take Mr. Berkowitz down to his resting place."

"Which one is Mr. Berkowitz?"

"The one on the right," Ruben said.

"Great, thank you," David said, then he thought maybe he was being too informal, so he added, "And bless you for the work you do."

David waited until Ruben was engaged in conversation outside with the hearse driver before he opened the coffin completely. He noticed a few things almost immediately. The first was that he wasn't quite sure what he was looking at. Obviously, there was a body in the coffin, a head, a neck, a chest, he could make those out . . . but the head was missing its ears. And it wasn't like they'd been severed in some kind of accident. David could see the jagged cuts that were made around the ears, even with all the dried blood that was gathered there. Though, that wasn't what killed him. Getting his eyelids slit off hadn't killed him either, nor had the cigarette burns on his face. All were survivable wounds.

David didn't know anyone who could survive without a throat, however, and they'd done a good job with that, cutting Paul Bruno's neck in a full circle, likely using piano wire from the front, the way Fat Monte always liked to take out snitches, so they could see it happening.

Bruno the Butcher. Poor bastard. He'd been snitching for years, but no one really gave a shit, since he only dimed out the people the Family wanted him to dime out, the loose threads, the idiots who were working on the fringes, guys like Lemonhead, who'd tried to blackmail a straight-edge city councilman over some prostitution shit. Ronnie was always smart about letting people like Paul Bruno do the dirty laundry for them.

What the fuck was going on in Chicago? He'd known Paul Bruno his entire life, could remember playing jacks with him out front of the butcher shop while his dad and Paul's dad talked shop inside. Paul's dad gave them turkeys every

Thanksgiving, free of charge, after David's mom disavowed the Family and money got scarce; Paul's mom always brought over soups and casseroles and magazines and books. Jennifer's family was tight with them, too; the Frangellos and the Brunos bowled and played bridge together, just like regular people.

Paul so confused growing up; David remembered that, too. Tried to be a tough guy. David remembered Jennifer telling him how she'd always known he was gay, from back when they were kids.

And now here he was. Not just done ugly. Done ugly and personally—the cigarette burns, the eyelids. And that Paul was here, not just thrown into a ditch somewhere, told David that whatever information Paul had given out was not the negligible shit of the past, because the Family would make an example out of him if that was the case, leave him somewhere as a message to other snitches. This was private and personal, and that gave David pause.

David closed the coffin and wheeled it back into the morgue. "Miguel," he said, "you need to clean this body."

"The man?"

"Yes, the man," David said.

"I'm sorry, Rabbi, but Ruben said that the family requested he not be touched, which I understood to mean that he wasn't to be cleaned."

"And I'm telling you to clean him."

"I'm sorry, Rabbi," Miguel said, "but I'm not sure I understand."

"I don't care what you understand," David said.

Miguel started to say something, stopped himself for a moment, then said, "I'll do it right away, Rabbi."

"And I want you to fix all these wounds," David said. "You understand that?"

"Yes, Rabbi, that's no problem."

David went back into the waiting room, grabbed a chair, and slid it into the morgue, where he watched Miguel wash down Paul Bruno's whole body, from the top of his head to the bottom of his feet.

CHAPTER NINE

S pecial Agent Jeff Hopper was always surprised by how pleasant prisons looked from the outside. The state penitentiary in Walla Walla, for instance, had a beautifully manicured front lawn, perfectly squared shrubbery, lines of evergreens, a sturdy redbrick facade. If you cut and pasted it into another part of the city, you might have mistaken it for one of the buildings at Whitman College.

Stateville was the same way. Just thirty-five miles west of Chicago down Interstate 55, it was situated in the middle of verdant fields and farmlands, two miles from the new Prairie Bluff Golf Course. To get into the prison, you had to drive a quarter mile along a tree-lined road with a median of green grass and circular planting beds that, in the spring, were filled with roses, though which today, the first Sunday of 1999, were covered with a thick blanket of snow and ice, the result of a brutal, two-day storm that dumped nineteen inches of snow on the city and plunged temperatures to an arctic negative thirteen. From the outside, the administration building, a four-story made of red and yellow brick, looked like an old Chicago hotel, the kind of place with a bottom-floor restaurant that served only steaks bloody-rare. In fact, if you could ignore the thirty-foot-tall cement walls and sniper towers, Stateville Correctional Center looked downright inviting.

Richard Speck and John Wayne Gacy probably wouldn't concur, Jeff thought, but then they got to see the place from the outside only once. Same as Neto Espinoza.

"Do you ever wonder how people end up doing the things that put them in there? The process by which they decide to become that kind of person?" Matthew asked as they walked out of the administration building, back into the biting cold of the winter day, and down the long gravel road toward the parking lot. Matthew didn't say much the entire time they were inside, waiting for the official paperwork on Neto Espinoza's final days at the prison, and, before that, most of the ride out from Chicago.

Jeff had learned what Matthew's demeanor meant over the course of the last several weeks. Sometimes, he was silent because he wanted to listen carefully to what was being said around him—like when they'd been with Paul Bruno—so that he could figure out how to play a particular situation. Some-times, he was silent out of simple necessity: He didn't know enough about being an agent to argue Jeff's thoughts on an issue, though that didn't mean acquiescence. No, it actually meant he'd attack the topic an hour or a day or a week later, after he'd formed a determined opinion. It was one of Mat-thew's most admirable qualities, Jeff thought, and one not all that common in field agents.

Other times he kept his mouth shut so he could contemplate an issue he found difficult to parse. Like when they found out that Neto Espinoza, Chema Espinoza's brother, died of a heart attack while in custody at Stateville. That wouldn't have been all that vexing if Neto hadn't been twenty-six at the time of his death, or if he hadn't been, according to his death certificate, otherwise physically fit. And then today, after the prison released Neto's death-in-custody report to them and it showed exactly what Jeff thought it would show: nothing. Just a regular heart attack for a completely healthy young man.

"That's the reason I became a cop," Jeff said, "and an FBI agent."

"Really? I thought you just wanted to catch bad guys."

"That was part of it, sure," Jeff said. "But after a while, you see enough stupidity, you have to begin to wonder about the root causes. You don't have to be evil to make the wrong choice. Don't need to be good to make the right choice. You could save a kid from choking to death at McDonald's one day and that night, to celebrate, you go out and get sloshed at the bar and plow your car through a bunch of disabled orphans. Next thing you know, you're the worst person on earth."

"Maybe people are just fucked-up," Matthew said.

It was hard to argue that point. It had taken Jeff and Matthew weeks to find out the exact disposition of Neto Espinoza for just that reason. Finding out he was dead was easy—it was public record, after all—but when Jeff and Matthew went to question Neto's mother, she was unwilling to talk to either of them. It didn't matter that one of her sons was dead and another was missing. Jeff didn't bother to tell Mrs. Espinoza what he knew about Chema, figuring that information would only get her killed, too. Not that he imagined many people in the Family would come down to Twenty-Fourth and Karlov to handle their business, the idea of rolling into the heart of the

Gangster 2-6 territory probably not all that enticing even if the Family did employ many in their ranks. The Gangster 2-6 needed the drugs the Family provided, but their allegiance was to each other, not a bunch of Italians, and certainly not a bunch of Italians who may have killed some of their boys.

None of that mattered to Mrs. Espinoza. That Jeff and Matthew were investigating at all was the problem: The entire Espinoza family was gang-affiliated—Neto and Chema's father, an OG in the Gangster 2-6, was doing fifteen at Logan—so Mrs. Espinoza wasn't going to say a thing to anybody.

They had to move through back channels, Jeff calling every contact he had in the prison system to try to get anything beyond confirmation that Neto was dead in hopes of gleaning information that might lead to the Family's attempts to cover their tracks with Sal Cupertine. If Neto had been murdered, that would mean another link in the chain, another person who could provide information, another cracked window. Problem was, no one wanted to give him anything, not with all the heat that had come down on the Illinois prison system recently, the stories of graft and obstruction of justice so regular that they began to dwarf the crimes of the men and women who got sent away.

So Jeff did the one thing he didn't want to do, which was contact Dennis Tryon's office. Dennis was an old classmate from UIC who'd moved into prison management at Stateville just in time for a decade of corruption scandals to erupt around him. Stateville's history of laxity—which included Richard Speck himself appearing on a videotape with mounds of cocaine and handfuls of money, talking about what a great time he was having in prison, before taking time out to give a blow job to another inmate—now made even the smallest corruption possible front-page news. So asking Dennis to give him anything on the side was strictly verboten.

Lying to him, however, wasn't. At least in theory. So Jeff called his office the previous day and simply asked for whatever documents could be mustered for what he described as a "wide-ranging FBI investigation." It was a common code for a federal fishing exhibition, a nice exchange of information that the bureau and the prison carried on fairly regularly. He didn't bother to mention to the clerk that he was on paid administrative leave. Jeff hoped the form would reach Dennis's desk and Dennis would just sign off on his old friend's request. It's how business was usually conducted between people who trusted each other.

Still, Jeff had spent enough time visiting Stateville in the past several years to know that any number of nefarious deeds were possible in that shit hole. They'd cleaned up some in the last few years, though not so much that a death connected to the Family, or the Gangster 2-6 for that matter, might occasionally go uninvestigated if the price was right . . . which is what the absence of paperwork on Neto Espinoza confirmed. He was a disposable person in a family of criminals. The kind of person Dennis Tryon probably didn't give one shit about.

Jeff took out his cell phone and tried calling Paul Bruno. He'd spoken to him twice after their visit, once to tell him that Neto was indeed dead, and once to ask him if he had any contacts at the slaughterhouses still, see if anyone might give him any information on anything that seemed shady in the last several months. And then . . . nothing. It was general policy not to leave messages on a CI's voicemail, so at first Jeff just called and hung up, then eventually left a message anyway.

"Shit," Jeff said, and he closed his phone.

"Nothing?" Matthew said.

"Says his voicemail is full," Jeff said.

They walked a few more yards in silence, the crunch of ice beneath their boots the only soundtrack to what both were coming to realize.

"Tonight," Jeff said, "we're going to have a conversation with Fat Monte. You ready for that?"

"I was ready a month ago," Matthew said.

A horn honked, and Jeff turned to see a black Dept. of Corrections Cutlass, the official car of any decent prison, coming up behind them. Jeff and Matthew stepped off the road to let the car pass, but instead it pulled to a stop, and Dennis Tryon stepped out.

Dennis was a few years older than Jeff and had worked in criminal justice since he was eighteen. Jeff remembered that. It was one of those things Dennis used to say when they were in school, the ultimate trump card, that he'd been working with bad guys since he was a teenager. Now, though, he had the paunch of a man in his sixties and the sagging neck to match, even though he wasn't yet fifty. He wore navy-blue wool pants and a blue-and-white striped shirt that bulged out over his belt, a red tie, a blue sport coat. Jeff liked Dennis a decade ago, though he wasn't sure he still did.

"Shouldn't you be behind a desk somewhere?" Jeff said.

"You didn't come by the office to say hello," Dennis said.

Jeff wagged the envelope containing Neto Espinoza's report in front of Dennis's face. "I got what I came for."

"Did you know you're on paid administrative leave?" Dennis said.

"I was aware of that, yes," Jeff said.

"You failed to mention that when you asked for Neto Espinoza's death records."

"I didn't think it was important," Jeff said.

"Of course not," Dennis said. A shiver went through him and he pulled his sport coat closed. He couldn't button it over his gut, so he just held the two sides together. "Christ, it's cold as hell out here. I hear Chicago is socked in. That right?"

"There something you want to talk about, Dennis?" Jeff asked.

"I called your office," Dennis said, "and they said you are on an extended vacation. Stateville isn't the kind of place most people visit while on vacation. Even fewer people do independent investigations into the natural death of drug mules." He paused and looked at Matthew, who was watching the whole interaction with something close to amusement. "And you," Dennis said to Matthew, "who are you, exactly?"

"Just a friend," Matthew said.

"I'm sure," Dennis said. Another black Cutlass pulled down the road, and Dennis straightened up, tried to look dignified. The Cutlass slowed as it went by, so Dennis gave it a wave, as if to let the driver know Jeff and Matthew weren't escapees. "Jeff always was great about making friends," Dennis said, once the car passed. "You keep in touch with anyone else from school?"

Jeff didn't keep in touch with many people. That he kept in touch with Dennis Tryon had mostly to do with their infrequent meetings at the prison, though Jeff had no delusions that Dennis was simply one of the good guys or one of the bad guys. You work in prison management, those roles are generally pretty fungible, which made everything about Dennis questionable. He'd helped Jeff on a few occasions, Jeff had helped him on a few occasions, and even those interactions were strictly business, albeit salted with periodic attempts at familiarity, Dennis always going on about his wife, Lisa, who worked at the zoo in Chicago, and his son Devin, who had some developmental problem, or showing Jeff photos from his hunting trip; Jeff promising that the next time he came out, they'd get a beer in Crest Hill afterward, really catch up, that sort of thing.

Not exactly a friendship. More like two people with a tacit understanding that they should treat each other better than common strangers. *The debt you pay for shared experiences,* Jeff thought.

"No," Jeff said. "I don't want to ruin the possibility of chance reunions."

Dennis laughed. "See?" he said to Matthew. "Jeff has friends everywhere." He walked back to the Cutlass and popped open the trunk, then came back holding a bulging manila envelope sealed with packing tape. "You left this," Dennis said, and he handed the envelope to Jeff.

"If whatever is in this envelope is bad enough that we gotta go through all of this," Jeff said, "then I'm not sure I want you to give it to me."

Dennis said, "I read about that Family business in the paper, figured that was your people. I probably should have called you, but I thought you probably didn't need to hear from anyone else."

"I didn't hear from anybody," Jeff said.

"That's the problem with this business," Dennis said. "Everyone's too damn proud." He patted Jeff on the shoulder.

Dennis Tryon got back into his Cutlass. He pulled back up

the street, made a U-turn, and came to a stop across from where Jeff and Matthew were still standing. He rolled down his window, motioned Jeff over.

"Yeah?" Jeff said.

"Listen," Dennis said. "Don't get yourself killed. No one would come to your funeral for fear of being recognized." He extended his hand out the window, but Jeff didn't take it right away. "Shake my hand," Dennis said.

"I don't know if I should," Jeff said.

"Thing is, Jeff, it's probably no worse than what you expect."

"That's the problem I'm having," Jeff said. "You didn't need to give me this stuff. I already knew something was crooked."

"Well," Dennis said, "be that as it may. I see some stuff here that makes me sick. But I've got five more years until I can take early retirement. When that day comes, there's gonna be no second thoughts, that much I can assure you."

"So maybe you should hold on to this," Jeff said, "in case you need to blackmail someone."

"I won't lie. I thought about that," he said. "I reckon that makes me no better than the animals I've been tending." Dennis took a balled Kleenex from his pocket and blew his nose. "Whatever you do with that," Dennis pointed at the envelope, "just know that maybe five years ago that boy would have been a chew toy in this place."

"All I'm going to do is read it," Jeff said.

"Well, good, then," Dennis said. "You think you'll get back into the bureau?"

"No," Jeff said. "Not now, anyway. So don't worry, I'm not here to cause any problems for you."

"I know you're not," Dennis said. "I didn't say anything to your office, you should know."

"It doesn't matter, really," Jeff said. He paused and thought about the steps that had brought him to this moment, the litany of mistakes that he accumulated trying to be the good guy. "Just tell me I'm not going to find out Ronnie Cupertine is an honorary guard or something."

Dennis laughed in a way Jeff didn't find in the least bit authentic. "Well," Dennis said, "next time you come through, call first. We'll have lunch."

"I'm not ever going to come back this way," Jeff said.

Dennis rolled his window back up, gave Jeff a two-fingered salute, and was gone.

■

It was amazing to Jeff how much paperwork accumulated during a cover-up. He and Matthew were parked across the street from the Four Treys Tavern in Roscoe Village, waiting to meet up with Fat Monte. They'd made him hours earlier, walking out of his apartment, which was only a few blocks down Damen, and decided to follow. When he ducked into the Four Treys, likely to watch the Packers and 49ers play in the Wild Card game, they decided to let him percolate a bit before they made their move. Besides, they had plenty of reading to do.

"No wonder Stateville is always ankle-deep in problems," Matthew said. "They're meticulous in their record keeping of negligence."

What Dennis gave them wasn't exactly the *Pentagon Papers*. In fact, to the layman, most of what he gave them would appear meaningless and mundane. Neto Espinoza was sent directly to Stateville on a parole violation and pending his trial on drug-trafficking charges—he was arrested near the Canadian border with over fifty pounds of heroin hidden under the bed lining of his truck—and was looking at serious time, particularly with the gang enhancement charges saddled on top of everything else.

Normally a person like Neto, with gang affiliations and Family ties, too, would find himself segregated from the general prison population while he awaited his hearing, since the danger level was high. Both the Family and the 2-6 would want to make sure he wasn't going to snitch, and there was a good chance they'd want retribution for losing so much product, since fifty pounds of heroin was worth a cool million dollars, maybe even more during the colder winter months when distribution slowed down.

On the other end of the spectrum, the state would want to keep Neto segregated for the very hope that he *would* snitch, a kid like him easy bait for a decent interrogator. That's how Jeff had found the CI Sal Cupertine killed, after all. And he was sure that if given the chance, he could have turned Neto Espinoza, too, if only he'd been aware of his existence.

All of which made the fact that he was put into the general population exceptionally suspicious. His first cellmate was a career bank robber named Kyle Behen who was also awaiting trial, but he was moved out last April in favor of Thomas "Lemonhead" Nicolino, a career Family member (and, notably, a part of Fat Monte's crew) whom Bruno himself had dimed out a few years before. Five days later, Neto was dead. Ten days, he'd already been cremated.

The autopsy report came back with huge sums of cocaine and heroin in Neto's system, enough to cause a perfectly healthy person to die of a heart attack. Problem was, the report also indicated that Neto had injected the drugs.

Into his chest.

Approximately, the report said, thirty-seven times.

Matthew shook his head in disgust and handed the papers to Jeff. "It's a joke. That's what that is."

The autopsy report showed that the "injections" managed to crack Neto's sternum in five places, not exactly a common self-inflicted wound. Jeff flipped through the stack of papers to see when the autopsy report was filed: June 27, 1998. Nearly three months after Neto's death and cremation. Just another drug-induced heart attack. No mention of any likely complicity via a third party.

And who was going to complain? Not Neto's family. Not Neto's public defender. Certainly not Neto's coworkers in the Gangster 2-6 or the Family. The benefit of killing someone like Neto Espinoza in prison was that he existed beyond the law; the only people who cared about him were criminals. That was always the challenge when dealing with organized crime: You had to force those who suffered the most—the living—to turn their back on an entire way of life. Jeff thought he'd made some headway with Jennifer Cupertine, but the truth, he realized, was that Jennifer had already turned her back on the Family. That wasn't the issue. The problem was that she hadn't turned her back on her husband.

Neto Espinoza was murdered in prison for what he might do or say when he found out his brother, Chema, had been murdered. Simple as that. Jeff didn't think of Lemonhead Nicolino as the killing type, but who knew anymore. The whole world was a Ponzi scheme.

Matthew cracked the knuckles on his right hand, then his left. Grabbed his chin and popped his neck and shoulders. He shook out his arms and legs, every joint along the way snapping audibly. Jeff watched him for a few seconds, imagined what it would be like to see that running at you on the lacrosse field, holding a stick. It wasn't that he looked angry, it was that he looked ready to uncoil.

Matthew turned on the radio to check the score of the game. The 49ers were leading the Pack by three with a couple of minutes left. "What do you think?" Matthew said.

"He should be filled with joy right now," Jeff said. He reached into the glove compartment and pulled out two guns, handed one to Matthew, and stuffed the other in his ankle holster. He didn't think they'd need to shoot Fat Monte, but it never hurt to be prepared.

"Let me do this one," Matthew said.

"Are you afraid I might lose it on him?"

"I know you liked Paul Bruno," Matthew said.

"I still do," Jeff said.

"Right," Matthew said. "Let me hook him. If you feel like you need to get into the conversation, feel free, but let me hook him."

■

The Four Treys was one of those neighborhood taverns that didn't seem all that concerned about looking like anything more than a place to get drunk and watch sports. There was a long rectangular bar in the middle of the main room surrounded by brown vinyl high-backed bar stools, a few three-top rounds, and then a larger room with a pool table and space for someone to stand up with a guitar and butcher "American Pie" on Open-Mic Monday nights. Weekends, the place would fill up with twentysomethings who lived close enough to stumble home, softball teams, and the odd bachelor or bachelorette party. Jeff remembered coming here on a date once, even, after a Cubs game, Wrigleyville just a twenty-minute walk away.

It wasn't the kind of place you expected to run into a Mafia enforcer like Fat Monte, but there he was, sitting by himself at a three-top, a pitcher of beer in front of him, staring at the football game on the big-screen TV, just like the fifty other people in the bar. There was just over two minutes left, and the Packers were driving.

"You mind if we take a seat?" Matthew said.

"Go ahead," Fat Monte said, without even looking away from the TV. "Favre is going to win this ball game. Unbelievable." They sat and watched, and sure enough, a few seconds later, Brett Favre threw a looping pass to Antonio Freeman in the end zone. "Cocksucker," Fat Monte said. He slammed his hand on the table twice. He finally turned and looked at Jeff and Matthew. "Where was the defense?"

"Plenty of time on the clock," Matthew said.

"49ers can't beat the Packers. It's just how it is," Fat Monte said.

"Gotta admit," Matthew said, "if Favre were on the Bears, you'd love him."

"I don't have to admit shit," Fat Monte said, though not in a threatening way. Just a couple of guys talking football in a bar. "Favre couldn't hold Jim McMahon's dick."

"Didn't McMahon back up Favre a few years ago?" Matthew said.

"I dunno," Fat Monte said. "Couple years, I didn't follow football."

Yeah, Jeff thought, *must be hard to keep up with the movements of second-string quarterbacks while you're in prison.* The Packers kicked off, and Fat Monte turned his attention back to the game. The last time Jeff saw Fat Monte was in surveillance photos from late 1997, right before he got sent up for six months on a possession beef, Jeff trying in vain to stick the murder of James Diamond, a Cicero drug dealer who was shot to death outside his house, on him, lining up witness after witness . . . only to have each and every one of them disappear or change their stories. Unlike Sal Cupertine, whom no one ever saw, Fat Monte was spotted everywhere back then. He was over six foot and, back in 1997, weighed at least three hundred pounds. That he drove a black Navigator on twenty-inch tires didn't exactly make him inconspicuous.

Now, though, he was slimmer, more muscular, probably from hitting the weights and the steroids while in prison, probably still hitting the steroids, Jeff noticing that Fat Monte had pimples crawling up the back of his neck, odd for a guy in his late thirties unless he was juicing. Jeff also saw that Fat Monte had a wedding ring now, too, which explained why he was living in Roscoe Village. Even the mob gets gentrified eventually. In fact, that Fat Monte was sitting inside the Four Treys instead of one of the Family's video poker bars in Bridgeport was probably all Jeff really needed to know to understand how the world was changing.

"Finally," Fat Monte said. "You see that? Young's been avoiding Rice all day. Jesus Christ."

"You got any money riding on this?" Matthew asked.

"None of mine," Fat Monte said. "Besides, no one here wants to bet with me." Fat Monte laughed at his own joke, or what Jeff presumed Fat Monte considered a joke. Maybe he was laughing at his general state of affairs: sitting in a yuppie bar in Roscoe Village with absolutely no action on the biggest game of the year. There was a timeout in the game, under a minute left, and Fat Monte took the opportunity to stand up and stretch his legs.

"You look like you've lost some weight," Matthew said.

"Yeah? You seen me before?" Fat Monte said, interested now, and not in a good way, Jeff saw.

"A few times," Matthew said. "Though they say surveillance cameras add fifteen pounds. You, it looked more like fifty."

Fat Monte looked over his shoulder and then around the room, probably for uniformed cops or at least a few guys wearing FBI windbreakers, Jeff watching him calculate what this all meant . . . and probably calculating the odds of doing something stupid, like pulling out his own gun. Jeff was sure Fat Monte was packing, probably had a piece in his jacket, which was hung over the back of his chair, though not even someone like Fat Monte was dumb enough to try to shoot someone in the middle of a bar, particularly not someone who was probably law enforcement. And, on top of that, law enforcement that had the jump on him.

"Whatever this is," Fat Monte said, "I'm gonna watch the end of this game first. You don't like it, just go ahead and shoot me in the back of the head and get it over with."

Matthew gave Jeff a shrug. What the hell. Jeff asked a waitress for a couple of glasses, refilled Fat Monte's beer, poured one for Matthew, one for himself, and sat back to watch. Steve Young completed a pass to Terry Kirby for a couple of yards, then another to Garrison Hearst, the 49ers moving down the field, fourteen seconds left, the whole bar screaming and yelling at the TV right until a time-out was called and Jeff heard fifty people expel the same breath. Fat Monte saw the beer, took a sip.

"Answer me this," Fat Monte said, "am I going to jail tonight? Because if so, I'm gonna get a shot. You guys want shots?"

"We'll see how things go," Matthew said.

"You federal?" Fat Monte asked. "Because I'd know you if you were local."

"Yes," Jeff said, figuring that was his spot to interject.

"Fed guys working a Sunday night," he said. "I must be pretty special." He took another sip of his beer and turned back to the TV. What did Jeff really know about Monte Moretti? He liked to hurt people. He wasn't one of Ronnie Cupertine's new-breed gangsters, guys who made money and didn't do a lot of outside damage. No, he was the guy Ronnie turned to, still, to keep that cliché alive, the guy who broke arms and talked tough and did time. On the organizational chart, Fat Monte Moretti was listed as a capo, but in truth he was more like a high-ranking soldier, since he still liked to do his own grunt work, since he couldn't keep himself out of jail for more than a year at a time. He had his own rackets, and then he did work directly for Ronnie, like this whole Sal Cupertine issue.

On the TV, Steve Young stumbled back from center, the clocked ticked from eight seconds, to seven, to six . . . and then he threw a strike to Terrell Owens in the end zone. Fat Monte jumped up from his chair and shouted, "Fuck the Packers! Fuck the Packers!" and soon the rest of the bar joined in, until there was a chorus of drunk yuppies and one Family enforcer chanting together, which then turned into a series of high fives, hugs, and fist pumps. The Bears hadn't even made the playoffs, but the Packers had lost, which was enough for the bartender to announce one-dollar shots for the next half hour. Fat Monte pulled out twenty bucks, handed it to a waitress, and told her to bring ten shots of whatever and keep the change, baby girl.

Fat Monte eventually took his seat, threw back the rest of his beer, and leaned back. "Now," he said, "who the fuck are you guys?"

"We're looking for Sal Cupertine," Matthew said. "Have you seen him lately?"

"Last I heard," Fat Monte said, "you guys found him toasted to a crisp in some landfill."

"Nah," Matthew said. "That was Chema Espinoza." The waitress swooped by then and dropped off the ten shots. Fat Monte immediately downed one, paused, took down another, Jeff not saying a word, watching Matthew set his hook, going about it real smooth, letting Fat Monte make the next move . . . though downing two shots of what smelled like Jägermeister probably qualified at least as a tell if not a move.

"Maybe I need to have my lawyer here," Fat Monte said eventually.

"*Maybe*," Matthew said, his voice low, not angry, not loud, just matter of fact, telling Fat Monte how it was going to be. "*Maybe* I just put the word out that Fat Monte Moretti now spends his Sunday nights in Roscoe Village taverns surrounded by a bunch of accountants and their tucked-in polo shirts. *Maybe* I drive down to Logan and tell Chema and Neto Espinoza's father that Fat Monte Moretti and his wife live in an unsecured walk-up on Damen, and *maybe* one night you and the wife are sitting on the sofa eating popcorn and watching *Friends*, and *maybe* four or five 2-6 Gangsters roll up on your place, tie you up, and rape your wife in front of you, then *maybe* get a little cornhole practice on you, too, just to make sure they still remember how to survive in prison."

Fat Monte took this all in without saying a word. He took another shot and then examined the empty glass, then pointed at Jeff. "I know you," he said.

"Oh yeah?" Jeff said.

"Yeah, I couldn't place you at first, but now I remember. You were the one who kept trying to pin that Diamond murder on me, right? Hopper? That you?"

Jeff tried his best not to seem surprised, tried to figure out how the hell Fat Monte knew he was the one moving the pieces around that investigation, then realized that it made sense. The Family kept records, too. Interesting. "That's right," Jeff said.

"Never did get that to stick, did you?" Fat Monte said.

"No, never did," Jeff said. "Fortunately there's no statute of limitations."

"No witnesses plus no statute of limitations equals you walking around holding your dick," Fat Monte said.

"Between us?" Jeff leaned across the table, so that he was only a few inches away from Fat Monte's face, so close he could smell Fat Monte's acrid breath, the creepy bastard actually breathing out of his mouth in these short, quick pulses. "I didn't mind you killing a drug dealer. One less piece of paperwork I had to worry about. But what gets me, Monte, is why you'd kill Chema and Neto Espinoza. My guess is that Chema saw whatever went down with Sal." He paused for just a second, tried to think of his next words carefully, see how Fat Monte reacted. "Probably saw the trade go down. Or he could have just been the driver, since I can't imagine Sal Cupertine sitting by while your fat ass drove him around in the dark. Okay, fine. You can't be leaving witnesses around. But Neto? He was already in prison and wasn't going to be leaving any time soon, not with a million dollars of H on his ticket. That just seems . . . sloppy . . . to me. Because then I gotta walk that back, see who Neto is down with, see that he was on your crew, and that up in Stateville he somehow ends up rooming with Lemonhead Nicolino. You couldn't have farmed the job out to the Aryans?"

Jeff sat back, took a sip of his beer, and let Fat Monte process the information.

"You don't know what the fuck you're talking about," Fat Monte said.

"Thirty-seven times, Monte? You think I wouldn't notice Neto was stabbed thirty-seven times in the chest?"

Fat Monte had another shot halfway to his mouth but thought better of it. He set the glass back down on the table. Jeff thought he saw a little shake in his hand. "Maybe you think I'm a little bitch like your friend Paul Bruno," Fat Monte said. "See, I don't scare. Prison doesn't scare me, either, so why don't you just go ahead and call your assault team down to secure the bar and take me in."

Hearing Paul Bruno's name immediately gave Jeff pause. That Fat Monte knew he was a snitch made Jeff reconsider a few things. It shouldn't have been a surprise, not with Ronnie Cupertine's connections. Maybe he had a guy in the bureau. Or maybe he just bugged all the cars he sold and serviced out of his shop. Most likely, though, he was keeping tabs on Paul Bruno. It's what Jeff had predicted for Bruno's fate, he just didn't want to believe it could come to pass so quickly.

"You want to be on the hook for Paul's murder, too?" Jeff asked, just to see how Monte reacted. "Because I'm happy to add that to your ticket."

"You'd need to find a body first," Monte said.

"Funny thing," Jeff said, "I didn't even know he was missing."

Fat Monte started to say something, stopped, and then started to laugh. "Maybe he committed suicide," he said. "You never know."

"Pretty hard to hide your own body," Jeff said.

"I got somewhere to be," Fat Monte said. He took another shot, slammed the glass onto the table, and then started to stand up. Before Jeff could even make a move, Matthew reached out with his right hand and grabbed Fat Monte Moretti by the balls and yanked down. Fat Monte shrieked and fell to both knees and then onto his side. Matthew stood up as though to help him back up, but in the process managed to also kick Fat Monte in the face. Not too hard. Just hard enough to break his nose.

"Whoa," Matthew said, as friendly as can be, "easy there." He reached down and seized Fat Monte by the back of his neck and hefted him back up onto his stool. Fat Monte's face was a bloody mess, his nose now pointing to the right, his eyes filled with tears. "Maybe you should go a little easy on those shots." A waitress came rushing over with a rag filled with ice, which Fat Monte took without saying a word.

"Is he going to be all right?" she asked.

"He'll be fine," Matthew said.

"Do you want me to call an ambulance for you, Monte?" she asked. *Monte*. She knew his name; he was a regular at the Four Treys now, the kind of guy who the servers knew by name, the kind of guy who wasn't likely to make a scene now because this was where he actually came to chill out, where he came to not be who he was during business hours . . . whenever those happened to be for members of the Family.

"Yeah," Fat Monte croaked out, "call 911."

The waitress turned to Jeff. "Is he being serious?"

"I don't think so," Jeff said. "But then, you probably know him better than I do."

"Are you being serious, Monte?" she asked. "Do you want me to call your wife?"

"No," Fat Monte said.

"No you don't want me to call your wife or no you're not being serious?" the waitress asked.

"Both," he said. "And bring me some Tylenol, doll, if you could."

"You're not gonna sue or anything, are you, Monte?" the waitress asked. Fat Monte shook his head, which looked like it hurt. "All right then," she said, and she walked away.

"Nice girl," Matthew said once she was gone. "You sure you don't want her to call your wife, Monte? How about your mommy?"

"Fuck you," Fat Monte said, though there wasn't much behind it. It occurred to Jeff that this might be the first time in his adult life that Fat Monte had actually been on the other end of a beatdown, even if a single punch hadn't been thrown. That was the thing about being trained how to fight versus just picking it up on the streets. You learned how to do the most amount of damage with the least amount of exertion. Matthew managed to emasculate Fat Monte in two distinct ways. "How the fuck am I supposed to explain to my wife how I ended up with a broken nose?"

"Maybe you should ask yourself how you'll explain it to Ronnie Cupertine," Jeff said.

Fat Monte pulled the rag from his face, examined all the blood—as if he thought looking at it might somehow fix the situation—then pressed it back up against his nose. "What kind of feds are you?"

"Tell me about Sal Cupertine," Matthew said, "or one day you'll be walking down the street and I'll be inside of a building with a sniper's rifle, aimed right here." Matthew reached over and touched a spot on Fat Monte's back. "You feel that? That's the part of your spine that controls your bladder, your bowels, all your sexual functions. That's where the bullet is going to go. And you know what? It will be perfectly legal because you're a known criminal with a gun and I'm an FBI agent. You'll be shitting into a bag for the rest of your life, trying to make your limp dick work. Maybe I'll just go ahead and do it when you walk out of this place tonight, because I'm sure you've got some heat on you and you're surely on probation. Save us all some time."

"I want my lawyer," Fat Monte said.

Matthew actually started to laugh. Jeff thought Matthew was enjoying this a bit too much. Here was Fat Monte Moretti, one of the most feared gangsters in all of Chicago, a man probably responsible for a dozen or more murders, asking for his lawyer, undone by a broken nose and the realization that sometimes you really don't have any rights.

"Let me put it to you this way," Jeff said. "You're free to go any time. But understand that as soon as you walk out the door, you're a dead man. Either my partner here will shoot you, or it's gonna be the Gangster 2-6, or it's going to be someone in the Family, once we put out the word that you were seen at this nice bar consorting with the FBI. You could say we're actually here to help you."

"Help me?" Fat Monte said. "This asshole broke my fucking nose and now wants to hobble me."

"I know you helped get rid of Sal Cupertine," Jeff said. "I know you killed Chema. I know you had Neto killed. So that's two bodies on your sheet, plus aiding a fugitive who murdered federal agents. And now I'm pretty sure you killed Paul Bruno, too, because you opened your stupid mouth. You want that weight? You willing to spend the next five hundred years in prison? Because that's what you're looking at, Monte. No more in and out in a year. No more Ronnie greasing things so you're living like a kingpin somewhere. Because now you're a liability to him. So I'm talking the rest of your life in a supermax, solitary confinement for twenty-three hours a day. That's if you live through the week. All that, and your wife will have a bounty on her ass from the Gangster 2-6 for you killing two of their boys. You ready for that?"

"I talk to you," Fat Monte said, "what can you do for my wife?"

Matthew shot Jeff a quick look. Fat Monte hadn't just taken the hook, he'd swallowed it all the way down. Jeff wasn't totally convinced this was the case, actually, though if there was something to be gleaned from all this, it was that Fat Monte understood what Jeff said was entirely true. Though, if Fat Monte actually went to his lawyer, well, there could be some problems . . . namely that Matthew was impersonating an FBI agent . . . though the odds were fairly good that Fat Monte Moretti would probably have some problems alleging that his civil rights had been violated, particularly since he was a known felon.

"We can get her protection right away," Jeff said, which was a lie. But it was a lie he'd figure out how to make good on, if need be. He still had a few friends, somewhere.

"Like a house in Phoenix or some shit?" Fat Monte said. "Maybe a little place on an island? Get her some new tits, also? Maybe you put her up in business, like an ice cream shop or some little boutique place selling sweaters and scented candles?"

"This isn't TV," Jeff said.

"So don't play me like I'm on TV," Fat Monte hissed. He pulled the rag from his face and picked up a napkin from the table and dabbed at his nostrils to check for bleeding. It was down to just a few trickles, though once he saw himself in a mirror, he wasn't going to be pleased. "Unless I see some marshals in this joint, you don't even have the authority to make that kind of promise. You're not the first feds to come knocking on my door with offers of immunity and shit."

Jeff had long worked under the impression that Fat Monte wasn't very bright. Of all the members of the Family he'd investigated, he was the one clear liability, the one part of upper management prone to common stupidity—over the years, in addition to his notable felonies, Fat Monte was pinched for drunk driving, got nicked for beating down a valet he accused of stealing three dollars in change from his car, even once tried to get on a commuter flight with a vial of cocaine in his pocket—never mind his propensity to kill other humans. Now, though, sitting here with him, Jeff was beginning to understand that Fat Monte wasn't very bright, but he'd acquired some level of institutional intelligence.

"Okay, then," Jeff said. He stood up and put his coat back on, Matthew followed suit, and then Jeff asked a passing waitress for a pen, scribbled his cell phone number on the back of a napkin, handed it to Fat Monte. "You call me, and I'll get an ambulance for you."

"That's it? Your pit bull breaks my fucking nose, threatens me, and then you leave?"

"You don't need to be Ronnie Cupertine's bitch," Matthew said. "You tell us where Sal Cupertine is, that's all, and maybe we'll forget about Chema and Neto."

"They're already forgotten," Fat Monte said.

"Just like you'll be when you're not of any use anymore," Jeff said. "I'm not asking you to tell me what crimes Sal Cupertine committed. I have that information. I'm just asking for a location. You point to a spot on a map, and your wife is safe for the rest of her life."

"While I do . . . what? Five hundred years? That what you said?"

"You chose this life, Monte," Jeff said, his voice rising, and it was all he could do not to grab Fat Monte by his collar and shake him, but he managed to stay calm, managed to extend a single finger in Fat Monte's direction instead of his gun. "Your wife didn't. She could ask Jennifer Cupertine about that, see how life really works when your old man is left to sway in the wind by the Family. See how far the omertà goes when she can't afford to flush the toilet."

"Fuck you," Fat Monte said again, and there still wasn't much behind it.

"That's what Ronnie Cupertine does," Jeff said. "You don't believe me, just you wait until he sees you with your twisted face and your story about how the feds roughed you up. He's gonna have a lot of questions about why you're not in jail, and next thing you know, we'll be pulling your crispy body out of the landfill, too."

Jeff started out the door, Matthew a few steps behind him, and it was only then that he realized how quiet the bar had become, primarily because he'd shouted at Fat Monte Moretti, killer of men and a regular at the Four Treys Tavern in bucolic Roscoe Village. Bad form, sure, but whatever.

∎

Even though they'd been gone less than thirty minutes, the inside of Jeff's Explorer was already freezing once they made it back, the steam rising from both men fogging the windows. Jeff took his gun from his ankle holster and put it back in the glove box. Matthew didn't seem to notice. Jeff checked his reflection in the rearview mirror, wiped a speck of dried blood from his forehead.

"I could do it, you know," Matthew said. "Put one right in his back."

"I know," Jeff said.

"I want to do it now. What's stopping us from doing it right now?" Matthew said.

"Put your gun away," Jeff said.

"We should take it to the next level," Matthew said. He took his gun out, examined it for a moment. "I want to hurt him." He looked at his hands, wiped them on his pants. "I've got his blood all over me."

"You violated his civil rights," Jeff said. "If you were still working for the FBI, I'd have to fire you."

"I want to hurt him," Matthew said again, like maybe he was trying to make sense of his own revelation. He dumped the gun in the glove box.

"I know," Jeff said. He pulled off Damen, turned right on Roscoe, then came back down Wolcott and onto Henderson, headed back toward the bar.

"What are we doing?" Matthew said.

"I want to see what he does," Jeff said. "If he walks home, back to the wife, we got him. If he sits in there and calls a couple of his boys, starts plotting how he's going to kill us, we'll need to make different arrangements."

"He doesn't even know my name," Matthew said.

"He could get it," Jeff said. "He knew who I was."

"Do I need to worry about my sister?"

"We'll know soon enough." Jeff parked half a block away from the bar, in front of a blue walk-up that had both Cubs and Sox banners flying out front. Jeff took out his cell and tried Paul Bruno's phone again. Voicemail still full. Shit.

"Anything?" Matthew said.

"No," Jeff said. Matthew nodded, kept staring out the window, waiting for Fat Monte, or a bunch of guys in sweat suits, to appear. "If he's dead," Jeff said, "that's on me."

"It's on him," Matthew said. "What did you say to Fat Monte? That he chose this life? Same thing for your friend."

"Maybe so," Jeff said, though he didn't want to believe that.

Jeff dialed 411 and got the number for Paul Bruno's mother. Mrs. Bruno picked up on the third ring.

"Ma'am," Jeff said, "my name is Jeff Hopper. I'm friends with your son. I was wondering if you'd heard from him recently."

"Are you friends from the neighborhood?" she asked.

"No," Jeff said.

"You one of his boyfriends, then?"

"No," Jeff said. He tried to figure out a polite way of telling the truth and then just decided he'd tell the truth as it was. "I knew him from his work with the FBI."

"Oh," she said. "You were his handler, is that right?"

"That's right," Jeff said.

"Oh," she said again. Jeff heard her sigh, and he wondered how much she actually knew about her son. "I haven't heard from him in weeks. He normally called every other day or so. More often since his father passed. It's been almost a month. Do you think he's all right?"

"No," Jeff said. "Ma'am, if I were you, I would file a missing person's report. Get an investigation going."

"Oh, I see," she said. "Maybe I can ask you a question?"

"Sure," Jeff said.

"Do you think I'm stupid?"

"Ma'am?"

"I just want to know if you think I'm stupid," she said. Her voice sounded choked, and Jeff realized she was crying.

"Of course not," Jeff said.

"Then please don't call here again," she said, and she hung up.

Jeff set his phone down. It was 1999, a whole new century was about to start, and people were still too scared to do the right thing. Chicago was still the kind of place where people feared the authorities and respected the crime bosses, even after all this time. "Paul Bruno is dead," he said quietly.

Matthew nodded. "What do you want to do about it?"

"This whole thing," Jeff said. "It's stupid. Right? Isn't that what you tried to convince me of? Back at the White Palace? That this was a fool's journey?"

"I'm here, aren't I?"

"Where else do you have to go?"

"You know who killed him," Matthew said. "You just sat there and had drinks with him. I've got his blood all over my pants."

"That's what gets me," Jeff said. "What makes Sal Cupertine any different? Why bother looking for him if it all just perpetuates? Could be any of these assholes who work for the Family."

"The FBI any better right now? They let Sal Cupertine walk," Matthew said. "You said it yourself. They'll wait until it's convenient to start looking for him. And you know what? They won't find him. And the czars at Stateville? Doesn't someone have to do the right thing? I mean, isn't that what this is about, Jeff? Doing the right thing?"

"I don't know anymore," Jeff said.

"You better figure that out," Matthew said, "because I'm riding with you now, and I can't just throw my life away. I need to find this guy if I want to have a career, or else I'm going to be the most qualified security guard at Citibank."

Ten minutes later, as Jeff and Matthew sat in the front seat of Jeff's idling Explorer, a single woman crossed the street in front of them and entered the Four Treys. She came back out less than a minute later, hand in hand with Fat Monte Moretti.

■

Jeff was woken up at four o'clock in the morning by the sound of his cell phone ringing. He picked it up and looked at the number on the caller ID, but he didn't recognize it. He hoped it was Paul Bruno, calling from Canada or something, but was fairly certain that wasn't going to be the case.

"Hopper," he said.

"Why do you law enforcement people always answer the phone like that?" Fat Monte said. "Anyone ever teach you to say hello?"

"It's FBI policy," Jeff said. "Always smart to identify yourself, takes the mystery out of things."

"Yeah, I bet," Fat Monte said.

"Something I can help you with, Monte?" Jeff asked. "Or are you just making sure I gave you a working number."

"You know," Fat Monte said, "your people aren't that sharp. There was another body in that dump."

"Oh yeah?" Jeff said.

"A white guy," Monte said. "About the same height and weight as Sal. But you find the faggot Mexican and make *him*. That's why you're never going to win, you get that?"

"What's to win, Monte?" Jeff said.

"Tonight," Fat Monte said, "why didn't you just take me in? Why bust me up and let me go home? That's not how you guys normally do business."

"New policy went into effect," Jeff said, "right after one of your guys killed three feds." He sat up in bed and turned on a light, looked around for his minirecorder, since it wasn't every day that a member of the Family called in the middle of the night with, it sounded like, a few things to get off his chest. Jeff was pretty sure he'd left the recorder outside in his car, and he wasn't about to go running outside in his underwear when it was zero degrees outside. He fumbled through his nightstand and came up with a pencil but no paper. He'd write on the wall if he had to. "You want to talk to me about that day, Monte? That why you're calling?"

"You gotta make me a promise," Fat Monte said. "I tell you some shit, you go back out to the dump, and you get that fucking body. Because I can't have that on me."

Jeff tried to remember if there'd been any chatter about any guys from Fat Monte's crew missing around the time of Sal's disappearance, but part of his brain was still in REM. And anyway, Chema Espinoza wasn't listed in any of the files. The FBI didn't care much about the guppies, not when there were whales like Fat Monte swimming around.

"It's been months, Monte," Jeff said. "Whoever you threw in there has probably been picked clean by the rats."

"Don't fucking say that," Fat Monte said. "Jesus Christ, don't say that shit. Get some of those cadaver dogs and get out there tomorrow, right? Tomorrow. Promise me you'll get those cadaver dogs out to the dump, or this phone call is over."

"Okay," Jeff said. He was startled by the desperation in Fat

Monte's voice. There was something happening here, and it wasn't good. "Okay. I'll get them. I'll get dogs and radar and everything, okay? Whatever you need, we'll get it. We'll go out together if you want."

"Nah, nah, fuck that," Fat Monte said. He was silent for a moment, and Jeff heard what he thought was the clink of ice in a glass. "One other thing. You keep my wife's name out of this. She's got family and cousins, and they don't need to know what kind of life she was living, okay?"

"There's no reason to bring her into anything," Jeff said. That Monte said "was living" immediately bothered him. And he didn't say "keep my wife out of this," he said "keep my wife's name" out of it. "Where are you right now, Monte? Why don't I meet you, and we can talk."

"Like I need another beatdown? My balls finally stopped hurting."

"It won't be like that," Jeff said. "We'll sit down, have a cup of coffee, you can tell me whatever is on your mind."

Fat Monte laughed at that. "Look," he said. "I'm going to tell you two things, and that's all I got with this. You walked into my life today and ruined it, you get that? Ruined it. Nowhere I can go now, you get that?"

"I get that," Jeff said. "But I'm giving you a chance that Neto and Chema didn't get." He paused. "Or my guys that Sal murdered. I'm giving you a chance to get out of this with your life."

"You don't really believe that, do you?" he said. "Because maybe that's the line you gave Bruno when you flipped him and now he's dead. You know Ronnie don't forget, right?"

"So then what is this?" Jeff said.

"Making my own bed," Monte said. He cleared his throat, and Jeff heard the clinking of ice again. "First thing, you get that body from the dump, you call my mother. You got her phone number?"

"Yes," Jeff said. He had phone numbers for every extended member of the Family, and the FBI had bugs on most of them, too.

"You call her, tell her you got my cousin Neal. She's gonna lose it. Don't play with her, don't dig on her, no pressure, okay? She's not in the game, never has been, she just tried her best, you know? That kid was practically a retard, not a evil bone in his body, just real sweet, wanted to start a puppy farm, always had gerbils and hamsters and shit, used to wash them . . . Ronnie always had this idea that he was the perfect guy to have along for things because, well, fuck, what did he know? Right?"

Jeff had only passing knowledge of Neal Moretti: He was inconsequential to even the smallest investigations Jeff had been party to, his most notable trait being his last name and that he was frequently used as a driver.

And now he was rotting in the landfill.

Fat Monte rambled on about his cousin, his words running into each other, and Jeff realized this wasn't just a confession of some kind, it was maybe a coda, too, that Fat Monte was winding down toward something dreadful, trying to get his mind right. This was not good.

"Okay, okay," Jeff said. "I'll call your mother. We'll find Neal. We'll do whatever we need to do to get that to happen right away."

"He was like my brother," Fat Monte said finally. "I've done plenty of bad things, you know that, right? You know that?"

"I know that."

"But I was never like Sal. I tried to be this cold-blooded motherfucker, and maybe most of the time I was, that steroid shit, that made it worse for a while, but I tried to get off that when I met my girl, and all of a sudden, all this shit, it starts visiting on me, like flashbacks. So I get back on it, get that rush, you know, invincible. Most of the time, I can put it in the back somewhere, but Neal, Neal, he was like my brother, right? And I had to do him. There's no returning from that, that's what I keep thinking about, thinking about how my wife, Hannah is her name, you knew about her, right? What if she found out about that? She'd never be able to see me like she saw me before, and that, that, that, that wouldn't be something I could deal with."

"It's going to be okay," Jeff said. He was throwing on his pants, had already slipped into a sweatshirt while Monte was going on, was looking for his shoes, trying to figure out how he'd call 911 while he was on the phone, trying to figure out how he'd explain to the cops—shit, to the FBI—how it was that he was on the phone with Fat Monte Moretti and the tenor of their conversation. He'd need to figure that out. But at that moment, his biggest concern was getting to wherever Monte was, since he was becoming increasingly aware of how much Fat Monte was talking about his wife as if she didn't exist anymore.

"Yeah, yeah," Fat Monte said.

"Why don't you tell me where you are," Jeff said. He found his car keys and was walking out into the frigid darkness. "Why don't you tell me where we can meet and talk, Monte. Just man-to-man. No bullshit."

"Kochel Farms," Fat Monte said.

"You need to tell me where that is," Jeff said.

"I ain't there, but you'll find it," Fat Monte said.

"Okay," Jeff said. "Let's just do one thing at a time. I'm getting into my car right now. Why don't you let me buy you some steak and eggs over at the White Palace. You know where that is?"

"It's too late," Fat Monte said.

"No, no, it's not, Monte," Jeff said. "We can figure out a good solution here. Get you out of town, into a program, you and Hannah into a house with a lawn and a garage. Send you out to California, whatever you want. Okay? We can do that. I have that authority."

"Just get him out of that dump," Fat Monte said, and then the next thing Jeff heard was the distinctive blast of a .357, followed by the unmistakable sound of a body hitting the floor.

CHAPTER TEN

R abbi David Cohen hated to wait. In Chicago, if he had to sit on someone in order to take him out, well, that wasn't really waiting. That was working. It was part of a process with a discernible end point. Now, however, it was a completely different story. Since his coming-out party at the Hanukkah carnival, he'd become, it seemed, the go-to rabbi/problem solver for any Jew in Las Vegas under the age of fifty—and he'd have to drop everything, get over to the temple, sit in his office, and wait for them to show up.

Most arrived on time, but then once they were in his office, his new congregants had no compunction about staying longer than their allotted appointment. So David would have to wait for them to get to the point of their problem, which was tiring because it required mental focus in addition to the monastic ability to just sit and listen. Stillness was of paramount importance, according to Rabbi Kales, who was strict about this, telling David over and over again that most people just wanted someone to listen to them, that it wasn't really up to him to solve their problems as much as provide them the road map to their own decisions.

He was to do this by dispensing as many nuggets as possible from all his readings—the Torah, Midrash, Talmud, whatever—though he'd found that if he paraphrased Neil Young or Bruce Springsteen it generally had the same effect.

That probably wasn't going to work today, not with Claudia Levine. She was a New York Jew who'd moved to Las Vegas five years earlier when her husband, Mark, took a job in the accounting department at the Rio and then moved a few streets over to the Palace Station, but that was just too dirty for his taste—physically dirty, as in they didn't clean it often enough—so he moved up the street to a new resort in Summerlin, which was good because it cut down his commute, since they were living in a charming little townhouse over at the Adagio on the corner of Buffalo and Vegas, just a few blocks down the way from the temple, though, for Claudia's taste, there were a few too many strippers living there, too, which made her fear the pool.

David still had no idea of the exact nature of Claudia's problem, and he was due to meet with Jerry Ford in fifteen minutes. Their little business operation had taken off in the last few weeks. After the holidays, there were far more bodies to be disposed of from natural deaths—old people, David had found, were all about holding on through the holidays before biting it, since no one liked to have Grandpa keel over during Hanukkah or on New Year's Eve—and unnatural deaths. It made sense: David couldn't ever remember killing someone on Christmas, or even the week after. Even hit men took that time off.

But once the second of January rolled around, it was open season. By the middle of January, David had already presided over fifteen funerals, equally divided between real people and hit jobs.

It was the suicides that left David unnerved. It was one thing to bury some old lady who'd been alive since before there were paved roads and then another thing altogether when he had to eulogize some UNLV student who threw him or herself out of a dorm window. Usually, Rabbi Kales stepped in because of the long relationship he had with the families, but more and more often, David found himself being thrust into situations that weren't criminal in the least, Bennie telling him it was part of their long-range plan, the selling of this long con.

Which is why he was now listening to Claudia Levine's tantalizing story of . . . what? Shit. He didn't know what she was saying, but he knew he needed a way to cut her off. Problem was, he'd found that he really couldn't fake his way with New York transplants: They were more *Jewish* than the average temple member, which required David to stay as focused as possible. It was exhausting.

"So I say to Martin—you know Martin Copeland, don't you, Rabbi?" Claudia said, and David realized that he'd done the one thing he was trying not to do: He'd let his mind wander.

"Martin Copeland," David said. He put a finger up to his lips—this was something Rabbi Kales did frequently, and it immediately impressed David with how it made the rabbi look contemplative and, at the same time, passively judgmental, as if all the world in front of him was not quite up to snuff—and left it there for a moment while he attempted to pick up the thread of conversation.

He did know Martin Copeland. He'd provided the seed money for the Dorothy Copeland Children's Center, gave the temple a check for two hundred thousand dollars to see his dead wife's name on a wall. Bennie said he'd been setting numbers in town for a generation, but now he didn't know where he was half the time. "He's a quart low," Bennie told him, "but had more oil than all of us to start with." David met with him a week earlier to talk about the deep moral questions that were now plaguing him, particularly if all his years working in the gaming industry was a *shanda*, even if it wasn't mentioned directly in the Torah. Martin was concerned that maybe Bugsy Siegel had set them all on a bad path, that maybe Siegel was a *golem*, and now that we were only a year away from the turn of the millennium, there was a real chance it was all a terrible omen for the destruction of the Jewish people. Bennie told David to listen to and agree with every word Copeland said, make sure he wasn't planning on changing his will in any way, since as it stood, the temple was in for a cool million. "He starts giving any hints that he's spending more than his living expenses or looking to donate to Gamblers Anonymous or something," Bennie said, "drown him in the toilet if you have to."

"Yes, yes, Martin Copeland," David said, finally. "I fear, Claudia, that Mr. Copeland is not a person you should be going to for advice." Not that David knew what the hell she was talking about.

"He said you'd say that," Claudia said.

David tented his hands and leaned back in his chair, stole a glance out the window, and saw that Jerry Ford was standing on the sidewalk talking to Bennie Savone, their kids running around on the sidewalk together. Which was fine, generally. David had made the executive decision to let Bennie know all about the deal he'd made with Jerry, and Bennie didn't care provided he got his beak wet. So they'd gone about it legally, getting the morgue staff trained to harvest tissue, even got all the proper forms, which they then doctored for use with those "clients" whose bodies could still be harvested, which wasn't many of them. *So many amateurs out there*, David thought. No honor in their work.

The mortuary hadn't received its first official payment yet—Jerry said his company paid on a net-sixty after processing the tissue, which sounded reasonable to David, even if he wasn't exactly sure what it meant—though already Jerry had made a nice donation to temple, a check for five grand last week, a promise for another five grand this week, which indicated to David that whatever *net-sixty* meant, it was going to be a nice payday.

Still, David didn't like seeing Bennie and Jerry together on a public street, where anyone could snap a photo of them, particularly since that shit over at the club with the tourist getting stomped half to death was becoming a larger problem than Bennie could have imagined.

He'd followed David's advice and gave up his bouncers, even offered to pay for the victim's health care, which seemed to appease Metro, but word was that the feds were taking a hard look at the Wild Horse now, seeing as how both the bouncers were called "mob associates" in the *Review-Journal* over and over again. And the offer to pick up the medical costs didn't exactly appease the family of the guy, who were now getting ready to sue the Wild Horse for, Bennie told him, "fifty-cocksucking-trillion-billion-dollars."

Then one of the weekly papers did an exposé about how half the strip clubs in town were fronts for organized crime, explained in precise detail how the families had moved from the casino business into the legal skin business, it being more profitable to sell lap dances and overpriced Cristal than to illegally pimp out girls for sex. The house charged patrons twenty bucks just to walk in the door, then took 20 percent from every girl's cash take, plus another 40 percent from the credit card charges; the girls then had to tip out the bartenders, bouncers, the DJ, the house mom, bathroom attendants, and anyone else who happened to work the room . . . and then those people had to tip the house 20 percent on their take, too, plus 40 percent on *their* credit card tips. And then there was just the normal grift: charging twenty-dollar lap dances at a hundred a pop, charging a grand for a bottle of fifty-dollar Champagne, and if the customer complained to management, maybe management responded to the complaint with a hammer to the knees. If the person was smart, maybe they'd go home and dispute the charges at a safe distance from Bennie's boys, but then who was smart at 3 a.m. in a strip club staring at a couple grand on their corporate American Express?

Credit cards. It made David's head spin thinking about how Visa and MasterCard were bankrolling a big portion of Bennie's crew.

Cash was another matter. A strip club was the easiest place on earth to wash hard cash, particularly when you could generate paperwork that said Champagne was legitimately billed at five hundred dollars a bottle. It was no fun to wash money twenty bucks at a time, but it was the easiest way to move it around in the mob.

He'd done it again. Claudia was still staring at him, waiting for his rabbinical ruling on . . . something . . . and he was zoned out, thinking business, making *her* wait. "Yes, well," he said. He looked around his office for something to pull from, some bit of arcane wisdom that might solve whatever issue this woman was having, while not actually displaying to her that he had no idea what she was talking about. His eyes settled on a book of poetry about Jews that Rabbi Gottlieb had left. He retrieved the book from the shelf and paced the office for a moment in silent contemplation. "Yes," he repeated. "Are you familiar with Longfellow, Claudia?"

"The only Longfellow I know well is the song Neil Diamond has about him," she said. "We played it at our wedding, even."

David sat down on the edge of his desk, only a foot from Claudia, close enough that he could smell the chemical reaction between her nauseating perfume and her hair spray, and he flipped through the pages of the book of poetry with what he hoped looked like solemn appreciation before settling back on the one poem he'd actually read. The key was to make it look like divine inspiration.

David tapped his index finger on his nose, trying to get the pose right. "In his poem 'The Jewish Cemetery at Newport,' Longfellow calls our people trampled and beaten as the sand, but unshaken as the continent." David hoped Claudia never managed to stumble on the poem, since he was taking a lot of liberties with the line in terms of context—though context, Rabbi Kales had told him, was rarely important when making a point. He set the book back down on his desk and leaned toward Claudia. "That's very powerful, isn't it?"

"It is," Claudia said. She closed her eyes, and David saw a tear trying to escape from the corner of her right eye. Crying women had no timetable, this much David knew. He needed to get her out of his office.

David reached over and clasped Claudia's hands. They were ice-cold. Maybe her problem was really poor circulation. "Trust in the Torah," David said, his voice just above a whisper. "That's where your problems will be solved. I think you know that."

"What I don't understand, Rabbi—" Claudia began, but David cut her off.

"Suppose a dream doesn't come true," David said, hoping Claudia wasn't much of a Springsteen fan, or if she was, that she favored his later records. "Is it a lie? Think about that, Claudia." David stood up then, which made Claudia stand, too, which then made it very easy to usher her out the door of his office and into the hallway . . . where instead of Jerry Ford, David found Bennie Savone waiting for him. Surprisingly, he wasn't on his cell phone. Instead, he was standing there holding his daughter Sophie's hand and looking impatient. Claudia just gave him a polite nod and made her way down the hall.

"You got a minute?" Bennie asked.

"I'm supposed to be meeting with Mr. Ford," David said.

"Yeah, he had to cancel." Bennie and Sophie sat down inside his office, Bennie in the chair Claudia had just vacated and Sophie on the floor, where she immediately opened up her backpack and started pulling out dolls. Sometimes it was difficult to tell if Bennie was speaking in code or not, though since David had just seen Bennie outside chatting with Jerry, he assumed that it was true that Jerry had to cancel; particularly since neither Bennie nor his daughter were covered in blood.

Sophie was Bennie's youngest—she was only five; he had another daughter, Jean, who was thirteen—and, from what David had sussed out during his time at the temple, she was blissfully unaware that her father was a sociopath. She favored her mother in the looks department, which would also serve her well for the long term, and from what he'd experienced with her when the Tikvah Preschool visited the temple every Thursday for lunch, she was an unusually lucid conversationalist.

It was David's job to come by and smile at the children, say a few words to each, make them feel like God had just strolled in for a bite, thus ensuring their parents wrote out a big fat check at the end of the month for no other reason than their children were happy. In truth, it was David's favorite time of the week. For the hour he spent going kid to kid, he didn't have to pretend. He just sat down next to them and asked them about their day, their life, how things were *going* and never how things *had been*, which was different from what he normally dealt with. With the people of parenting age, it was always about their childhood, how someone had fucked them up and only God or David could help them deal with the past, like it was some constant growling beast that lived next door that needed only to be fed and watered and everything would be okay. The senior citizens all wanted to bitch about how things were better back then, and wanted assurances that they were right, that the world had turned to shit but that they, of course, weren't to blame.

Sophie seemed mostly preoccupied by her mother's health—last week, when David sat with her for a moment and chatted her up, she told him that her mommy might need to have a "hystericalectomy," which David found both oddly charming and terribly sad, not sure if she'd put the words together or if she'd overheard her parents talking.

David closed his office door and sat down behind his desk. "What can I do for you?"

"I got a call last night," Bennie said. "Seems there's been some developments in Chicago. You know a guy named Fat Monte?" David cut his eyes over to Sophie. She was deep into a conversation between Barbie and Ken about the need for them to get a horse. Bennie didn't seem to care, which was presumably the subtext he was trying to impart to David.

"I did," David said.

"Pulled his own roots a couple weeks ago," Bennie said. "Put one in his wife's head while she slept and then one in his own. Wife's a vegetable. He's dead."

"I didn't know he had a wife," David said. Fat Monte used to be the kind of guy who liked to fuck hookers and strippers, said it was better than having to deal with any bullshit afterward. Fat Monte had a kid living down in Springfield, he remembered that, though he wondered if anyone else did.

"What's this got to do with me?"

"You know a fed named Hopper?"

Hopper. That was the Donnie Brasco reject on the hotel bill. "I heard he died," David said.

"No such luck," Bennie said. "Apparently, he's been looking for you on his own time. Fat Monte spent his last minutes alive talking to him on the phone. He's got his snout in a bunch of business up there, trying to figure out where you are."

"I thought I was dead," David said.

"Yeah, well, you are. This Hopper didn't seem to care about that."

Maybe that explained Paul Bruno showing up in ribbons. And if Fat Monte felt enough pressure that he had to kill his own wife—or at least attempt to—and then himself, that meant this guy was digging closer and closer to something Cousin Ronnie wouldn't like, something that made Fat Monte fear enough for his own life that he cut out the middle man.

This didn't make sense to David. Why would the feds be looking for a dead man? And if the feds knew he wasn't dead, or at least one of them knew, or suspected, then maybe his wife knew, too. Or suspected. Particularly if Chema hadn't made it back to give her his wallet. He doubted he had. What was it Rabbi Kales had said? *Dismembered and burnt.* If Chema and Neal were dead, and now Fat Monte was dead, who was left that knew enough about that last night, other than Ronnie? And it still didn't explain Paul Bruno getting it, unless that was just for talking.

"I got something to worry about," David said.

"Not yet," Bennie said.

"That's wasn't a question," David said.

"This Fat Monte, he a talker?"

"He's a company man," David said. How many falls had Fat Monte taken? Three? Four? Enough to earn some serious credit in Ronnie's book, plus however many blood jobs he'd done—the kind of stuff David stopped doing years ago, the arm breaking, the eye gouging, all that baseball bat and screwdriver shit—but if he was snitching on the murder of FBI agents, there wasn't enough credit in the world for that. That was the thing. David just didn't see Fat Monte doing that on his own accord. Which had to mean this Hopper had enough on Fat Monte to prosecute him for some big-league tickets. "I don't make him for a snitch, really."

"He's just the kinda guy who pumps one in his wife and then puts his brains on the floor?"

"I don't know," David said. "It doesn't make sense."

"Between this shit at the club and this asshole, we may need to do some housekeeping," Bennie said.

"Daddy," Sophie said suddenly, which made David flinch. He'd practically forgotten her. "You said a bad word."

Bennie looked down at his daughter. She was still on the floor with her dolls. "Two, actually," he said.

"That's two dollars," she said.

"You shaking me down?" Bennie said. Just a dad talking to his baby girl.

"We have a deal," she said. She stood up and put one hand on her hip, the other out flat. "Pay up."

Bennie pulled out his wallet, thumbed through the bills, came up empty. "All I've got is fifties," he said. "You got any small bills, Rabbi?"

David didn't have a wallet anymore. For the first time in his life, he was now a money clip guy, because he'd given Chema his wallet to give to Jennifer and then never felt right getting another. His mind turned over the connections: the dead feds, Chema, Fat Monte, all that shit, right down to Bennie's kid asking for money and Bennie asking David for it. It was some kind of Talmudic parable. What had he read? *The treasures which my fathers laid by are for this world, mine are for eternity.*

David peeled a five from his fold and handed it to Sophie. "I heard him say three bad words yesterday," David said.

Sophie squealed in delight and then immediately went back to her dolls. Bennie watched her for a few moments, a smile etched into his face like granite. "A real shakedown artist," he said.

"It's in the genes," David said.

"On her mother's side," Bennie said. "Speaking of which. This housekeeping. You up for a spring cleaning if it comes to that?"

It wasn't a question of whether he was up to do his job—he'd do it. The issue here was scale. What Bennie was alluding to, apparently, involved closing the circle even closer . . . which would likely mean the end of Rabbi Kales. Maybe not now. Maybe not next month. But at some point. That would have ramifications beyond the usual, since Rabbi Kales was Bennie's father-in-law. Bennie also had something on the old man, that much was certain, though Rabbi Kales had never been as candid with David as that day after their first meeting at the Bagel Café, at least not about matters concerning anything other than the Jewish faith, and Bennie hadn't betrayed any secrets, either.

The issue with Rabbi Kales knowing the truth about David and about the money being pushed through the temple in all its illegal forms wasn't that he was likely to suddenly be investigated by the feds and break. No, the issue David had gleaned over the last two months had more to do with something far more common: Rabbi Kales felt profoundly guilty. He was beginning to take stock of his life, and that made a man do stupid things. And now here Bennie was floating out a series of potential problems that vaguely included Rabbi Kales, too, probably just to see how the good Rabbi David Cohen would act, even in front of a kid. David wasn't sure how much Bennie intuited about Rabbi Kales's emotional state, though he wouldn't be surprised if Bennie had the temple bugged, too.

For fuck's sake, David thought. That was probably true. Bennie probably knew the entire temple's secrets, though David couldn't imagine Bennie had the time to sit around like the FBI, monitoring a wire for the slightest hint of something illegal.

"Whatever mess needs to be cleaned," David said, "I can clean it."

Bennie sighed. "All this crap," he said, "you're the only guy I trust right now. You're the only guy who can do what needs to be done."

Bennie reached into his jacket pocket and pulled out two envelopes and placed them on David's desk. One had the logo from Jerry Ford's company on it—LifeCore—and the other was plain white. David slit open the envelope from LifeCore and saw that it contained a check for seven thousand dollars, payable directly to the temple's performing arts fund, along with an official letter from Jerry Ford thanking the temple for its dedication to the arts.

"Something wrong?" Bennie said.

"You tell me," David said. He showed Bennie the check and the letter.

"Tax write-off for the business," Bennie said. "Last year, the Wild Horse donated ten grand to outfit the entire Little League. All legal in this town. Isn't that the rub, Rabbi? Twenty years from now, there won't be any need for people like us. Everything will be on the level."

David opened up the other envelope. Inside was a photocopy of a driver's license for a man named Larry Kirsch. He had a Las Vegas address, and his fortieth birthday was coming up in April.

"I need you to clean that up," Bennie said.

"Who is he?" David asked, which was stupid. He never asked that question. But this didn't seem like some random job, since he was the first person Bennie had asked him to kill since Slim Joe, and in light of the shit going down at the club, he knew Bennie was trying to keep his criminal activity on the down-low.

"He built your face," Bennie said.

"I thought you said that guy had an accident."

"That was the guy who did your jaw," Bennie said. "Make it look like a house fire or a cougar attack or something. Last thing we need is another ring on the chain. Know what I'm saying?"

He did know what he was saying. If there was someone who needed to be killed and it was just some civilian, someone like this doctor, that made it a murder, not a mob hit, and that meant you couldn't have some monkey do the job, because they'd invariably fuck it up.

"Just tell me when," David said.

"Soon. You do it before Valentine's, maybe I can surprise Rachel with a cruise or something." Bennie tipped his head back and closed his eyes, kept them closed while he talked. "I'm sleeping four hours, if I'm lucky, what with Rachel being up half the night. She doesn't sleep, I don't sleep."

"She still not well?" David didn't know how to properly address this issue, nor did he want to, but it seemed like Bennie wanted to talk about a whole host of things today. The strange thing was that more and more, Bennie was coming into his office for conversations that started first as business and then spiraled into whatever was going on at home. "She still got that problem?" he finally continued.

"Yeah," Bennie said. "Two beautiful daughters, I'm not complaining, right? I just thought, down the line, maybe we'd try for one more, see if we could get someone I could throw a football with. Doctor's telling us no. And then there's the pain. You can't just take a Tylenol for what she's going through, so she's stoned on Ativan half the time."

"He who bears his portion of the burden will live to enjoy the last hour of consolation," David said.

Bennie whipped forward, his eyes open now.

"It's from the Talmud," David said. "Moses."

"I know what it's from," Bennie said. "My father-in-law likes that one. You believe that crap now?"

"No," David said. "It's something I read that stuck with me. I've got all kinds of quotes at the ready."

That was true, mostly.

What was also true was that David kept finding himself with

these tiny earthquakes of epiphany, particularly when he read about the sanctity of life. He wasn't particularly well-read in his former life—mostly *Sports Illustrated* and whatever paperback he picked up at the grocery store to flip through while he waited on a job, though he was particular enough to know that he hated Tom Clancy and anything about the Mafia, so he stayed away from those true crime books, too, since he was also somewhat worried he'd find something he did in one of them—and thus the mere process of digesting all these religious texts was filling his brain with whole new pathways of thought.

He wasn't sentimental about most things, and he'd been good about keeping Jennifer and William on the back burner as much as possible; but every now and then he'd read something in the Talmud or the Midrash that he'd immediately be able to apply to his own issues, and suddenly he'd have a way to deal with what he'd previously thought was a problem only he'd ever had. Which, he also recognized, was ludicrous.

"She wants to take you to lunch," Bennie said.

"Who?"

"Rachel. You listening to me, Rabbi?"

"I don't think that's a great idea," David said.

"She needs someone to talk to who isn't going to just throw pills at her, give her some spiritual advice."

"And that person is me?" David said.

"You're having lunch with her tomorrow at Grape Street," Bennie said. "This isn't a negotiation." His cell phone rang then, and Bennie looked at the incoming number with something close to disgust. "My lawyer," he said under his breath, so his daughter wouldn't hear. "I gotta take this. You watch Sophie for a minute?"

"Sure," David said. Bennie stepped out of the office, and in few seconds David could see him pacing out on the sidewalk, always pacing. He was a man with problems, that much was true, though David sort of admired him, all things considering. He had this long con rolling, he had the strip club, he had this in with the Jews, which gave him some protection in the court of public opinion—even Harvey B. Curran was taking him light in his column lately, talking about how people who go to strip clubs can assume that the bouncers aren't all a bunch of clergymen and should treat them accordingly and how Bennie Savone was doing so much for the community—and then, well, there was this little girl sitting on the floor talking to her Barbies.

Over the years David had found it difficult to hate someone who cared about their kids. It didn't mean he wouldn't still kill the person, only that it made him wonder who the person was before they got tossed up in a situation with the Family.

One day, David's own son, William, would get curious about him. David knew that. And what would he find out? That he was a psychopath. Jennifer would try to tell him otherwise, but the kid, he was smart, sensitive, too, like Jennifer was, and he'd figure out his father was a piece of shit. And then maybe he'd figure out his grandfather was, too, because no good man gets thrown off of the IBM Building. How far back would William take it? To the beginning of Chicago? David's own father used to tell him that their great-grandfather was one of the guys running liquor when the World's Fair came to town in 1893, but who knew, really? Maybe William would find out all of it and realize he came from a long line of criminals and he'd become a fed and would one day knock on the temple door to arrest his old man.

Some things, David thought, *kids just didn't ever need to know about their parents*. David moved from behind his desk and sat down on the floor next to Sophie.

"What are Barbie and Ken up to?" David asked.

"They're going to clean houses," Sophie said, "just like you and Daddy."

CHAPTER ELEVEN

Rabbi David Cohen never returned to the scene of a crime. It's how people ended up getting fingered by previously forgetful witnesses or caught on surveillance cameras. And yet here he was pulling into the same parking spot Slim Joe had used in front of the tanning salon on his last day alive. Of course, no one had bothered to report Slim Joe missing, since he was the kind of guy most people were happy to not see again—and David never bothered to ask Bennie about Slim Joe's mother, but it was safe to assume she was on a permanent vacation now.

Since Bennie had instructed David to never set foot inside a casino on account of their facial recognition software, David couldn't really complain about Rachel Savone's desire to meet at a neighborhood restaurant like Grape Street even if it happened to be in the same shopping center as Slim Joe's favorite tanning salon. It was one of those restaurants David would never visit on his own—he had a standing policy that forbade him from ever going into a joint that had a chalkboard outside, and this place, he saw when he got to the front door, had two, one with a list of the day's specials, another with a list of appropriate wine to go along with each special.

David walked back to his car and, as discreetly as possible, removed the butterfly knife he kept in his sock, and put it in the glove box. No need to tempt fate, particularly since the idea of spending an hour anywhere talking to Bennie's wife without some kind of medication—be it in pill or liquid form—had him considering ways to potentially kill *himself*, not to mention anyone who might make him, something he was always wary of when out in public, even though he still didn't recognize himself in the mirror.

This all had the potential to turn black quickly. But before he could make a break for it, Rachel pulled up in her little silver Mercedes convertible, the top down even though it was only about sixty degrees outside. She was on the phone, and when she saw David she waved at him but didn't hang up.

David watched her for a few moments, tried to decide if he found her attractive or if it was just that he hadn't spent any time alone with a woman—in a physical way—in almost a year. It was easy for him to dismiss these thoughts at the temple, since most of the women there were so wracked with worry or guilt or some kind of existential crisis that he wasn't able to look at them as women at all. They were just bundles of problems clothed in expensive leisure wear.

With Rachel, though, David felt a small sense of familiarity. It wasn't that she reminded him of Jennifer exactly. As far as he could tell, they were completely different from one another in almost every plausible way—Jennifer would no sooner drive around in a convertible Mercedes while talking on a cell phone than she would ride on the back of a motorcycle with her ass hanging out—except in one sense: They were both married to bad men.

It took a special kind of woman to decide that hitching up with a mob hit man and freelance professional killer (or, in Rachel's case, a Mafia boss who probably didn't kill a lot of people with his own hands anymore but likely had done a fair share of that sort of thing back when they were dating) was a fun way to spend not merely a few dates but also the rest of her life.

Maybe it was exciting at first, when everyone was young and stupid and watched a lot of dumb movies, but once things got solid, once bills came due and there were kids and broken radiators and car payments and funerals, along with all the other tiny disasters that made up the daily life of a married couple, you had to want it. You had to call what you had love. You had to look at that person in bed next to you and respect him, even if you knew the truth about what he was.

"Sorry I'm late," Rachel said when she finally reached David. "It's been a crazy day." She was wearing a light blue sweater set, black trousers that widened around her ankles, so that David couldn't see her shoes, no sunglasses. She had on the same jewelry she always wore—diamond earrings, the simple gold necklace, the nice wedding ring he'd first noticed at the Hanukkah carnival—and carried an expensive-looking handbag.

"I just got here," David said.

"If you're anything like my father," she said, "you'll just love this place."

"What about Mr. Savone?"

"Oh, he won't come here," she said. "He won't go anywhere near a wine bar."

■

After ordering, it took Rachel twenty minutes to finally address the purpose of their meeting, filling up the time with idle chatter about the temple before letting them both get in a few bites of their Caesar salads. "I'm sorry," she said. "I'm just sitting here babbling. You must get so tired of listening to women babble."

"It's fine," David said, because it was, for the most part. She hadn't yet asked him to solve anything, which was different than every other conversation he'd had over the last two months.

"No, no, it really isn't," she said. "When my father was your age, he didn't have to deal with what you have to deal with. He could come home at the end of the day and not feel like he'd been party to every single injustice of the world, just the ones facing the Jews." She took a sip of wine—she ordered a bottle of Merlot immediately upon sitting down, and most of it was gone—and then stared at David for a long moment. "Why don't you have a wife yet, Rabbi, if you don't mind me asking?"

"Married to the job," David said. It was a line he'd used about ten thousand times since taking his position at the temple, every young mother in the place wanting to set him up with a single friend, every old-timer wanting to introduce him to their daughters or granddaughters.

"Everyone says Las Vegas is a great place to be single," she said, "but I don't believe that. It can be pretty lonely if you're looking for a girl to start a family with."

"Well, that's not my priority right now." David tried to smile at Rachel, but it didn't feel natural. It never felt natural. It wasn't that his face still felt like a mask, though it did; rather, it was that he'd spent so many years trying not to smile, growing up so hard, anything that was happy had the elastic snap of shit, so it was easier to just treat everything evenly. Once he got in the business, he didn't want to be one of those assholes who ended up with a nickname like "Smiley" or "Gums."

"If it becomes one," she said, "let me know."

"I will," he said.

"My father says you're an excellent young rabbi," Rachel said.

"Your father is a kind man."

"My father can be an asshole," Rachel said, without a trace of anger, "but I love him." She took another sip of her wine and then refilled her glass with the rest of the bottle. "I'm sorry we haven't had the chance to talk much, because everyone says you're an incredible listener. Claudia Levine thinks you're wonderful."

"Yes, well," David said.

This got Rachel to smile. "My father teach you to say that?"

"It's taught on the first day of rabbinical school," he said, and they both laughed.

"This feels good," Rachel said. "I don't remember the last time I laughed."

"If you could just laugh and cry in a single sound," David said.

"Maimonides?" Rachel asked.

"Springsteen," David said. This made Rachel laugh again. David took a sip of his wine, felt his face get a little warm, felt the muscles in his shoulders relax a bit. It wasn't like drinking Scotch, but at this point, it was better than drinking water. Maybe things would turn out okay today.

Three tables over, David saw a familiar face. "Is that Oscar Goodman?" he asked.

Rachel looked over her shoulder. "Everyone comes here," she said.

"Looks like he'll be mayor," David said, trying to make conversation, but also trying to figure out just how connected the Savones were.

"It will be good for the city," she said. "He was on the board at Beth Shalom for years, so he knows what it's like to work with intractable ideologues."

So that answered that.

"What has my husband told you about me?" Rachel was still smiling, but David could see that something had hardened inside of her, that she'd moved on to the part of the conversation she'd been dreading, too. He found that to be somewhat of a relief. For once, even ground.

"Nothing, really," David said.

"I'm sorry," she said, "but I find that hard to believe. He spends more time with you than he does with anyone, except for his lawyer."

"What we talk about is . . . ," David began, but Rachel waved him off.

"I know, I know," she said. "It's confidential."

"Actually," David said, "it's mostly business related. Your husband has been very good to the temple. I really can't thank him enough." These were sentences David had practiced a thousand times in preparation for anyone asking about his relationship with Bennie Savone. "We've also had many interesting talks about his faith, which, as I'm sure you know, is a constant challenge."

Rachel shook her head and laughed again. "Rabbi," she said, "I appreciate that you're trying to be polite, but you don't need to be. I know who my husband is."

"He's said you're unhappy," David said.

"Understatement of the year," she said, "and we're only in January, so maybe I should include last year, too."

"And that you're not well, physically."

This time Rachel didn't laugh. "I'm glad he's aware of these things. I'm glad he can talk to you. It would be nice if he could talk to me."

"He's a complicated person," David said, because he didn't know what else to say.

"He's not complicated," she said, "he's a liar. There's a difference, if you don't mind me saying, Rabbi."

Thankfully, their waiter arrived and dropped off their lunch. David ordered the chicken Marsala on Rachel's recommendation, though now he realized he probably wasn't going to get a chance to enjoy it since Rachel was already dabbing at her eyes in a futile attempt to save her makeup from the tears. He took his handkerchief out of his breast pocket—the advantage of wearing a nice suit every day, David now realized, was that you were forced to be a gentleman around crying women, even if you didn't want to be—and slid it across the table.

"Thank you," she said. "Look at me. Crying in the middle of a restaurant."

"The Talmud tells us that even when the gates of heaven are shut to prayer, they are open to tears," David said.

"I'm going to leave him," she said.

David looked around the restaurant, tried to figure out if there was any way Bennie might have bugged it. The guy behind the bar pouring wine into tiny tasting glasses, maybe he was wired up. Maybe the waiter. Maybe Oscar Goodman, walking out right then, was headed off to report directly to Bennie.

"I'm sorry," David said. "Did you say were considering leaving Mr. Savone?"

"Not considering it, doing it," she said. "That's why I wanted to talk to you. My father, he won't listen, tells me to just suffer through it. I can't talk to my girlfriends about it. I can't talk to anyone, really, except for you." She reached across the table and took David's hand. Everyone always wanted to touch his hand, as if whatever wisdom he might have could be delivered through the sweat of his palm, which, in this case, might have been closer to the truth, since David was certain he was sweating like a Baptist preacher. "I'm not a young woman anymore, Rabbi. Don't I deserve to be happy? Don't I deserve to be loved by someone capable of love?"

"You're still a young woman," David said.

"I'm thirty-nine," she said. "I'll be forty in six months. That will make it official."

"I think you need to consider all of your options here," he said.

"That's what I'm doing," she said. She covered his hand with both her hands now, making a minifurnace that was heating his entire body.

David examined the table for something sharp, but the waiter had taken the steak knives from the table. He didn't know what he was looking to cut, anyway, other than maybe his own arm off at the wrist. At this point, he could probably do the job with a spoon.

"You have to consider your children," David said, figuring that was a good place to start, a good way station for Rachel while he figured out what he was going to do with this information.

"They wouldn't miss him," Rachel said. "Sophie might, I guess, but Jean knows what kind of man her father is. Thirteen going on forty-five, that one. I'm not going to wait another ten years for Sophie to get the picture, Rabbi. I can't do that."

David flipped through his mental Rolodex looking for some kind of Talmudic interpretation of divorce that would make Rachel realize the error of her ways. Not that the Talmud forbade divorce—the Jews were pretty forthright on it, much to David's surprise, allowing that a life in a bad marriage was no life at all and that a divorce, while not a great option, was nonetheless an inevitable one. And this wasn't even a modern interpretation.

Still. This was not acceptable.

"Have you thought about marriage counseling?"

"He's not the marriage counseling type," she said.

"Yet you think he's the divorce court type." Rachel flinched in her seat, and David realized he had slipped into his old voice, that his cadence was off. Shit. Still, it gave him an opening to remove his hand from her grip. He cleared his throat. Took a sip of wine. Grabbed a waiter, asked for a knife. Cut a piece of chicken, dipped it in the Marsala sauce, put it in his mouth, chewed as deliberately as he could . . . and all the while, Rachel stared at him in something like muted wonder.

"Maybe I can't divorce him," Rachel said, her voice sounding resigned. "But that doesn't mean I can't leave him."

"Do you think you'll just run off? You think you can do that?" He cut another piece of chicken, swirled some pasta onto his fork, swallowed it all down without even chewing. There was that voice again. "How will you survive?" Dammit. "Financially. How will you survive financially if you just run off? That's something to consider." Another bite of chicken. A gulp of wine.

"Well," she said, "eventually I'll inherit the funeral home from my father." She sat back from the table and exhaled. "It's not a business I'm interested in, but it's not like there's ever a down season, if my father is to be believed."

"Rabbi Kales is a long way from being dead," David said, though he wasn't entirely sure that was true. Was it possible that Bennie didn't know this salient bit of information concerning the funeral home? David didn't imagine Rachel would want to be the owner of a funeral home that was laundering money . . . and bodies . . . for the Mafia. And then there was the new tissue business . . . and whatever else David and Bennie could dream up. More importantly, it was the cash cow that was going to get David back to Chicago, back to Jennifer and William, back to Sal Cupertine.

Oh, he thought, *this will not do.*

"Of course, of course," she said. "But you know he's been slipping, mentally, for a while now. I'm sure he hides it well when he's at work, but, Rabbi, there's a reason you're here now, obviously."

"Obviously," David said.

"My point is, my father is not going to be able to run the business for much longer regardless," she said. "I'll need to get power of attorney, so if need be, I can step in to handle his affairs. I don't want to, but if my husband won't support his children, what choice would I have?"

That Rachel wasn't aware her father was not running the funeral home, even now, was a concern. If she began digging— or had a lawyer start digging—that would not be good. David didn't like the idea that he might need to kill Bennie's wife. He also didn't like the idea of going to prison.

"Let me think for a moment," he said.

"Of course, of course," Rachel said.

David had learned that if you really wanted to get people to listen to you, it was important to pretend that you needed a moment to listen to God before coming up with a proper answer to something. David did this by closing his eyes and breathing slowly. Except when he closed his eyes, he wasn't talking to God as much as he was trying to figure out how not to choke the life from the person sitting in front of him.

In this case, he was trying to decide if it would be better, all things considered, to simply follow Rachel out to the parking lot, and as she was walking up to her car, shoot her once in the back of the head. Except he didn't have a gun on him. Just that knife, which was now in the car. He could stab her in the throat with a fork, but that felt too personal, and, generally, people tended to notice a person geysering blood from her neck in the middle of a crowded parking lot.

And, he didn't kill women. It seemed like an irredeemable trait, even among a series of what would normally be highly irredeemable traits. Yeah, the Russians and the Kosher Nostra in Chicago did it, but they did it for reasons completely unlike this one. This was an issue of preservation, not to collect a debt, which, actually, sounded like a better reason on the face of things. But, still. He had to take that option off the table. What else was there?

Reason, he supposed. He could attempt to reason with Rachel. Or maybe he could lead her to see the folly of her ways by pointing out how fucked she was if she even thought she could walk out on Bennie Savone.

"It was my understanding," David said, his eyes still closed, "that your husband helped your father purchase the funeral home. Is that correct?"

"That was years ago," she said. "That debt has been paid, I'm sure." David couldn't tell if there was any sarcasm in Rachel's response or if he was looking for . . . something, anything, to get an idea of what Bennie had on Rabbi Kales.

He opened his eyes and tried to be as soothing as possible, tried to make Rachel change her mind based solely on answering simple questions. It was a tactic he learned from some old hard knocks in the Family when they tried to get information out of people before whacking them. "Are you certain?"

Rachel exhaled deeply, again. "I guess I'm not," she said. "Bennie isn't exactly forthcoming with these sorts of matters." She paused. "I guess I could ask my father, but he's already advised me that I'm being foolish, for any number of reasons, even considering this. But you understand, don't you, Rabbi Cohen? I have a right to be in a marriage that I find fulfilling, don't I?"

"Of course," he said. "Let me ask you a question. Do you think any of this has to do with your recent medical problems?"

"No," she said . . . too quickly in David's opinion.

"Because I know how going through the change of life can make one start to reevaluate one's choices from a place that is more emotional than reasonable."

"How do you know that, Rabbi? Do you have a lot of experience going through the 'change of life,' as you put it?"

"Talmud tells us to look not at the pitcher but at what it contains," David said.

"It contains bullshit and recrimination and lies," Rachel said. She flagged down a waiter and asked for another bottle of wine, this time a Chianti. "Rabbi, I'd be curious what you know about your body betraying you. Do you know I'm going to need a hysterectomy? Do you know that? Don't you think that I'd like my loving husband around when I was going through that? Doesn't that sound reasonable to you?"

"Lower your voice," David said. This time, he used his old voice intentionally.

The waiter came by and refilled Rachel's glass and then left the bottle in the center of the table. Rachel picked it up and examined the label. "Last good thing that came out of Italy," she said quietly. "Do you know where I went to get married?"

"No," David said.

"Florence," she said. "This was 1982. I was twenty-two, and Bennie, he was a big shot, thirty years old, money falling out of his pockets, that's what I thought, anyway. But you know, when you're young, someone with a thousand dollars seems rich. I wanted to get married at Temple Isaiah when it was still down on Oakey, but because Bennie wasn't Jewish, they made a real stink about it. My father was a rabbi there, so he didn't care, obviously, but the board wouldn't let it happen for political reasons, which is just a fancy way of saying they didn't want to have Bennie's family showing up in photos inside the temple, not when one of their members was about to run for the Senate. So Bennie says, *Fuck them*. He said that to me. I remember it clear as day. He said, *Fuck them*. So he flew my family, all of my friends, all of his friends and family, plus anyone who was a member of Isaiah that wanted to come, flew everyone to Florence, and I got married at the Great Synagogue of Florence."

"That sounds like a good time," David said.

"It was," she said. "But it took me until recently to realize he didn't do it out of a sense of justice, or even to make me happy. He did it out of spite. Maybe I should have seen that back then, but what do you know when you're twenty-two?"

"You think you know everything," David said.

"That's right," she said. "That's so right, Rabbi. You think you know everything. You think your whole life is going to be what it is at that very moment, can't imagine anything ever being different, can't imagine you'll ever feel differently about the things you don't care about, if that makes sense. A year later, my mother would be dead from ovarian cancer, and all of a sudden, I realize how young I am. That all I want is my mommy. So here I am now, with these two girls, and I'm realizing my entire marriage is based mostly on spite. That is not a pleasant experience, Rabbi. I don't want my daughters to look back and think that their mother let them live a horrible life."

The problem David faced on a semiregular basis when talking to his congregants was that he just couldn't relate to their issues, but Rachel's problem was one that David had become intimate with since the night he found himself in a frozen truck filled with meat and nothing but time to think. It was hard, after having a kid, not to start thinking about your legacy. Though, admittedly, David hadn't really started contemplating what he was leaving behind for William until he was already gone, which was strange since he'd been thinking more and more about his own father, and his trip off that building.

Still, he couldn't very well just let Rachel sneak out in the middle of the night, particularly since he was pretty certain he'd be the one who'd have to chase her down.

"My advice," David said, "is that you need to look inside yourself first and see precisely what you're dissatisfied with. I think you may find, ultimately, that your husband is not at fault here. Let the Torah speak to you."

Rachel pushed her plate of uneaten bow-tie pasta and vegetables to the side of the table so she could make room for her purse, which she turned over and dumped onto the table. Among the items was a Saturday night special, a little silver-and-black Lorcin .380, a piece of shit, really, mostly a paperweight.

"Do you see this?" she said.

"The gun?"

"Of course the gun," she said. "Why aren't you freaking out?"

"It's not pointed at me," David said. "And I'm not scared to die." He picked up the gun and examined it on his lap. Nice weight to it, actually, though David couldn't believe Bennie allowed his wife to leave the house with anything less than a nine. Then it occurred to him: He probably didn't even know she was packing . . . and that was probably the point of this little exercise. David wrapped the gun in his napkin, wiped it down, and then set it back on the table with the napkin on top of it. "It would be a good idea to put the safety on, otherwise you might kill your purse."

"I have to carry a gun because of my husband, Rabbi. Today, I'm going to pick up Jean and take her to softball practice, and I'm going to have a killing machine in my purse. Because of him. And because I think people will try to hurt me when I'm with him," she said. "Or hurt my children. So don't tell me this is somehow my fault. Okay?"

Half the restaurant was already eavesdropping on their conversation now, never mind all of the staff. Peopled tended to notice the word "gun," and if the restaurant had anything approaching halfway decent lighting, they would have all been under the tables after she dumped the .380 next to the salt and pepper. "I'm a mess. Jesus. I'm a mess," Rachel said quietly. She patted her face with powder from her compact, which made it look like she was trying to hide something. "How's this?"

"Better," he said.

Rachel gathered herself, even tried to smile. "I'm not asking for your permission, Rabbi, I'm asking for your guidance. So please, Rabbi, please, give me some idea of hope."

He needed to get out of this conversation and this restaurant. "Okay," he said. He was in an absurd situation, he recognized. Here he was, a man who'd spent his entire life killing people, sitting across from a woman with a gun, attempting to convince her that the world was a safe and good place, even in the face of what he knew was a terrible decision on her part, a terrible decision that could ruin his own life even more. "Your husband is not trying to hurt you," David said calmly.

"How do you know that?"

"Because if he wanted to hurt you," David said, again, calm as can be, "my understanding is that you'd already be hurt." Rachel's eyes widened, but David kept staring into them, hoping she'd get the subtext he was trying to impart, without revealing too much about himself in the process. "So my idea for hope is this: Live your life for yourself and your children, but do not put yourself in a position where your husband is forced to act . . . irrationally."

"Jesus Christ," Rachel said. "He's gotten to you, hasn't he?"

"No one has gotten to me," David said.

"You're lying."

"Mrs. Savone," David said, "I have never been more honest than I am right now. I'm a rabbi, I'm not an idiot. I get the same newspaper as you. It's all right there."

Rachel stared at David for a long time, then chuckled to herself. "I should have seen it," she said. "I don't know how I missed it."

"Seen what?"

"Nothing," she said. "Nothing at all." Rachel looked at her watch. "I need to go," she said, a smile wide across her face now, as if she'd discovered something particularly fantastic. "I have an appointment."

"Don't do anything stupid," David said.

"I was going to get Botox, if you must know," she said. She stood up and came around to David's side of the table, kneeled down next to him so he could really see her face. "Do you see these lines around my mouth?"

"No," he said.

"You *are* a liar." She touched him lightly on the face, just under his left ear, where his beard still didn't grow correctly. "You almost can't see your scars anymore." She let her hand linger on his cheek for just a moment, then smiled again, this time in a way that seemed terribly unhappy. "Dr. Kirsch did my face, too," she said.

■

That afternoon, David sat on a chaise lounge out by his pool, smoked a cigar, and tried to figure out the best way to escape. It had warmed up into the low seventies, the sky was a deep blue, and in the distance he could hear the sound of children laughing.

David got up from the chaise lounge and walked the perimeter, tried to gather his thoughts into a straight line, see if he might be able to make some decisions. If Fat Monte was really dead—and David didn't doubt the veracity of the information Bennie had given him, only that sometimes people in the Family who were presumed dead ended up alive—that was one less impediment to his returning home, or at least one less person who might hurt Jennifer and William. Not that Ronnie wouldn't be happy to farm that out to the Gangster 2-6, or just some tweaks willing to kill a family for a grand a head, maybe less.

No, if he wanted to get back to Chicago and be assured of his family's safety, he'd need to have Ronnie put out to pasture. Because the more he thought about it, the more David began to suspect that none of this was an accident, that there'd been a plan in place to get Sal in trouble, that preyed on his desire for a better life, a dangling carrot that moved him out of the shadows (where he frankly enjoyed working) and into what amounted to a business meeting with the FBI. Sal Cupertine *should* have died that day. Four against one. But once he was out on the streets, Ronnie must have moved on to plan B.

Jewish custom said to meet all sorrow standing up, and that's what David was trying to do. Ronnie clearly wanted him gone, which meant there was something he didn't want him to learn, something that would eventually matter enough to David that he'd kill his own cousin.

Problem was that Ronnie was nearly impossible to get to. He was never alone, even out in public, kids on the street running up to get their pictures taken with the used-car salesman/gangster from the TV. And no one local would be dumb enough to take the contract, not even one of the scads of crooked Chicago cops, half of whom were on Ronnie's book, anyway.

David was getting way ahead of himself, indulging in the same fantasy he'd been having for months now. He needed to handle Las Vegas first, then worry about Chicago. Except for one thing: He needed to get some money to Jennifer, let her know somehow he was still alive without tipping off the feds. Ah, the feds. Jeff Hopper, another dead man that was suddenly alive. Another person he needed to handle.

A brown Southwest plane flew overhead, and David traced its path as it descended down toward McCarran Airport. Every forty-five minutes, the same brown plane would pass overhead, either coming or going, David wondering if anyone ever bothered to look at what was really underneath them: a fetid sunburnt bowl of dust in the middle of nothing. Just another Pleasure Island, filled with liars and thieves.

Money. That was the first order of business. He had to figure out a way for Jennifer to get a good sum, in case Ronnie cut her off, because now that Monte was dead, he'd be tightening the noose in order to keep her quiet.

Problem was, he didn't quite know how to get her money in a way that wouldn't be tracked. This would take some finessing.

What David also knew for certain was that Dr. Kirsch needed to disappear, though David couldn't very well make it look like an accident, not with Rachel aware of . . . something. And what did she know? That he'd had plastic surgery? What did that prove? Nothing. Nothing at all.

Except Rachel Savone knew her husband was in the Mafia. And now she thought she knew something about him, something that wasn't possible to prove, because there was no David Cohen. He didn't exist. Yeah, he had all the right papers, but how far would those papers take him? If Bennie wouldn't let him go inside a casino for fear of the facial recognition cameras, he sure wasn't about to go into the airport or even out of Las Vegas.

David needed to have a conversation with Rabbi Kales. A candid, open conversation where David made it clear that he had no problem killing him unless Rabbi Kales let him know what Bennie had on him. And then, if need be, he'd handle Rachel, too. He wasn't about to let Bennie know about her plans, however, because then it would be an *order* to make her disappear. No, first, he'd make sure the funeral home was willed properly, see that it was left to the temple, not to Rachel, and if that meant he did it with a gun to Rabbi Kales's head, then so be it.

But how long would it take for the feds to start sniffing up the freeway from the strip club and into Bennie's personal life? How long before they saw how much money he'd donated to the temple? How long before there was a subpoena to look at the temple's books? David figured that Bennie was smart enough to avoid that sort of impropriety—he was sure of it— but that didn't mean the feds wouldn't want to eventually sit down and talk to him just to make Bennie sweat.

David went inside the house and came back out a few minutes later with a yellow legal pad, a ballpoint pen, a glass of Macallan 30 year, and his copy of the Torah. He made a list of all the people he needed to deal with locally—including, eventually, the bouncers who'd beaten the tourist in the first place, since they were out on bail pending trial, and who knew what they might say—then ripped off the page and made a list of all the people in Chicago he needed to deal with, with Jeff Hopper's name on the top. He tore that page off the pad and folded both it and the Las Vegas list together and shoved them in the Torah, so he'd have easy access to them, a reminder as to why he was doing all this in the first place.

He then made a short list of all the materials he'd need: guns, some decent knives in case he decided to go that route, steel-toe boots, gloves, bleach, some S.O.S pads, hollow-point bullets, a length of rope . . . It had been a long time since he'd put together a decent murder kit, so he had to remind himself of all the important instruments he liked to keep nearby.

Which reminded David of one other important detail. He went back inside and came back with the bottle of Macallan, the Yellow Pages, and the telephone. He poured himself another drink and flipped through the phone book, finally landing on the listing for building supply outfits. The first one listed was A & A Construction Supply, which David thought was cheating, since he was sure there was no one there actually named A or A, so he scanned down the page until he landed on Kerby's Machine Tools Direct & Rental. The store was located out on the other side of Craig Road, about ten miles away. There wasn't much development out that way yet—a casino, of course, and an overpriced movie theatre, but no decent houses, which was perfect, since no decent houses meant the Jews weren't thick on the ground. Last thing David wanted was to run into one of the Israelites while he was busy doing his other job. He'd practically screwed the pooch with Rachel today, and that was when he was at least quasi-prepared.

Kerby's answered on the first ring.

"Yes," David said, "I'd like to rent a portable foundry."

CHAPTER TWELVE

Rural southern Illinois had become one blurred grain silo and field of dirty snow. Jeff Hopper sat in the backseat of a black Chevy Suburban driven by Senior Special Agent Kirk Biglione, marking time by the distance between cities he'd never visit—Pontiac to Normal to Lincoln and beyond. A person could hide out here forever.

"You comfortable back there, Hopper?" Biglione asked. Jeff didn't respond. "Be happy you're not in cuffs," Biglione said, which made the guy sitting next to him up front, an agent named Lee Poremba whom Hopper worked organized crime with years previous in Kansas City, turn and glare. Turns out no one found Kirk Biglione amusing.

They'd been driving south on I-55 for nearly five hours, headed for Kochel Farms, located between Divernon and Farmersville, the middle of the middle of nothing. The plan was to meet up with the U.S. Marshals to serve a warrant right around kickoff of the Super Bowl, hopefully ensuring that no standoff would occur, the FBI always preferring to do their raids on days when they knew family would be around—Thanksgiving,

Christmas, Super Bowl Sunday—or when they knew even the worst dirtbag on the planet was likely to be home sitting on his sofa. Not that Jeff believed they'd roll up on the place and find the farm's owner eating chips and salsa with Sal Cupertine.

Kochel Farms had been owned by a man named Mel Kochel Jr. since 1979. The farm and the thirty thousand head of cattle that were routinely slaughtered to fill up grocery stores and fast-food restaurants around the country had been around much longer than that, started by Mel Sr. back in 1959, but the day-to-day operations of the farm had been transferred recently to Mel Jr.'s son Trey.

There wasn't a hint of criminal activity related to the Kochel family, unless one considered Trey's speeding ticket in 1992 an act of domestic terrorism. In the weeks since Fat Monte's suicide, every conceivable avenue into the Family's involvement with the farm had been investigated, and all the FBI had been able to prove—and even this could be met with some reasonable doubt—was that one of the Family's bars in Bridgeport, the Sidewinder, occasionally bought ground beef from a distributer who occasionally got meat from Kochel Farms. In essence, the only relationship was one of mere happenstance.

That didn't mean there *wasn't* something, Jeff understood, only that it was buried so deep it didn't exist on paper. Fat Monte didn't just throw out the name *Kochel Farms* because he saw it on the side of a truck and thought it would be a funny joke to play on the FBI, not after he'd already buried a bullet in his wife's head, and not while he was working up the guts to put one through his. Jeff knew that much. What Kochel Farms really meant was another matter.

Could be Sal Cupertine was now a Big Mac, but that just didn't make a lot of sense. He couldn't see Ronnie Cupertine engaging the services of civilians to help get rid of one of his dead bodies. There was just too much risk involved in having some ten-dollar-an-hour farm employee shove a human being into the slaughterer, even if Ronnie had Fat Monte hand over a stack of bills in compensation. Could be it was Chema Espinoza or Neal Moretti who did the honors—not that they'd found Neal's body in that landfill, nor did Jeff think they ever would—but, still, why would Ronnie bother making them do it all the way out here, when they could have used whoever was doing the job Paul Bruno used to do? Not that they'd found his body, either.

If Kochel Farms was somehow involved in the disappearance of Sal Cupertine, Jeff thought it was a more passive experience . . . a point he'd been trying to elucidate to the FBI for the last several weeks to little avail. Which also made perfect sense, since the leadership of the FBI in Chicago weren't exactly charter members of the Jeff Hopper Fan Club, not after the Fat Monte suicide hit the *Sun-Times* and *Tribune*.

It took a few days for everything to come out due mostly to the fact that Chicago was more interested in dealing with the fallout of the blizzard that had drilled the city than the suicide of a gangster and the attempted murder of his wife. But once the city began to thaw and journalists could actually get to their offices, what had been a page 3 blip turned into a front-page embarrassment with "confidential sources" confirming that "Family enforcer" Fat Monte Moretti's last conversation had been with an FBI agent, who, it turned out, was currently on paid administrative leave for misconduct. Those same "confidential sources" were happy to suggest that the agent in question was Jeff Hopper and that it was believed he would soon be relieved of his duties completely, particularly in light of the murder of four people under his supervision the year previous and his now questionable relationship with a known crime figure.

Jeff was pretty sure that the "confidential sources" named in all the stories was in fact Kirk Biglione, who at the moment was trying to explain to Special Agent Poremba how much he was going to enjoy Chicago once spring came around, now that Poremba had been hired ostensibly to replace Jeff. "Lots of great restaurants," Biglione said. "And if you like to hunt or fish, it's just a couple hours to some great spots in Wisconsin. I've got this place I've been dreaming about building in Fond du Lac."

"I don't hunt or fish," Poremba said.

"What do you like?" Biglione asked.

In the time Jeff had worked with Lee Poremba, that was the one question everyone had about him: He didn't seem to like anything other than his job, which made him, at the time, seem like one of those guys ready to stab you in the back. Except it just happened that he was a fairly boring guy who had a pretty firm vision of what his life would be like, one where he caught bad guys and then went home and tended to his three springer spaniels. This was information Jeff had learned only after being asked to do some background on him when he was up for a promotion in Kansas City, as the FBI was typically concerned with agents who didn't seem to exist outside their jobs. It wasn't normal not to leave some kind of footprint, somewhere.

It had been several years since he'd done the background report on Poremba, but Jeff still remembered the most salient details of his life: a brother in Tampa, an ex-wife in Santa Fe, and, as far as Jeff could find, no one else. Incorruptible, Jeff had said about him in his report, because his tastes are so base. A good book, his dogs, a place to sit, a matinee movie every Saturday afternoon when he wasn't working. And if he was working, he'd see a matinee on Sunday instead. Preferred romantic comedies and anything with talking animals.

"I like to read," Poremba said.

"You still have springers?" Jeff asked.

Poremba turned in his seat and stared at Jeff for a few seconds. "Yes," he said finally. "They're still in Kansas City at a kennel. Can't have them living with me at the Comfort Suites."

"Last I knew," Jeff said, "you had three of them. You'll need a place with a yard in Chicago. Probably need to look out in the suburbs. Batavia is nice, I hear."

"I don't know how long I'll be staying," Poremba said.

"Oh yeah?" Jeff said. "I thought you were permanent."

"I have a feeling I'll be moving around some in the next few weeks," he said.

"I wouldn't be so sure about that," Biglione said. "We may find what we're looking for today, and then you're knee-deep in moving boxes by the end of the week."

"Maybe," Poremba said. Biglione was technically Poremba's equal in rank, but it was clear to Jeff that Poremba had been brought in to fix a potential nightmare for the FBI. Once word got out that the body in the dump wasn't Sal Cupertine, or that there was another body somewhere in the dump that they couldn't find, big questions about the FBI's investigation into the Family would begin to be asked. The only reason the press hadn't discovered this information already had a lot to do with the present situation Jeff Hopper found himself in.

As soon as Jeff heard Fat Monte's body hit the floor, he knew that the rules had changed. In all his time working organized crime, he'd never run into a made guy killing himself outside of prison, and even then it was rare. That he tried to kill his wife, too? That didn't happen, ever. He also knew the fact that Fat Monte was on the phone with him would be the sort of thing that the press would eventually discover, which meant it was the sort of thing the FBI would offer up to them in form of sacrifice—a juicy tidbit that might keep them from digging much further into the real story, namely why Sal Cupertine was allowed to disappear. As it happened, it wasn't that much different than the Family offering up the body of Chema Espinoza. Tit for tat, everyone stays in business, and the world keeps spinning.

It was how business was conducted in Chicago. And it made Jeff Hopper sick to know he was going to need to cut a similar deal if he wanted to protect the one person with something real to lose: Matthew. The only way to do that was to push the FBI into a corner. Jeff knew he had the one thing that the FBI needed: information.

If the public learned about the FBI's decision to let the body of Chema Espinoza stand in for Sal Cupertine's, even to the point of having what was left of the body cremated and delivered to Jennifer Cupertine simply so they could solve the murder of their three agents and CI without compromising their long-term investigation into the Family, there was a good chance Roosevelt Road would be filled with people carrying torches. Worse were the families of the dead men, all of whom had been led to believe that justice had been served, even if it had been meted out on the streets. You couldn't ask for more than having the man who killed your husband or brother or son found disemboweled and burnt . . . particularly since Jeff was certain Special Agent Biglione had intimated to the families that it was more like vigilante justice that caused the body to be found versus the Family trying to smooth out a bit of salve.

Let the families believe the FBI took care of the problem Old West–style, and everyone goes home feeling a little better. It was the sort of thing Biglione would do. Hell, it was the sort of thing Jeff would have done, too.

So, that frozen night, after Fat Monte blew his head off, Jeff made two calls. The first was to 911, to report a likely suicide, maybe a murder-suicide, all of which put Jeff on the public record. The next call was to Kirk Biglione at his home in Barrington. He could have called Biglione's cell, but Jeff wanted to make sure his number showed up on Biglione's home phone records, something easily subpoenaed, and wanted to make sure it showed up within minutes of Fat Monte's death. Plus, there was a good chance Biglione's phone calls were monitored, if not actively, at least passively, just like everyone else's in the FBI. It was a fucked-up thing to do, Jeff realized even as he was dialing Biglione's number, but if there was one thing Jeff Hopper knew, it was that the FBI would happily bury him alive. He needed to make sure he had a way to breathe underground.

"Who is this?" Biglione asked when he came to the phone.

"It's Jeff Hopper," Jeff said. "I wanted you to know that Fat Monte Moretti just killed himself."

"What? How do you know this?" Biglione was just coming awake, and Jeff could hear the slow dawning of recognition in his voice. "Who is this?"

"It's Special Agent Jeff Hopper," Jeff said, "reporting to you that I was just speaking with Fat Monte Moretti on the telephone when he shot himself. It sounded like a .357, but I could be wrong. You'll need to check ballistics. I suspect he killed his wife, too." Jeff could hear Biglione's breathing. It sounded somewhat labored, so Jeff continued. "I was with him earlier this evening, at a bar called the Four Treys in Roscoe Village, where he essentially admitted to killing Paul Bruno, not that I expect you care about someone as insignificant as him, not with Sal Cupertine allowed to run free. About that, incidentally. Fat Monte confirmed for me Sal Cupertine's body was not disposed of in the landfill, and that, in fact, there were two bodies placed there, namely, uh, let me see here, one Neal Moretti and one Chema Espinoza. Seems like we found Espinoza but not Neal. Somewhere at the bottom of the landfill is another body."

"Hopper," Biglione said, "I'm going to hang up."

"Also," Jeff said, "I might have beat this information out of him. When you get his body, if there's not a hole in the middle of his face, you'll probably want to know how his nose got broken. That was me. I did that."

"Hopper," Biglione said again. This time it sounded more like a plea. "I'm hanging up. Do you understand? I'm hanging up."

"One more thing then," Jeff said. "Fat Monte indicated to me that Kochel Farms is somehow related to Sal Cupertine's disappearance and that we should begin investigating them in earnest."

"You're fired," Biglione said.

"I know," Jeff said, "so I'm going to go ahead and call some friends at the *Tribune* and see if they might like this information."

"We have an investigation, Agent Hopper," Biglione said. His voice was oddly calm now, and then Jeff remembered he used to do hostage negotiation back in the day, that he'd risen up in the ranks quickly after managing to get some lunatic in a Memphis bank to let twenty-two hostages go without anyone getting hurt. "If the Family finds out we're still investigating Sal Cupertine, it has the potential to ruin nearly a decade of work.

You *know* that. And if the Family knows we're looking for Sal Cupertine, it will make it that much harder to find him. You *know* that."

Of course Jeff knew that. This was all for the public—and private—record, Biglione likely coming to the same realization Jeff had in making the phone call in the first place. Asses needed to be covered.

"See, that's the problem, Kirk," Jeff said. "You're not looking for Sal Cupertine. No one is. Or was. But I have been. And do you want to know what I've found out? Or do you just want to read about it in the paper?" Biglione didn't respond, but Jeff's call waiting beeped. He pulled the phone from his ear and looked at the display—it was Biglione's cell phone. Jeff didn't bother to click over and instead just hung up. He'd expressed what needed to be expressed. They both knew he wasn't going to call the *Tribune*. At least not yet.

It was 4:42 in the morning, sunrise not for another two hours at least, when Jeff got into his Explorer and headed along the snow-packed streets of Chicago toward Matthew Drew's apartment building. It was one of the first times having a four-wheel drive SUV in the city actually made any practical sense, one of the few things that morning that did. As he drove, he tried to take stock of where the last several months had taken him. Had he committed any crimes? No, he had not. Had he done anything morally reprehensible?

He slammed his hand against the steering wheel. He was sure he had. He'd caused another human being to kill himself. It didn't matter that Fat Monte was a criminal. Jeff had to hope Fat Monte hadn't shot his wife. He slammed his hand again. What was he thinking? What *the fuck* was he thinking? An innocent woman was probably dead because he got it in his mind that he was going to do the right thing, that he was going to catch Sal Cupertine, who murdered four innocent men.

But, no. That wasn't true. Those four men weren't innocent. Those four men had taken part in a sting. For three of them, it was their job to be put in that situation. For the fourth, it was a result of getting caught being a criminal. No one was exactly innocent in that situation. It was a point Jeff had started to believe—an implied risk of doing this business was that they might very well die. The fault didn't rest with Jeff for leaving his name on the bill. And the fault hardly even rested with Sal Cupertine, when you really thought about it. No, he'd tried to convince himself, the fault resided in the implicit rules of the game. People die doing illegal things.

It took Jeff nearly thirty minutes to make the ten-minute drive to Matthew's building, and by the time he got there, he realized what a bad idea it would be for all involved if he was found on the apartment's closed-circuit security cameras, so he continued up the street to the White Palace and called Matthew's cell from the pay phone inside.

"What time is it?" Matthew asked when he answered.

"A little after five," Jeff said. "Do you know who this is?"

"No one calls me but you," he said, already catching on and not saying Jeff's name. Not that Jeff thought Matthew's cell phone was tapped, but you never knew. Matthew cleared his throat. "What's the problem?"

"Fat Monte is dead," Jeff said.

"Did you kill him?"

It was a reasonable question. "No," Jeff said.

"Did I?"

"Not unless you forced him to shoot himself in the head."

Matthew didn't respond for a long while, and then, when he did, all he said was, "Where are you?"

"The White Palace."

"I'll need to get a cab. My car is under three feet of snow."

"No," Jeff said, "wait, listen. You need to pack some clothes and get out of town for a few weeks. Your sister, too."

"That's not going to work," he said. "My sister can't just leave school. Do you hear what you're saying? Jesus. What's going on?"

Jeff told him what Fat Monte had said, told him about the phone call Jeff made to Biglione, told him that maybe Fat Monte's wife was gone, too. "I don't know what's going to happen next," Jeff said. "We could all be in danger if the Family decides to make a move."

"Give me thirty minutes to get my sister up and fill her in," Matthew said. "Order me a shake." Before Jeff could protest again, the phone was dead. Jeff made his way to a table and sat down. When the waitress came by, he asked her for a chocolate shake and if she might have a piece of paper and a manila envelope somewhere in the place that he could borrow. The waitress looked at him strangely, but it couldn't have been the most outrageous request anyone had made of her, particularly since she had a tattoo on her throat that said *Robert* and one on the back of her hand that said *Fuck All Men*.

The waitress came back a few moments later with the shake, a padded mailer, and a piece of college-ruled paper. "The manager says I have to charge you for the envelope," she said.

"Okay," Jeff said.

"You look familiar to me."

"I used to come here a lot," Jeff said.

She cocked her head. "Are you a cop?"

"FBI," he said, for what would be the last time in his life.

"Are you allowed to say that? Isn't that supposed to be a secret?"

"Nope," Jeff said. "That's the CIA."

"You all look alike, I guess," she said. "Enjoy your envelope."

Jeff took his car keys and cell phone out of his pocket and shoved them into the envelope, then scrawled a note to Matthew:

My truck is parked behind the restaurant. Take it. Pack your stuff up and be out of town before the morning news, if at all possible. Only use my phone. The charger is in the glove box. I'll call you tonight. Get out of Illinois. Tell your sister I'm sorry and that she'll be home in a week.

Jeff looked over the note, tried to decide if it was absurd or cautionary or just honest. It didn't matter in the long run, Jeff supposed, since what was most important here was that Matthew and Nina be safe, but also that the FBI had no ability to scapegoat Matthew. This was weight Jeff was willing to carry, and he had a plan.

He gathered up his heavy winter coat and gloves and walked to the cash register, where he waved the waitress over and handed her the envelope. "In a couple of minutes, another FBI agent is going to walk in here with a young woman. Give him this envelope," he said. "And the shake, too. That's for him."

"Am I on some hidden camera show?" the waitress asked.

Jeff looked around the White Palace. There was a camera above the register, another over the door, most likely a few around the outside of the building, too, everyone and everything captured, just in case anyone wanted to take a look. "Probably," Jeff said.

He walked out of the White Palace then and stood on the corner of Canal Street and Roosevelt. The FBI's offices were just two miles away down Roosevelt, a good twenty-minute walk in perfect weather, probably an hour through the snow-drifts that lined the street. Just enough time to get everything straight, so that when he stepped foot back inside the bureau, he'd know exactly what kind of deal he was willing to take.

■

It occurred to Jeff now, in the backseat of Biglione's Suburban, that he probably should have held out for a better deal. One that didn't involve him spending time with Biglione. As it was, agreeing to be fired—he didn't agree to be excoriated in the press, though he should have expected it—and hired back as an independent consultant with the proviso that the bureau would investigate the leads he'd found into Sal Cupertine's disappearance was probably more than he could have hoped for, but that was the agreement he made in exchange for not going to the press with any of the information he'd gleaned while on leave. Biglione didn't even mention Matthew while they negotiated the terms. In fact, it wasn't until three days later, when Biglione was going over the report Jeff had typed up on the information he'd learned (or, rather, the informa-tion he decided to share; Jeff had made a promise to Dennis Tryon regarding Neto Espinoza and he intended to keep it) that Matthew was brought up.

"So, where was Agent Drew in all of this?" Biglione asked. He had his glasses on and was still looking at the report, though Jeff could see he wasn't really reading it. Jeff knew that Biglione couldn't afford to find Sal Cupertine yet, which meant unless Cupertine showed up on their doorstep, they weren't going to go above and beyond to get him into custody. They'd follow the leads they had, because they had to. Fat Monte's wife was sitting in a hospital with a bullet wedged into her head. Alive, but only barely. Her eyes were open, she was breathing, but there wasn't much else going on. Just enough for her family to keep her alive and to keep the pressure on the FBI about Fat Monte's last hours alive.

"I'm not sure I get what you mean," Jeff said, though he was certain he knew exactly what he meant. The bureau had likely combed through all his affairs from the last few months, and it wouldn't have taken them long to see that he'd written Matthew checks every month.

"I got a witness at the Four Treys who says he overheard Agent Drew threaten to kill Fat Monte," Biglione said. "You care to explain that?"

"You line up every person in Chicago who threatened to kill Fat Monte," Jeff said, "you'd need to rent out Wrigley for the occasion."

"Let's not bullshit, okay?" Biglione said. "I know he was working with you."

"So what?"

"The Family might like him dead," Biglione said. "And I'm frankly not exactly comfortable with him threatening to kill people while in the company of an FBI agent."

"Well, that's been rectified."

Biglione put the report down on the table and rubbed at his eyes. "I know he was impersonating an FBI agent," he said. "I could get proof if need be."

"What would the need be?"

"Newspapers are starting to pile up in front of his door, and his sister is about to miss an important test in her Western civilizations class. She gets below 3.0, could be a problem with her *federal* student loan," Biglione said.

"He's safe," Jeff said. "He and his sister are on a road trip."

"Is he looking for Cupertine on this road trip?"

"No," Jeff said. In fact, Matthew and Nina were already safely at the Marcus Whitman Hotel in Walla Walla, the one town in America Jeff was reasonably sure did not have a tendril of the Family in operation.

"I can't protect them if I don't know where they are," Biglione said. "The Family decides to send a blackout team for them, they're on their own."

"Matthew can handle himself," Jeff said.

"How do you handle yourself when ten guys shoot automatic weapons into your house?"

It was a good question, but the larger issue was that Biglione seemed to know what was becoming more and more evident: The Family had a way to get the names of the FBI players. Jeff doubted there was mole in the bureau. That was some cloak-and-dagger shit that frankly was above the Family's general purview. Nevertheless, Jeff was sure that there were CIs playing both sides, along with guys doing deep cover who would shovel a bit of helpful information to the Family if it meant keeping their own asses covered. And as it related to Matthew, his association with Jeff was enough to make him the sort of target they'd be willing to go a bit soft on if they didn't think there was a good chance of him getting hurt. Give up the name of someone inconsequential, basically, just to have the act of giving up information. The same cat and mouse the bureau and the Family had been playing since Capone and Ness.

"He deserves another shot," Jeff said.

"You renegotiating your deal?"

"No," Jeff said. "This Cupertine thing, that's it for me. When he's in custody, I'm done. But Matthew, he did good work. He's a real agent."

Biglione didn't say anything then, and now, weeks later, as they headed to Kochel Farms, and Matthew was still in Walla Walla, his sister back in Chicago but with an FBI tail, just in case, Jeff wondered if maybe he should have made Matthew's rehiring a condition of all this. Even though Matthew wouldn't let him, telling him that the only leverage Jeff had anymore was that Matthew was out there . . . somewhere . . . with all the knowledge Jeff had, including everything he hadn't shared with the bureau. Sadly, it was true.

"Here we go," Biglione said. Up ahead, parked on the side of the freeway, about two hundred yards up from an exit, were three black Lincoln Navigators and a black Lincoln Town Car, the marshals always good about keeping the nice-seized vehicles for their own use. Biglione slowed down and flashed his brights twice and then pulled behind the marshals and followed them out toward Kochel Farms.

"What's that smell?" Jeff asked.

"The cows," Poremba said. He tapped on the window. "They've probably got most of them behind a windbreak or in a barn, because of the cold, but with thirty thousand head, it would be hard to keep them all inside, even now."

Jeff could see a few cows now as they drove, grazing on what looked like freshly dropped bales of hay. In the spring months, though, the field would be a solid black mass of animals, constantly walking and grazing, shitting and pissing on everything, the ground churned over and over by 120,000 hooves a day. *A pretty good place to leave a body*, Jeff thought.

Jeff sat stewing in the Suburban for forty minutes while the marshals and Agents Biglione and Poremba cleared the house, which proved to be a bit of a task since the Kochels were having a Super Bowl party for about twenty-five people, most of whom came walking out of the house looking as though they'd been kicked in the stomach. The marshals hadn't bothered knocking on the front door, opting instead to burst in using a door ram. That's how it always was with them—always with the Wyatt Earp shit. Jeff was of the opinion that if you wanted to achieve anything with a suspect, you had to make sure you didn't start off at an escalated emotional level. It's what concerned him about Matthew, how quickly he'd gone from having a conversation with Fat Monte to beating him. How easy it was. How much he'd liked it.

Biglione left Jeff with a radio so he could hear everything that was going on—a nice concession on his part, since Jeff wasn't allowed inside during the raid—and, after the chaos, they began going through every person at the party to determine who was who and if anyone happened to be Sal Cupertine, which, of course, none were. Most were business associates or employees of the farm—a meat distributer (and his wife) in town from Chicago, the operations manager of the slaughterhouse, the farm's marketing director and her husband and newborn—or just friends of the family. Once the marshals and Biglione and Poremba managed to sort the players, letting all the guests go on their way, Agent Poremba walked outside and stood in front of the main house and took several deep breaths, his frozen exhalations rising up in plumes and disappearing into the air.

Poremba took a handkerchief from his pocket, blew his nose, and then absently waved Jeff out of the car. As Jeff made his way over, four marshals came strutting out of the house, one holding the ram, the other three holding shotguns, each wearing Kevlar vests that said U.S. MARSHAL across the chest and back.

By the time Jeff reached Poremba, the marshals were already in one of the Navigators and pulling away.

"They find Jimmy Hoffa in the guacamole?" Jeff asked Poremba.

"Not today," Poremba said. He blew his nose again and pointed at the warehouse-size barn that stood about fifty yards away. "That's where they keep the packaged meat. They move three, sometimes four truckloads a day, every day, except Super Bowl Sunday and Christmas."

"What about Thanksgiving?" Jeff said.

"One shipment," Poremba said, "to a local food bank."

"You find that all out in forty minutes?"

"No," he said. "I got all that before I came out from Kansas City. Meat industry in KC is just as corrupt as ever. This place is a model of efficiency."

"Still the Sicilians out there?"

"Almost seventy years they've been running the meat business in Saint Louis and KC, running the unions, and here we are, freezing to death at a cattle farm on Super Bowl Sunday." Poremba laughed in an unfunny way. "These are working people," Poremba said, "and we just crashed into their house. This isn't even a union farm, Jeff."

"I know what Fat Monte told me," Jeff said.

Poremba folded up his handkerchief and examined it for a few seconds. "Your father keep a handkerchief?"

"My dad was military," Jeff said. "He blew his nose on his arm."

"Mine didn't either," Poremba said. "It's like something from antiquity, right?" In the distance, Jeff could see a white paddy wagon heading toward the farm. Poremba noticed it at the same time. "Wishful thinking on Special Agent Biglione's part, no doubt."

"You need to let me in to interview these people," Jeff said. "I know I can get . . . something. Fat Monte wouldn't have spent his last breath telling me I needed to get out to this place for nothing."

"If the Family were connected to this farm, that would mean war with the Missouri boys by now, don't you see? These people, they're too successful to be connected. Can you imagine Ronnie Cupertine standing out here in one of his mohair over-coats, filling his nostrils with this lovely aroma?"

Jeff couldn't. It was true. But there was something in all this that kept worming in his mind, had been for weeks now. There was no evidence anywhere that the Family was in the meat business. They'd gotten out of it in the 1920s, when John Giannola moved down to Saint Louis to be with his brothers and started up the Green Ones, the only decent agriculture-based organized crime syndicate in the country, which is why the Missouri families still were in it, presumably, even in a minor way.

"If there's so much money here," Jeff said, "there's no good reason the Sicilians in Missouri wouldn't move up a few miles and at least get in on the trucking, right? We're ninety minutes from their operation in Saint Louis. What reason would they have for *not* being in this place? This farm has been here since the 1950s, and you mean to tell me no one in Missouri has ever tried to get their hooks into it?"

Poremba started to say something, then stopped. It was a simple question. "Saint Louis is weak," he said finally. "Lucky to hold on to what they have."

"Yeah," Jeff said, "but if they have the meat industry, and the Family doesn't give a shit about it, wouldn't they cut a deal? Isn't that what they do now? All one big happy crime family?"

The paddy wagon pulled up in front of the house then, and a young marshal got out and looked around, as if he expected to see all the original Five Families lined up and cuffed, the history and future of organized crime snuffed out on a farm in southern Illinois. "Am I in the right place?" he asked.

"You can go home," Poremba said.

"I drove for five hours," the marshal said. "From Chicago."

"You can go home," Poremba said again. "Or you can go inside and talk to your superior officer and have him tell you to go home."

The marshal didn't say anything. He just walked back to the paddy wagon and got inside but didn't bother to pull away.

"I think someone in the bureau is giving the Family information about this case," Jeff said. "I think from the beginning, from before Sal Cupertine took out my guys. Because the more I learn about Cupertine, the more unrealistic it seems to me that he'd have been the guy to be meeting our people. It just doesn't make sense. I think somewhere down the line, someone tipped Ronnie Cupertine that we were getting close to his operation, and he put his cousin up for sacrifice, and then everything turned upside down. Everything has been too convenient. Even this, here, today."

"Probably," Poremba said.

"That's it?" Jeff said. "Probably?"

"When you were running your unit," Poremba said, "how many CIs did you have?"

"That I trusted? Maybe two."

"So why should any of this be a surprise? The guppies have always been sacrificed so the big fish could swim." Poremba took his handkerchief back out of his pocket, blew his nose again, then wadded it up and threw it into the snow.

The door opened behind them, and a young woman stepped out, a little boy in a Bears winter coat holding her hand. She couldn't have been more than twenty-five, which meant it was probably Tina Kochel, the elder Mel Kochel's niece. A college student out in Springfield, if Jeff was remembering the files correctly. Jeff didn't know who the kid was but immediately felt terrible that this whole day was going to be something he'd possibly remember: the day men with guns showed up during the football game.

Tina took a few steps forward with the boy, but when she saw that Poremba wasn't going to let her pass, she said, "Am I allowed to walk out of my own damn property?"

"Is this your property?" Poremba asked.

"It's my family's property," she said. "You don't have any right to do this, you know."

"Actually," Poremba said, "we have all the rights we need, or else we wouldn't be here. That's how the federal government works. You can rest assured that if we show up somewhere with a bunch of guns, we have the right to do it. The warrant helps, too."

Jeff was surprised to hear Poremba's rather snippy response—the girl was obviously scared and of no concern to the FBI, so he was just doing it to keep up appearances. Unlike Biglione,

Poremba still appeared to wear human skin, so this all seemed unneeded.

"My son is scared out of his mind," Tina said. "I'd like to get some of his toys out of my car. Is that against the law? Do I have the right to do that?"

"Sure," Poremba said. "Where's your car?"

"The carport," she said. She pointed to a covered area adjacent to the barn where there were five Ford trucks parked.

Poremba took a step to one side, but just as Tina was about to pass, Jeff put a hand on Tina's arm and stopped her. "For security reasons," Jeff said, "why don't you leave your son with us."

"This is infuriating," Tina said.

"Policy," Jeff said, which wasn't true, because outside consultants didn't have any policies. What was true, however, is that he was certain he hadn't read anything about Tina Kochel having a kid. He would have remembered that. What was also true was that it wasn't illegal for him to question the kid, but it was illegal for Poremba to do so. The FBI couldn't interrogate a preschooler—Jeff thought the kid was maybe four—but there was nothing wrong with a stranger doing it.

"Fine," she said. She kneeled down and took her son's face in her hands. "I'm going to leave you with these nice men for two minutes. I'll be right back. Be a good boy and don't bother them."

"Okay!" the boy said. Or, essentially, shouted.

Tina stood back up and glared at both Jeff and Poremba. "I know you're just doing your job, but this is bullshit," she said.

"Federal agents were killed," Poremba said, "so we need to follow all leads. As a taxpayer, I'm sure you can appreciate that."

"It's the Super Bowl," she said.

"So imagine how little we want to be here, too," Jeff said.

Once Tina was out of earshot, Jeff said to Poremba, "Don't listen to this," and then he kneeled in front of the boy, so that he was at eye level, and said, "What's your name? Is it Mel?"

"No!" the boy said, and he stomped his foot. He didn't seem exactly terrified. What he seemed, in fact, was fairly entertained. Either that, or shouting was his default setting. "That's my uncle! I'm Nicholas!"

"That's right," Jeff said. He looked over his shoulder at Poremba, who was watching this unfold with something like curiosity mixed with horror, but knew enough not to say a word. "That's right. Your uncle is Mel. Who is your daddy?"

Nicholas stomped his foot again, "My daddy is my daddy!"

"That's right," Jeff said. "But do you know his name?"

"Daddy," Nicholas said, but he didn't sound terribly convinced that this was true. Odd.

"Where does your daddy live?" Jeff said.

"Heaven," Nicholas said.

Jeff thought it was somewhat possible that he'd forget Tina Kochel had a kid—she didn't matter to him in the least, so maybe he'd just seen that she was going to school in Springfield and left it at that—but there was no way he would have overlooked a dead husband. Twenty-five-year-olds didn't have dead husbands anymore. Or dead fathers of their children, at least.

"Finish up," Poremba said calmly. "She's at the car right now."

He needed about thirty minutes with the kid, really. Maybe with a good child psychologist. But that wasn't going to happen. "How long has your daddy been in heaven?"

Nicholas shrugged. "Ten years!" he said.

Shit. Shit. Shit. The problem with kids and time is that until they're about six or seven, the concept of past, present, and future can get fairly muddled. Nicholas was maybe four. Nothing he said was reliable. Nothing he said was admissible, either.

"What did he get you for Christmas?"

"Nintendo," Nicholas said, "and G.I. Joe and five games and popcorn."

"Was that the last time you saw him?"

Nicholas nodded once.

"Can you tell me what your daddy looks like?"

"He's big!" Nicholas said.

"Bigger than me?"

"Bigger than everybody!"

"Taller than me and bigger than Santa?" Jeff said, and he stood up and pushed out his belly.

"Bigger than Santa!" Nicholas said.

"Is your daddy's name . . ." Jeff paused, tried to decide if this was what he really wanted to do to this kid, if this was what he wanted to do to Tina Kochel, if this was what he wanted to give the FBI. Could Fat Monte be this kid's father?

"Lucy is in heaven, too," Nicholas said before Jeff could finish his sentence.

"Who is Lucy?"

"My cat," Nicholas said.

Poremba tapped Jeff on the shoulder once. Jeff turned and saw that Tina was only about thirty feet away now. She was smoking a cigarette and had a small backpack shaped like a tiger slung over one arm. She was pretty, Jeff decided, but not overly so. Her hair was blonde—a dye job, Jeff guessed, since her kid had reddish-brown hair—and she was skinny, with long legs. What did Jeff know about Tina? Nothing, really. Just that she lived and went to college in Springfield. But she was twenty-five. Shouldn't she have been out of school by now?

"Were you good?" Tina asked Nicholas when she got to the porch.

"He was," Jeff said. "He told us all about his father."

Jeff watched the color drain from Tina's cheeks, which was quite a feat, since it was freezing outside, and her face was flushed red from the wind. "He doesn't know his father," she said.

"No?" Jeff said.

"I don't know who his father is, either, if you have to know," she said. "And I'm sorry, how is this any of your business?"

"He volunteered the information," Poremba said. There was nonchalance in his voice that Jeff found oddly comforting. He liked that Poremba understood what was at stake here, too, without anything being spoken.

"He said his father was dead," Jeff said. "That seems like a strange thing for a kid to say, don't you think?"

"That's what I've told him," she said. She reached down and took Nicholas's hand and started to make her way inside.

"Wait," Poremba said, and Tina did. He lifted his chin at Jeff. "He has a few other questions for you."

How could Tina Kochel have any connection to Fat Monte? Jeff had about two minutes to figure this out before it became obvious he was fishing.

"Where do you work?" Jeff asked.

"Why?"

"Because I'm asking you. I know you're a student at the university in Springfield. Now I just need to know where you work. You can either tell me, or I can just run your social. It's up to you how much you want to cooperate. What kind of example you want to set."

Tina looked down at her son and sighed. "The Kitten Club," she said.

"That a strip joint?" Jeff said.

"I've been trying to pay for school, okay? I don't want to be a farmer, so here I am."

"What are you majoring in?"

"Social work," she said.

"Okay," Jeff said. "Who watches your son when you're dancing?"

"I bring him here some nights," she said. "Some nights a girl-friend watches him. Are we done?"

"Your family know about the dancing?" Jeff asked.

"No," she said. "They think I'm bartending. I'd like to keep it that way, okay?"

"Sure." He smiled at her. "Your son is very sweet. You must be very proud of him."

"Are we done?" she said again.

"Sure." Jeff reached over and opened the front door, and Tina and Nicholas started back inside, where the marshals and Agent Biglione were going through the house, room to room, looking for evidence Jeff was pretty sure they weren't going to find.

Special Agent Lee Poremba stood beside Jeff and watched Tina and Nicholas disappear as the door closed.

"Who runs the Kitten Club?" Poremba asked.

"Last I knew, a guy named Timo Floccari," Jeff said. "If he's not dead, he's in prison by now and will soon be dead. If he's alive, you might want to get him into protective custody, wher-ever he is."

"Soldier?"

"Yep," Jeff said. "Moved oxycodone for Fat Monte."

Poremba looked at his watch. "Why don't you get a ride back in the paddy wagon. We're going to be here a while."

"Okay," Jeff said.

They were both silent for a few moments, Jeff working out the math of it all, trying to figure out what Poremba's move would be.

"I can give you a week. Ten days at the longest," Poremba said. "And then I'm going to need to act on this. What do you need from me?"

"A shipping manifest for all the trucks that left here the night of the killings," Jeff said. "And then any payload transitions those trucks made. I want to know where every single piece of meat this farm shipped out that day ended up. Someone saw something."

"What else?"

"That kid," Jeff said, "doesn't need to know his father was a gangster."

"That's out of my hands," Poremba said.

"His birth certificate is probably clean," Jeff said. "It can stay that way." Poremba didn't say anything, so Jeff continued. "Get a deal for the girl," Jeff said. "You can do that."

"I'll try," Poremba said. "You get Cupertine, you can probably dictate all the terms."

"Then I guess that's what I'll do," Jeff said. He measured his next words out in his head before he said them, certain he needed to know the answer. "Why are you doing this for me?"

"What happened with those men at the Parker House," Poremba said, "that could have happened to any of us. It was a clerical error."

"It was my error," Jeff said.

"Are you in charge of the accounts payable section of the FBI now? Come on."

"As soon as I knew it was Sal Cupertine they were meeting with, I should have known to call it off. The only reason the Family would send Sal Cupertine anywhere, in broad daylight, would be to have him blow up. That's on me. That will always be on me."

"You can't think like that," Poremba said.

"Yeah," Jeff said, "my therapists have said the same thing."

This made Special Agent Lee Poremba laugh. Jeff was pretty sure it was the first time he'd ever seen the man show any emotion other than basic placidity and occasional irritation. "Did I catch a plural there?" he asked.

"It's been a hell of a year."

"A week," Poremba said. They shook hands, and Poremba went back inside, an agreement sealed.

It took Jeff another hour, sitting in the back of the paddy wagon, before he had reliable enough cell service to call Matthew in Walla Walla. "Pack your bag," Jeff said after filling him in on the details.

"Where am I going?" Matthew asked.

Jeff looked out the window of the paddy wagon. To the east, he could see nothing but fields of white, to the west, the same thing. Where would they ship Sal Cupertine? Where could a man like him, the most proficient killer the Family had ever employed, be comfortable? Where would they send him where they knew he couldn't just come back, kill them all, grab his wife and kid, and run away? Somewhere they had a connection, where they weren't competing for the same dollars. Far enough away that he'd need to fly home, most likely, since the Family wouldn't risk the idea that Sal Cupertine might decide to sneak out of wherever he was living at midnight and show up on their doorstep at 6 a.m. with a pipe bomb. That ruled out Detroit, Cleveland, and Nashville.

If the Family had really sold Sal Cupertine, as Bruno had suggested, the only likely trading partners were families who had the capital to spend and the ability to keep Cupertine either confined or busy or both. Where did the Chicago Family still have pull? They were getting pushed out of Miami by the New York families, none of whom needed help. They still had connections in Las Vegas and Reno, for sure, and in Los Angeles, where they had tendrils in pornography, strip clubs, and some of the entertainment unions, as well as in the burgeoning Indian casinos that dotted the desert outside Palm Springs, where regulation was difficult to manage in light of the Indians' sovereign status. Nothing to speak of in San Francisco, where the organized crime element had shifted to the Russians and Asians.

Palm Springs was a possibility, but Jeff didn't see that sticking for long, not with the corporations taking over all the golf courses and resorts, leaving the Italians with the restaurants and clubs, but that was little more than skim money, and the gambling money was a split, if that, with the Indians. The cartels and Mexican Mafia coming up with the cheap cocaine and weed had pretty much everything from the border up into L.A. locked down, drug-wise.

The Family's union juice in L.A. couldn't last much longer, either. Their best shot for long-term survival was in their bankrolling of skin flicks, provided they could keep AIDS under control, not that Jeff thought the Family was likely to run a clean shop.

Las Vegas was an open city, but they still had some historical allegiances to Chicago, even with Splitoro dead and Angelini doing time. But on the whole, Las Vegas was weak, unconnected guys working the streets and talking like they were big guns but who were really just idiots at cell phone stores trying to act tough. All the big business in Las Vegas was being run through the strip clubs, though Jeff didn't see that as a place Sal Cupertine could exist in. What was he doing? Working as a DJ? Chatting up the drunks? Working the door in a tuxedo, shaking down bachelor parties? That wasn't Cupertine's scene. There hadn't been a significant mob hit in Las Vegas since Herbie Blitzstein got his in 1997, and it took four guys from Buffalo and L.A. to do the job. Cupertine wouldn't work like that. It had to be a small outfit, not too flashy. The sort that needed a middle manager who could also do some contract work. Someone who knew about the Rain Man and saw the potential he possessed.

An outfit, too, that just so happened to need a lot of frozen meat. The manifests would be key. This was going to take some finessing, and they didn't have much time. He wanted Sal Cupertine alive.

"Somewhere warm," Jeff said.

CHAPTER THIRTEEN

Dr. Larry Kirsch kept a busy schedule. First thing in the morning, he'd leave the Meadows at Sahara, his exclusive guard-gated McMansion development in Summerlin, and get to his practice on the corner of Harmon and Eastern twenty minutes later, do a couple boob jobs before lunch, maybe work on a tummy tuck or a rhinoplasty, and then he'd usually head over to Piero's for a bite. Some days he'd follow up Piero's with a beer at Champagnes, the kind of bar where no one knew your name, and then he'd make a round up the street at Desert Springs Hospital to see any of his surgical patients. He'd come back to his office around three, do some Botox and chemical peels, close the day with a face-lift, followed by a lap dance at the Olympic Gardens or Cheetahs, never the Wild Horse.

Sometimes he paid a girl to go out to his car and jerk him off in the parking lot, sometimes he'd just do it himself.

Then he'd spend an hour or two at his ex-wife's house helping his eleven-year-old son with his homework, grab a burger from Sonic, and then head back to the Meadows at Sahara. Kirsch's ex and kid had a house in the Scotch 80s, an old Las Vegas neighborhood where mobsters and city officials used to live next door to one another without the need for any kind of gates. If someone was going to kill you, they'd just drag you outside, shoot you in the face, and then bury you in your own backyard.

It wasn't that easy anymore, unfortunately. David watched the doctor for almost two weeks trying to figure out the best time and place to kill him, but the asshole was never alone. Plus, everywhere he went had cameras and people, and David, for the first time in his life, needed to leave a little bit of a mess.

So, on the morning of the Super Bowl, David called Dr. Kirsch's cell.

"This is a friend of Bennie Savone's," David said when Kirsch answered.

"Oh, okay," Dr. Kirsch said. "Any friend of Bennie's is a friend of mine."

"Right," David said. "We need some work done tonight."

"This work," Dr. Kirsch said, "does it require immediate medical attention?" He lowered his voice. "Is it a bullet wound?"

"Minor procedure," David said. "No nurses or anything."

"Of course, of course, I understand," Dr. Kirsch said. "It's just that I have plans tonight. It's the Super Bowl, as I'm sure you're aware, and . . ."

"You're either at your office at 7 p.m.," David said, "or the *Review-Journal* gets a stack of pictures of you whacking off in public."

Silence.

"When all of your security cameras are off," David said, "pop your office door open, the one facing Harmon. Any questions?"

"No," Dr. Kirsch said.

"If you're even two minutes late," David said, "your ex-wife gets the pictures, too."

"This isn't how Mr. Savone usually speaks to me," Dr. Kirsch said.

"This isn't Mr. Savone," David said, then he dumped his burner cell into his portable foundry—an expense that was already paying for itself—and took an inventory, made sure he was prepared.

Rubber gloves.

Wet-Naps.

Knife.

He'd even made himself a silencer for this job, something he was generally adverse to, since it spoke to a kind of weakness. But the difference between killing someone in Chicago and killing someone in Las Vegas came down to simple acoustics: Chicago was *loud*, between the L and all the traffic and the howling wind and the sound of about three million people going about their daily lives. In Las Vegas, though, once you got off the Strip, everything fell quiet, the desert surrounding the city a valley of echoes.

He didn't have much choice about guns, so he'd taken a nine from the cache in Slim Joe's closet, filed off the serial number, and cleaned it meticulously, though he didn't bother to wrap the handle with duct tape, since that just made it more likely he'd trap a finger print. And he was going to melt the gun anyway. He'd have a cab take him to Desert Springs and then he'd walk the mile to Kirsch's office and wait for him.

If everything went according to plan, he'd be home in time to prepare sufficiently for the Monday morning *minyan*. If it turned upside down, someone else would be making prayers.

■

At sixty forty-five, David watched from across the street as Dr. Kirsch parked his green Jaguar in his personalized space—there was no bigger honor in Las Vegas than having your name painted on pavement; even the temple sold spaces for seven hundred and fifty bucks a month—and headed inside through his private office door. Fifteen minutes later, he stepped outside, looked both ways, and then propped his door open.

When David walked in, Dr. Kirsch was sitting behind the desk in his office, a wall-to-wall mahogany affair lined with bookshelves filled with framed photos of the doctor with various celebrities. Danny Gans. Wayne Newton. The captain of *The Love Boat.* The guy who played Dan Tanna on *Vega$.* A white tiger. That one was signed.

Dr. Kirsch didn't seem surprised to see David, even though he said, "I wasn't expecting to see you again."

"You've never seen me," David said.

"Right, you're right, no," Dr. Kirsch said. He looked over David's shoulder. "Is Mr. Savone here?"

"No," David said. "I'm alone. You want to close your blinds?"

"Yes, right," Dr. Kirsch got up from behind his desk and closed the matchstick bamboo blinds behind him, though David could still make out the passing lights of traffic. Didn't anyone have decent curtains anymore? "The man who called said there was something minor to be done," Dr. Kirsch said. "Are you having some issue with your skin? That area around your ears was difficult."

"Yes," David said. "My cheeks don't move right. And I've got a lot of jaw pain." Which was true. If he clenched his teeth too hard, it was like getting a nail through the eye.

"Any bleeding?"

"Not that I've seen," David said. "But I can taste blood in the back of my mouth sometimes."

"Okay then," Dr. Kirsch said, "let's check it out." He walked David out of his office and down a long hallway lined with photos of showgirls, models, and a lady who did the weather Saturday nights on Channel 8. He stopped and unlocked an exam room. "Lay down on the exam bed, and I'll take a look, Rabbi."

David saw the doctor give an inadvertent twitch, like he'd been shocked, which he probably had been at his own stupidity for addressing a man he'd supposedly never met. He began to turn around, which was a mistake, since he ended up getting half his face blown off when David shot him.

Dr. Kirsch dropped to the ground, his jaw and most of his nose completely gone, but he was still alive, twitching on the tile, half of his face splattered all around him.

The upside of this, David considered, was that now it *really* wouldn't look like a professional job, which had been the point all along. He'd planned on shooting the doctor in the neck, the kind of thing people who aren't used to killing ended up doing all the time, and if the doctor didn't die instantly, he'd be dead soon enough and would never know the difference. But David had seen guys survive a face shot, even stay conscious. The human body, man, it wanted to live.

Not that it looked like Dr. Kirsch was long for this world.

David snapped on his rubber gloves and leaned over Dr. Kirsch, tried to figure out what exactly he was breathing from, since he didn't have a mouth or much of a nose anymore, and decided just to cover what was left of his face with both hands until the twitching stopped. He could shoot him again, but he didn't want to have to dig a slug out of his head. Thirty seconds, tops. If that. The guy was probably already comatose.

David pressed his hands over the gaping maw in the center of Dr. Kirsch's face, but all that seemed to do was help staunch the flow of blood, which was the exact opposite of the point. The other problem was that Dr. Kirsch seemed to be coming to. His eyes fluttered open, and his arms started swinging wildly. David didn't know if it was adrenaline or actual fight, if the doctor was even aware of what was happening. If he knew that he didn't have a face.

"Stop moving," David said quietly. "Just let go."

Dr. Kirsch focused on David then, another unintended outcome, and then he tried to scratch at David's face, swiping at him with both hands, until David decided *fuck it*, sat on his chest, pinned his arms down with his knees, grabbed his throat, found a thick gold chain there, which was helpful, and strangled him, face-to-face, eye-to-eye, just like he'd done that Donnie Brasco fuck in Chicago. That guy who wasn't Jeff Hopper, the guy who'd started this whole problem, except that Dr. Kirsch was harder to kill.

David stood there for a moment and collected himself. He had a plan, and it had gone slightly astray, but, all things considered, it was a minor inconvenience. Dr. Kirsch was dead. Time to move to phase two. There needed to be an order to things, or else he'd end up tracking blood all over the city.

The bullet that took off most of Dr. Kirsch's face kept going and lodged in the wall, so David dug it out with his butterfly knife and put it in his pocket. It made the scene look authentic; even the dumbest fucks were smart now about not leaving slugs and shell casings around, those forensics shows acting like Mr. Rogers for a generation of crooks.

He stepped back over to Kirsch's body and jabbed his knife into the doctor's rear pants pocket and cut his wallet out from the fabric, never once touching the actual body, cut his car keys and cell phone from his front pocket; that would all melt easily enough. The doctor didn't wear any rings, didn't even wear a watch, just that thick gold chain that was now garroted into his throat, so he sliced that away, too . . . and that's when David noticed the pendant on one end.

David should have known what he'd see when he looked down, yet he was still taken by surprise. Two Hebrew letters, ח and י, crusted in diamonds, forming the symbol יח, the edict to live, the edict to be ethical, the edict of power: *Am Yisrael chai.* The people of Israel live.

It hadn't even occurred to David that Dr. Kirsch was Jewish. A year ago, it wouldn't have mattered. A couple of months, even, it wouldn't have registered. But now, these were his people, the *chai* a part of his daily life, as much as the omertà used to be. That was the thing: Omertà was a made-up code to keep crooks quiet, a false loyalty born out of movies, dumb fucks like Slim Joe adopting it as a religion in place of something with actual meaning. Maybe most Jews didn't believe even half of their religion, but he hadn't met one who didn't understand the struggle to survive, faith or no faith.

Dr. Kirsch had to die. But it all boiled back to that day at the Parker House, that hotel room, those four guys Sal Cupertine had to kill. Wasn't he a different person now, Sal only a thing of his past? And Sal *had* to kill those men. There'd been no other way. He'd come across false witnesses, and he'd done what he had to do. Even God considered that entrapment. What was it the Torah said? *Then you should do to him as he plotted to do to his brother, and you shall thus abolish evil from among you.*

David stuffed Dr. Kirsch's wallet, keys, and necklace into his pockets. It was 7:07 p.m. He was running two minutes behind schedule, yet Rabbi David Cohen suddenly found himself muttering Hebrew—*Yit'gadal v'yit'kadash sh'mei raba*—the Burial Kaddish slipping from his mouth with what had become his usual ease, though David knew Dr. Kirsch would never actually be buried. At least not most of him.

■

After cleaning himself up, David walked up Eastern to Flamingo and then back onto the campus of Desert Springs Hospital, where he'd been dropped off earlier that evening, to hail a cab. The walk gave him an opportunity to get his adrenaline in check. Normally, he liked a meal after killing someone, but his night was still a work in progress, albeit one with a strict timeline.

The entrance to the emergency room came up on David's right. There were a few people standing outside talking on cell phones or smoking, and through the sliding doors David could see that the waiting room was packed with people. In the last two months, David had visited the hospital at least once each week in his official capacity, sometimes two or three times in a day if there was someone particularly wealthy or particularly ailing that Bennie wanted him to see. The last time, he'd gone with Rabbi Kales. One of the members of their temple, Bert Feinstein, had suffered a stroke while playing craps at the Mirage and was taken to Desert Springs already in a coma. The family had asked for Rabbi Kales to come when it appeared the last hours were upon them, and Rabbi Kales had asked David to come, too.

"I guess I need the practice," David said.

Rabbi Kales didn't respond at first, he just stood in the doorway to David's office and stared at him, incredulous. "Then you should stay here," Rabbi Kales finally said, his voice hardly above a whisper, and stalked he out of David's office.

David caught up to him in the parking lot. It was just after noon, and the kids were all outside on the playground, laughing, shouting. "Wait," David said. "I'll take you."

"Don't bother," Rabbi Kales said. "I forget that you pretend to have no soul."

David paused. Rabbi Kales knew the right words for every occasion, the bastard, so David looked for his own right words, settling on, "I'm sorry." David tried to remember the last time he had actually apologized to anyone.

"This is not someone who has done wrong," Rabbi Kales said. "This is someone's father, someone's husband, someone's friend. They are looking to us for comfort. If you cannot provide that, if you cannot treat the death of a man honestly, for the first time in your life, then stay here."

"I can do this," David said.

"Then get your yarmulke and your Torah."

They were met in the hospital lobby by Bert's granddaughter Elissa. David had seen her at the temple plenty of times, since she came after school and worked as a tutor for the younger kids. But seeing her at the hospital, David was struck by how little she looked like the young woman he remembered. She'd been crying, so her eyes were puffy, aging her in the bad hospital light.

Bert's room was crowded with people—Bert's wife, Lois, who'd once made David eat a cookie made of applesauce and coconut and something he presumed was straight lard; Elissa's parents, Jack and Rochelle, as well as her aunt and uncle,

Margaret and Carl, and their two teenage sons whose names David couldn't remember, since they showed up at temple only on the rarest of occasions—all of whom turned and gazed upon Rabbi Kales with a mixture of melancholy and relief.

Rabbi Kales immediately went to work: He touched each person gently as he made his way toward Lois, whom he hugged while she sobbed into his shoulder. And there, in the middle of the room, was Bert Feinstein. He had an IV in one arm, but there were suspiciously few machines beeping in the room. David thought maybe it didn't matter at this point, that there were no heroic recoveries to be made.

It occurred to David that he'd been surrounded by plenty of dead people in his life but very few in the process of dying a natural death. His own father was murdered. His mother? She could be dead by now, too, he supposed, which brought a wave of sadness over him. How could he not know? How could he live the rest of his life not ever knowing? And would she die alone? Would she be in some hospital by herself? And what of Jennifer? William . . . he couldn't bear to even let his eventual demise enter his head.

"Rabbi Cohen," Rabbi Kales said softly, "will lead us in the Mi Sheberakh."

"In English, please," Lois said. "Bert never understood Hebrew."

David had said the Mi Sheberakh many times over the course of the last several months, but never in a situation like this. It was a prayer made for the ill, and it was usually done during services. He knew it in Hebrew phonetically, just like a kid at his bar mitzvah, but because people concerned about the life-or-death situation of a loved one tend to like to know what is being said, he'd found that more often than not he was asked to read it in English, and each time he found himself moved that the prayer was asking not just that the person be healed physically—and if it came down to someone needing the prayer, it was usually a grave situation—but that, too, their spirit be cleansed.

"Of course," David said. Bert Feinstein made it through only the first half of the prayer, but David kept reciting, sending Bert's healed soul into whatever came next.

David and Rabbi Kales spent the next several hours with the family, helping them with the details of death, so that when they finally headed back to Summerlin, it was rush hour. "You did very well today, Rabbi Cohen," Rabbi Kales said. The red glare from all the brake lights gave everything a spectral glow.

"It was just a prayer," David said.

"No, it was more than that," Rabbi Kales said. "Your being there was a comfort to the younger ones. They look up to you. It's a special gift, David, even if you don't want it."

"Here's what I'm trying to understand," David said. "I feel like I'm pretty acquainted with death, but seeing that man there just slip away, no thrashing around, not gasping for breath, he just . . . he just stopped. It didn't seem right. Why doesn't the body fight more? "

"We fight every day," Rabbi Kales said.

David supposed that was true. But for what? "So, tell me, what happens next?"

"He'll be at the funeral home in the morning."

"No," David said, "I mean what happens *next*."

"Eventually, when the Moshiach returns, we'll all live in peace, in our most perfect state, and all the world will be Israel."

"I know that," David said. "I know what the books say. But what happens to me, Rabbi Kales? What about me?"

Rabbi Kales sighed. "Sal Cupertine," Rabbi Kales said, "he is already gone. Rabbi David Cohen still has a chance."

"He's not gone," David said. "He'll never be gone. As long as my wife is still alive, Sal Cupertine is still alive. Because I'm going back to her at some point, Rabbi. You can believe that."

"I can believe that," Rabbi Kales said. "But for the choices we've made," he continued, "we're likely to rot together."

David repeated Rabbi Kales's words in his mind again as he walked up to the main entrance of the hospital. In truth, he'd thought about those words somewhat constantly over the course of the last several weeks. Was his eternity going to be spent with the people he'd worked alongside, the Fat Montes and Slim Joes he'd spent all these years running with, or was he going to have Jennifer and William there? What about his own father? Would he be there? David had never even considered the idea of an afterlife until he'd fallen in love, and even then it wasn't until he thought that he might not ever see Jennifer and William again that it mattered.

For the first time in his life, he actually had some kind of purpose. There were days when he'd spend hours—hours!—listening to other people's problems and offering them advice that they seemed to find useful. At first, he hated that shit. And if he had to choose how to live his life, he wouldn't choose to spend his time doing that. And yet. Those same people would come back a few days later and tell him how much his words had helped them figure out how to plan their daughter's wedding, or deal with their taxes, or figure out whether to have the holidays at home or to fly back to Portland to see the kids. They were mundane problems, the issues he dealt with, but David had come to learn that it was the mundane shit of life that sent people into ever-widening spirals of anxiety.

There was a line of at least fifteen people standing in front of the hospital's entrance, waiting for cabs, just like in front of one of the casinos, so David stood in the back of the line and bided his time. When he finally reached the head, there was a young man dressed in all black. He blew a whistle, and a yellow cab pulled up.

"Where to, sir?" the young man asked.

"That park off Rancho," David said. He checked his watch. He was running a few minutes late for a meeting he'd scheduled with Gray Beard, the "doctor" who'd snipped the wires out of his jaw.

"Twin Lakes?"

"Yeah, that's the one."

"Are you sure?" he asked.

"Yes," David said. "Is there some kind of problem?"

"I only ask because, at night, that's not a great part of town, sir, so if you're looking for a nice place to take a walk or something, I can recommend several lovely places in Green Valley."

"I look like I can't handle myself in a park?" David asked.

David got into the cab without another word.

"So, Lorenzi Park?" the cab driver asked. "That's Twin Lakes. Everything here has two names."

"Yeah," David said, and he heard his old self creep back into his voice. "Unless you think it's too scary."

The cab driver looked at David in his rearview mirror. "I think you'll be fine, buddy."

◾

David had the cab driver drop him off on the opposite side of Lorenzi Park from where he was meeting with Gray Beard and told him to wait. He'd come down to the park earlier in the week with a proposition: If David could get him some decent medical gear—even if it was just an autoclave from this century so that he could sterilize his tools over something other than the fucking grill—would Gray Beard be willing to do him a couple of small favors?

"I'm a doctor," Gray Beard had said, "so I won't be killing anybody, right? I stick to the Hippocratic."

"Yeah," David said. They were inside his RV, and Gray Beard's partner, whom David had learned was named Marvin, was in the back bedroom smoking a blunt and watching a kung fu movie. "I see that."

"What kind of equipment are we talking about?"

"Whatever you need," David said. "You'll only be burdened by how long you want to take raiding the joint. I assume it's not against your Hippocratic to do some robbery?"

Gray Beard nodded toward the bedroom. "Marvin isn't a doctor, so we're good."

"That's a relief," David said.

"What about the drugs?"

"You'll have the run of the office," David said. "Take the photocopier and fax machine if you want, doesn't matter to me."

Gray Beard considered this for a moment. "Could be I bring another associate on this, that bother you?"

"Yes," David said. "That bothers me."

"Guess I'll just be selective," Gray Beard said. He extended his hand, and the two shook on it. David didn't mention that they'd need to move a body, too, but he had a pretty good idea this was the sort of thing Bennie had used Gray Beard for in the past, in addition to his medical needs. Knowing a guy with an RV is useful in a number of ways.

At any rate, even though Bennie trusted Gray Beard, it didn't mean Gray Beard wouldn't suddenly get some sense of morality and roll on David, so he did the extra diligence of casing the park a bit.

David came around the corner and saw Gray Beard and Marvin sitting outside, a portable TV on a chaise lounge in front of them, the sound off, a cooler of beer at Gray Beard's feet.

"Didn't think you were going to make it," Gray Beard said when David walked up.

"Got a little hung up," David said.

"Saw you moseying around the park earlier," Gray Beard said.

"Had to make sure I wasn't walking into an ambush," David said. "No offense."

Gray Beard frowned. "You ever hear of 'First, do no harm'?"

David reached into his pocket and took out Dr. Kirsch's keys and handed them to Gray Beard, along with a slip of paper with the address of the office. "These will get you a car and an entire medical office," David said.

"I don't have any need for a car."

"It's a Jaguar," David said.

Gray Beard looked over at Marvin. He gave the tiniest shrug of acquiescence. "I guess we could sell it," Gray Beard said. "What do you want in return?"

"There's a body inside the office," David said. "I'm going to need you to clean it up and deliver it here."

David gave Gray Beard a business card for the funeral home. Gray Beard looked at it once and then handed it back to David. "I know the place," Gray Beard said. "What do you want done with the body?"

"It doesn't have much of a head anymore. I'd like it not to have any head whatsoever. Or hands or feet."

Grey Beard again looked over at Marvin, who again shrugged. "What else?"

"Soon as possible, get it on ice," David said, "and don't fuck with the organs."

"We don't get down like that," Gray Beard said. "You want something done, we do it. Otherwise, we keep it professional. Rubber gloves, scrub for foreign bodies, black light for fluids, whatever you want. What else?"

Good. Finally, someone who took pride in his work.

"Don't clean up the mess I made," David said. "I want the cops to know there was a body there. Make it look like a robbery. Break some needless shit. That sort of thing."

"Easy enough," Gray Beard said.

"Best case, how much profit do you stand to make?" David asked.

"Depends what we come upon in the office," Gray Beard said. "Plus what we can get for the ride. Why don't we cut a fair percentage."

"I think you'll find it lucrative," David said. "So once you see what you have, make me an offer. Bennie trusts you, I trust you."

"You shouldn't," Gray Beard said, but they shook on it anyway.

"Maybe you'll be able to expand your business," David said, "get an RV in Reno, too."

"Reno isn't my style."

"Maybe take your show on the road, then," David said carefully.

"I could go on a vacation."

"Good," David said. "You handle this cleanly, you make me a reasonable offer for your takeaway, and then maybe I'll periodically have an errand for you to run."

"I like to help people," Gray Beard said, "but I got limits, you understand."

"Good," David said again. "I like to help people, too."

David looked at his watch. It was almost nine. "I need you to get that body to the funeral home by one a.m. You got a problem with that?" David looked at Gray Beard's partner, now that he'd figured out the power structure for this side of the job.

"Naw," Marvin said. "No hands. No feet. No head. No problem." He reached into the cooler and pulled out another beer, twisted off the top, took a long sip, and leaned back in his chair.

David started to walk away then, figuring the deal was sealed, but Gray Beard called after him. "You want me to take a look at your mouth?" he asked.

"Why?" David said.

"I ask because your bite is off," he said. "I can see it from here. You having any jaw pain?"

In fact, like he'd told Dr. Kirsch, he was. David just figured it was one of those things. You get your entire face rebuilt, you'll have some lasting soreness. "Little bit," David said.

"Hold on," Gray Beard said. He got up from his chair and went into the RV, leaving David outside with his partner. That's how David thought of him, anyway. He didn't see an extra bedroom in the RV, so maybe they were a couple. David couldn't figure out a good reason for them to be hanging out with each other otherwise. Though when David had his wires snipped, Marvin did assist with the procedure, gave him water to swish with, stuffed some cotton against his gums when the bleeding got bad, that sort of thing. So maybe like Gray Beard was a defrocked doctor, Marvin was an ex-EMT.

Gray Beard reappeared with a handful of papers. "These are some exercises you can do," he said. "You probably have a case of TMJ."

"TMJ?"

"Temporomandibular joint disorder," Gray Beard said. When David didn't respond, he added, "Your jaw is out of whack. Those exercises will help."

David examined the pages. The exercises seemed simple enough—put your tongue on the roof of your mouth while opening and closing your jaw—and David felt relief of a small, nagging problem was within reach. "Anything else?" David asked.

"Try to avoid clenching your teeth during stress," Gray Beard said. He sat back down next to Marvin and cracked open a beer for himself, swallowed most of it down in three gulps. "Maybe try to avoid stress, too."

"That's what I'm doing today," David said. "Taking care of some stress."

"No hands, no feet, no head, no stress," Marvin said. He held his bottle up, and he and Gray Beard toasted.

"One a.m.," David said. "Don't be late."

"I'm never late," Grey Beard said. "If you're not punctual in this business, someone can die, right?"

■

As David walked back across the park, he considered the fact that he might have to eventually kill both Gray Beard and Marvin, though that point seemed a long time away, and something about them seemed more trustworthy than they probably were. Maybe it was just Gray Beard telling David he shouldn't trust him. It was the kind of honesty David liked, because it admitted probable fallibility, though David was certain Gray Beard knew that fucking up was not really an option here, or ever, as it related to his work. If the next twenty-four hours turned out for the best, maybe David would see Gray Beard and Marvin only once or twice more; that would be okay, too.

For everyone.

CHAPTER FOURTEEN

The cab dropped Rabbi David Cohen back at Temple Beth Israel a few minutes after nine thirty, just in time for David to see Rabbi Kales step out of the administrative offices to light a cigarette. In the months that David had worked with Rabbi Kales, he'd never seen him smoke, never even smelled smoke on him. It was, in David's opinion, somehow undignified for his position, never mind that David himself liked a cigar periodically.

"I've been calling you all night," Rabbi Kales said when David walked up. He looked panicked. "Where have you been?"

"I left my phone in my car," David said.

"Where have you been?" Rabbi Kales repeated.

"You don't want to know," David said. "Let's just leave it at that."

"I thought the worst."

"The worst about what?"

Rabbi Kales waved him off. "He's in jail," Rabbi Kales said. "Benjamin."

"Jail? What the fuck are you talking about?"

"The FBI raided the Wild Horse this evening," he said.

Fucking feds. If it was Super Bowl Sunday or Christmas or Thanksgiving, you could expect a knock on the door. "What did they get him on?" David asked.

"Conspiracy," Rabbi Kales said.

Shit. That was a federal charge. When the feds wanted to have the freedom to poke around until they found something worthwhile, they always went the conspiracy route, since they could convict a boss for what his soldiers did, or what his soldiers covered up, or even what his soldiers were *thinking* about doing.

David tried to collect his thoughts. If it was the conspiracy he and Rabbi Kales and Bennie were involved in with the funeral home and the bodies, Rabbi Kales would already be in cuffs, too. If it had anything to do with David whatsoever, there'd be feds and marshals and cops and reporters lining the street like the Macy's Thanksgiving Day Parade. And if it was just some local shit—the building commission or something equally mundane—David was sure Bennie had enough people in his pocket to take care of that, at least forewarn him about a raid on Super Bowl Sunday. Bennie didn't talk much about the political side of his life, but it was in the papers every day which "reputed mob figures" or "jiggle-joint owners" (or whatever euphemism the *Review-Journal* came up with that particular day) were donating to which races for mayor, city council, judge, sheriff . . . hell, even the dogcatcher was getting checks from guys with vowels at the end of their last names.

All of which made Bennie no different than Ronnie Cupertine when it all came down, both of them selling rides of one kind or another and peddling influence so long as no one got hurt.

And there it was.

"The tourist," David said.

"You're really blaming a paralyzed man for this?"

"I'm not blaming him," David said. "I'm blaming the situation." One of those bouncers rolled, said something to someone; had to be. The FBI doesn't get out of bed on Super Bowl Sunday unless they think they've got something for the newspapers. That's how they work. In Chicago, everyone involved would already be in a body bag, that's for sure: the bouncers, the victim, maybe the victim's family, and then maybe they'd burn down the club, too, just to clean the slate entirely . . . the realization of which made David actually catch his breath.

It wasn't the first time he'd come to the conclusion that he should be dead for his role in the fuckup at the Parker House. But it was the first time he realized that he *wasn't* dead for some specific reason. Cousin Ronnie got David's ass smuggled out of Chicago and killed either Chema or Neal, or both, just to make it look good . . . and then had Paul Bruno killed . . . and then Fat Monte put a bullet in his wife's head, and then another in his own, rather than deal with whatever Hopper had said to him. It had taken a while, but Ronnie wasn't just cleaning the slate, he was pouring lye on it and burying it in Siberia.

David had told Bennie to give up the bouncers, which he had, got them good attorneys, everything, and yet, the Wild Horse still got raided. The bouncers didn't know enough to give up anything other than what the feds already knew—that maybe Bennie Savone wasn't exactly an angel—and David was certain Bennie told the boys he'd take care of them if they ended up doing time, provided they kept their mouths shut. And they were likely to do time for the crime they'd obviously committed, and deservedly so in David's opinion, particularly with the beating caught on camera. So it had been about keeping them from getting a longer sentence, keeping them from being recognized as part of an organized crime conspiracy, which didn't give the bouncers any good reason to start putting Bennie's name on the street. Might as well come out of prison with some money in their pocket. David just didn't see the feds getting enough from a commonplace beatdown—even if the guy ended up paralyzed—to actually move against Bennie Savone.

Which meant they got their information from somewhere else, from someone who knew enough about Bennie's operations that they could ring up the feds and offer some kernel of information that would get the suits up and running.

"Where's Rachel?" David asked.

"Home, with the girls," he said. "Benjamin hasn't been arraigned yet, so there's not much that can be done until tomorrow when the bail is set."

"If there's a bail," David said.

"He's just a businessman," Rabbi Kales said.

"Never been arrested?"

"Never," Rabbi Kales said.

"Pays his taxes?"

"Yes, of course."

"His business taxes, too?" David thought of all the bosses who'd gone down not for murder but for ducking the IRS. That was the one lesson Ronnie Cupertine had imparted to everyone in the Family: Pay your taxes. You like driving on nice streets? You like taking the L places? You like breathing fresh air? Pay your fucking taxes. You like staying out of prison? You don't want a visit from the Rain Man? Pay your fucking taxes.

"How should I know?" Rabbi Kales said.

"Because you know everything else, seems like."

Rabbi Kales tossed his cigarette onto the pavement and ground it out under his shoe, fished in his pocket, and came back out with a pack of Camels and a lighter and lit back up. "I haven't smoked in fifteen years," he said. "I don't know why I ever stopped."

"This will get resolved," David said, though who the fuck knew. If they had Bennie on a conspiracy charge, that meant they probably convened a grand jury first, secured an indictment, maybe for conspiracy to obstruct justice or something similarly minor compared to everything else Bennie Savone had actually done during the course of his life. "Bennie's got a good lawyer. The thing to concentrate on right now is Rachel."

"She's fine," Rabbi Kales said. "You don't need to worry about Rachel."

"She didn't sound fine when she was telling me she was planning on leaving her husband," David said. "She didn't sound fine when she told me you knew."

"You don't need to worry about Rachel," Rabbi Kales said again.

"Maybe she should worry about me," David said.

Rabbi Kales took a long drag off of his cigarette and then exhaled through his nose. He flicked the still-burning cigarette into the parking lot and for a few moments watched it burn. "Do you think you frighten me?" he said eventually.

"I think I probably should."

"Your son's name is William," Rabbi Kales said. "He is in preschool at Mt. Carmel Academy, though your wife is having a hard time paying his tuition. Your wife, Jennifer, recently took a loan out on your home, even though it was paid off, in full, a few months after your death. Unfortunately, your wife is having a difficult time finding a job, since the name Cupertine doesn't exactly make her easy to hire, since people either think she is related to your cousin, who I understand is a reputed mob figure, or was the wife of Sal Cupertine, who killed several federal agents. That must be a difficult weight to carry simply by virtue of who she fell in love with as a teenager, wouldn't you say?"

"Shut the fuck up."

"Your father," Rabbi Kales said, "was thrown off the IBM Building. Do you know the circumstances that required he be thrown from the building? Because I would be happy to tell you, Rabbi Cohen."

"I told you to shut the fuck up."

"I heard you," Rabbi Kales said. "We've all got secrets, Rabbi Cohen. Just know that I'm aware of all of yours."

"You think it's that easy? That you can just say shit like that to me and suddenly your daughter is off the hook? If she ratted out Bennie, she's just a couple moves away from figuring out that her father is piece of shit, too."

"She is already aware of that."

"I don't think she's aware of the fact that you're burying murder victims in the cemetery she thinks she's inheriting," David said. "Or that everything here is a fucking grift."

"How is it you think she ended up marrying Bennie Savone, David? You think the daughter of a rabbi is going to just marry Bennie Savone? Do you really think everything you see here is by happy accident? That Benjamin lucked into this arrangement?"

David figured that Bennie had something on Rabbi Kales, figured that there was some weight that Rabbi Kales bore for the opportunity to have his own temple. Rabbi Kales had told him that day after their meeting at the Bagel Café that he'd made mistakes with his life. That Bennie had given him a tremendous opportunity. David had just assumed that Bennie had something on Rabbi Kales, when, maybe, it was the other way around. Bennie clearly adored his wife and kids. Or adored them as much as Bennie Savone was able to adore anything.

So that was the pact. Rabbi Kales knew that Bennie loved his daughter, held that over his head, and made a deal. Bennie got to marry the woman he loved; Rabbi Kales got his own temple, his own people. He couldn't have imagined what Bennie would do next. Who could? And it was why Rabbi Kales wouldn't just let Rachel divorce Bennie, wouldn't let her just walk away, even when he knew it was the best thing she could ever do with her life. And why he wouldn't just call the cops and tell them he was getting shaken down by the mob. In return, Bennie couldn't do anything at the temple without going through Rabbi Kales, which is why it became important for there to be someone like David at all.

A mob boss who had to answer to a rabbi.

What an elegant fucking con, David thought, both sides ripping the other off.

In the short run, David answered to Bennie. Bennie hadn't said anything definitive about taking Rabbi Kales out, but David wasn't stupid. He knew it was coming, some day, and probably someday soon. And the thing of it was, Rabbi Kales wasn't stupid, either.

"It doesn't matter to me," David said. "All that matters to me is what Bennie tells me to do."

"That's not true," Rabbi Kales said.

"If it was Rachel who went to the feds on this," David said, perfectly calmly, "I'll kill both of you. Because what matters to me is one day getting the fuck out of this place and back to my family. And I can only do that with your cooperation, Rabbi Kales. And I count Rachel's cooperation as your cooperation."

Rabbi Kales smiled at David then. "Bennie was right about you," he said.

"Yeah, in what way?"

"He said you had a singular focus."

"I pay attention," David said. Except once. And that's what had brought him here, on this night, in front of this man, this man who was probably fairly decent, a man who spent 90 percent of his time in service to something larger than himself. The other 10 percent was given over to the management of a criminal enterprise, the benefit of which gave every member of his temple hope that their own lives weren't meaningless. Rabbi Kales had essentially sold his daughter to Bennie Savone so that he could build an empire for the Jews in Summerlin.

What was the cosmic algebra on that? If you did a little bad for a greater good and the only people who got hurt were people who decided to get involved with a bunch of gangsters, wasn't that a net positive? Because, surely, Rachel Kales, at twenty-two, had fallen in love with the wrong person. A choice was made. And then her father had bartered with a criminal for what he wanted out of the deal, and, in the long run, the members of Temple Beth Israel were content.

The way David saw it, the only person with a viable complaint at this point was David himself, now that he understood all the people he was doing business with were shysters, which, he realized, was like a boxer complaining about how often he got hit. Except it hadn't been David's choice to be in the ring with Bennie Savone and Rabbi Kales. He thought for a long time that it had been his choice to be Sal Cupertine, a man who killed people for a living, but really that was a choice Ronnie made for him. This was a different sort of madness he was involved in now.

Jennifer had chosen to be the kind of woman who married a hit man, the kind of woman who has a child with a hit man, the kind of woman who, one day, knew that she'd be alone because she'd married a hit man. Those were the choices they'd made together, if not explicitly, at least tacitly. So Rabbi Kales could threaten him all he wanted. It didn't matter. David was who he was, and his wife knew. His father's death, that was something he'd figure out on his own, because he doubted Rabbi Kales knew all the reasons . . . but when it came right down to it, the reason was simple enough: Someone in the Family wanted him dead.

And that person was probably Ronnie Cupertine.

It was a truth David had tried to keep from confronting directly for a long time, but in the last few weeks it had come easier and easier for him to accept. Ronnie had also most likely wanted him dead, too, and then had to find a work-around when he got the jump on the FBI motherfuckers. There was no way Ronnie thought he'd get out of that meeting alive once he realized who the players were, four against one, impossible odds even for Sal Cupertine.

Ronnie never played to lose anything, so he was probably sitting in his house waiting for a phone call that said Sal was dead, only to get a call from Sal himself. No wonder he sounded so surprised. Ronnie wasn't used to failure and had to find a work-around that wouldn't end with Sal killing everyone in Chicago.

But the rub on that deal was that Sal Cupertine was alive, well, and prospering. It was the prospering that was beginning to bother David. That he'd been set up to succeed. It just didn't make sense. It wasn't how Ronnie did business.

Rabbi Kales's cell phone rang, and the old man—because that what he was, David saw, an old man standing outside a place of worship chain-smoking filterless Camels—took it from his pocket and examined the screen. "It's Benjamin's lawyer," Rabbi Kales said.

"Give it to me," David said.

"I don't think that's a good idea," Rabbi Kales said.

"I wasn't asking," David said.

"When you're at Temple Beth Israel," Rabbi Kales said, "you work for me, Rabbi Cohen." He answered the phone and turned his back to David. Rabbi Kales still had a full head of silver hair that he kept cut short in the back, so you could see three or four inches of neck between his hair and his collar. David could shoot Rabbi Kales in that spot, and he'd be dead before he hit the ground, his hair still perfectly coiffed while he waited for the Moshiach to come stomping back to collect all the Jews and bring them to the Mount of Olives.

With five pounds of pressure exerted on the trigger of his gun, David could end Rabbi Kales right here. That was it. Five pounds of pressure. Less pressure than it would take to slap the man. David could feel his gun pressing against the small of his back, beneath his now ever-present suit jacket. He could draw his gun in a second, second and a half if he really needed to take some time with it. At point-blank range, the bullet would take just a fraction of a second to pierce that spot between Rabbi Kales's head and neck. And for what? The hubris of wanting to give his community a place to gather and of not realizing the consequences of his actions?

Yom Kippur wasn't for another eight months, yet David couldn't help but think of what he'd learned about the Day of Atonement, about how almost a hundred years earlier, Rabbi

Hertz had written that sin was not an evil power whose chains one must drag behind oneself for the rest of one's life. We can always shake off its yoke, Rabbi Hertz said, and we never need to assume the yoke in the first place.

The Talmud taught that Jews live in deeds, not years, and in that way, David understood the paradox of all the things he'd learned during these months of rabbinical study: You could never quite unfuck yourself, when it got right down to it, but that didn't mean you couldn't be a better person after making a bad choice.

Rabbi Kales turned back around then, the phone pressed to his ear as he listened intently to whatever was being said to him, so David very calmly took out his gun and placed it directly against the rabbi's forehead. "We all have a boss," David said.

David thought he saw the wrinkle of a smile begin to play at the edges of Rabbi Kales's mouth, though he couldn't really be sure. What he didn't see was fear. And that, above all else, made David's assumptions about the power structure between Bennie and Rabbi Kales crystallize. He wasn't scared because he knew it wasn't his time to die yet. If Rabbi Kales was found with a bullet in his head on the same day Bennie Savone was arrested, everyone would go down.

"You're in luck," Rabbi Kales said. "Benjamin's lawyer would like to speak with you." He handed the phone to David and then fished out another cigarette and lit up.

David stuffed his gun back into his waistband, cleared his throat, collected himself for a moment, tried to decide which voice he wanted to use, and then said, "With whom am I speaking?"

"Who the fuck is this?" Bennie's lawyer said.

"This is Rabbi David Cohen," David said.

There was a pause on the other end for a moment, and David thought he could hear Bennie's lawyer thinking. "Okay," he said. Another long pause. "Okay."

"I am Mr. Savone's rabbi," David said.

Another long pause. "This is Vincent Zangari, Mr. Savone's attorney. I wasn't expecting you to sound like you sound."

"How do I sound?"

"Calm," Vincent said.

"Yes, well, I am very concerned about Mr. Savone," David said.

"He said you might be." Vincent chuckled then, or let out what amounted to a chuckle. There was something strangled about what the man found amusing. David wondered just how much he knew. Maybe everything. David had never met Vincent Zangari, but he knew all about him from the news and the papers and the commercials he had on television. That was one of the weird things about Las Vegas: You'd be watching the news, and they'd be reporting on some guy cannibalizing his wife and kids, and they'd cut to the scene in front of the courthouse, and there was someone like Vincent Zangari, ten-thousand-dollar suit on, telling everyone how misunderstood his client was, how it was a simple accident involving cooked humans. They'd cut to a commercial, and there was that same lawyer, wearing the same suit, striding the neon streets of Las Vegas, letting you know that if you got "jammed up," he was the guy to get you unjammed.

Zangari's commercials had slightly higher production values and always featured him getting in and out of a Bentley. There was one specific commercial that seemed to run on a loop during the eleven o'clock news broadcasts: Zangari's Bentley pulls up to a crime scene, and the lawyer steps out of the backseat, cell phone to his ear, and approaches a line of cops standing in front of a band of yellow crime scene tape. As soon as they see Zangari, the cops lift up the tape and let him stride into the crime scene, like he's chief of police. He turns to the camera, the phone still at his ear, and says, "Keep your mouth closed. You have rights." That's it. *Keep your mouth closed. You have rights.* Simple but effective, David guessed, since Zangari seemed to be the go-to guy these days for the crime family types now that Oscar Goodman was running for mayor. The benefit of Las Vegas being an open city, David imagined, was that there was always plenty of work for guys like Zangari.

"How long do you expect him to remain in jail?" David asked.

"Depends," Vincent said. "They might not give him a bond hearing for another seventy-two hours, then they'll arraign him after that. If there's a bond, we'll get him out right away. That's no problem. But with a federal case, they might claim he's a flight risk and hold him without bond, or postpone his arraignment for thirty days. Maybe even sixty, if they end up tacking on some RICO. I've seen worse. Could be ninety."

"But what do you think?"

Another long pause. "I think Mr. Savone has a good reputation locally," he said. "He has many, many friends in all parts of local government. I think that will help him, but it won't save him from the feds doing their best to elongate the process. At this point, I don't even know what he's allegedly conspired to have done. On the outside, I would guess the feds will try to get at least thirty days on him and that they won't give him bond, based almost entirely on his last name. I'll need to make a fuss. Even still, thirty to sixty, then probably they spend the next year watching him. This isn't going to be a cakewalk. We get him out, first things first, and then see what the government has. They probably have dick, if I know these guys."

"Yes, well," David said, "Mr. Savone should know that he has the support of Temple Beth Israel."

"He knows that," Vincent said. "That's why I wanted to speak with you. Mr. Savone wanted to convey how important it was for you to make sure his wife and children were well taken care of while he's away."

"Of course," David said.

"He'd like you to keep a close eye on Rachel, specifically," Vincent said. "She might feel like Las Vegas is not a safe place for her and therefore might be considering leaving. You should make her feel safe."

"Of course," David said.

"That's good," Vincent said, "because Bennie was concerned that Rachel might be thinking of leaving town, but he knew you wouldn't let that happen if she knew you were there to watch her. Keep her safe."

"No," David said, thinking: *Fucking Bennie.* He knew everything. Probably had his own fucking house bugged. "I wouldn't let that happen."

"Because Mr. Savone wanted it made clear that if he knew *your wife* was planning a surprise trip, well, he'd let you know well in advance, just out of common courtesy. In case you wanted to buy them travel insurance or something. You understand?"

"I understand."

"He also wanted you to know, specifically, the faith he has in your work and that you shouldn't be concerned about his devotion to the temple and to your work. And that you should absolutely stay in Las Vegas."

"I wasn't planning on going anywhere," David said.

"It's not always something people plan on," Vincent said. "Sometimes, you just decide, what the hell, maybe I'll take a vacation. That wouldn't be the right course of action during this trying time."

This trying time. For fuck's sake. "Bennie doesn't need to worry about that," David said quietly.

"That's good," Vincent said. "He would also like you to keep a close eye on business affairs of the temple, for which he's made such sizable investments. He trusts your judgment on the projects while he's indisposed. Things Rabbi Kales probably isn't quite as sharp on. You are in charge. Is that clear?"

"You covered all of this ground tonight?" David said.

Vincent Zangari chuckled again. It sounded like someone swallowing chicken bones. "Let's just say we've had some discussions on the topic recently. Always good to have a contingency plan."

"You mean other than 'Keep your mouth closed' and 'You have rights'?"

"That's the best contingency plan of all," Vincent said. "One last thing. Mr. Savone did relay to me this evening how important it was for you to plan on an efficient way to clean the house. Not tonight, or even tomorrow, but shortly. Do you understand?"

"I understand," David said.

"Very well," Vincent said. "I'll be in touch with news as it comes. And Rabbi? Answer your phone, okay? I don't like having to call all over town looking for you. Seriously. You're lucky to be alive right now."

■

David found Rabbi Kales sitting behind his desk reading the Torah. Rabbi Kales's office was twice the size of David's and had a sitting area with two sofas facing each other, a low coffee table between them set with an ornate porcelain tea service, though David had never seen anyone drinking tea in the rabbi's office, not even the rabbi. David sat down on one of the sofas and picked up the samovar. "Where did you get this?" David asked.

"It belonged to my parents," Rabbi Kales said. "And before that, it belonged to their parents, in Russia."

"Where in Russia?"

"Ukraine, to be exact," Rabbi Kales said. "But I wasn't sure you'd know the difference."

"I know the difference," David said, wondering if Rabbi Kales remembered telling him about his family once before, when they first met. Maybe Rachel was right. Maybe he was shedding some space. "When was this?"

"They came here in 1909," Rabbi Kales said, though David remembered him saying it was 1919. Maybe it didn't matter.

"And they brought this all the way over from the Ukraine?"

"Yes," Rabbi Kales said.

"And you never drink out of it?"

"It's very fragile."

"How fragile could it be if it's lasted all this time?" David asked. He picked up one of the teacups. It was decorated with a pastoral scene—a green field filled with blooming flowers, and in the distance, the blue of the sea—and was rimmed in what felt like actual gold. "You should use it. Your grandparents didn't bring it all the way over from the Ukraine just to be a decoration."

"One day, it will be Rachel's, and she can do with it as she chooses," Rabbi Kales said.

David set the cup down. "So that's how it works? It's an inheritance?"

"No," Rabbi Kales said. "I received it when I got married, as did my parents. It did not seem right to pass it on to Rachel when she married."

"Because of Bennie not being Jewish?"

"My wife didn't approve, no."

"You never talk about your wife," David said.

"You never talk about *your* wife," Rabbi Kales said.

Fair enough, David thought. "Listen," David said, "there's going to be a transition here."

"I'm aware of that," Rabbi Kales said.

"Whatever you and Bennie have, that's between you two. I've got a job to do."

"As you indicated earlier," Rabbi Kales said. He rubbed at his eyes and then walked over to the sofas and sat down across from David. "How long do you expect it will take?"

"It's already happened," David said.

"No," Rabbi Kales said, "I mean how long until you're expected to kill me?"

"I guess that will be up to you," David said.

"You think that?"

"I don't see you running to the cops. I trust you will help me keep Rachel's mouth shut," David said, though he wasn't convinced she hadn't already run her mouth. "I don't have any orders right now."

"But you are aware that the orders are coming."

"Rabbi Kales," David said, "they are always coming."

"How would you do it?"

"Painlessly," David said.

"I believe you," Rabbi Kales said. He shook out another cigarette and lit up right there in his office.

"Might be the best thing would be to get cancer," David said. But then he had an idea, something that was already right in front of him. "Alzheimer's wouldn't hurt, either."

Rabbi Kales cocked his head. "Pardon me?"

"Maybe not Alzheimer's, exactly," David said. "Maybe just dementia. You got any history of that in your family?"

"They used to just call it being senile. My father was senile. His mother was senile, I remember that, her babbling in Russian about going back home to where she felt comfortable." Rabbi Kales sighed. "Half of the people in the parking lot at Smith's, at any given time, are probably senile. It's very sad."

"It doesn't have to be," David said. "Could be that you just wake up one morning and you're a little confused. Not sure where you are, go outside with two different shoes on, whatever. Think of it as an early retirement."

Rabbi Kales stared at David for a long time without speaking. "How much time will that buy me?" he said finally.

"Could be forever. If Bennie doesn't think you're a liability, there's no need to get rid of you."

"Is that what he thinks? That I'm a liability?"

"You know too much," David said flatly. "That's how it works. One day, he'll decide I know too much, and someone will come for me, too."

"You're too valuable," Rabbi Kales said.

"For now," David said. "But this whole place is changing. Whole world is changing. Not a lot of room for gangsters anymore. Everything that used to be illegal is legal now." David hadn't minded being a hit man—it was a legit job in the field, as it were—but the idea that now he was, for all intents, also an undertaker was showing him just how little a skill set like his was really going to be needed in the future. You didn't need a gun to rob someone anymore, you just needed a spreadsheet.

"How old are you, David?"

"Thirty-five," David said. Shit. No, that wasn't true. He was thirty-six now. He'd had a birthday in September. How had he forgotten to celebrate his own birthday? And now he was halfway to thirty-seven. Damn. Time fucked with you in Las Vegas.

"You talk like you're my age."

"I've seen some shit," David said.

Rabbi Kales stubbed out his cigarette on the underside of the coffee table and then picked up one of the teacups. This one was covered in vines that spun out from the handle, where a fine drawing of a tree sprouted. "This one was always my favorite," he said. "My nana used to let me hold it for one minute at a time, but only if I was sitting and only on carpet." Rabbi Kales chuckled lightly. "She's been dead for sixty years, and I still think about her. Isn't that odd?"

"Not so much," David said.

"But you see, she wasn't given a choice about when she was to die, so every day could have been her last."

"That's true for everyone," David said.

"That is not true," Rabbi Kales said. "I can't tell you how many of my relatives died in the camps, David. Do you think they had any choice?"

"They could have fought back," David said. "Maybe they did. You don't know."

"They killed the entire village my family came from in Ukraine. Not a Jew left standing. Unless they had tanks and planes, no amount of fighting would have saved them from that."

"All respect," David said, and he actually meant it, "this is a choice you made to enter into this life, with Bennie, with me, with all of this shit. And now I'm giving you a choice of how to leave it. You can either wait for me to show up one day with a gun, or you can fade away and buy some time."

"That's not a choice. It's an ultimatum. Act like I've lost my mind, or you'll kill me?"

"Call it what you want, Rabbi Kales," David said. David knew that Bennie wouldn't have anyone else take out Rabbi Kales, so if it came down to it, he'd see about implying to the rabbi that a nice cocktail and a handful of Percocet might be a good way to leave the world. "I'm offering you a lifeboat."

"You're taking everything from me," Rabbi Kales said.

"I'm giving you a chance," David said. "It's more than I need to give you."

Rabbi Kales considered this. "When would this madness have to begin?"

"Depends on how long Bennie is locked up," David said. "A stressful time like this, a psychotic break wouldn't seem that unusual. So let's say a week from today, you maybe tell Rachel that you've been feeling disoriented."

"She'll take me to see a doctor," he said.

"Great," David said. "Even better."

"Won't the doctor know that I'm lying?"

"Rabbi," David said, "how old are you?"

"Seventy-two," Rabbi Kales said. And then he nodded, getting it. "And that's it? Am I still allowed to come here?"

"Of course," David said, though he suspected Bennie would feel differently.

"Anything else?"

"One thing," David said. "Before you start losing your mind, you need to update your will. The funeral home needs to be left to the temple."

"That was to be left to Rachel," Rabbi Kales said.

"Yeah," David said, "that won't work. I'm sure Mr. Zangari can recommend an estate lawyer to you."

"You're taking everything away from me," Rabbi Kales said again.

It was true, David realized. In one day—in one hour—he'd stripped Rabbi Kales clean. It wasn't his proudest moment, but the end result was that he'd let him live. That was worth something, wasn't it?

"You've had a good life, Rabbi. Why not relax? Spend time with your granddaughters. Play golf." David understood it was hard to do those things while simultaneously drooling on yourself and pretending to be lost, but it could be a slow descent, he supposed. Rabbi Kales *was* seventy-two. Rachel had said he was slipping, but David hadn't believed it, chocking it up more to the secrets Rabbi Kales had to keep than some actual cognitive deficiency. Now, thinking about the last nine months, it seemed more than plausible, even though the rabbi still looked fit and able. "This thing," David said, "could be a *mitzvah*."

"Sal Cupertine," Rabbi Kales said, "what did he believe in?"

"Family," David said. "Duty, I guess. Retribution."

"Nothing else?"

"Everybody dies," David said. "That was sort of my motto."

"What about Rabbi David Cohen?"

"He believes in the articles of our faith, Rabbi."

Rabbi Kales smiled at David and then got up, walked over to his desk, emptied a small file box of its contents, and then came back and filled the box with the tea set, save for one cup and saucer—the one with tree branches—which he handed to David. "Does your wife drink tea?" Rabbi Kales asked.

"Sometimes," David said. "If she can't sleep."

"When you see her next, give her that cup and saucer as my regards," Rabbi Kales said. "That will be the *mitzvah*."

■

Just before midnight, David walked across the street to the funeral home to call Jerry Ford. In the time they'd been in business, they'd fostered a positive working relationship with no real sense, at least on David's part, that Ford considered him anything more than a rabbi. David tried to keep the flow of work to Ford's firm within reason in case anyone bothered to look into the business of either side of the transaction. All the paperwork was legit—or at least looked legit when it involved the bodies Bennie took in—and everyone seemed happy. David wasn't exactly sure when it occurred to him that it was no happy accident that Jerry had appeared on the scene with this wonderful offer to help the Jewish faith by moving corpse tissue, though the afternoon he saw Jerry and Bennie chatting amiably out in front of the temple confirmed what he probably should have always known: that Bennie was involved from the get-go. It was simply another layer of secrecy: If David didn't know that Bennie had the initial idea, it was one less potential witness for the prosecution.

The endeavor needed a rabbi . . . and that was never going to be Rabbi Kales, nor the late Rabbi Gottlieb. And who knew what Bennie had on Jerry Ford. Probably nothing, once he thought about it. Guys like Jerry, they wanted to work with the mob. Made them feel like they were doing something out of a movie. It wasn't like that in Chicago too much because the stakes were too high. People in Chicago were much more open about killing you. Here it just helped get you into nice strip clubs, maybe a little extra grind for your twenty bucks.

Thus, David was under the impression that Jerry Ford might be willing to do him and the temple a little favor. So David sat down in the funeral director's office and called Jerry Ford's cell phone.

He picked up on the first ring. "How you doing, Ruben?" he said.

"This isn't Ruben," David said. "It's Rabbi Cohen."

"Oh, sorry, Rabbi," he said. "Ruben calls me so often in the middle of the night, my wife is beginning to think something is up."

"Yes, well," David said.

"Not that my wife has reason to worry otherwise, you understand," he said. In the background, David could hear music and people talking. It was midnight on Super Bowl Sunday, and it didn't seem like Jerry was keeping vigil at one of the local hospitals.

"Listen," David said, "a man has taken his life and has asked that his body be buried in a traditional Jewish ceremony, with conditions, however, and so I'm hoping you might be of some help."

"How'd he go?"

"He shot himself in the head, I'm afraid," David said.

"Okay, I'm listening," Jerry said. If Jerry was completely above board, he would have already hung up, but David could hear the man making calculations in his head. Internal organs were big business . . . and not a business he was normally privy to . . . and a bullet to the head wasn't the sort of thing that spoiled a kidney.

"He'd like only his hands, feet, and head to be buried and for the rest of his body to be disposed of," David said.

"Strange," Jerry said.

"Yes, well, he was not right in his mind," David said. "And while I'd like to respect his wishes, I'd hate for what was an otherwise healthy young man to not pay forward the gift of life, particularly if someone could use a kidney or a liver or heart."

"Of course," Jerry said. David could hear that Jerry had stepped outside now, the music gone, replaced by the sound of traffic. He was probably on the Strip or, worse, at one of the local casinos playing cheap poker with guys in satin jackets.

"Unfortunately Ruben is gone for the evening, and thus you'd need to handle the harvesting on your own. I trust you would dispose of the internal organs in an appropriate fashion."

Jerry paused for a moment and then said, "Yeah, I can take care of all of that. No problem. No problem in the least. I've got a guy who can do that."

"Because I know you can't handle the organs yourself," David said.

"Right," he said. "The extremities, you got that part handled? Avoiding the long bones, that would be best. I'm talking femur, tibia, humerus. Keeping those intact would be, uh, helpful, in terms of paying it forward."

"Yes," David said. "One of our technicians has taken care of that. But he isn't certified for the other work. So if you think you can handle this, I'd be happy for the help. Though I think it might be wise for you take caution here. You'd hate to lose your license."

"I'll take supreme caution, Rabbi. Absolutely."

"Good." David paused for a moment and thought about everything that had transpired that day and over the last few weeks, tried to figure out just how to say next what he wanted to say, and then decided being simple and direct was probably the route to go. "I'm not sure if you heard, but Mr. Savone was arrested today."

"Yeah, yeah, tough stuff there," Jerry said. "Saw him getting perp-walked on the news tonight. Terrible."

"Yes, horrible. Horrible indeed. We're hoping to help get him bonded out, of course, so it would be helpful if you could bring cash with you tonight instead of waiting sixty days."

"Cash? How much are we talking about?"

"Whatever you think is the correct amount."

"And this is for Bennie?"

"In light of everything," David said. It was one of those terms he'd heard Rabbi Kales use periodically that seemed to comfort everyone while saying absolutely nothing.

"Right, okay, " Jerry said. "For the temple."

"Yes, for the temple."

"No problem, Rabbi," Jerry said. "I'll cash a check at the Bellagio, and we'll be good to go. Everything will be above board. What time should I be there?"

"Ninety minutes," David said. That would be enough time to get Gray Beard and Marvin back out the door, get the body refrigerated, and make sure there were no bumps in the road. Like another actual body being delivered for non-nefarious purposes. "I'll have all the paperwork waiting for you, too. Please don't be late."

David hung up and leaned back in the chair. Ruben's office was small and tidy—a desk, a computer, a phone, a Rolodex, a file cabinet, a framed copy of his funeral director's license, another of his diploma from a mortuary school in Arizona—and smelled like lemon Pledge. There were photos on the desk of a little boy dressed in a Little League uniform, another of Ruben with a woman, presumably his wife, and the same child wearing Hawaiian shirts, the blue waves of the Pacific Ocean crashing behind them, a sunset of orange and pink hovering above the horizon.

What did he know about this asshole? Nothing, really. He worked with him on a daily basis and didn't even know his last name. He looked at Ruben's diploma. *Ruben Topaz.* He sounded like a fucking magician.

In the photo, Ruben's wife wore a diamond ring that could be seen from Russian satellites (which went well with the diamond-crusted watch Ruben had on in the photo, which must have been his vacation watch, as opposed to the nice gold number he wore to the office each day), a diamond pendant necklace, a diamond tennis bracelet, and diamond studs in her ears . . . all of which helped David understand why Ruben was the only other person on the planet Bennie trusted, even a little bit.

Mostly, the photo just made David feel . . . sad. Yes, that's what he was feeling. Sadness. He felt bad for calling Ruben an asshole in his head, that was one thing, but there were other more specific things pinging around in there tonight, too. He'd been gone now almost a year . . . and did Jennifer even have photos of him? He wasn't real big on his image being snapped, for obvious reasons, but now it seemed like a terrible thing. And then: Could he even remember Jennifer's voice? Would he even recognize William? Would either of them recognize *him*?

It was 2:15 a.m. in Chicago. Jennifer would be asleep on her right side, the blankets pulled up to her neck, her sketchbook on the nightstand, the remote control on top of it. William would be asleep on his stomach, his bed filled with army men and *Star Wars* action figures. Or maybe he'd be into something new. Almost a year.

David picked up the phone.

Fuck it to death.

He punched in the first nine digits of his phone number. All that was left was the number 5. That was it. Just the number 5, and he could hear Jennifer's voice, tell her he was alive, tell her that he was coming back, eventually, and that she needed to wait for him. Tell her that he was going to take her and William away from Chicago, that they'd go to Hawaii or Barbados or, hell, Green Bay if that's where she wanted to go. Tell her that he was out of the game just as soon as he finished cleaning out the closet . . .

"Oh, excuse me, Rabbi Cohen, I didn't know you were here."

David whipped around in his seat, the phone clattering from his hand, and found Miguel, the tech who'd worked on Paul Bruno, standing in the doorway dressed in a suit, holding one of the saws they used to cut open the bodies.

"What the fuck are you doing here?" David said before he could catch himself.

"It's my night," Miguel said, but the look on his face said something entirely different. That didn't explain the fucking giant saw.

"Your night?" David was still rattled, things weren't computing right, and there was about to be a fucking headless, footless, handless torso delivered to the funeral home in an RV. Not exactly standard practice. When the bodies came in from the other families, it was always Ruben who checked them in. He'd let Miguel or the other techs work on them, but shipping and handling was his area of expertise.

"Super Bowl Sunday," Miguel said, "can be a busy night. People lose a lot of money." David just stared at Miguel, trying to figure out what the fuck he was saying. "You know, people have heart attacks, or they jump off something. It's an emotional night. So we always have someone on that night, in case of emergencies."

"What are you doing with that saw?"

Miguel looked down at his hands and seemed surprised to find he was still holding the saw. "I thought someone had broken in," Miguel said.

"And you were going to cut them in two?"

"I guess I didn't know what I was going to do," Miguel said. He gave David a sheepish grin.

David smiled back. Just two guys in a mortuary, one with a saw, the other with a gun stuffed in his waistband.

"How long have you been here?"

"Bus dropped me off around ten," Miguel said. "I might have fallen asleep in the back, so I didn't hear you come in."

"No, I mean, how long have you worked here?" Though, actually, he meant both things.

"Oh, three years in June."

"You like your job?"

"It's cool," Miguel said with a shrug. "I like the responsibility."

"Did you hear my phone conversation?"

Miguel looked confused. "I'm sorry?"

"I was on the phone," David said. "Did you hear me talking?"

"I heard voices," Miguel said carefully. "That's what woke me up."

David examined Miguel closely. His suit was olive green and cheap—probably bought from one of those places in the Meadows Mall called Suitz or Stylez or Fashionz. His watch had a leather band. No rings on his hands. His shoes were brown and didn't really match his suit, and he wasn't wearing a belt. In his whole life, he'd probably never made over fifteen bucks an hour. What did this Miguel know about him? Probably nothing. What did Miguel know about Bennie Savone? Probably an awful lot.

There was a single bead of sweat on Miguel's upper lip.

David could see Miguel's pulse beating in his neck.

He kept swallowing.

"So, yes or no," David said, testing Miguel, because he knew the answer just from looking at him.

"I guess," he said. "Yes. I guess."

"You have a wife?"

"No," Miguel said.

"Kids? You got some shorties running around? Is that what you call them now? *Shorties?*"

Miguel shook his head. "No, that means *girlfriends*. Actually, it means both things. Depends how you say it. Like the context of the word."

"You got either one of those?"

"No, not right now."

"So, no wife. No kids. No girlfriend. What the fuck do you have, Miguel?"

"Rabbi?"

"What the fuck do you have?"

"I'm afraid I don't understand what you're asking," Miguel said.

"It's a simple question, Miguel: What the fuck do you have?"

David knew that what was throwing Miguel off was that one word—*fuck*—that he'd dropped early into their conversation and now felt married to using a few more times, just because it felt good saying the word out loud after having it run through his mind pretty much constantly, in different derivations, for the last nine months.

"I guess nothing big," Miguel said.

"Nothing worth losing your life over then, right?"

Miguel swallowed hard. "No, nothing worth dying over."

"Then if you think this place is ever getting robbed," David said, "run out the back door. Because *nothing* is worth dying over . . . particularly not something you might have *thought* you heard."

"Yes, Rabbi," Miguel said. He now had a good seven beads of sweat on his upper lip, and David was somewhat concerned that if his pulse didn't slow down a tick, Miguel would stroke out.

"Go home," David said.

"I'm on until six."

"Put that saw down, and go home," David said, and this time Miguel didn't bother to disagree. He set the saw down on the desk, nodded once at David, and then left.

David picked up the phone, which had begun to bleat from the incomplete call, and examined it for a moment. He'd been so close. One number away. But nothing here was worth dying over. That much was absolutely true.

■

At 12:57, Gray Beard and Marvin pulled up to the receiving bay of the funeral home in a white cargo van that said lincoln medical supply & uniform on both sides. At first David thought he'd failed to account for something important, but then he saw Marvin behind the wheel and realized that Gray Beard wasn't shitting him: They did everything professional.

The van backed up to the building, and Marvin came around to the rear of the vehicle. He held a clipboard and wore a crisp white uniform with the Lincoln Medical logo on the back of his shirt. He even had a name tag, except it said Alex.

"We have a delivery," Marvin said.

"Okay," David said.

Marvin opened up the van's rear double doors and pulled down a short metal ramp. He then climbed into the cargo hold and pushed down a large cart topped with freshly laundered towels. "Everything you ordered should be in the cart," Marvin said.

He peeled back several layers of towels to reveal that the cart was filled with ice and, in two body bags, what was left of Dr. Kirsch. David had thought getting shipped across the country in a freezing cold meat truck was a bad lot, but he supposed there was, in fact, worse ways to get from point A to point B.

"If you just want to sign off here," Marvin handed David the official-looking clipboard, "we'll be on our way."

According to the paperwork, they'd been making deliveries all over town for the last few hours, including a stop at the Marshall Brothers mortuary a few miles away, where the goyim seemed to gather for the afterlife, and which made David ponder just what the future might hold in terms of revenue streams if he had to stay in Las Vegas for the long term. David signed his initials where indicated, figuring that if they were going to go this far with putting on a show, he'd keep it up, too. He gave the clipboard back to Marvin, who silently nodded his ascent and headed back to the front of the van.

David walked around to the passenger side, and Gray Beard rolled down his window. He was also wearing a Lincoln Medical uniform. "Everything okay?" Gray Beard said.

"Looks like it," David said.

"You left a real mess there," Grey Beard said. "But we managed pretty well. Took care of some hair we found, some fibers, that sort of thing. No charge." Gray Beard smiled. "On account of you maybe giving me an early retirement."

"Be discreet," David said.

"Always am," Gray Beard said.

"You got a ballpark figure for me?"

"Why don't we go a flat twenty thousand now, more later once I'm able to move some machinery and that Jaguar. Don't know who might want an X-ray machine and bunch of surgical equipment, but I'm gonna find out."

"That works," David said, making calculations in his mind. Twenty thousand dollars was the kind of money that could make a difference for a little while. Maybe another eight or ten from Jerry Ford, that would make an even bigger difference. Fifty thousand, now that would be the kind of money that a person and a child could maybe live a year on, particularly if they didn't have a lot of other bills. "But if you can get me fifty in the next day or two, we'll call it square for the whole job."

"Give me until Wednesday," Gray Beard said. "Tuesday night if you're in a rush."

"I trust you," David said.

"After what I've seen," Grey Beard said, "I'm glad that's true."

■

Thirty minutes later, right on time, Jerry Ford showed up in the refrigerated LifeCore truck.

David already had Dr. Kirsch's head and extremities set for burial tomorrow, and the rest of Dr. Kirsch was on a gurney and ready to go, so when he saw Jerry pull up, he met him outside with the body.

"Just you tonight, Rabbi?" Jerry said.

"It's Super Bowl Sunday," David said.

"Better than Christmas," Jerry said. He unzipped the body bag and examined Dr. Kirsch. "He's been kept cool?"

"Yes," David said.

"The whole time?"

"As soon as his body was discovered, yes," David said.

"The major organs, those are probably shot, but we'll see," Jerry said. He pinched the skin on Dr. Kirsch's bicep. "Everything else looks good." He zipped the bag back up and then loaded Dr. Kirsch into the back of his truck and closed the doors back up.

David handed Jerry a thick manila envelope filled with all the needed paperwork for the transfer of one Gabe Krantz to the good people at LifeCore, which Jerry didn't even give a cursory glance to. He just reached into his pocket, took out a banded, half-inch stack of hundreds, and handed them to David.

"Everything look in order?" Jerry asked.

David flipped through the cash, just to be sure it wasn't filled with singles, and suddenly it was like the old days, back when he did collections, back when this all seemed pretty glamorous, back when he thought his cousin Ronnie was the coolest man alive, back when he and Fat Monte were friends, hanging out, going on double dates. Back when none of this seemed even remotely plausible. Way back when.

"Yes," David said.

"*L'chaim*," Jerry said, and then he got back in his truck and was gone. It occurred to David then that there was a pretty good chance Jerry Ford wasn't really a Jew. Not that it mattered.

Rabbi David Cohen locked up the funeral home and mortuary and then, for a long time, he stood in front of the entrance to the cemetery and stared up at the sky. Most of the time, it was impossible to see any stars, the light pollution from the Strip giving everything a strange green glow at night. In Summerlin, though, there were still ordinances about that sort of thing, and this close to the Red Rocks, if you faced away from the Strip, you could actually imagine you were somewhere else.

It wouldn't always be this way, David knew. The newspaper had stories every other day about new casino developments getting approved on this end of town, along with huge shopping centers, to satisfy the needs of the one hundred thousand people who were supposed to eventually inhabit Summerlin.

It wasn't a bad place to live. In the last nine months, David had grown warm to the convenience of the villages of Summerlin. He had his coffee place. He had a pizza joint he liked— a Detroit pizza, of all things—called Northside Nathan's. He'd come to depend on the Bagel Café for decent corned beef and a pretty fair bagel. He even had a few places he liked to knock around in: a pub called the Outside Inn that had cheap whiskey and salty prime rib and no Jews (owing primarily to their hunting motif, David thought); a shopping center called Best in the West a few streets down, off of Rainbow, that had an ice cream shop where some angry kid mixed flavors on a slab of marble. He'd go into that store sometimes and imagine what flavors Jennifer and William would choose.

The idea that she was struggling to pay the bills made David sick. He wasn't sure if Rabbi Kales had said that to make him feel that way. Once David got the money from Gray Beard, he'd get her some cash, and she'd be okay for a bit. A little breathing room was all she'd need while he figured out the plan.

And maybe the plan was changing. Maybe it wasn't about getting back to Chicago anymore. Maybe it was about getting Jennifer and William to Las Vegas, where he could protect them. Get William into the Tikvah Preschool here. Keep him in all the way through high school. Get him into a good college. Maybe he'd become a doctor or a lawyer, or just the kind of guy people weren't afraid to strike up a conversation with at a bar. What must that be like?

What would Jennifer make of this new life? It dawned on David then that in just nine months he'd been able to set up an entirely new life, here in the desert, and while it wasn't perfect, it was a life and it had room for his wife and kid, for sure. And for the first time in his life, he was on top. Bennie was in jail, at least for a while. And then, who knew? Maybe he'd end up doing a year or two or ten, or just six months. Whatever. He wasn't physically present, which meant that the only person who knew the truth about David was Rabbi Kales, and he was soon to be out of the picture, too. The day-to-day operations of two legit businesses—the temple and the funeral home and attached cemetery—would be under his control.

There would be so much money: all the donations, and the tuition, and the general operating budget of the temple, and then the money moved through the funeral home. The real business alone was lucrative. The murder business was a windfall, and they hadn't even gone outside the Italian families. If they started talking to the Chinese or the Russians or even the Mexicans and blacks . . . well, there were a lot of potential markets that weren't being tapped, mostly because Bennie didn't like dealing with anyone outside the traditional families. He just wasn't thinking forward. The Bloods and Crips were killing each other at a pretty remarkable clip just a few miles away.

In Chicago, the Family farmed out a lot of their drug trade to the Mexican gang—the Gangster 2-6—and that had worked out well enough, so at least there was a working template . . . though it wouldn't exactly be easy to explain the sudden influx of dead Jews who were also Chinese or Mexican or black, David supposed. So that could wait.

Maybe what he'd do, David thought, was just kill Bennie Savone and keep it all for himself and . . .

He'd been set up to succeed. And tonight, after nine months, he had done just that. Wasn't that all he ever wanted?

"No," he said aloud.

And there it was.

There was only one person alive who could predict how Sal Cupertine might react to this new life, one person who might benefit from knowing that Sal Cupertine wasn't just efficient, wasn't just ruthless, but was also *adaptable*, who could be taught to have a new life.

Only one person who might, after all this, figure out how to profit from sending Sal Cupertine to Las Vegas to become Rabbi David Cohen.

Only one person who knew where he was.

Cousin Ronnie.

It all made so much sense now.

CHAPTER FIFTEEN

J eff Hopper loved Las Vegas. When he was still living in Walla Walla, he'd drive out to Pasco and pick up a flight to Las Vegas on a Friday afternoon and be playing blackjack at the Sahara by dinnertime. Sometimes he'd go with friends, but Jeff mostly preferred to go by himself. Once he settled in Chicago, his trips became less frequent, but he still managed to get out at least once a year . . . except for this last year, which had been completely lost to him.

He had a whole system: He never stayed at a casino—which meant he ended up staying at some shitty hotels over the years, invariably called the Royal Plaza Inn—so that once he went off to bed, there was no temptation to play just one more hand. He always had a cheap steak dinner at the Barbary Coast's Victorian Room. And, without fail, he always played a couple of hands at the Frontier, just to see if the Culinary Union was still on strike there, as they'd been since the early 1990s.

The hotel was a microcosm for just how terminally screwed up the city really was: Howard Hughes had purchased it, the Desert Inn, the Sands, and a handful of other casinos in the

1960s as part of his quest to clean the Mafia out of Las Vegas, only to turn those places into his own strange fiefdom. And then a few years after his death, the Frontier was sold to the Elardi family, who promptly gutted the casino, tried to bust the unions, and ended up with picketers for the better part of a decade. And no one even got killed in the process.

Now, though, four days after the Super Bowl Sunday raid on Kochel Farms, as he drove away from the Strip toward the tony suburb of Summerlin—a place built by the Howard Hughes Corporation, too, in the ultimate coup de grace for old Las Vegas—Jeff couldn't help thinking it was better back then because the Mafia would never have put a Gilley's in the Frontier. The idea of a mechanical bull on the Strip as absurd as the giant sword of Excalibur jutting into the sky, or the laser beam from the top of the Luxor. Hard to imagine Frank, Dean, and Sammy doing their show in a glowing pyramid. Of course, the Mafia was still operating out here, they just couldn't afford to run the casinos anymore.

Not the big ones, anyway. There were a few silent partners still involved with the sportsbooks, though the FBI was content to keep their eyes averted since they weren't breaking tourists' legs or getting involved in point shaving (at least not as obviously as they used to), and there was some decent grift going on with the prevalence of video poker machines in every bar and restaurant in town. All victimless crimes. No one seemed to be running to the FBI to complain they'd lost at video poker.

The Mafia in Las Vegas these days was all about secondary markets: the booming construction business that had spoked out in every direction from the Strip; the warehouse-size strip clubs that promised huge cash hauls on a nightly basis; the resort drug trade of ecstasy, coke, and pills. They didn't bother with the hard stuff or the easy stuff, leaving the heroin, crack, and weed to the Bloods and Crips, who mostly operated out of the slums of North Las Vegas.

The strange thing about Las Vegas, the part that Jeff really loved, was that the local press treated everyone with an Italian name who got nicked for a crime like they were John Gotti. The front page of both the *Review-Journal* and the *Sun* this week ran a huge story on someone named Bennie Savone, a local hood who wasn't even connected to a family, just running his own crew out of a strip club in town called the Wild Horse, who'd apparently overseen a series of wholesale beatings and shakedowns of his customers, plus some run-of-the-mill credit card scams. Jeff hadn't bothered to read the whole story—it was bush-league stuff. That was the thing about open cities like Las Vegas: If you were criminal minded, no one was going to tell you what you couldn't do, particularly if you were good for the ecosystem, and that included the local media. What else were they going to report on?

Las Vegas had always been the second home for the crime families, with the Chicago crews running huge swatches of the city for decades before eventually receding into the background through the unions, particularly the Teamsters and Culinary Union, though with the corporatization of the casinos, they simply weren't as prevalent anymore. Turns out, not even the Mafia can muscle an entire corporation.

Not as prevalent, however, didn't mean gone. Which is why Jeff was in Las Vegas in the first place. The delivery trucks that exited from Kochel Farms on that night the previous April had gone all over the country—as far east as Vermont, as far west as California, but nothing south of Missouri, which made sense considering how the Kansas City crews still had so much influence in the steak world—but the largest concentration was in Nevada and California, home to countless hotels and steak houses. There were only a few probable locations, based on where there was actual organized crime taking place and where the trucks had stopped, at least according to their logs, which could have been falsified.

"You think Cupertine is living inside a Sizzler?" Matthew said to Jeff on the phone the morning after the raid, after Agent Poremba was able to get the trucking information Jeff had requested.

"Someone saw him," Jeff said. "I know it. That's enough to get us moving in the right direction."

"What about the drivers?"

"We can't get to them yet," Jeff said. "They've got no reason to speak to you and me. In a week, maybe the FBI will pick them up, but what will they say? They'll be lawyered up long before any questioning."

"Maybe one of them has a conscience," Matthew said. "Could be waiting the week is the way to do it. What's the hurt in waiting?"

"Because this is ours, Matthew," Jeff said. "This is what we've been working toward. And it's what I'm paying you for." Matthew sighed on the other end of the line. He was still in Walla Walla; Jeff was still in Chicago, sitting at Midway, waiting to figure out where he was going to fly to. "We can only make a dent if we do this separately."

"This is about that night at the Four Treys. You don't trust me anymore," Matthew said.

"I don't trust us together," Jeff said.

"You know the bureau would have given Fat Monte a deal," Matthew said. "Would that have been better?"

"His wife is showing some signs she might come out," Jeff said.

"So, what, she can have Ronnie Cupertine toss her into Lake Michigan? She's better off staying in a coma the rest of her life."

"If she can talk," Jeff said, "we'd have another chip in this. We have a week to get something solid, and if that happens, it's all yours. I'm done."

"That's a big if," Matthew said.

"It's what we're left with."

"What's your hunch?" Matthew asked.

Kochel Farms had over a hundred accounts in Nevada—sixty-nine in Las Vegas, seventeen in Reno, another dozen in Tahoe, another seven in Carson City—and over a hundred and fifty in California—thirty-two in the San Francisco Bay Area, seventy-five in and around Los Angeles, twenty in Palm Springs, and then a few more spread out in San Diego, the California side of Tahoe, and Silicon Valley.

Jeff examined the list of businesses: Kochel Farms trade was in either supplying high-quality meats—prime rib, porterhouse steaks, and the like—or low-quality meats—ground beef, rump roasts—so they worked with high-class hotels and pricey restaurants, but also with schools, ethnic meat markets, and crappy burger stands.

There was no way they'd stick Cupertine in Tahoe, he'd be too obvious, and the Mafia there was like a boutique business these days, mostly running low-level slot machine scams, the odd bit of prostitution, the occasional loan sharking business. Too family-oriented. No room for tough guys. And no one out there could afford whatever Ronnie's asking price would have been.

He had to be strategic about this.

"I know Las Vegas," Jeff said, "so I'll start there, then move up to Reno. You ever spent any time in L.A.?"

"I went to Disneyland when I was eleven," Matthew said. "So I could stake out the Haunted Mansion if you think that will help."

"What about Palm Springs?"

"My grandparents have a time-share," he said. "You think the Bonannos bought Cupertine and he's calling bingo numbers now? Is that our best shot?"

"It's not impossible," Jeff said.

"You have some metric on how to approach this list of places?"

"One by one sounds like the only way, starting with any places that have strong old-school union or criminal ties, people who still might be willing to do a favor for the Family or who might actually need someone like Sal Cupertine," Jeff said. "We need to shoe-leather this, Matthew. Hand out photos. Talk about the people he killed. Get anyone who might be scared of talking feeling comfortable that they'll be protected."

"Will they?" Matthew asked. Then: "Will I? Because that's a question I have."

"I know," Jeff said.

"I want to live a long life, and I don't want to spend all of it looking over my shoulder if we somehow muck this up."

"Look," Jeff said, "after this, you're done. Okay? I'll pay you your whole nut, and we'll consider it a done deal, with or without Cupertine."

Matthew didn't say anything for a moment, and Jeff assumed the kid would say no, no, he was in for the long haul, that this was his obsession, too, and that he'd chase this white whale around perdition's flames if need be. Instead he said, "Okay."

Now, three days after that conversation, Jeff merged onto the Summerlin Parkway feeling no closer to Sal Cupertine and farther away from Las Vegas in general. He'd spent the last days working the Strip, Downtown, the joints clustered around UNLV, then down into Green Valley and Henderson, and it was, frankly, depressing. Sometime in the last few years, the Las Vegas he remembered had turned both into a place to bring the family—the number of people he saw pushing strollers down the Strip was truly appalling—and a place to descend into absolute, opulent, asshole-fueled debauchery. $3.99 prime rib had been replaced by $100 artisan burgers. The strip clubs were essentially legalized prostitution, twenty-four hours a day, twenty bucks to get a girl to bounce on your lap for five minutes at a time. And inside every restaurant or bar or casino or strip club, there was a group of five or ten unsmiling guys trying to look tough, wearing too much cologne and jewelry, calling cocktail girls "bitch" and tossing money at them, like they were acting out characters in a movie.

He hit several of the big old-school hotels—Circus Circus, the Sahara—some that probably had contracts with Kochel Farms dating back twenty years and which historically had strong ties to the old Culinary Union, places that might still stand up and take notice if Ronnie Cupertine needed something. But the people he met in food service there were in their twenties and early thirties and were mostly Mexican; the managers were fresh-faced corporate types, guys who'd shit themselves if someone stuck a gun in their face or would just call the cops if someone tried to shake them down. If someone higher up came down to the loading dock to pick up some gangster out of the back of a truck, there'd be fifty witnesses, none of whom would likely be willing to put their own life on the line for fifteen bucks an hour. Plus, the level of security was astounding: Cameras and armed private security guards were everywhere. The casinos were, after all, just giant banks when it came right down to it.

The newer luxury hotels that had contracts with Kochel Farms—the Monte Carlo, the MGM, the Bellagio, even the revamped Caesars—barely even let Jeff in the door, which didn't make it likely that they off-loaded a hit man, either, and the restaurants inside them were all corporate jobs for the most part, none of them connected to any known crime figures.

He hit up the bars and the dives and the mom-n-pop joints on the list, and the reaction he got was the same each time, usually some variation on, "Why the fuck would we be hiding that guy? Get the fuck out of my business." He event went off the map a few times, rolling into venerable (and reputed Mafia) businesses like the Venetian, the twenty-four-hour pasta spot over on Sahara, and Piero's over by the Convention Center, just to get the feel for the city again, listen in on conversations, that sort of thing, but all he heard were tourists quoting *The Godfather* while they ordered dessert.

And now Summerlin, Howard Hughes's landgrab that had turned twenty-five thousand acres of scrub desert into high-end suburbia, replete with private golf courses, McMansions, man-made lakes, and millions of dollars' worth of plastic surgery patients. Hughes wanted to rid Las Vegas of organized crime, and he did a pretty good job of it. But he'd replaced one kind of criminal with elements just as immoral and ruthless: real estate developers and elective surgery outlets.

Jeff exited on Buffalo, then headed west on Vegas Drive and then up Hillpointe, past gated developments with names like Adagio, Cielo Vista, and Painted Shadow Canyon, signs for the TPC golf course and vacant lots that promised "unique, timeless homes at exclusive members' pricing!" Jeff couldn't help but think of Paul Bruno.

There were six places in and around Summerlin Jeff needed to visit today, and he figured he'd knock the easiest one out first—the cafeteria at the Tikvah Preschool and Dorothy Copeland Children's Center at Temple Beth Israel—before going to a bar called Bananaz, a couple delis, a new resort in Summerlin, and then two different country clubs.

The idea that a private preschool might need its own meat distributer seemed absurd on the face of things, until Jeff saw the sprawling campus of Temple Beth Israel unfold in front of him. On one side of the street was the temple, with a lattice-work of adjoining buildings and green spaces forming a crescent against the road. Aside the crescent of completed buildings was another series of buildings—the signs said it was a private K–12 school called the Barer Academy—which looked to be about 80 percent finished and which at the moment was filled with construction workers.

On the other side of the street was a funeral home, a cemetery, and even more construction—a learning center and another park that promised tennis courts and an aquatic center by 2001. Jeff thought of Paul Bruno again—a guy like him could have made a billion dollars selling real estate in Las Vegas.

Jeff parked in the temple's lot and gathered up his materials— a notepad, a pen, a stack of photos of Sal Cupertine, his cell phone, and his gun, but then thought better of it and stuffed the gun in the glove box of his rented Pontiac, figuring that bringing a gun into a house of worship that was also filled with kids was a bad idea. No need to court anxiety and trouble where it wasn't needed, particularly not for an exercise that would probably be over in ten minutes or less. The bars and delis, well, those he'd come strapped in. You never knew who was hiding in the back of those places.

He walked through the temple, poked his head into their little Judaica shop, which was well stocked but didn't seem to have anyone actually working in it, and then made his way down a long hall to the temple's administrative office . . . where he sat for fifteen uncomfortable minutes, waiting for someone with a little authority to come and speak with him, since the receptionist was no help whatsoever. It was nine thirty in the morning. If he wanted to get everything done that he planned for the day, he'd need to bounce in another fifteen minutes, come back the next day, or just cross it off the list as cleared.

He'd shown the receptionist, a woman in her late fifties named Esther, several photos of Sal Cupertine, and she hadn't recognized him, and she said she'd been there every weekday for the last three years, except for holidays and when she went on vacation to the Hotel del Coronado in San Diego.

"Rabbi Cohen should be here any minute now," Esther said.

"Is Rabbi Cohen the only person who can take me over to the cafeteria?"

"Oh, yes," Esther said. "We have very strict rules about strangers coming onto the campus during school hours. Rabbi Cohen or Rabbi Kales must be with you at all times, for safety purposes. We can't very well have strangers with the children, you understand."

"Is Rabbi Kales in?"

"Oh, no, he's out ill. Rabbi Cohen should be here any moment now," she said, a touch too sternly for Jeff's taste. "A cup of coffee would probably make the time pass faster, that's what I've always found."

"Okay, thank you," Jeff said. Esther stepped away then, so

Jeff got up and looked out the window to the construction going on across the street. What a strange combination of facilities: a funeral home and a Jewish cemetery surrounded by an aquatic center, tennis courts, and, at least according to the signs, a performing arts center. The entire circle of life on one street.

"Can I help you?"

Jeff turned around. Standing in the doorway was a man in an expensive black suit, a thick salt-and-pepper beard, glasses, close-cropped black hair that showed just a hint of gray at the temples, a black yarmulke on the back of his head. He was maybe six foot, lean in the body but had some weight in his face, like maybe he ate a few too many cookies. Jeff guessed he was in his forties.

"I'm waiting for Rabbi Cohen," Jeff said.

The man cocked his head, like he hadn't quite heard him. "Did you have an appointment?"

"No," Jeff said. "I'm actually here on some sensitive business that I hoped to discuss with him." He stepped back over to the uncomfortable chair and gathered up his materials. "I'm actually wondering if anyone here has seen this man." He handed the man a photo of Sal Cupertine. He stared at it for just a moment, then handed it back.

"I didn't get your name," the man said.

"Jeff Hopper," he said, and he extended his hand.

"Rabbi David Cohen," the man replied, though instead of shaking Jeff's hand, he clasped his hands behind his back. "I'm afraid I've just come back from a funeral, so my hands are covered in dirt."

"Oh, of course, right," Jeff said. It was one of the few things Jeff knew about Jewish funerals: Everyone threw dirt on the casket. It was both touching and a little creepy, though of course *someone* had to bury the dead. What must it be like for this man, Jeff wondered, who had to throw dirt on the graves of people every day? What must it be like to be so intimate with death? Jeff wasn't a religious man, so he never gave much thought to people like priests and rabbis, never considered that when it all came down to the end of things, they were always there to handle the worst of it. How do you not take that home with you at night? Four people had died because of Jeff's actions—or his inactions, anyway—and he wore their memories like chain mail. And then there was Paul Bruno . . . and Fat Monte . . . and who knew what the hell would happen to Fat Monte's wife, a still-living vegetable?

"I can come back," Jeff said, because suddenly he realized just how fruitless it was to be at Temple Beth Israel, of all places, bothering this rabbi.

"No, it's fine," Rabbi Cohen said. He smiled then, but only half of his mouth seemed to work just right. Like maybe he'd had a minor stroke at some point.

Esther returned with a cup of coffee and the morning's *Review-Journal* under one arm. "Rabbi Cohen, this nice man has been waiting to speak with you," she said.

"Of course," Rabbi Cohen said. He gave Esther that same crooked smile. No, it wasn't a stroke, Jeff decided. The guy just didn't seem comfortable smiling. "Why don't you take Mr. Hooper to my office while I wash up. Is that fine with you, Mr. Hooper?"

"Yes, that's fine," Jeff said. "And it's Hopper, not Hooper."

"Of course," Rabbi Cohen said. There was that smile again. There was something funky about his teeth, too, Jeff thought, like maybe his bite was off, his teeth not quite matching up. "And Esther, if you could do me a small favor," Rabbi Cohen continued, "if you could run down to the Bagel Café and pick up an order of lox for Rabbi Kales and take it to his house, I would appreciate it. I was to bring him lunch this afternoon, but this morning has been a trying one, as you can imagine, with Mrs. Goldfarb, and I thought we'd close the offices until this afternoon's funeral."

"Oh, yes, Rabbi Cohen," she said. "I'll do that right away." She nodded solemnly, like the rabbi had just asked her to put down his dog. This was not a world Jeff understood, clearly.

The rabbi excused himself then, so Jeff followed Esther down the hall to a small, neat office. It had chest-high bookcases lining one wall, the books all spine out and at the front edge of the shelf, not a single one out of place. There was a wide oak desk that faced the door, a high-backed black leather chair behind it, two less-comfortable-looking chairs in front of it. There was a window behind the desk, too, and it was open just a crack, and Jeff could hear the sound of children playing nearby. Recess, probably.

On the other side of the office, there was a large dry-erase calendar filled with events affixed to the wall—Jeff could only guess what the *Valentine's Day Kugel Off!* might possibly entail, never mind the *Y2K&U* talk that was scheduled for the end of the month—and beneath it was a wooden cabinet topped with a few knickknacks: a teacup and saucer, a framed diploma from a rabbinical school on a metal stand, a menorah. There wasn't a speck of dust anywhere.

Esther set Jeff's cup and newspaper on the edge of the desk.

She kneaded her hands together in what appeared to be honest worry.

"Esther, are you okay?" Jeff asked.

"Rabbi Cohen has never entrusted me with an errand before. It's a big step. He didn't specify if he wanted bagels as well and I certainly don't want to assume, since you know what that does!"

"I say go ahead and get the bagels," Jeff said. "Who was ever upset to get a bagel, even if they didn't ask for one?"

This brightened Esther considerably. "That's an excellent point." She patted Jeff on the knee. "Thank you. That's such a wonderful way of looking at the world."

After Esther left him in the rabbi's office, Jeff tried to imagine what it would feel like to have bagels be the weight of your world.

He'd give the rabbi ten minutes, and then he'd head off to Michelangelo's Deli, one of the more promising locations on his list for the day, since Jeff had never known an Italian deli that wasn't hiding something. The joint was an old Las Vegas establishment dating from the 1960s that had just opened a new storefront in a strip mall on Lake Mead and Rock Springs. Their old location, across from the Commercial Center on Sahara, was one of those places Jeff used to like to visit when he came to gamble, since they weren't exactly hiding the fact that there was something other than meats being served, at least not with the number of guys in sweat suits who kept walking in and out of the kitchen counting cash.

Jeff picked up the newspaper and examined the articles. Russian astronauts were going to point giant mirrors at the sun, which would then bounce light onto parts of the Earth for a few minutes. Questions were being raised by a recent spate of U.S. bombings of Iraq. The president of Chechnya announced his country would now be ruled under sharia law. Jeff flipped to the local news section. Construction on the spaghetti bowl to snarl traffic for weeks. $75 million wagered on super bowl, casinos rake in $2.9 million in profits. Local plastic surgeon presumed dead. And then there was a photo of that Bennie Savone character again, this time next to a column by Harvey B. Curran, the mob's own town gossip:

> The street is still buzzing about jiggle-joint operator **Bennie Savone** getting nicked on conspiracy charges related to the beatdown two of his bouncers gave **Lewis McDonald**, 42, a dentist from Nebraska, that left the tooth-man paralyzed and missing an eye. The indictment is sealed, but word is that Savone ordered video from the club's security system destroyed, then sent a friend over to Ace's Pawn to see about acquiring their tapes. All this after offering the family of McDonald serious seven-figure cash in hopes of keeping them quiet on the criminal front and forestalling what would likely be a crippling civil suit against his gentleman's club, **The Wild Horse**. The feds are also closing in on Savone for what one source says are "credit card irregularities," which might be anything these days, but if you've ever been to the Wild Horse, you know that a glass of water costs $10, $100 if you want ice. Savone's got pit bull legal eagle **Vincent Zangari** on the case, so he's surely been told to "keep his mouth closed" and that "he's got rights," but that might not keep the feds from taking a closer look at some of the sweetheart construction contracts Savone has made on both sides of the Strip. Savone hasn't found any trouble over the course of last decade, so it's a good chance he'll be back in no time for his weekly brunch at the **Bagel Café** with his father-in-law, **Rabbi Cy Kales**, to talk about the expansion of **Temple Beth Israel**, Savone

Construction Partners' ambitious project in Summerlin. For wiseguys like Bennie Savone, "no time" to the feds usually means **60 days until they'll get around to setting a bond.**

Jeff sat there for a moment and tried to reread the column. His heart was beating so hard that he wasn't quite able to focus on the words. Jeff had never heard of Bennie Savone prior to arriving in Las Vegas. It was impossible not to know about the Wild Horse, since they had advertising all over the city—on top of cabs, inside the weekly rags, guys wearing Wild Horse T-shirts walking up and down the strip and handing out flyers that promised "the most Wild ride in town"—and the club itself was the size of a football field . . . a football field covered in topless women, no less.

All the words in the column were ones Jeff knew, but he'd never seen them put together before. *A wiseguy. A strip club. A rabbi. A temple.* It was like the beginning of a bad joke. It was also the first time since last April that Jeff Hopper felt like Sal Cupertine was anywhere near his grasp. He didn't know how the dots connected yet, didn't have even the faintest idea how it had come to pass, but what he did know was simple and tangible: Last April, on the same night Sal Cupertine killed four men in the Parker House in Chicago, a truck departed Kochel Farms and ended up at Temple Beth Israel in Las Vegas, maybe fifty yards from where Jeff was sitting, seven days later. That was a fact. It was also, apparently, a fact that one of Temple Beth Israel's rabbis was the father-in-law of a reputed wiseguy named Bennie Savone, who, if the gossip column was to be believed, was spearheading the development of the temple's sprawling campus.

There was nothing illegal with that, at least not on the face of things. Nor was there anything illegal in getting meat delivered, though Jeff wondered when Temple Beth Israel had begun to use Kochel Farms. In fact, there was no proof yet that this Savone guy had done anything wrong, though legitimate businessmen didn't usually let their local newspapers call them wiseguys.

Jeff stood up and looked out the window. He could see the parking lot, a bit of a playground that was filled with children now, and then, in the distance, tractors moving land, maybe thirty construction workers in the midst of various tasks, a water tank, and acres of undeveloped land that hadn't even been graded yet. How much did this kind of development cost? Millions. Multi-millions. Where was that money coming from? And how would Sal Cupertine fit into this? Or was he buried underneath that high school? There was that, too, he supposed. He needed to find out from Agent Poremba all he could on Bennie Savone and how the hell he ended up married to the daughter of a rabbi. The local Las Vegas boys would know more than Poremba, but it wasn't like he could just walk into the field office anymore. He was little more than a rent-a-cop at this point. Then he'd call Matthew, get him to drive up from Palm Springs, only four hours south, and start getting eyes on this temple.

"Beautiful view, isn't it?"

Jeff startled at the sound of Rabbi Cohen's voice, turned, and saw that the rabbi was standing directly behind him, just inches away. The office door was closed. Christ. When had he walked in?

"The construction?" Jeff said.

"No," Rabbi Cohen said, "the children playing."

"Yes, yes, I suppose it is," Jeff said.

"But they can be a bit loud." Rabbi Cohen reached past Jeff, slid the window closed, then closed the thick brown curtains, too, descending the office into half-light. "Please, have a seat, and I'll see if I can help you."

Jeff sat down. He needed to settle his thoughts, take this point by point. There was nothing here yet, just some words in a newspaper article. He needed to be meticulous, as ever. "Right," Jeff said, mostly for himself. He took the photos of Sal Cupertine back out of his notebook and set them on the rabbi's desk, next to the newspaper. "As I said, I'm looking for this man. Have you seen him?"

"And who are you?" the rabbi said.

"A private consultant for the FBI," Jeff said. It was a mouthful. And not one that Jeff particularly cared for.

"What does that mean?"

"I'm working on a special project for them," Jeff said.

"They don't have enough agents?"

"Not for this, no," Jeff said.

"There seem to be quite a few agents in Las Vegas," Rabbi Cohen said. He pointed at the newspaper, which was still open to the column about Bennie Savone. "If what Mr. Curran in the *Review-Journal* says is to be believed, at any rate." Rabbi Cohen picked up the photos of Sal Cupertine then and carefully looked at each one. "He doesn't look familiar, I'm afraid," he said eventually.

"He would have been here in April," Jeff said. He flipped through his paperwork. "The twenty-second, to be exact."

"Doing what?" Rabbi Cohen said.

"We're not sure," Jeff said. "But there's some indication he might have been transported via the company who delivers meat to your cafeteria. Kochel Farms."

"And what did he do that he needed to escape inside of a meat truck?"

"He murdered three federal agents and a confidential informant," Jeff said.

"Oh, I think I read about this," Rabbi Cohen said. "In Detroit, wasn't it?"

"Chicago," Jeff said.

"I see," Rabbi Cohen said. "And it's your belief he is now standing in our cafeteria, waiting for you?"

"No," Jeff said. "It's my belief he went from here to somewhere else, but I'd like to talk to your staff and see if they recognize him, remember any details about the day in question."

"This man," the rabbi said. "Does he have a name?"

"Sal Cupertine," Jeff said.

"Oh," Rabbi Cohen said. "Now I understand." He picked up the newspaper and spent a few moments looking at the article about Bennie Savone. "This is the only city in America where it's illegal to be Italian, apparently. As you can imagine, Rabbi Kales is sickened about all of this. That's the father of his grandchildren and the husband of his only child that this . . . this . . . *golem* . . . is libeling."

"If he's innocent," Jeff said, "he has nothing to worry about."

Rabbi Cohen opened a desk drawer and pulled out a pair of silver scissors and began to cut the story out of the newspaper. "Talmud says that there are those who gain eternity in a lifetime, others who gain it an hour," he said, and he continued cutting up the story until it was little more than confetti, then he very carefully scooped the pieces up and dumped them in his trash can. "How long do you think an article in a newspaper lasts?"

"Bennie Savone is not my business," Jeff said.

"And yet here you are," Rabbi Cohen said.

Rabbi Cohen tented his hands together at the fingertips but didn't speak for a moment. Jeff couldn't quite place the inflection in the rabbi's voice, couldn't tell if he was annoyed or intrigued or simply bored. He didn't seem surprised by the appearance of someone working for the FBI, which most people are, and that seemed odd. The more he stared at the rabbi, the more Jeff also got the sense that maybe he'd been in some kind of accident, because the skin on his neck and along his hairline seemed slick. Not like he'd had a facelift, exactly, but like he'd had something reconstructed. Maybe he'd been attacked by a dog or something. That would account for the weird way his mouth wouldn't quite wrap around a smile. And then there was the way his beard didn't quite connect with his sideburns . . . must have been an accident, maybe a burn? It was impossible to tell what the skin around his mouth looked like under his thick beard.

"You're wondering about my face," Rabbi Cohen said.

"I'm sorry?" Jeff said, because he didn't know what to say.

"I see you looking at my face," Rabbi Cohen said, "trying to figure what's wrong with it. It's all right. You're not the first person. Turns out children frequently have the same question."

"I apologize," Jeff said. "I just . . ."

Rabbi Cohen waved him off. "No need," he said. "You can't be more candid than you are with your own face, now can you? Talmud tells us that we cannot expect the Torah to live in only the most beautiful people. Eventually even the best wine spoils in gold chalices." He tried to smile again. "Well, in light of everything, Mr. Hopper, I'm afraid that I can't let you search our grounds without a warrant. While I trust your intentions are pure, you'll pardon me for not trusting the FBI right now."

"I'm not an FBI agent," Jeff said.

"Then you're just trespassing," Rabbi Cohen said, "and I'm afraid I'll have to ask you to leave."

"This is how you want to do it?" Jeff said. "You want twenty guys in here tomorrow? That's what you want?"

"If you'd like," Rabbi Cohen said, "I'm happy to take you on a tour of our public facilities. Show you that all we're hiding here is dirt and sand. And if tomorrow you come back with a warrant, Temple Beth Israel will be happy to let you do as much searching as you'd like."

Jeff knew one thing for certain: Poremba wasn't going to be able to get a warrant to start searching a temple in twenty-four hours. He'd be lucky to ever get one. And Jeff wouldn't be in on the search even if they did. Tomorrow, he and Matthew would do this on their terms.

Jeff stood up. "Show the way, Rabbi."

CHAPTER SIXTEEN

Christianity, unlike Judaism, Rabbi David Cohen learned, was about rejecting the idea of luck. It was a consequence-based process. If you led a pious life, good things would happen. If you led an evil life, bad things would surely follow. If you led a pious life and bad things *still* happened, then that was the hand of God, it was meant to be, and in the afterlife you would be rewarded with the gift of God's eternal love. He created humans, gave them free will, only to demand fealty, or there would be hell to pay. Nothing was chance. All was either reward or punishment.

It wasn't unlike being in the Mafia. Except at least with God, if you waited until the last minute and said that you were sorry, and you really did respect his authority, you could go on living your life in everlasting peace. David was not under the impression his cousin Ronnie, nor Bennie Savone, operated under those same rules. He was certain that the FBI wasn't about to accept his apology for knocking off their agents, especially not this Jeff Hopper, a man he thought he'd killed.

And yet here they were, two men raised from the dead, walking through a cemetery, David pointing out where the aquatic center would be housed, the bluff they were constructing so that the performing arts center could be seen from the bottom of the street, all the better to attract natural light, you see, to catch the brilliant colors of the desert sunset, as it was in Israel. "For the Talmud tells us," David told Agent Hopper now, "whoever did not see Jerusalem in its days of glory never saw a beautiful city in their life."

"You'll pardon me, Rabbi," Agent Hopper said, "but it's still Las Vegas." David heard a hint of boredom in the agent's voice, which was good. They'd spent the last thirty minutes walking the perimeter of the temple and its property, David narrating the entire time, filling Agent Hopper with the arcane and the minute, explaining every plan Temple Beth Israel had for the future. The agent had stayed largely quiet, apart from every now and then muttering some empty platitude.

As they walked, David let the agent stay at least a half step in front of him, let Agent Hopper feel like he was guiding the tour, when in fact David was pushing him the entire time. They were inching toward the far end of the cemetery, blocks from the street and the bustle of people, where later that afternoon David was scheduled to bury a man named Alan Rosen who'd been brought up from Palm Springs that morning, but who David guessed was an Indian. The grave was already dug, a mound of dirt covered by a green tarp in the distance, the simple green shovel they used in burial ceremony placed at the ready for the mourners who preferred not to use their hands. All that was missing was the body.

"Where there is the temple, there is Israel," David said.

"I'm sure that's true," Agent Hopper said. "But don't you have a difficult time believing in the sanctity of your faith in a town like this?"

"Chicago is any better?" David asked.

Agent Hopper chuckled once. "Tell me something, did you always believe?"

"Does anyone have absolute faith?" David said.

"My family was not particularly religious," Agent Hopper said. "Personally, I never bought into any of it."

"So you think the world is just wicked?"

"That's what the evidence suggests," Agent Hopper said. He stopped walking then and turned around, a field of the dead before him. "Did any of these people die with any faith left? Any pride?"

"And you have yours?" David said, doing something Rabbi Kales had taught him, to answer questions with questions, as the Jews have always done.

"I don't know," Agent Hopper said, "but I'm still alive."

"*Mazel tov*," David said. He reached into his pocket and felt the butterfly knife there. It hadn't been luck that made him carry the knife every day, nor faith; it was fear. God told Abraham that Israel had no *mazel*, and so the Jews created their own. A single *mitzvah*, done without question, done without the need for recognition, was the door to finding *mazel*. Luck didn't happen because of *mazel*, luck was the embodiment of it: Everyone was able to transcend the merits of their life and, for at least a moment, find prosperity and unfathomable happiness. A wedding, a baby, a new job? *Mazel tov*. Jews had forgotten what the term really meant. It was only the moment that was blessed. You still had a chance to fuck up what came next.

And wasn't that what David's life had been? He'd found true love, had a baby, been given a new job. And then, *mazel tov*, the FBI showed up. It was someone else's good luck. David would have to make his own.

Agent Hopper walked over to the hole that had been dug into the ground for the Rosen funeral and looked down.

"Is it really six feet?" Agent Hopper asked.

"Jewish custom requires ten handbreadths," David said. He stepped beside the agent and examined the grave. "It seems deep enough, doesn't it?"

"Off the record, Rabbi," Agent Hopper said, "you ever seen anything funny here?"

"How would I know?" David said.

"You seem like a man who pays attention."

"This person you're looking for," David said, "is he a monster?"

"He's just a man," Agent Hopper said. "Nothing special about him."

"Then he shouldn't be very hard to find," David said. He'd spent all this time observing Agent Hopper. He wasn't wearing Kevlar and didn't have a gun on his belt or slung over his shoulder. Just a notepad, a file filled with pictures, and a hunch. This was the man who'd made Fat Monte kill himself? If he knew anything, he would have come with an assault team. If he knew anything, he'd still be an FBI agent, not a consultant. If he knew anything, he'd start running.

"You happen to remember where you were last April 22?" Agent Hopper asked.

David shook his head. "Do you know where you were?"

"Yeah," Agent Hopper said. "A funeral for one of my friends."

"Talmud tells us we have two faces," David said, "one that lives in sorrow, one that lives in joy."

"Didn't Bruce Springsteen say that?" Agent Hopper said.

Shit. "Did he?" David gripped the knife in his pocket.

"Yeah," Agent Hopper said quietly. He took a step away from the grave, a curious look on his face.

David was no more than a foot away from Hopper, but he'd need to lunge for him at this point. David needed to be closer.

"You know, you haven't answered a single question I've asked."

"I hope you find your man," David said. He extended his hand, but Agent Hopper took another step, this one to the side, near the mound of dirt and the shovel.

"You didn't tell me what happened to your face."

"All is vanity," David said. He tried to smile, but his mouth wouldn't follow directions.

"Then I'd think you'd want a better plastic surgeon."

The Talmud said that if someone comes to kill you, you should wake up early and kill him first. David doubted Jeff Hopper knew that edict in the religious sense, but he surely knew it as an FBI agent, or else he wouldn't have made such a sudden move for the spade.

As soon as he did, David was on him.

He plunged his knife into Hopper's back once, twice, three times, the blade snapping off in Hopper's rib cage as David tried to pull it out so he could cut the agent's throat. They both fell to the ground, deep in the dirt.

David stood up then and rolled Jeff over onto his back, his eyes wide open, his mouth opening and closing like a fish. David had seen this before. He wouldn't need to use the shovel. At least not to kill the man.

"I found you," Jeff Hopper said, his voice barely a whisper.

"You shouldn't have come here," David said.

"I would have let you live," Jeff said.

Jeff Hopper tried to take a breath, and then another, but they wouldn't come; his body tensed and he tried to raise his head, tried to fight what was coming, and then he relaxed, his eyes fluttering. "I found Sal Cupertine," he said.

"You did," Sal Cupertine said, and then he leaned over and squeezed Jeff Hopper's carotid off so that he'd pass out before he drowned on his own blood.

A *mitzvah*.

■

Sal Cupertine parked Jeff Hopper's rented Pontiac across the street from Wingfield Park in Reno and then walked a few blocks down Second Street, looking for a place to make a phone call. It was midnight, and though he'd spent the last seven hours on the road from Las Vegas, Sal didn't feel tired. In fact, for the first time in a good nine months, Sal Cupertine felt positively alive.

Though it was a Thursday night, and not much more than thirty degrees outside, there were people streaming in and out of the hotels, casinos, and restaurants along Sal's path. There was also music—country, rock, rap—that bleated out of each passing car, each open door into each casino, each set of head-phones of the people who brushed too close to Sal. But that was fine. How long had it been since he'd let anyone actually near him? Actually touch him? Plenty of people at Temple Beth Israel hugged him or kissed him on the cheek or felt the need to have some kind of human contact with him after receiving his counsel, but it was never Sal's choice, never something he actually courted.

Though, in that way, he supposed, it was a choice. He wanted to save physical interactions for the two people whose touch he actually missed. But today, his first day back among the living— and his last day for a good long time, too, he recognized—Sal went ahead and let people bump into him, let people look him in the eye, even let people smile at him.

Not that many did any of those things. He was still Sal Cupertine, after all. Still the Rain Man. Still the last person you ever wanted to show up behind you, anywhere, at any time. These days, though, when Sal Cupertine was going to kill a guy, it really didn't matter which way the guy was facing.

Sal had spent much of his time driving between Las Vegas and Reno trying to find an upside to all this, other than the fact that he probably wouldn't have to kill another person for a while. And that was good, since killing Jeff Hopper hadn't given Sal any gratification, had in fact upset him a great deal, at least for a time, since he realized just how far down the road he'd been sold. That he'd once again done what someone else should have done.

And now, thanks to a small alteration in the deal he'd made earlier with Gray Beard, Jeff Hopper—or at least a portion of him—was on his way back to Chicago. Seemed only fair since Chicago had sent Paul Bruno to Las Vegas, and after going through the paperwork Sal found in Jeff's car, Sal thought there was perhaps a tad bit of poetic justice in that.

It had been a long day, and Sal needed a drink, maybe a big piece of fish, since he couldn't quite handle the idea of cutting into some bloody piece of meat for the second time that day.

Sal didn't know if the casinos in Reno had the same facial-recognition software as the ones in Las Vegas, but he wasn't taking any chances, so he ducked into a bar called the Brass Nickel. It was in between a pawn shop and a Vietnamese restaurant called Pho Saigon that Sal recognized from Hopper's list of Kochel Farms clients. It was the kind of place that had grainy pictures of their dishes taped up to the window, so Sal spent a moment looking at something called *bo luc lac*—which didn't look like much more than some meat, onions, lettuce, and white rice—and thanking God he hadn't ended up on that plate.

There were a dozen or so people inside the Brass Nickel. Sal went up to the bar, ordered a Johnnie Walker Black on the rocks, got five dollars in quarters, and headed over to check out the pay phone. It was between the men's room—distinguished by the painting of a cowboy with his gun drawn that covered the door—and the ladies room—woman with her dress pulled up, revealing sexy garters, of course—in a back hallway that smelled of Lysol and beer piss. Not the kind of place people tended to spend much time waiting around.

Perfect.

Sal punched in the numbers, deposited a buck seventy-five for five minutes, and listened to the space between his past and present close around the sound of a phone ringing.

Ronnie Cupertine answered his cell phone on the third ring by saying, "Who the fuck is this?"

"It's your dead cousin," Sal said.

There was a pause on the line, and Sal could hear *SportsCenter* on in the background—someone on the Lakers was "cooler than the other side of the pillow"—and the sound of water running. Ronnie was probably in his favorite spot: watching TV from the shitter in his basement.

"Good that you called," Ronnie said. "Save me the trouble."

"I figured," Sal said.

"You somewhere safe?"

"Safe enough," Sal said.

"You in Chicago?"

"You'd know if I was in Chicago," Sal said.

Ronnie laughed. "I suppose I would."

"You fucked up," Sal said.

"You think so?" Ronnie said, and then Sal heard a toilet flush.

"I had to clean up your mess, again," Sal said.

"I knew you would," Ronnie said. "It's what you've always been best at. It's why you've always been so valuable to me. To everyone."

"I don't work for you anymore," Sal said. "Let's make that clear. I work for Bennie Savone."

"See, I heard someone dimed him out to the feds," Ronnie said. "Seems like that strip club of his is doing some very shady things. Real shame."

"He'll be out in thirty days," Sal said, though he didn't believe that. "Maybe less."

"Could be someone dimes him out again," Ronnie said. "Could be every few months, the feds learn something else about your boss. Could be they eventually start looking into that Jew business, too, because I know I've been looking at my business model, and while cars and drugs are lucrative, they're nothing compared to God and death. Now that's a long-range business. Could be you need some protection out there now that fed charges are sitting on your boss. Could be I make sure the fed's phone doesn't ring for a while."

"Snitching on yourself," Sal said. "Where'd you learn that?"

"You don't stay in this business for as long as I have without learning a few tricks," Ronnie said. "Sometimes, it's just easier to have the feds take care of my problems. Could be you've learned that yourself these last couple days."

"Could be," Sal said, "you get into your car one morning and I'm in the backseat."

"And then what? I'm dead. So what? I'm dead. *Your* best-case scenario still involves the gas chamber, if you're lucky. We might as well enjoy our time together, you and me."

"How much?" Sal said.

"Your boss, he's got quite the scam out there," he said. "Do you know what he charges just to bury a body? I can get some Mexican to dig a hole for a whole lot less."

"How much?" Sal said again.

"I can't tell you how much until I get a look at your books," Ronnie said, "and I'm not planning on making a trip to Las Vegas anytime soon. Probably wouldn't look good, you know? So why don't we just agree that I'm in on this now. Full partner. You're my guy in Las Vegas."

There it was. He'd known it already, of course, but he wanted to hear it, wanted Ronnie to admit it.

"I'm not your guy," Sal said. "I'm your cousin. We're family."

"Of course we are," Ronnie said.

"Just like you and my father, right?" Sal said.

"That what this is? You want to talk about your daddy? Fine. But I charge a copay for that." Ronnie laughed. "Isn't this what you always wanted, Sal? You're the big man now."

"No," Sal said, "I'm a dead man. But you know something?

I'm not gonna be dead for long. And when the FBI realizes that, and they will, Ronnie, and soon, you're gonna wish you were, too. As long as they know I'm alive, you belong to me. Because you know what, Ronnie? I know where all the bodies are. Every single one of them. And they all belong to you."

Sal hung up before Ronnie could respond, took a few sips of his Johnnie Walker, and made his second and final call of the evening, this time to the *Chicago Tribune*. He'd need to make it quick, since he still needed to get a cab to the airport, boost a car from the long-term parking lot, and then drive back to Las Vegas in time for his 2 p.m. meeting with Barbara Altman, Camille Lawerence, and Phyllis Gabler to talk about the teen fashion show they wanted to do at the temple come spring. Maybe, in a month or two, he'd see about getting an assistant rabbi, someone he could train, since the temple really needed two rabbis if they wanted to get business done. There was the book fair coming up, the opening of the new school, the never-ending brisses, weddings, funerals, bar mitzvahs . . . and then there was the business Sal knew Rabbi Cohen would need to make sure didn't lag while Bennie was away . . . and maybe he'd need to get creative with that, too, maybe periodically *make* some business locally . . . could be the other six temples in town could face some tragedies in the coming year. Who could say when Temple Beth Zion might have an electrical fire? Or when one of the conservative shuls might lose a rabbi to some kind of blood poisoning? And who was to say that the cemetery needed to remain Jewish only? Yes, those were all possibilities to consider, and like that, as the phone began to ring, Sal Cupertine could see miles and miles of empty desert turning into roads paved toward his wife, Jennifer, and his son, William. Ronnie would remain a problem, so he'd need to keep Jennifer and

William safe, somehow, but that was the next step. For now, he just had to set the ball rolling.

"*Tribune* City Desk, this is Tom."

"Tom," Sal said, "my name is Jeff Hopper, and I have some information concerning the murders that took place last year at the Parker House that I need to discuss with someone."

March 1999

Jennifer Cupertine sat outside the Artists Café on Michigan Avenue and tried to make sense of the front page of the *Chicago Tribune*. She'd stopped in for lunch after spending the last three hours down the block at the Museum of Contemporary Photography, where she'd been employed part-time for the last two months, combing through a huge box of photos taken in the early 1900s in France that consisted mostly of people not looking at the camera, still lifes of various breads, and very little else of artistic or historical merit. It was like that sometimes, which was fine. It was solitary yet concentrated work, which kept her from drifting too far in her mind to other, more upsetting things. Like her missing husband—who the FBI had helpfully informed her recently was probably still dead, but was not the ashes they'd given her the year previous, which apparently belonged to someone named Chema Espinoza, a fact every local news station was having an absolute field day with—but also the more pressing issues like the light bill, like the price of new clothes for William, or that she didn't know what she was going to do with the rest of her life.

But it was hard to avoid the headline that screamed from the bottom of the front page of the paper she'd purchased to keep her and her chicken salad sandwich company:

REMAINS CONFIRMED TO BE EX-FBI AGENT

The badly decomposed severed head discovered last week in a trash bin along Ontario St. has been identified through dental records as Jeffrey Hopper, 45, the former senior special agent in charge of the city's FBI Organized Crime Task Force. Hopper was first reported missing shortly after contacting this paper in February regarding the federal cover-up concerning the murder of three federal agents and a suspected confidential informant allegedly perpetrated last April by Family associate Sal "the Rain Main" Cupertine. Hopper alleged that the FBI, under the direction of Senior Special Agent Kirk Biglione, had willingly led authorities (and family members) to believe Mr. Cupertine had been found dead in the Poyter Landfill on or about April 17, 1998, when, in fact, the body discovered in the landfill belonged to Jose Maria "Chema" Espinoza, a reputed foot soldier in the Gangster 2-6. Cupertine has subsequently been at large despite direct evidence linking him to the April 1998 murders, as well as possibly two dozen additional murders dating back as far as the mid-1980s . . .

It was easier on Jennifer to think there was a good chance Sal was dead, even if she didn't choose to believe it was true. She could fool herself that way, could entertain the idea of moving on with her life, but now that wasn't possible, not with Special

Agent Hopper dead. Because if that man was dead, it surely meant her husband was alive.

Jennifer felt sorry for Special Agent Hopper. He seemed like a nice man. That he was dead now didn't give Jennifer any joy, though she did wonder what had become of his partner . . . was he decomposing somewhere, too? Or was he still out there, looking for her husband? Had Sal done it? Was Sal in Chicago? It didn't seem plausible to her, not with the amount of pressure the authorities had been putting on Ronnie and the rest of the boys since Hopper's story had hit the front page the month previous. It all sounded absurd, the stories she'd heard . . . that Sal had been smuggled out in a frozen meat truck . . . that Ronnie had gotten rid of anyone who knew anything . . . and now it wasn't so much about whatever the Family's role in this had been as much as it was the FBI's cover-up, and just what they were hiding besides the identification of bodies they'd turned up. But wasn't that what Special Agent Hopper told her all those months ago? That it was bad PR?

Jennifer set the paper down and looked out to the street. It was sunny for the first time in weeks, and though the air was still cool, the people walking along Michigan Avenue had taken off their heavy coats in favor of light sweaters. It would be overcast again tomorrow, she knew, would probably snow again sometime before April, but today was one of those afternoons when Chicago was perfect, the kind of day she and Sal would spend in the backyard with William, doing yard work, raking leaves, tinkering with the sprinklers, complaining about how crappy their rain gutters were, neither of them ever really willing to climb up on a ladder to clean them out, much easier just to bitch about it. William hardly even talked about his father anymore, and maybe that was better, too.

What frightened Jennifer, however, was how much the child had begun to remind her of Sal. It was just little things—the way he tended to curl his thumb into his fist when he felt nervous or worried, the bits of green that were showing up in his eyes, how sensitive he was, how meticulous, how singular his focus could be—but Jennifer knew she needed to find him role models that weren't criminals. Maybe that would mean she'd need to start dating. Maybe that would mean she'd need to sell the house and move, just like Special Agent Hopper had suggested. Maybe it meant she needed to watch William more closely, make sure he knew that his father was not a good man but was a good husband and father, a distinction that she'd only just started to make herself, but which she wouldn't allow to happen to her son.

She could not lose them both.

Jennifer finished her sandwich, paid her bill, and headed back toward the museum. Yes, she would make some changes, she had to, that's all there was to it. But she would stay in Chicago, if for no other reason than days like today, when everything seemed to remind her of how good it used to be, how even the wind blowing through her hair reminded her of Sal, reminded her of how he used to tuck her hair behind her ear when they were facing each other in bed, which she hated, but which she wished she could feel just one more time.

Jennifer Cupertine was headed up Michigan Avenue, back toward the museum, when she came across a large, black-and-gold RV parked near the corner of Harrison, taking up three parking meters. Two black men sat outside in folding chairs right in the middle of the sidewalk, like they were having a picnic. As she got closer, she noticed they had a little portable grill out with them too, which one of the men was trying to ignite, no easy task with the wind.

"Beautiful day," one of the men said when Jennifer got close. He was the older of the two, with a long gray beard, glasses, nice shoes. The other man was too busy with the grill to even look up.

"Yes," Jennifer said. She didn't know why she responded to the man. She never spoke to strangers on the street, or anywhere, for that matter, and she immediately regretted it when Gray Beard stood up and blocked her path. She stuck her hand inside her purse, where she kept one of Sal's old guns now, because she didn't know who might come for her some day, too. Not that she knew how to use it. And not that she'd probably need it at this moment, considering there were hundreds of people walking around her, though Jennifer tended to always feel alone in crowds these days, as if she were the one person no one could see.

Gray Beard smiled at her, though, and for some reason that put her at ease. "It's polite to stand up when a pretty woman walks into your house," he said, and then he stepped out of her way. "You have a nice day, now," he said.

"I will," she said, and she conjured her own smile. It came hard, but there was something oddly comforting about common kindness.

Jennifer made her way across the street and into the museum. Her little cubicle—which she shared with a graduate student from Columbia College named Stacy, whom she never actually saw, since they worked opposite days—was up the stairs from the first-floor exhibit hall, inside a tiny administrative space that also included a broken photocopier and a minifridge. She set her purse down and then noticed a thick manila envelope on her chair, her name printed on it in thick block letters. There was no postage on the envelope, no note indicating who it was from, no "handle with care" stamp, which was pretty much what every package sent to her attention at the museum came affixed with.

Odd.

The envelope was sealed with so much duct tape that it took Jennifer a good thirty seconds to cut across the top with her crappy scissors—the museum made a point of stocking dull scissors, in Jennifer's opinion, to avoid the accidental cutting of precious items—and dumped the contents on her desk.

Or at least attempted to, since the banded stacks of hundred-dollar bills inside the envelope wouldn't budge through the little opening she'd made.

"Jesus," she said. She reached into the envelope and started pulling the stacks out. One, two . . . three . . . four . . . five . . . six . . . seven in all. "Jesus," she said again. At the bottom of the envelope was a single piece of paper, folded once, lengthwise. And there, in her husband's precise cursive, was a note:

> I will send more when I can. I love you and William. I always have and I always will.

Jennifer shoved the money into her purse, grabbed the manila envelope, and then ran out to the information desk at the front of the exhibition hall, where another graduate student—this one named Chad—sat reading a textbook.

"Did you put this envelope on my desk?" Jennifer asked. She tried her best to sound calm, but waving the envelope like a crazy person probably wasn't helping.

"No," Chad said, "I put it on your chair. The guy who dropped it off said he wanted to make sure you didn't miss it."

"Right," Jennifer said, "right." She tried to breathe. Tried to feel her fingers. Tried to concentrate on not drawing any attention to herself, in case anyone was watching. "The man. What did he look like?"

"Just some delivery guy," Chad said with a shrug. "Black guy with a gray ZZ Top beard."

"When?"

"Right after you went to lunch. Are you okay? You look sick."

"Chicken salad," Jennifer said, already pushing her way through the museum's double doors back out onto Michigan Avenue. She ran halfway down the block toward Harrison, though she could plainly see the RV was already gone. She knew it would be, knew her husband wasn't sitting inside watching her walk by, knew that the man with the gray beard was just a messenger, but she wanted to be near someone Sal had been near, wanted to tell that man with the gray beard to deliver a message back to her husband: that she would wait, that she would be right here waiting, for as long as it took . . . and to never send money, ever again. That she didn't want it. That she would rather be destitute than take one more dime that came with another man's blood on it.

Never again, Jennifer Cupertine thought as she turned and walked slowly back to the museum, aware suddenly of the weight seventy thousand dollars and a gun made in her purse, *after this one time.*

ACKNOWLEDGMENTS

I've been blessed by the help of so many people during the years I wrote this book: Dan Smetanka, editor extraordinaire, should have received hazard pay for the work he did on this novel— I am so grateful for his careful, inspired, and insightful notes, thoughts, deletions, additions, strong-arm tactics, and hour-long phone calls to keep me off the ledge. Likewise, I'm so thankful for the steady hands of my agents Jennie Dunham, who has been by my side since the start and who always provides wise counsel, firm editorial advice, and just the right amount of forceful intervention, and Judi Farkas, who has navigated so many rough seas for me she should probably have her own boat by now.

This novel came out of a short story entitled "Mitzvah" that I wrote for *Las Vegas Noir*, edited by Jarret Keene and Todd James Pierce. I owe both Jarret and Todd a huge amount of gratitude for knowing that I could come up with something dark and violent about Summerlin. I don't know if any of these characters would exist if I hadn't been asked to write that story, so I thank you both for including me in your book. And thank you to Stacy Bierlein for her astute editing of the story when it appeared in *Other Resort Cities*, a line change that opened up an entire novel in its wake.

Mark Haskell Smith, for his great notes and his continued moral and ethical support; Gina Frangello, for her help with all things Chicago and life; Daniel Krugman, for answering all of my odd questions about funerals and undertaking; Geoff Schumacher, my former editor at a variety of defunct Las Vegas newspapers, for his excellent book *Sun, Sin, and Suburbia: An Essential History of Modern Las Vegas*, which was an invaluable resource; Vitaly Sigal for his insight into Russian Jews, criminals, and criminal defense; the poor rabbis who responded to my tortured metaphorical and existential queries on AskMoses.com in the middle of the night (really, they are there all night long); Ross Angelella, for his middle-of-the-night support and wisdom, and for giving me a better title; Carl Beverly and Sarah Timberman for believing in the idea long before it became a novel; my siblings, Lee Goldberg, Karen Dinino, and Linda Woods, who travel this same path as I do, and whose unending support means the world to me; Agam Patel, my partner in crime at the University of California, Riverside, who everyone thinks knows how to bury a body, but who actually knows how to keep one upright; all my talented and smart colleagues at UCR Palm Desert Low Residency MFA, whose tremendous work inspires me, and all my students, whose promise and dedication embolden my spirit; Rider Strong and Julia Pistell, my Literary Disco partners and dear friends, who are also my de facto literary therapists twice a month; Mechtild Dunofsky, for sanity, and her insight into the motivations of people. Mikayla Butchart, for catching all my mistakes—there are few things more valuable on the planet than a copyeditor.

I am not a rabbi, so I am deeply appreciative to a variety of sources for the spiritual wisdom included throughout this work, including, obviously, the Torah, Talmud, and collected works of the Midrash, but also, namely: *A Book of Jewish Thoughts* (Bloch Publishing, 1926), Selected and Arranged by Rabbi Joseph Herman Hertz, the edition that once belonged to my grandparents, and then was handed down to my mother, and then, when I needed it most, to me; *Holy Mountain: Two Paths to One God* (Binfords & Mort, 1953) by Rabbi Raphael H. Levine, given to my mother when she graduated from high school; *A Treasury of Jewish Humor* (Doubleday, 1951) edited by Nathan Ausubel; and *Judaism: An Anthology of the Key Spiritual Writings of the Jewish Tradition* (Simon & Schuster, 1991) edited by Arthur Hertzberg. My fictional interpretation of the meanings found in all of the above isn't to be taken as actual Jewish law, or even as my own beliefs, which is not the fault of the wonderful writers, scholars, and religious leaders who wrote the above. Also, thank you to the United States Treasury Department, Bureau of Narcotics, for keeping such assiduous records and compiling them in *Mafia* (Harper Collins, 2007), an indispensable compendium of bad guys.

Finally, my beautiful wife, Wendy, whom I write all of these books for, and who reads every word, but has to live with them for much longer. I'm coming to bed now.

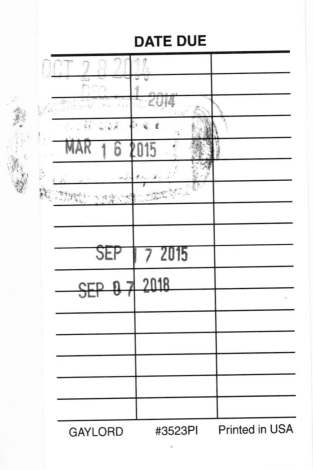

DATE DUE

OCT 2 8 2014	
DEC 1 2014	
MAR 1 6 2015	
SEP 1 7 2015	
SEP 0 7 2018	

GAYLORD　　#3523PI　　Printed in USA